Praise for

A SWORD OF BRONZE AND ASHES and ANNA SMITH SPARK

'Weaves a spell that will consume you.'
Barnes and Noble

'Literary *Game of Thrones.*'
Sunday Times

'Spark blends Celtic mythology and grimdark fantasy into an enthralling tale of female power. [Her] poetic prose gives the adventure a mythic feel that enhances its folkloric and folk horror elements. Balancing the violence of war with emotional depth and thematic explorations of motherhood and legacy, this gripping outing is a testament to Spark's power as a storyteller.'
Publishers Weekly

'Anna Smith Spark has done it yet again with this cracking read, and I hope there are many more stories to come in this multi-layered and captivating world.'
Out of This World SFF

'It is a mind-blowing book. I don't think I've ever read anything quite like it. It's a story about the ragged, tearing wound you get when high myth gets stitched to the grind of mundane life. It's incredible.'
Adrian Tchaikovsky

'Lushly poetic Heavy Metal mythology.'
Peter McLean, author of *War for the Rose Throne*

'Fusing together a Tolkienesque level of worldbuilding with Celtic folklore, *A Sword of Bronze and Ashes* is hauntingly beautiful…a masterpiece.'
Shauna Lawless, author of
The Children of Gods and Fighting Men

'Anna Smith Spark's unique poetic literary fantasy delivered an *absolute experience*.'
Grimdark Magazine

'Anna Smith Spark wields a shining sword of beauty and destruction. Her books aren't there just to be read; they have to be consumed with all of your soul.'
Spells & Spaceships

ANNA SMITH SPARK

A SWORD OF GOLD AND RUIN

BOOK TWO of THE MAKING OF THIS WORLD RUINED

This is a **FLAME TREE PRESS** book

FLAME TREE PRESS
6 Melbray Mews, London, SW6 3NS, UK
flametreepress.com

US sales, distribution and warehouse:
Simon & Schuster
simonandschuster.biz

UK distribution and warehouse:
Hachette UK Distribution
hukdcustomerservice@hachette.co.uk

Thanks to the Flame Tree Press team.

The cover is made by Flame Tree Studio, working with the fine and wonderful artist Broci who created the cover and inside illustrations especially for this book. The art is © Broci 2025. The font families used are Avenir and Bembo.

Flame Tree Press is an imprint of Flame Tree Publishing Ltd
flametreepublishing.com

A copy of the CIP data for this book is available from the British Library and the Library of Congress.

1 3 5 7 9 8 6 4 2

HB ISBN: 978-1-78758-969-8
ebook ISBN: 978-1-78758-970-4

Printed and bound in Great Britain by Clays Ltd, Elcograf S.p.A.

MIX
Paper | Supporting responsible forestry
FSC® C018072

ANNA SMITH SPARK

A SWORD OF GOLD AND RUIN

BOOK TWO of THE MAKING OF THIS WORLD RUINED

FLAME TREE PRESS
London & New York

To Jenny

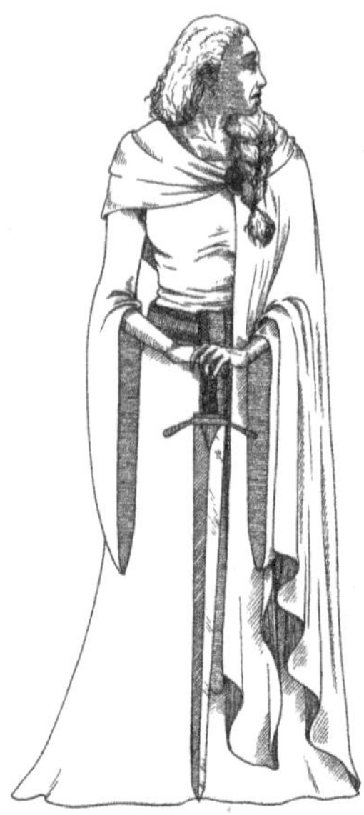

CHAPTER ONE

The crocuses were in bloom.

A gray sky, that gray that suggests rain and softened weather. The storms of winter are almost now the first spring rain. A bird was singing in a tree still bare, yet the song was calling a mate or singing that she had one, in the single note there repeated there was spring blossom and summer sun and hatching eggs. The ground was cold mud and bareness, yet from the mud with the snow's melting fresh on it the crocuses were in bloom purple and white and yellow, and beneath the ground the world was waking to burst up green. And the bird flew low and brown with twigs in her beak to build her nest.

But the air was far colder than Kanda had expected, biting at her face and hands, stinging her throat as she sucked it down into her lungs. Stepping out of the door with her coat loose and unfastened, her face turned bright to the sky. The cold made her gasp. Pleasant, refreshing: the taste, the feel of the winter cold in her mouth stepping out from hearth smoke: that was a thing she loved. But the smell of the air, the light that streamed in pale through the hall's high windows – they had made her think of warm days and warm sweet flower air and she had relaxed herself for the warmth on her face.

Almost unbalanced, walking in the biting cold feeling – knowing – that it was spring. The bird there singing, even if the trees were bare, knew it was spring. And the crocuses she waded through knew.

Winter is not a good time for fighting. And not a good time for burying the dead.

The earth is too cold in winter to bury the dead. Spring is the fitted time for these things.

From the slopes of the mountains before her on the far horizon, smoke was rising. The wind blew the wrong way for her to smell it. Thin columns. Many columns. Kanda put her hand on the hilt of her sword. More smoke rising on the horizon than would soon rise from the slopes of the mountains where she stood.

"Ah, it's cold." The voice made her almost jump. She turned. Laughed.

"If you insist on going out in your shirt, Gallyn."

"Look, you can see my breath." He huffed out into the gray air.

"No, you can't."

"No, you can't. Bah." He puffed out his cheeks, blew out like blowing a war horn. "It should be cold enough for that."

Kanda looked at him. "Have you even been to sleep?"

"That's for after all this, when the excitement's died down. We fight, we celebrate, then we sleep."

"Gallyn…we haven't started fighting yet. This is still the boring bit."

"We celebrate, we fight, we celebrate again…then we sleep. Bah, it really should be cold enough to see my breath."

"Gallyn…." His face was such a boy's face. So young. Celebrating for him almost meant cakes and games and running about. Kanda thought, looking at him: why could our Lord not have made me as young as that? Her hair was red as fire, her skin was brown as earth, her eyes were blue as sweet deep water, on her brow she wore a circlet of bronze; out of good sown earth and wildfire and red autumn berries, the Lord of Roven had shaped her. But he had not, in his great wisdom, made her beautiful and young.

Gallyn, *Great Leap*, silver trout and green willow leaves, golden sand on summer beaches, the babble of a snowmelt river, dragonflies in a buzz of rainbowed wings. His helmet had a young stallion rearing in the dance as its crest.

"Go inside and put your cloak on before you catch a cold and miss the battle entirely," Kanda said.

"A cold! A mere cold keep me, Lord Gallyn of the Six Swords of Roven, from fighting?"

"Yes, but.... Go inside and put your cloak on before you catch a cold and have to ride into battle with a sore snot-crusted nose beneath your helmet."

Laughter. "That might bother Morren. But not me. However – it is far too cold to be without a cloak, yes."

If it was Morren, Kanda thought, she would say now, "Are you... have you been drinking before the battle?' and fret over him. But Gallyn skipped off back into the hall only young and foolish and in such high thoughtless good spirits. He shouted from inside the hall: "And sneeze so hard I almost fall off my horse mid-sword thrust! Spray snot all over the enemy even as I cut off his head!"

"Get on with you, Gallyn." Ah, he was by far the best of them!

A trumpet rang from behind the hall. A long, mournful note.

Gallyn said, "Oh." He came back out, cloaked now in shining white. His face was grave now. A boy's face, shocked by war and death.

Kanda thought: our Lord of Roven in his wisdom made him young and innocent. Thus every time the battle ends and the dead are gathered, the cost of war comes new to him. Poor sweet Gallyn.

A bow shot's distance, perhaps, or a little more, or as far, perhaps, as a man could run and not be winded, or as a horse could run for the sheer pleasure of its running, or as far as Gallyn could leap. Up to the crest of the hill on which the king's hall was built, down the other side one hundred, two hundred, three hundred steps. There in the lee of the king's hill a pool lay very clear, perfectly round and black like the eye of a prized milch cow, fringed in dark rushes. In the middle of the pool was a black rock. On the rock was a pyre. Birchwood that seemed to be not wood but white bleached bone against the black water and the black rock. On the pyre, quiet, almost sleeping, was a body wrapped in a fine red cloak.

The king's hall, the king's hill, the king's pool in which the king must bathe on his crowning. The king's cloak. The king's son.

The horn blew its one terrible note. Comfortless, pitiless in its grief as the scream of a gull or a hawk. In answer, pitiless and comfortless also, the women raised the lament.

Mare. Mare.
Henket.
How young he was. How splendid.
So beautiful he was, and fierce, and strong.
Night has covered his eyes.
There is no joy in his face.
His arms are as stones in the empty field,
His eyes are as stones,
As stones, as cold ashes, his face.
Mare. Mare.
Henket.
Henket.

Mare, that is only *despair. Mighty ceaseless quenchless all-consuming sorrow. Grief.*

Henket, that is only *death.*

One woman, face veiled in white, her voice louder than the rest, out of their rhythm. Ended with a shriek. She fell to her knees, tore at her clothes, fell to lie prostrate tearing at the cold ground. Mud clawed beneath her fingers.

Kanda stared, then looked away. Stared. Looked away. Gallyn beside her stiffened, she heard his breath fast and shallow, frightened. Like a mother comforting her child, Kanda reached out to touch his arm. "It's all right to feel upset, Gallyn. Not to want to look."

The boy shrugged her hand off. "They should not make her come out in front of them all like this."

"It's important to them. For her. Part of the grieving. They see and share her grief."

"It's horrible. It's not right." He said, "It's like…like making her show her private parts or something."

"Gallyn! It's nothing like that. Not to her. It's important for her that she does this." I hope.

Like a mother comforting her child, Kanda thought: and what would I know of mothers and children? What would I know of death? Of grief? She said after a time: "Don't look, Gallyn, then."

"I won't. I can't." The boy stomped off a few paces, toward the hall he had just left. He turned back, almost ran to Kanda. "If we had come… Just a day earlier…. Curse it!" Kicked at the purple crocuses and the white crocuses and the crocuses as yellow as egg yolks.

"He might still have died in the battle, Gallyn, even if we had been there at his side." Or his father the king, or his sister, or…. Look, Gallyn, many parents' children lie dead on the field of battle, they too are all mourned and missed. We cannot be everywhere, saving every life. We are warriors, Gallyn. Tomorrow we will be there, and many still will die – and some of them, we will kill. But you would say: *but we will kill the enemy! Not our friends!* And I would say: *they are still someone's friend.* But you would not understand, because our Lord in his great wisdom made you so bright and young.

Oh our Lord made you too innocent, Gallyn. For our Lord made us only to kill.

Gallyn said with a sob: "He could have been…my friend."

The worm that lived in Kanda's heart, the worm shifted, thrashed its tail, bared its teeth. *I would our Lord had made me as young and ever innocent as you, Gallyn. It was cruel of our Lord, the way he made me and you*, it said. Kanda said, "You could go down there. Join them."

Two women had gathered the queen between them, held her as she beat and slapped and screamed. The king was coming now with the torch to light the pyre. He waded into the cold water up to his waist. Kanda saw the cold shudder through him. His left arm was bandaged. His shoulders were hunched with grief. The crowd shifted as the torch was raised and dropped onto the pyre, a great wall of weeping howling silence, and one voice wailed, and one voice, a young woman's, cried wildly, "No! He can't be dead! No!" All thin and hunched and cold they looked, bent like trees on a high moor stunted and battered trying to grow.

She looked at Gallyn. Tall, splendid: his skin gleaming black, his hair silver curls, his big clear dark eyes, the strong muscles of his arms, his legs, his chest. His cloak was pure white silk trimmed in white marten fur, the man who had woven it for him, who loved him deeply and truly and without shadow, had spoken a charm of happiness and comfort into every warp and weft of the thread. His shirt was white silk, his jacket was combed wool dyed leaf-green and sewn all over with gold beads in the shape of winged horses. He wore a torc of gold at his throat, his boots were buckled in gold, his belt had a buckle of gold in the shape of a flower burst, his cloak pin was a disc of gold as big as a man's fist. His leggings were soft deerskin dyed scarlet. In the king's hall his armor waited for him, his corselet and his helmet were bronze covered in silver, his sword had a golden hilt and a golden scabbard. Pale fire ran along the length of the golden blade.

Gallyn looked down at himself so splendid. "I'll stay here until it's done," he said in a quiet voice.

From the pyre the smoke was rising. The water of the king's pool rose up in steam. The body and the mourners both were blotted out.

In the first bright morning of the world the Lord of Roven summoned the Six of Roven to him. Roven, the great hall roofed in gold whose name means *Peace*. In that hall there is set the cauldron Helle, that is *Health*, which can never be exhausted by any hunger, and the throne Thalle, that is *Hope*. The gates of Roven are always open, any who pass near to her walls are welcomed in. By the gates stands her Lady, looking out upon the world in welcome. On the throne sits her Lord, who has no name but in whose face is all that is kind and wise and good. Yet even in that first bright morning of the world there was grief, and pain, and evil, and thus the nameless Lord of Roven in his wisdom called the Six to him. From the play of sunlight on water, from the snow that falls pure and clean, from the wild high places and the rich tilled fields, from the stones of the earth and the wood of the trees, from birdsong and flowers and the sky's bright fire, he made them. He clad them in shining armor, into their hands he placed matchless shining blades. Each night they feasted in the Hall Roven. Each day they would ride out across the world.

From the south the call came: a quiet kingdom in a green valley, surrounded by great snow-capped mountains. The snowmelt rushed down cold and sweet to the rich black earth of the fields, the sun lingered long on the mountain's slopes. Quiet, sheltered, hidden, its people poets and singers, farmers, dreamers. Even its king – the custom of that place was that for ten years he would rule, then he would hand the crown to another, chosen by the people, and settle to till the fields again in peace. This the messenger told the Lord and Lady of Roven, gasping out her words, stumbling on them, choked by tears. *For now war has come to our kingdom, an army squats in the high passes, above the peaks of the mountains things that are not birds have been glimpsed flying on heavy wings. The outer farms and the summer pastures in the mountains are burned: what burned them we do not know, for no one survived the flames to speak. Why they were burned…who can say why? Our cattle were butchered, our sheep. The carrion birds that came down to feed on the ruins…cruel hands caught them, butchered them; even the crows, even the rats and the flies, have been killed. Why would anyone, anything, do this?*

Help us, my Lord of Roven. Please. Send the Six Swords of Roven to fight for us.

Of the Six:

One had ridden east to slay a dragon.

One had ridden west to find a stolen treasure.

One had ridden south to free a city from a tyrant.

One had ridden north to rescue a handsome prince.

Two remained in Roven, one content in being courted by a new lover, one itching to be off on a quest. The youngest and the oldest of the Six. Within an hour of the messenger's desperate arrival, they were riding out through the gates of Roven to the kingdom's aid.

Arrived to grief beyond measure, the enemy in the field, the king's young fine son newly dead. "We must surrender," fearful voices pleaded.

"We have come to aid you. To help you," Kanda told them. They were fearful, stared suspicious. Wary even as they welcomed Kanda and Gallyn in.

"Where is your king?"

"He is weeping."

"Where is your army?"

"It is cowering away in shame and grief."

"But you defeated the enemy, you won the victory?"

"But the king's son who led us to that victory is dead."

Kanda said: "I will command you." Greatly she pitied them. They did as she bid them, but they did not look at her face, and the fear streamed like sweat off them.

A day and a night for the burial. Then a day to sleep. Then a night to sleep. Unsleeping, Kanda and Gallyn watched over them. Dawn broke. A lone bird in a bare tree was singing. A trumpet blew – no human mouth blew it. It blew to mourn. It blew to feast. It blew three times, the third note was to draw swords for battle. The wound of the sun was red.

Kanda armed herself in bronze armor worked with glinting gold. A golden helmet with a red plume upon her head. Her sword was Iath, that is *Kind Strength*; its blade was gold. Gallyn armed himself in bronze and silver, put on his helmet with its silver stallion as a crest. His sword was Neir, that is *Joy in Eagerness*.

Again, the trumpet sounded. Loud and urgent. From the mountains in the west a trumpet answered, lower, angrier, perhaps – hope and desire it – more frightened. Then from the shadow of the far mountains the drums began to beat. In the far distance the dawn light caught on spears, on swords, on great bronze-helmeted giants. Caught on things winged that were not birds. On banners blowing in no earthly wind. A single voice cried: "The enemy comes! The enemy wakes!" Fell silent at its neighbor's begging.

The sunlight broke then in a blaze of red and gold upon those far mountains beyond the crocus fields. Side by side, Kanda and Gallyn strode to the doors of the king's hall. The doors were thrown open by hands unseen. On the threshold Kanda said three words that need be spoken, Gallyn said three words that must be said. A breath of sweet spring air touched both their faces. In the bare tree the bird sang on. Ranks of warriors stood before them on the slope of the king's hill. A thousand nameless common women and men. All of them waiting grimly and in silence, fear in their eyes that their bronze helmets only half hid. Walls of bronze leading down the slope of the hill toward the crocus fields. In silence their ranks opened for Kanda to walk down among them. Like bronze doors opening. The crocuses yellow and purple and white beyond. The western mountains were alive with movement. On the slopes of the mountains the enemies' banners were very bright. The wind blew from the mountains into Kanda's face now. It smelled of smoke; when it blew from over the enemy's banners it smelled of blood.

Side by side, Kanda and Gallyn walked through the ranks of the army they had come here to lead to battle. "Do not be afraid," Kanda said to the eyes beseeching her through the bronze. "Lord Gallyn and I: we have come to help you win this battle. The enemy there – they can and they will and they must be defeated. And I know well how to defeat them."

Down through the bronze ranks to the perfume of the crocus fields. On the edge of the fields the petals already trampled down. A thousand faces watching Kanda and Gallyn. Desperate fear. Yearning. Eyes red with grief.

On the edge of the crocus fields the king bowed low before Kanda and Gallyn. "My lady. My lord. Grant us this victory." On the slopes of the far mountains the enemy was a dark tide rising. The king turned his face to stare. His army – Kanda's army – watched him. The king said, his voice trembling, "Please, my lady, my lord. Help my people live."

Kanda walked past him without speaking. Gallyn stopped a moment, touched the man's shoulder, went on. Together Kanda and Gallyn walked out into the crocus fields to stand between the army and the enemy as it came toward them. Two figures between the battle lines. The enemy was a dark tide rising. Men and beasts and shapes and shapeless screams. The enemy halted, drew back, at the sight of Kanda and Gallyn.

Yellow flowers bloomed in the tread of Kanda and Gallyn's feet. But shadows writhed in the tread of their feet, and their swords were naked in their hands and from their swords dripped blood.

The sunlight was extinguished.

"Ready! Be ready there!" Kanda's voice itself a war trumpet, a war drum. "Form ranks! Form up there! Now! Spearmen! Swordsmen! Archers – half draw! And – wait!"

The enemy crawled down from the far mountains. Came on running. In the air now, great invisible beating wings. Shadows, too hard to see in this daylight, shifting and flickering as blood spilled into a river shifts and is gone. Wolves behind and beside them, thin from mountain living, their pelts white as fresh-fallen snow on the high peaks. Wolves with men's faces, or men's arms holding sword and spear high above their wolf haunches, or wolves with wounds on their flanks raw and bleeding from which sharp teeth grew. Wild men with six eyes and the tusks of wild boar, antlers on their foreheads. Men with the heads and wings of eagles. Dead men heavy with grave soil. Men with knives in place of hands. A beast that might be a dragon, if dragons were gray loathsome toad things. A beast that might be all made of fire, if fire burned cold and vile and rotted. Fierce great men from the western side of the mountains, ragged in their hunger-strength, wrapped in the bronze-dipped fur of cave bears. Their axes were stone, their spears were stone. Like stone the young woman's face who led them. Kanda threw back her head, roared out her war cry. "Ready! Be ready there! Be strong! In the name of all that you hold dear, for this good sweet earth here in this valley, this life of quiet peace! Be ready! Do not fear them! I am the greatest of the Six Swords of Roven! I am sent by my Lord of Roven to defend you to my last breath! For all that is good, for all that you love in this world, be ready, do not fear – and – now – they come – fight them!"

And silence, the enemy holds also. Ready, hungry, fearless. Waiting. Straining. They twitch and claw for the coming blood.

"Hold!" Kanda shouting now. "Hold. Brace. Wait."

The Six of Roven, ever hopeful, ever foolish: never will one of the Six draw first blood.

The ranks of the enemy opened. A void, a mouth to swallow hope and fooling. From the enemy ranks too bright almost to look at there strode a man who shone like the sun.

"Geiamnyn!" Gallyn shouted. The boy's face was crumpled in revulsion. "See, Kanda, it is worse than we feared. What do you here, Geiamnyn, murderer, monster, beast?"

If Gallyn was a boy in first budding youthful splendor, Geiamnyn his enemy was a man in the first fresh bloom of adult strength. Long golden hair fell over his shoulders, his skin was white and gold, his eyes blue, his lips red. His face was as fair as a summer morning. His armor was gilded, set with gemstones; his cloak was crimson silk. He was so radiant in his beauty, so glorious was he that white light leapt from him as he walked. White flowers sprang up in his footsteps, and even his shadow was of light. A man of gold and crystal. Flawless. He moved like a great war horse, confident in his power and grace.

Gallyn hefted his sword, shook it. "Leave this place, these people, Geiamnyn, creep away back to the filth you came from. Or face me in battle man to man and let us end this."

Trumpets. The great man Geiamnyn looked at Gallyn and he laughed. The tide of the enemy came in and broke upon Kanda and Gallyn.

Killing. The blade of Kanda's sword was like a sickness. The wounds she made hurt her own skin. I had not thought I must destroy so many. She killed one two three four five six seven of them. She killed one two three four of them. She killed and she killed and she killed them. No choice. If she stayed her hand, they would kill all those she had come to defend. A woman went down at her left even now, chest cut wide open, eyes as wide open in surprise that she's dying. And a man – the woman's lover? brother? friend? – he runs forward howling, throws himself forward, he takes a beast hard on his spear, grips it, tears it, guts it. Brightness of vengeance. That killing smile. Eyes fall on her trampled body and the smile's fading. She's still dead. She shouldn't be still dead. And he pushes forward harder, and Kanda shouts for him to hold the line there, but he pushes forward, that delusion, if he kills enough, his woman will come back to him. And he pushes forward, and so of course before Kanda has a chance of helping he's down too beside his woman, he's opened up and stripped and dead. No choice, indeed, Kanda. These people, they are not blameless, but she must fight to defend them. Killing is a bad thing, and she…hates it, she thinks. But there are worse things than killing. She kills the beast that killed the man that killed the beast that killed the woman. She kills one two three four five six seven eight nine ten. One two three four five six seven eight nine ten. One two three four—

Gallyn shouted. Kanda spun around, blood dripping.

"Geiamnyn! Face me!"

She thought: no, no, Gallyn.

"Face me!"

The boy was in the slaughter-frenzy. "Face me, Geiamnyn!"

Kanda began to run. Choking. "Stop. Stop, Gallyn."

"Geiamnyn!" Gallyn shouted.

Geiamnyn rose up vast before the boy Gallyn.

"Face you? I'll kill you with one blow. With a knife, with my bare hands, I'll kill you with one blow, Gallyn."

His face was corrupt now. No beauty left until the battle ended. See him for what he was and is.

She meant Geiamnyn.

She meant Gallyn.

The two came together dancing. Gallyn made first strike. Like a child beating against the walls of a prison. Geiamnyn was all laughter. Struck his one blow. Roared not laughing as Gallyn blocked it, struck back. Gallyn struck back twice three times four times before Geiamnyn struck his second. Gallyn blocked it, and now both were bloody. Bloody their hands, bloody their monstrous faces. Gallyn had the better of it, one, two, three he had the better of it, now Geiamnyn was the child, Gallyn was all laughing. Gallyn was a beast, Geiamnyn was almost falling.

Gallyn slid his sword down for the death blow. But Gallyn could not strike it.

But Geiamnyn struck the death blow, and mightily and then weakly Gallyn shouted.

And Gallyn was a boy in his beauty, with his young face astonished.

"To me!" Kanda shouted. Leapt straight and proud over the body of *Great Leap*. Feet planted in mud and dust and bloodshed, her sword aflame. "Geiamnyn! Fear me!" The man was as a city wall towering over her. His shadow was on her. Hurt her. Bit like a serpent at her face, her hands, her feet. He roared like a stag in rut, Kanda let out her war cry thundering. Their swords clashed together so the blades rang like bells, one, two, three, four, blow struck, blow parried, music of blade against blade against blade. Twist, strike, ward, strike, duck, stretch, strike him, strike him! Gallyn with the death wound rolling like a child beneath their feet. One step back, hard blow, parry, strike harder, Kanda's teeth gritted against the pain in her arm, fire bursting from Geiamnyn's sword.

A horrible dead cry from Geiamnyn. He staggered back and his face was loathsome: like a toad, he looked, glowering in pain with the shame on him. *You, woman, you should be knelt in desire at my feet.* Blood on his fine body. A kind of wonder: *but you, you, woman, you….* He lashed out then wild, made weaker by fury, Kanda easily turned the blow away. She heard Gallyn alive with no wound on him roar to encourage the defenders. A beast all claws and sorrow crashed down burning, rose in frantic hunger, fell, did not could not rise again. Gallyn roared the kill cry, a woman's voice almost a child's rose beside it more ragged and more joyful. A mountain man and a shadow that rode his shoulders, axe huge as a bull's horns, a sword came up, a spear came up flashing, the man roared, the shadow bared its fangs – he and it together – in red pain they fell. The enemy fled with screams. Fell in silence. Threw out their arms to give way. Beasts and men and monsters. Gallyn gave the end cry. Called the warriors forward. Geiamnyn was crawling. Geiamnyn was sobbing. Kanda struck at Geiamnyn. Took off his fine handsome head.

"Victory!" Gallyn screamed. He danced and leapt with joy and with relief up to Kanda. He bent to spit on Geiamnyn's body. Spittle already on his lips. But Kanda grasped his arm, said quickly, "No, Gallyn."

"No." He bit his lip. Suddenly sobered.

"Come away," Kanda said.

The body began to twitch. Back crawling. The head began to roll. The head was grinning and laughing. "I'll be revenged!" Geiamnyn's head croaked. "I'll be revenged! I'll be revenged!"

"Leave him. Don't watch, Gallyn," Kanda said. She turned away, pulled Gallyn away. The remnants of the man in his beauty pulling itself from its death behind them. Crocus flowers crushed and staining him. His voice croaking a senseless idiot song. "Don't hear, don't see," Kanda said. "There is no point to it. Leave him." For the trumpets were ringing now a joy-song. The enemy was fled and broken. Gone like storm floods.

Gallyn looked at a single flower still somehow in bloom and undamaged growing in the killing ground. Golden. Gallyn looked up over the battlefield and a smile broke across his face. Said, delighted, amazed as if he had not expected it: "Kanda…it is won!"

Kanda sheathed her sword. Bile in her throat. She thought: bite back the sickness. She began to weep.

Gallyn said, "Kanda?" They had not been alone on a battlefield before like this, the only two of the Six. Sweet innocent Gallyn: how young and gentle still he looked!

"It's nothing." She blinked away her tears. "It's just…. When I sheath my sword, and it's ended…."

Gallyn looked down at the flower. Nodded, shifted his feet. "It's good," he said. "So good. Yes, I too could cry for the sheer joy of it having ended."

All across the crocus fields clots of warriors swirled around each other, cautious, they looked like birds after the storm has blown itself out. Two men met who were friends or brothers or lovers, they embraced, clasped hands. Then one's eyes, wandering over his companion's shoulder, saw something in the near distance, he broke away with a shriek, ran from his companion to another man who lay fallen, caught him up in shaking sobbing arms. His companion received another's shout of triumph, welcomed it, all the time watching his beloved grieving, all the time looking around them for his own dead. Two women embraced on the battlefield looking at nothing beyond themselves. An older woman pushed away any greeting, knelt alone wounded in the mud, until a tall young man came up to her, placed his hand on her shoulder, she turned then, looked into his face, and her face shone. Slowly they began to move together more thickly, came back together as the people of the mountain valley kingdom. Like birds gathering to fly together north to raise their young, and indeed it was almost, almost spring. The lover gathered up his grief-stricken beloved. A woman's voice rang out the victory song.

And the victory feast, there on the field of battle, treading the last few of the crocus flowers down. The sun shone with new warmth that was spring come early, or they felt warm after fighting and with the joy in them they could believe it was spring and summer come. The old and young and those who could not fight came spilling down onto the battlefield, "Thank you," they clamored around Kanda and Gallyn, "thank you! Thank you! Heroes!" They embraced, kissed, hugged their loved ones, "A feast! A dance! Victory!" they shouted. They drank barley beer and mead and winter milk pale as the moonlight, made wreaths of green pine boughs and brown budded twigs. But they did not crown Kanda and Gallyn with wreaths, nor offer them beer or mead or milk in wooden cups or clay cups or cups of fine-worked silver or fine-worked tin. Kanda saw them look askance, eyes flick from Kanda's shadow to the dead ready to be burned, from Gallyn's shadow to the victory feast. They danced, but they did not dance near Kanda and Gallyn. They whispered, and after a little while they began to make warding signs with their hands if Kanda or Gallyn came too close.

"We should go now," Kanda said to Gallyn. He sighed, but he nodded.

The people did not try to stop them. "You must stay for the feast, look, the meat is roasted, there are honey cakes almost baked," they said when Kanda went to get the horses, but they did not say it again as Kanda and Gallyn mounted up and rode away. As the two rode away the songs and the laughter grew louder behind them. "Victory! Victory!" the voices shouted; a voice called out too loudly in its relief, "Now we can gather up the dead." At the top of the king's hill a child threw a corn dolly before Gallyn's horse. It had been coated in honey, a stone was hung around its neck. "Ward," the child said. "Keep the evil away. Never may it come here again." Funeral smoke rose behind them, horses' hooves, the beat of drums. Kanda looked at Gallyn. Gallyn looked away from her in confusion.

"They would all be dead, Kanda," Gallyn said, "if we had not been there. All of them." He sunk his head low, slumped in the saddle. "I don't understand," he said.

The battle had lasted only a few hours; it was still only afternoon and the sun was long and almost summer golden, it lit gold the snow of the mountain peaks.

They rode back to the Hall Roven.

CHAPTER TWO

Long ago and far away, that battle happened, and the Six Swords of Roven now were themselves but words on the wind. But now, also, the crocuses were in bloom.

The sky was the perfect pale blue of winter falling into springtime, dry sharp clean cold enough to lay a faint frost; but the spring birds were singing, it was good weather, perfect weather, to build the new house. The timber for the frame was green pinewood. Six strong posts to hold the roof up, each three times as tall as Kanda and as thick each as Kanda's thigh (so: thick indeed! Kanda might think). Nine stronger posts to hold the six strong posts steady to stop the roof from breaking. The six strong posts and the nine stronger posts must be well sunk in deep round holes well dug in the deep spring mud. Calian, thirteen and almost a grown woman and almost a child, had loved that work digging many deep round holes. Green oak to peg the timbers, hempen rope rubbed with beeswax to bind the pegged joints, and, ah, the smell of new rope and beeswax and new-cut pine and new-cut oak! So yesterday the timbers were pegged and bound, the postholes dug and waiting, today they got up at dawn to pour a pot of beer into the bottom of each posthole and to raise the house up.

The house frames lay waiting, three of them, two long posts and three shorter posts bound and pegged together to make a shape like an arrowhead; when the beer had soaked away into the earth each frame was pulled up with strong ropes. The most dangerous part of the housebuilding, one two three up up up and steady, rocking, rocking, the smell of the ropes very strong now, the rope fibers creaked. Kanda was pressed behind Lela, milky-smelling, should she be doing this work? but her feet were strong planted while Kanda was half slipping; Gal behind Kanda was making a *click click* noise with his tongue on his lips as he strained and he was useless;

Kanda's husband Dellet was on the other rope with a wide happy sweaty grin. Rocking wood, creak of ropes, slowly, slowly, steady, hold there, steady, not too fast, not too strong there, hold it, hold it – everyone in the village gasped, and then such a cheer! Once, twice, three times, a frame for the east wall, for the west wall, and for the center of the house to hold up the weight of the long roof.

Now the house frames stood erect they looked strange and almost frightening, three great gateways open wide. Until the work started on the roof and the walls no one must walk through them or stand in their shadow. The ghosts of branches hung from the poles that had been living tree trunks, the air was filled with the sound and the scent of wet leaves, birds, insects. Thus the work could not be left like this. It was growing dark now, but quickly now they lit torches, worked to get up the ridgepole that would form the house's spine. Make it a house. The longest piece of wood Kanda had ever seen that was not a tree still growing, the trunk of a pine tall and strong as a warrior maiden, tended for many years to keep it right for this great work of being the spine of a house. The most difficult bit, raising the ridgepole, harder than raising the house frames even. Kanda thought: like trying to use a spear by balancing its end on a fingertip. She winced and bit her lip as it went up, certain it would fall and kill someone, at the least bring all the day's work raising the house frames down in a pile of firewood. She wanted to say, "Dellet, Calian, please, keep clear." She heaved and struggled with the rest, swaying beneath the absurd length of the ridgepole. It seemed to thrash like a serpent. A dragon's tail, even, Kanda thought. The wood creaking, crying: why have you cut me down? I hurt. I hurt. And then – wait, wait, nearly, almost, wait, no, wait, wait – and the cheers were deafening when they got it in place at last. And from the wood – peaceful silence. The shape suddenly of a fine house. The walls and the roof were there like mist between the house poles now. The ghosts of years of quiet daily life. Creak of old men's bones and young children playing. Damp smell of bodies sleeping, playing, eating, fucking, being alive so noisy and so quiet. The wood of the house sighed now with pleasure: oh, yes, yes, I see. Keep them safe, keep them warm, give them shelter. Yes, I do see, and it is a fine thing.

Now at last they could stop for the night.

Also now they could have a long victory drink of beer in the house before they turned in.

Several days' work now, steady: a latticework of smaller poles to hold it all together and make it solid, green pine for the long roof-sides north and south, willow withies woven together for the short wall-sides east and west. Thatching on the roof-sides, a vast treasure mound of dried reeds. Kanda had hoped at first to be part of gathering the thatch in, for she loved already the salt marshes that stretched away to the east of the village. But it had been gathered in the autumn and kept dry all winter, she had to content herself with helping to tie it into bundles and throw it to the three thatchers up on the roof working. "Watch out! Oi there!" the thatchers shouted. Reeds are vicious, cutting, wondrous things. Then the best of all: filling the withy walls with straw and dried beech leaves and dried bracken, then everyone in the village spitting into the daub, throwing off shoes to trample it beneath their toes cool and slimy, hold hands and dance triumphant on it, what a shriek when Kanda slipped. Dovei, Lela's man, grabbed Kanda's hand to catch her, they teetered, Lela shouted: "Get his knees!" and Kanda and Dovei were down in the muck. Calian roared with laughter until she almost fell over. Sal threw a lump of daub at Calian from where she sat with the other elders laughing and laughing. As if that was a signal, everyone in the village oldest to youngest started throwing the daub over the walls to cover the withies. That was best of best of all, and good for courting games and rivals' games and children making mock of all the adults. By the time the walls were finished even Sal and the other elders were covered in mud. It was dark by then. More victory beer around a makeshift house fire. They threw a cup of beer on each wall before they went off to wash and sleep. Kanda's legs were so thick with mud, Calian and Sal and Dellet all having a good aim, that she walked stiff as a baby with soiled clouts.

"Ruined my leggings," said Kanda.

Calian rolled her bright eyes: "What did you expect?" Said smartly: "These are the sacrifices we make, Mum."

The house was very almost a house the next morning. The night had worked its magic. The walls were drying, looked like walls, the daub rough and strong like the back of Dellet's hands. When they had dried fully, days and days away still, they would be washed with lime to protect them, but they were already definitely unarguably proper house walls. Now they must lift and tie the windows above the walls in place east and west. Stag hide stretched on a frame and rubbed with fish oil. It was gray that day, threatening rain – "typical, just as the daub needs to dry proper, you make all the offerings and more, put up with everything the reeds demand, but…ah, what can you do?" – but when the west window was in place and the last worker stepping off the bottom rung of her ladder, suddenly the sun came out. The hide looked black and in truth very ugly, and up close up the ladder it stank. But when the afternoon sunlight hit it the hide was pure light. The house was brilliant with light. So many sunbeams striking the far wall, and the house was filled with dancing dust motes. It was a house! A very fine house!

The porch for the door. The floor planks and over them the rushes and the strew-herbs: rosemary, chamomile, tansy, mint. The bed-benches around the walls in the west half of the house, the animal pens in the east half. The stone charms and the bone charms and a dried frog and a sprig of dried heather above the doors.

The furniture. Kanda carried in a good thick bearskin for a warm bedcover, Dellet a three-legged stool, Calian a clay cook pot, Sal a reed basket.

The hearth. The oldest person in the village was a woman with five great-grandchildren. She was almost blind, could barely walk. Lela her granddaughter helped her into the house, sat her down by the unlit hearth fire. The youngest village child – the woman's great-grandson, Lela's new one – was placed in her arms. Kanda had been chosen to beat one of the drums to call the luck down. Calian stood very close. The last person to die in the village was another great-grandchild, would have been the baby's older brother if he had lived. Tears in Kanda's eyes as Dovei the baby's father brought the tiny skull out of a safe place beside their own hearth, carried it to the beat of drums through the village. Around the bounds of the village, to the doorway of all the houses, to the fields, to the bank of the river, the fishpond, the village well, up to the bark of every fruit tree in the village orchard, to stop and lie a little while in the village burying place. Placed it in a basket of rushes, and in the basket there was besides the skull: the leg bone of a deer, the wing bone of a blackbird, an apple with one withered leaf, a snag of wool, a knapped flint, a broken bit of old pot. Outside the new house the man stopped, stood holding the basket. A hole had been dug on the threshold. Very deep. Dovei placed the basket in the hole, as he did so he let out a great sob and his eyes filled with tears.

"You could not be with us in life," Lela said. Her voice was strong and proud but full of heavy grief. "My son, my child, you will not sit by the fire here listening to stories, you will not tend the goats and the sheep in the pens here in the cold winter, nor will you lie in the summer warm watching the sun rise through the window in the east. Watch over this house now, watch over the village now, keep all who live here or who visit as guests seeking shelter – watch over us all, now and for many generations to come, as long as this house stands and longer. My son." She fell into her husband's arms weeping, he buried his face in her hair. The villagers hurried to fill in the hole, bury the basket. On the top to form the house's threshold they set a flat black stone they had dug up in the wood.

Kanda and the others beat the drums loudly. Inside the house, unkindled by any human hand, the hearth fire blazed up.

In the flames everyone saw clear as day a child's face smiling at them.

Now the house was alive, and a good place.

That night they feasted all together, roast meat and the last of that year's apples, small and as yellow as the autumn moon they had been gathered under, and sweet winter milk. They had not eaten meat or drunk milk since they started work on the house, and now the house was finished.

That night the whole village, the oldest woman, the youngest baby, Gal, Lela, Dovei; Kanda, Dellet, Calian, Sal; they all slept piled together in the new house. There had been a house on this spot long ago that had fallen ruined, and now there was a fine new house here again for the village to grow to fill.

CHAPTER THREE

The next morning, and the light through the east window made the thatch look like long rippling waves of hair. Kanda lay a little while and watched the smoke in the light and the thatch and listened to the sleepers breathing.

Her husband Dellet lay on his back. His skin was the rich bronze of a good axe-head, his hair was dark and curled like pine bark, his snores were like a blunt saw on hard wood. Del-my-heart, Kanda thought. He smiled in his sleep. He had loved the work on the house; the hard labor of hauling the great trees, raising the poles up, he had especially loved. His hands had new calluses he had shown her proudly; the muscles in his arms looked very strong.

Their daughter Calian lay beside him, pressed up to him close; her face also had a soft peace after such working to build the house. She had Del's bronze skin, Del's dark thick hair, Del's solidness. She was thirteen, bright as a jackdaw – but fierce as a jackdaw if she was displeased.

Sal lay between Calian and Kanda. Her hair was white silk, very beautiful it looked against her deep brown skin. Like mist in the dawn rising from a river, when the river itself is dark almost to black in the silver light. She was slender as a birch tree, fragile now because she was growing from older to simply old, often looked drawn and sad with age. But the village loved her as the kindest and best of the family, she was far closer and better and endlessly more patient with Calian than Kanda could ever manage to be.

The four were wrapped close. But there was a great space between where a ghost lay. Huge, that ghost. It would have cooed over Lela's baby, shrieked with joy at the daub-making, got in the way of the house frames going up, hurt its ankle falling in at least one of the postholes, dropped a pot that it had insisted it could easily carry into the house. It snuffled in its sleep, pressed its bird-thin arms against Dellet. Huge as the world, you see, that ghost.

Kanda had to get up now she had seen that ghost.

Carefully, not to disturb her family or any of the villagers lying asleep packed into the new house. Days of hard work, a late night, potloads of beer: it was no wonder they slept. Almost as if some kind magic had granted them all a deep peaceful sleep rich in dreams of summer sunshine, so that they might forever look upon the house as blessed.... Kanda thought: winter's injuries have healed, winter's illnesses were easily cured, Lela's baby was born safe and healthy, the livestock were safe all winter and the lambs were born as healthy as the baby, the sun begins to grow warmer, we have made a fine good house for people to live well in. Those are the best of things.

She picked her way over them to the double doorway. One side for the flocks, one side for the people. She knew the guardian smiled his baby smile as she stepped over the threshold, the door opened to the southeast and caught with joy the rising sun. And the sun was like a baby's face. And the charms hung at the threshold stirred and sang as Kanda passed them.

A fine village. Five houses now the new one was built, a frame for drying meat and marsh fish, a frame for drying hides, a dovecot, two small barns with deep storage pits beneath, apple trees and hazel trees and plum trees, a vegetable garden beginning to sprout up, all ringed around with a ditch and a drystone wall. Kanda walked to the edge of the village. Sat on the wall. She swung herself over to sit facing away from the village, looked out at the grass falling away new green to the sudden sharp line of the salt marsh where the marsh still wintered reed-black. Beyond the marsh to the north, pinewoods ran black as the reeds, and dark hills beyond. Kanda looked out at all this then she turned for comfort to look in at the village. Mist was rising from the roofs, making even the reed-thatch rare and beautiful. She looked at the sun through the mist to see a rainbow, the dew on the grass like diamonds. The villagers here had never seen diamonds, if they saw jewels they would say, surely, "They are almost as beautiful as the dew when the sun is shining." So Kanda could pretend. The doves were all waking in the dovecote, cooing. The gulls were calling and circling high overhead.

She said aloud, "Do you remember when you and I built our house, Dellet? You and me and your parents, your sister, her husband. Good strong stone walls, a thick turf roof. It took us the whole summer, I was half-afraid we wouldn't finish it before the winter came. A byre for our cows, a big bed for the two of us, a bed waiting for the children we wanted. A good big oven for baking bread for a horde of children, you said, and a larder to keep all the horde's food in. But I can't cook, I said."

A crow called in answer. She said gravely, "Good morning to you too, oh crow." She slid off the wall and went over to the village spring where the crow was sitting. The spring rose here, the village must have been formed around it. Water trickled through a gap in the wall into a stone trough, on the other side of the wall there was only earth. The wall here was overgrown with green stuff, even now still almost in winter Kanda had to push back green fern leaves to see the springhead, the stone was brownish green and slippery and gleaming, the lip was so worn it no longer looked like stone but like something warm and soft. It felt to Kanda like a caul. The water too was brownish, tasted of earth. Above the water a stone was set in the walling, carved with something so old and moss-covered and weatherworn it was almost lost. A bird, perhaps, winged body and what might be a beaked head; perhaps a crane, perhaps something as small as a song thrush. The stone was a different color to the trough and the wall stones, redder, warmer to the touch. The villagers said you should touch the stone before drawing water from the spring. Kanda did so now and it felt warm and good, and the water leapt to meet her as she dipped her hands to drink.

Kanda's family did not live in the village. They had left their own home behind them as the year turned to autumn, traveling with the birds, mist rising from the river they were following. No hurry and no particular destination, unless it was simply to travel away from where they had started until they reached the river's end and the sea. At the first village they had come to they had been received suspiciously, other recent travelers not having recommended the giving of a kind welcome; an isolated farmstead three long sad days later had thrown open its doors for Sal's sake, traded twenty days' work in the fields for a strong little pony to carry Sal to ease her legs. Then onward, treading out the bones of the land in a great curve west then north then east back almost the way they had come, the river always at their left hand, ragged bare hills appearing then falling away at their right, stopping here and there for a few days as seemed best or to wait out bad weather, pushing on in the shadow of coming winter, Kanda staring ahead hoping to smell the sea's salt before she smelled snow. Always keeping the river close unfailing as their guide – until one evening they had been drawn away onto the wrong path with the cold wind gnawing at Sal's bones. The droveway they were walking had turned away from the river, they had followed then left the droveway following a smaller pathway cross-country to get back to the river, then lost completely any trace of the path. Hopelessly lost, absurdly lost: a whole day wandering in circles, finding paths and streams all of which led only to the marsh, and always hills in the distance beyond, but nowhere they walked would ever run to reach them. Only animal paths, Kanda had begun to fear. Finally, despairing now, a wooden track over the marshes, a sign of human work, green from new summer's upkeep, and at last they had smelled woodsmoke, Sal's pony had pricked up its head at a sense of human life. A village like a place hidden from the world, though Dovei who had found them stumbling with snow in their faces had been amazed that anyone could have got so lost. "The River Wenet? Never heard of it. But there's a River Wend maybe an hour's walk back yonder. Path you're on led straight from it...." Turn back, walk one hour. One hour! Straight! But it was evening now, Dovei offered them shelter for the night in his village an hour straight farther on. Then the snow had set in hard the next morning, and everything was white and lost. The next day and the next and the next white and cold and lost in the snow. So they had set down their baggage, hung up their cloaks, joined in the work. Livestock to be kept warm in the cold nights, walls and nets and tools to be repaired, sickness and injuries to tend to, a woman suffering a long hard pregnancy after the death of her last infant. Then fields to be plowed as the snow retreated; winter's damages repaired; a new house to be built. Kindness and welcome and daily life. A good peace, a joy to stay and be helpful. Stay. Stay. Stay.

The crow called cheerily, flapped her wings. She was enjoying Kanda's company on this fine morning. Kanda dipped her hands into the spring, caught the water, let it run through her fingers back into the trough. Oh it sang like birds! When they first arrived in the village the springhead had been silver, ice-smelling, a cold skin on the water's surface, the green stuff tinged frost-rot-black. The bird carved on the well had seemed to Kanda to be flying away from the cold there; now this morning she thought it seemed to be flying home, to greet something good. She said gravely to the crow, "Your relation, is it, this bird here, oh crow? Where is it going?" That was a secret: the crow looked at her until she knew it was a secret, "I'll never know, then, alas, oh crow." She gathered up more water in her cupped hands, it ran through her fingers dripping over her clothes with a jolt of good cold, she drank the little that was left. The crow called loudly.

"Yes, yes, it is funny. I'm sure you can drink without getting soaked. But you'd laugh more if I put my head down to drink like a horse."

"I've a cup you can use. Unless you prefer to keep the crow amused."

Kanda leapt up, feet planted, right hand clutching at her belt. Lela stepped back with her left hand raised as she might to a startled child or a trapped beast. "I'm sorry, Kanda." Lela looked astonished and nearly really frightened.

"Oh!" Kanda too stepped back, lowered her hand, relaxed her stance. Hot embarrassed face. "You…I didn't hear you." She said awkwardly, "You're awake early, Lela." She had startled the crow, too, it had flown away.

"Baby's waking." Lela smiled. "Dovei is changing him." The woman dipped a clay cup into the trough, drank, handed the cup to Kanda. "Here you go."

"Thank you." The cup was ugly to look at but very pleasant to hold, perfectly shaped. It made a lovely sound when Kanda dipped it. The water tasted of earth, it was very soft in the mouth. Kanda did not in truth entirely like it. Never seemed to end, not somehow quite thirst-quenching. Not in a bad way, she'd tried to explain to Calian. Very good, sweet water, it wasn't that she thought it was dirty from the marsh. Just – it doesn't end in the mouth, like the land here doesn't quite end, you can't say, "the fields for plowing here, the water for the wild birds there," because of the marshes. Or like – the green stuff here around the well just grows and covers the stones up.

"Like the riverbank at home, then. Or our well with the moss covering the stones, or the sheep pond you dug in the muddy patch."

"No, it's just...." Water that ended hard as stone in the mouth when you swallowed. Like cold night air when you were fevered. That was how water should taste.

She drained the cup, handed it back to Lela. "Thank you. Delicious."

"It tastes of mud," said Lela. "I know it does." The crow called, or a crow called, from off in the trees, flew up and far away.

"You're leaving us," Lela said.

Kanda watched the crow grow smaller over the marshes. "Yes."

"You'd be welcome to settle here, Kanda." After a pause, Lela said, "Your...Sal, she was so good with the birth. Devad would have died too without her, I'm sure. I think I would have died."

Kanda smiled now. "Thank you. Sal's good with healing."

She should say: *"No, if Sal had not been there of course you and your son would both still have lived,"* but she did not like to lie about such things.

Lela did not notice, and had not truly meant that she would be dead now if these strangers had not ended up snow-trapped in her village, because she was alive and thus could not think truly of being dead. Lela said, smiling, "It would be good for the village to have new faces, Kanda. Your Calian: she's so happy here." But she paused again, thinking carefully, listening then to unspoken words, she said, "Sal.... That is, I mean...she could stay here, at least."

A silence. Come back to break the silence, oh crow, tell me good words to say. Kanda said at last, "We have to leave, Lela. Today. All fi—" Ah. Ah. Days, since she had last— "All four of us," Kanda said.

A burst of song from another bird somewhere in the sheep fields. Lela refilled the cup but did not drink. Lela said, "Is that…? No, I thought I heard Devad crying." She said, "I think it was a sheep." She looked down into the cup and Kanda thought she was looking a long long way down at something. She said, "Kanda: Sal…Sal and Calian…."

Kanda said carefully, "They are very close, yes."

Come back and laugh with me, crow.

Lela said slowly, "Kanda: when Sal was helping me when I was laboring…." She said quickly in a rush of fear, "The firelight, and I thought I was dying, and Sal said 'push', but I couldn't push, but I looked at the wall where Sal's shadow was, and I saw— She—"

The woman broke off staring down at the empty water cup. "Take care of her, Kanda."

Always. Forever, every moment of every day I live, I will take care of my daughter.

But the ghost was there in the plashing of the spring, the ghost of a child, and the ghost would not look at Kanda.

Always, forever, you have and you will take care of her, Kanda, your Sal, your *Shining* – apart from those brief few days that were the length of Sal's life.

Kanda said, "Sal—" And she had no idea what she was trying to say. There were no words that she could find to say. The ghost child knew the words, perhaps. But the ghost child didn't speak them. Could not speak and would not speak to Kanda or to Sal or to Calian. And even the crow had flown away silent.

And then, oh sweet relief, that was the baby Devad crying. And, ah, look, there was Calian coming down the hillside toward them, like any child might go if ordered to fetch a woman to stop a baby crying.

"The baby needs its mum's tit, Mum, Dad says!" Calian shouted.

There was Lela's milk making her dress wet, smelling muddy too. There was Calian standing in the puddle in her bare feet. There was the crow flying back cawing at them, and the doves cooing, and the sheep all starting to bleat. There was the ghost child, but the ghost was thinner and faded briefly.

Stay. Stay. Stay. But that's only the birds and the sheep and the wind in the trees and in the marshes. Other sounds now also, blown on another wind. Finer sounds now than these farm sounds and life sounds could ever now be to Kanda and Sal and Calian. *Go. Seek. Search. Find.* A golden sword as it is drawn in righteous anger. A crystal bell struck with a bronze spearhead. The ringing of silver trumpets.

A dead child, calling on the other wind, who says you can never rest now in quiet peace.

The whole village came to see the family off at noon, hugs and even tears from Lela and some of the others. Snow on the ground when they trailed in following the smell of woodsmoke, Sal bent on her pony shivering. The snowdrops and even the crocuses had opened and withered away again now, the birds had flown over the village laced like the smoke to begin their nests. The daffodils were golden now at the side of the trackway, the blackthorn was in bloom and the willows by the stream ahead of them were fuzzy with catkins. The air smelled now of leaving.

"You should stay tonight at least, sleep in the new house," Dovei said to Dellet. "All that work you put in." Lela took him aside, said things while looking over his shoulder every now and then in apology to Kanda. Dovei came back with the baby Devad in the crook of his left arm, in his right hand a lump of stone. He held the stone out to Dellet. Kanda could see it sparkle. Little flashes like sparks over it. "This is a good firestone," Dovei said. "You see how keen the sparks are to get out? You have it. Keep your family warm."

Dellet took it gravely. "Thank you. An honor." He had a good fire kit, and truly they didn't need a fire kit, it would be more use left with Dovei to keep Devad and his siblings warm. But Dellet took it and was glad and Dovei was glad also, for the gifting of a warm fire has great power to it for recipient and giver both.

The old woman Lela's grandmother was sitting on a stool outside the new house, well wrapped in sheepskin. Kanda went to say goodbye to her. Sal had helped another of her granddaughters care for her, mixed her herbs to help the pain in her joints – but Sal did not go up to her now, hung back waiting to be helped onto her pony. Someone must bid the old woman a formal farewell, there was a great power in that also, a promise and a sign to show that the village was a kind blessed place for someone to grow so old in. So it must be Kanda who bent to take her dry, frail, leaflike hands. The old woman raised her eyes to Kanda. Milk-mist eyes. A dog with such an eye can see the wind. She smelled of urine, her hand was cold, trembled with weakness. Then Kanda's face burned hot with shame, because this of course was why Sal did not want to say goodbye to the old woman.

I should have spent time with her, Kanda thought. Kanda squeezed the old woman's hand, thought to kiss her like one might kiss a child; the dryness of her skin compared to a child's sticky softness so surprising. The strength of fat and muscle worn down by a lifetime of work. Sal's skin was not yet like that. Soon enough, Kanda thought, Sal's skin would be like that. She glanced over at Sal and thought: I should have asked her, spent more time with her, tried to understand how it feels to be as old as this. Prepare myself. Like the mother of a newborn talking to the mother of three children, she thought. *Tell me it gets easier. Tell me what's best to do.*

Yet the milk-blind eyes met Kanda's and there was great joy in them. So Kanda squeezed the woman's hand tight and kissed her cheek, because the woman was indeed blessed beyond Kanda's dreaming because she had raised children and grandchildren and great-grandchildren to be well and happy, and had lived all her long life in quiet gentle peace.

"Come on, Mum!" Calian called.

The old woman smiled at the girl's cross voice. "Don't keep her waiting," the old woman said. Sal was mounted up on her pony, Calian and Dellet stood beside. Calian staring out skyward hungry to be going (and also stroking the pony's white nose). "Coming, coming," Kanda called. "No you're not! Hurry up, then!" Calian called back. Then Calian frowned and panicked, they were all fussing, "Wait, have you got—? No, it's fine, I've got it. No, wait, I'll just check—" "It's in the bag, I packed it yesterday." "Are you sure?" "Yes." "Sure sure?" "Yes! Okay, wait, I'll check again, wait—" "Argh, no, don't start unpacking the bag! Come on, Mum, hurry up!"

Eager to stay, eager to leave. Come on. Tarry. Get going. Stay. Wait.

There was one break in the wall around the village, no gate guarding the entry just a gap in the wall with the grass growing there thick with yellow flowers, a hawthorn tree not yet in flower but furzed with leaf buds, a puddle. Also a clump of nettles at each side by the wall ends that even last year Calian would have contrived to walk into. That another child, long ago now, as long ago and far away as last summer, would have contrived to fall into. There – the ghost – see? Sal sees it, Kanda sees, Calian sees. Dellet sees, his eyes are like stone one moment as he looks at Sal and Kanda and Calian. She shimmers golden, her face is almost visible in the puddle where the flowers are reflected gold.

The villagers sang and shouted: "Goodbye! Goodbye! Safe journey! Good luck!" Kanda shouted: "Thank you for everything! Good luck yourselves! Good luck to you back!"

The ghost child giggled and skipped by the wall, and wailed when she put her hand deep in the nettles, and Kanda would have gathered her up, seized her up golden and hot with outraged tears, but the ghost child was gone and Kanda could only wave more goodbyes.

She thought: I'm good at leave-taking.

"I really enjoyed building that house," Calian said. "It was fun. Our handprints will be in it forever! But—"

Calian's eyes were staring away over the fields and the marshes. Always looking beyond, that one. Fall over her own feet from staring at her dreams, one day, that one will. She looked at the horizon now where the sky was silver where it met the earth. The line of the sky at the end of her eye's vision. Onward, calling her, rushing toward and beyond.

Calian said with a shout that was filled with grief at the leaving and rage at the past, and was filled with courage to hope beyond that, "Don't look sad, Mum, Dad! Never mind a house: we're going to rebuild a world, remember!" And in Calian's shout the ghost child would be reborn and the world remade and many things almost forgiven. Thus the family went out of the village they had sheltered away the winter in hiding from themselves and what they were; as they went from that place the air around them changed, the earth changed, they were changed and they were made new. They left their shelter, came into the world that was their world to live in.

CHAPTER FOUR

To get back to the droveway from the village would take less time even than the two hours Dovei had mentioned when they first met him. Two different paths, a choice of paths, and one went on not back. Gal said, "I walk it often. Simple and straight." The Wend, that must surely be the Wenet (a thousand rivers, Kanda thought briefly, and all begin with the sound *when*! And that's an omen, if ever I heard one, for when, and when, and when, and when…), the droveway: if they followed the droveway onward westward indeed it did lead away from the river, but then – ah, listen to this great magic! – it led…back to the river again!

"Then there's a bothy," Gal had said, "near where the droveway meets the Wend again; a bit before it reaches the river; you can't miss it, if you reach the river first you've gone on too far north. Another two hours, maybe, from when you reach the droveway, you should be there well before dark. It's kept well stocked, food and firewood. But…your…." Gal had said, looking unhappily at Sal on her pony.

"*She'll* be fine," Sal had said. "She's itching to get going." Sort of. Yes, no, she is.

But when, and when, and when, but when….

Sal rode on now looking around her, the sun soft on her face. "I like it here," Sal said now. "I like the marshes. The salt smell. The size of the sky here where it's flat." Birthing Lela's baby had been a great thing for her. "I think we were meant to get lost, and find the village," Sal said. "Help deliver Devad, help build him a house. He'll live to be a hundred in that house, he'll sit in it with his great-grandson on his lap."

Calian said, "Do you think?"

Sal said, "I know it. Don't you?"

The track turned to the south, to the east, leading them to the very edge of the marsh. Calian and Sal and Dellet looked with interest; they had never seen salt marsh before the winter. Flat dark reeds stretching away, they were low now so that the world was lost behind the high reeds, the sky above was immense and seemed very low over them, everything seemed very low to the ground here, almost beneath the level of the earth with the sky pressed down heavy as a weight. But the sky seemed to go on forever above them also. The reeds were black and the sky was almost white; the reeds were a solid thing, not like the green plants in their own hills, stems packed together more solid even than a wheat field. The track ran on into the marshes, a wooden causeway leading in with reeds and deep water to either side, just wide enough to take Sal's horse. Kanda said, "I don't like this. Gal didn't say anything about going into the marshes. The path's going the wrong way."

Sal's horse snorted. It didn't seem comfortable here on the causeway. The marshes went on before them and the causeway went on and on. The rushes were now taller than Calian's head.

Kanda said, "I don't like this."

"Well, let's turn back then," said Dellet. He laughed mirthlessly. "*Hello Dovei, hello Gal, we got lost on the marshes again, can we stay another night?*"

"Yes, I know, Del. But." Six white geese were flying low across the marsh before them, so close together they might be joined with cords; their beaks were red. They called as they flew. "I don't like this," said Kanda. "I don't like this place."

"Dovei and Gal said the path led to the droveway, straight, they said, we couldn't miss it, and down the droveway was a bothy to sleep in." Dellet set off forward down the track with a quick step like he was pretending great confidence. He called back without looking, "The quicker we go now, the quicker we can be sitting round a fire having some dinner. Come on, girls, hurry."

Dellet then Calian then Sal and the pony disappeared into the reeds. Kanda drew a great deep breath like leaping into a dark tunnel. Set one foot on the track; the track was slippery, rotten wood, crumbling, taste of rot in her mouth, stink of rot, the wood crumbling to nothing beneath her, the mud rising up to swallow her away. Her bones wet in the wet earth, salt-crusted, her flesh eaten by worms, dead hands digging to try to reach the light.

Another step. Both feet on the causeway. The wood groaned beneath her weight. She thought: how have my children walked here? They were ahead, small, Calian turned and waved to her: "Come on, Mum! What you doing?" The causeway looked wide and strong for Calian. Kanda took another step. She wanted to shout back: "Come and hold my hand, Calian!" Calian skipped after Sal on the pony, disappeared into the reeds, her voice came back, "Hurry up!" Kanda thought with horror: shush, Calian! Another step, her foot slipping. I want to go back to the village. Lead a normal dull life as Kanda the farmer there. Her foot slipped backward, like the causeway itself was driving her back. The reeds were so tall and there seemed to be nothing else in the world now, this path leading on through the reeds, the whisper of reeds and water, the huge low sky overhead. A bird called, harsh and very sad, the rushes shivered and whispered. A great horror rose up in Kanda, mother's fear, warrior's fear, that the marshes were indeed endless, they'd been lost on them before, they'd be lost on them again. Forever they would wander the marshes, calling like the birds, circling like the birds, never resting, never able to escape.

She dropped her pack, bent with trembling fingers to untie the leather thongs. Hurry! Hurry! Get it open! They are coming! I feel them! I hear them! Her fingers shook, the thongs were knotted, and she thought in dumb horror: I didn't pack it, it is still hidden in the village, I didn't check! I should have rechecked!

There were four hidden in the pack Kanda carried, each one alone should have been heavy enough to weight the pack down awkward on her back.

The first was a corselet of bronze and black leather.

The second was a bronze helmet with a red crest.

The third was a bronze sword polished until you could see your face in it.

The fourth, that she sought now in despair ripping at the pack's bindings, was a black sword with a pommel in the shape of a snarling beast.

With this sword, she could kill monsters. If she hadn't left the sword hidden back in the village. If she could only undo the stupid knots. The bird called – it was not a bird calling. The reeds whispered – they whispered of slaughter and blood and death. The water was dark, with the blood on it. Her children's blood. They were coming. Ysarene, Geiamnyn, that third *empty* one. They had destroyed her home, two of her three children. A thousand years, she had fought those monsters, always they returned to make her fight them again. Never would she be free of them. Not until they had destroyed everything. The reeds whispered: that was Geiamnyn laughing. The bird called: that was Ysarene's laugh. The wind on her face was that third one's face pressed close to Kanda, bent with dead lips to kiss her lips.

The pack burst open with a sound of thunder. Kanda's hand closed around her sword hilt and her heart leapt. So joyful she was, more alive, like a winter tree suddenly burst into spring blossom, as she snatched her sword up. Black fire ran down its blade. The reeds and the wind cried out in pain as she leapt up holding it, the bird shrieked.

I will kill you! I will fight you! My sword hand sings to slaughter you, cut you down, cut out your hearts, cut off your heads. Monsters, evil, I will—

I will—

Calian's voice called, "Where have you got to, Mum? Come on!"

On the wooden causeway, the wind in Kanda's face smelling of mud and coming rain, the pack at her feet spilling out clothes and life-junk. Sal's best dress trailed over the side of the causeway, one sleeve in the marsh.

They are gone, Kanda tried to think. Defeated. A thousand years, the Six Swords of Roven had fought the monster Geiamnyn, *Burning*, always he rose up remade to fight them again. But with one stroke of Kanda's sword, Sal had killed him. Ysarene, *Hunger*, graceful and filled with laughter, ever desperate only to maim and kill as she had once been maimed; Calian had defeated and banished her, sent her fleeing. That third one, that *empty* one, no name he had but *empty* and *nothing*, whom

Kanda had once loved: Kanda had grieved to fight him, drawn back from fighting him, but at last she had defeated him, turned him into a toad and buried him deep beneath the waters of a lake. They were gone, all three of them, they could not return to harm her.

"Where are you, Mum?" Calian called from somewhere in the reeds. Loud enough to set two ducks up quacking.

"I'm…here. Coming. Coming!" Kanda called back. She looked down and thought ruefully that *they* or she had harmed Sal's favorite dress. The wild geese were flying over the marshes, the trackway bent round to the right, the reeds opened up and the marshes ended, thick green turf with a clear path running up drier and drier until there was no mud at all no water smell just good green stuff bursting out growing and the geese made an arrowhead pointing out the land and the dry and the light. And they went on and there was the droveway, wide enough for four, five, six cows to walk abreast, sheltered by arching trees from wind and rain, running north away from the marshes, leading on with strong confidence. A cold spring wind blew, a spring evening drawing slowly on gray and dull to cover the fire of the sun's wounding; before the evening they reached a good well-made bothy house just as it started to rain.

"I'll get a fire going," Dellet said, "test this firestone Dovei was kind enough to gift me. Been looking forward to that. Kanda, Sal, you sit down and rest a bit. You see to the pony, Calian girl."

"Dear Old White Nose! Bravest and best of horses! He's happy we're back traveling."

"No, Sal, you just sit down and rest a bit. Oh, don't kiss the horse's nose, Calian, don't, please."

"Plenty of dry firewood. Good, good. No, Kanda, wife, you sit down with your daughter a bit. Calian, once you've stopped messing with that pony – your mother just told you not to kiss its nose, girl, are you deaf? – once you've sorted the horse out, we'll get something on to eat."

The fire caught, sprung up. Strong flames. Smelled good. "Good firestone, this," Dellet said. "Very good. My thanks to you, Dovei my friend." There was bread and cheese and bacon in Dellet's pack, a pan clean and richly smelling of food hanging on the wall of the bothy house.

Dellet hummed to himself as he set the meat frying, enjoyed himself making the fat sizzle and spit when the flames caught it. "The best food," he said happily, "is cooked on a fire a friend gifted you. Nothing in the world seasons a meal like that." He made the fat burn, a rush of white flames. Kanda saw in it the shape of a long wide high building. A hall of brilliant fire, shining silver and gold.

In her mind, she heard a blare of trumpets. A crystal bell. A horn ringing.

The beast from which that horn came, she had hunted.

In her mind, she said the words that must be said.

CHAPTER FIVE

A good place, this: a good meal, a good place to sleep, bracken beds that were soft enough, and a stream to discreetly rinse Sal's dress sort of clean. But when the two girls were sleeping, Dellet said awkwardly: "Kanda… I…I think…I don't know whether to tell you this or not, but I think…I think maybe you'd want to know. You should know. I mean…. Anyway. Just listen, Kanda. Okay?

"A story Lela's grandmother told me.

"I think you need to hear it. So listen, yes?

"It happened long ago, she said. When her great-great-great-grandfather's grandfather was a boy. Odd story, but she swore it was true. And here and now I'm going to tell it to you.

"Just listen. You'll see.

"I didn't want to tell you the story earlier. Didn't seem right. But….

"You'll see.

"Anyway.

"Just listen.

"So."

He drew a breath, looked straight at Kanda. She said, "Del—" and he held up his hand to bid her hush.

"So.

"Once, long ago, that fine good village we've just been fool enough to turn our backs on, once upon a time that fine good village was destroyed by great violence. When they turn the soil for the plowing, they sometimes turn up bits of rubble, broken pots, cattle bones.

"Human bones. All cut and damaged.

"A warband came to the village once. Killed people.

"Their leader was a woman. She was as tall as the mountains and as terrible as lightning, with a red-plumed helmet on her head. The blade of her sword burned with cold fire, where she walked the ground behind her opened up and it was bleeding, just to look into her eyes was death.

"That's what Lela's grandmother said her grandfather had said about the woman, anyway. Then she laughed that lovely laugh of hers, 'How anyone survived to tell the story, if that was true, I don't know,' she said. 'But that's what everyone said about the woman.'

"The warband killed most of the villagers, apart from a few that fled and hid. Children, old people, they killed. And their leader, she was so mad with killing and ruining things, she set to smashing up the very houses of the village.

"She ran at the biggest longhouse, hacked at the house poles with her sword like a woodman's axe. She struck it and she stuck it, but the house was so well-made, she could not harm it. So well-seasoned and strong the wood, her sword was blunted against it. But she was so angry, so mad for destruction that she could not stop, and at last she tore at the longhouse with her bare hands, mad with fury, spitting and screaming, and her hands were red and torn on the strong good wood.

"One house pole of that longhouse, at last, she tore down before her hands were cut and bleeding so badly she could not use them, and then at last, seeing that she was defeated, she gave it up and went away with her men.

"When she had gone and they were sure she wouldn't return, the few that survived crept out of their hiding places. And they saw the damage she had caused, but they saw also that they had defeated her in the end.

"So they raised a spell against her. A curse spell. A promise spell.

"A death spell.

"They set the spell into the village springhead, for the water of a well-kept spring has great power in it to heal and guard its keepers' village. And the waters of the spring rose up in answer, like great wings beating, and a great dark fog came down over all the land around so that the woman lost her way and led her warband out onto the marshes. And a fear came over them and they ran mad, fought each other, until at last they all sank into the marsh and drowned. If you find a reed with a red flower on it out on the marsh, they say that marks one of the warband's graves.

"But the leader, the woman – she was so wicked that the marsh wouldn't swallow her body to bury it.

"So her ghost is lost out there still, wandering on the marsh, and on some days you can hear it crying, and on some nights you can see it flitting about between the reeds."

He looked at Kanda a long time, straight in her eyes like he did when they argued over some stupid thing like a broken plate. "So."

Kanda said, "So."

"I wasn't going to say anything, Kanda. I wouldn't have told you, except….

"I mean, it seemed like you should maybe know, and want to know. And I'd say you've made up for it now building that house, if your shoulders and your knees ache like mine do, buggered my knees right up, all that lifting, yours maybe the same, except I know you won't find that funny. And— Well—"

He shook his head. "These last months, in the village, felt like maybe all that that happened, wasn't real, you know. Like a dream. Or would do, except for…." A long dark frown, then, and she wanted to say it and he did too so very much, but for both of them even after everything they had been through together some things couldn't be said when the sun was in the sky or when the sun was setting in wounds and fire, or when the night had come and the sun was gone and its wound closing, or when the sun was waiting to rise new healed in the gloaming sky. So he said slowly, "It all seemed almost like a dream, everything that happened, I almost, sometimes I almost forget we were anything but a family together as guests in that village, sometimes it even seemed to me we could stay, live there in that new house. Sometimes it even seemed to me that when I thought about what happened it was all a tale you told one evening, that we had always lived there quietly in that village."

He shook his head again, fiercely, wearily. "You are what you are, and our children are whatever they are. And we're looking for a great new world I can't understand at all, for you and them. Terrible things have happened. Great things have happened. You've done great things, you've done terrible things. I don't understand much of it. Don't want to understand.

"The one thing of it I do understand, that – that I can't speak."

He poked at the fire. The fire sprung up. Strong flames. Smelled good. "Good firestone, that is," Dellet said again. "Very good. My thanks to you, Dovei my friend." Dellet stared at the fire. Kanda could see that he was thinking deeply. Then he burst out suddenly into laughter, so loud it made Sal start in her sleep. Bitter laughter and warm belly laughter both at once. "There was me desperate to go out for a piss. Out of nowhere, I was only sitting by the fire with her so I could have a tickle of that fat old baby, and she started telling me that story. What was I supposed to say in reply, eh? There's me, four cups of beer in, desperate for a piss, holding a baby, and she tells me that and looks at me like I'm supposed to say something back. And, I mean…what was I supposed to say?

"*'Funny, she sounds oddly familiar, that woman, let me see…wait, yes, I have it, she sounds rather like my wife'*?"

He laughed with all his bitterness and the fear and loss in him.

"But I thought….

"I didn't know whether to tell you.

"But I thought in the end you'd probably want….

"You'd probably want to know, I thought.

"So."

CHAPTER SIX

So:

Here, now, there were three women, all of great power, on a quest to remake the world.

One was a warrior, an *eagle*, fierce and savage and brave and wild as the storm wind.

One was a healer, her wisdom *shining*, the strength of a homestead when the storm howls outside the door but the children play safe within.

One was a great lady, who longed for glory, who longed for ruin, who longed to be forgiven, who longed to forgive.

In the first morning of the world, the Lord of Roven called the Six Swords of Roven to him. Fierce brave warriors, to fight for hope and peace. Lord Palle, *Calm*, wise and tall and strong as an oak tree in his glory, his skin rich and dark as oak bark, his hair the pale gold of new spring leaves when the sun strikes them. Lady Erenan, *Summer Harvest*, hair and skin and eyes pale as the morning, formed from sunlight and spring blossom and the water of the mere. Lord Morren, *Golden*, gold his skin, gold his hair, gold his armor, the best dancer, the best poet, a good swordsman but he did not like fighting. Lady Kestre, *Song*, her skin white as sea foam, her hair long and fair like a cloak about her, formed from birds' feathers and the wind in the trees and green wheat. Lord Gallyn, *Great Leap*, ever young and innocent. The first of them, their leader, was the woman who was now Kanda. The greatest, bravest, fiercest. She led them out in every battle. She took for herself the hardest and most painful quests. The Lord of Roven, she knew in her heart, loved her the first and the best.

The Six fought and were victorious. Many battles, endless battles, the Six fought. But peace never seemed to come to the lands beyond the walls of Roven. They fought, and there was no end to the fighting.

Until the woman who was now Kanda brought ruin upon the Six.

Three warriors came to her out of the darkness, whispered to her of the secrets she kept.

The first was a man, tall and strong and handsome. He was called Geiamnyn, *Burning*, a king of battle, glutted with pride in killing, drunk on bloodlust.

The second was a woman, Ysarene, *Hunger*, who delighted in her cruelty. "I am free to do only as I want," Ysarene crowed over her long knives. "Can you say the same, any of you Six?" A lovely creature, tall and graceful, long silvery hair and wide blue eyes. Some great cruelty had been done her once, for her face had been flayed open, her eyelids and her nose and her lips had been cut off.

The third was a man who was only *empty* and *nameless*, a dead man who refused his death. Hanged from a tree, drowned in the mire, throat cut, hands bound, he crawled his way rotted back into life.

Many times Kanda fought them. Never could she kill them, always she was killing them always they came back to life those three monsters. Many times she thought on them and on her Lord and on the Six of Roven and on the words those monsters said. Always a battle. Never an end to the fighting. She dreamed in her heart of an end.

Thus at last her ruin was cast upon the fields and the woods of Roven. Her fall was like the fall of a baleful burning star. As she had been the greatest of the Six she was the greatest of all monsters. Ikandera Thygethyn, that is *Great Warrior*. Queen of Destruction, her armies acclaimed her. Ysarene was her friend and rival, close as sisters. Geiamnyn was her blood-brother, her war-brother, fighting together back to back, nothing dared face the two of them. That third one, nameless, he was her husband, she loved him with all her body and her heart. She led her armies to the gates of Roven. As the Lord of Roven lay dying she spat in his face. She shouted as she destroyed Roven that she was at last free and had found her peace.

Of her companions the five remaining Swords of Roven, all five she fought and defeated.

So thus she found her victory and her peace.

Long years she stood beside those three monsters, she was the greatest of them and the three of them bowed to her. Long years she strode the world and set it to fear. Her golden sword she had lost, her swift horse she had buried, her name as one of the Six she could not recall. Her house was *Uncaring*, her sword was *Pain*, her hall was *Cruel Hate*. How happy she was, for long long great years! How glorious she was! But all things fade, as the light fades away in winter and the day is done. The stars are changed, the sea and the land change their places, trees are felled, fields are burned, the sun itself is driven down from the sky in the end. So Ikandera Thygethyn began to tire even at the last of killing. So her sword arm began to age and ache. So in her weariness she left those three monsters, even the one she loved who was her husband, left her hall and her house and her bed. Long years then she wandered, and the guilt of what she had done came down on her like winter snows. No peace was left her. Long years she lay sprawled upon the earth broken by her sorrow and her guilt.

A spring thaw came. The rising sun came. Hope came and love came, fragile as flowers. White petals easily trampled. She rose from her grief as only Kanda, she wandered on through a world changed and lacking. She felt the weight of her guilt on her, madness took her, she fled. She ran wild upon the mountains with a stone in her mouth and a stone in her heart and claws dragging at her heels. She ran through summer woods sweet with fruit and flowers, and her eyes were made of stone. She came to a valley where a stream leapt down from a mountain and the trees were turning to autumn; there she stopped to rest. Her madness faded. Weary, she looked around her, she saw fine good things.

A man to marry for his goodness, his kindness, the kind love in his plain good kiss. A house to build, a farm to work. Children to raise to be as kind and good as their father was. She buried her sword *Hate* on a mountainside where a stream burst out silver, and swore to live in quiet peace.

She bore three daughters, and they were indeed kind and good. Sal, *Shining*, Calian, *Eagle*, and Morna, still only an infant, who was all the family's *Golden*.

Those three evil ones found her. Geiamnyn, Ysarene, that third one, *nothing*, her first husband. They burned her home, they threatened her children, they stole her daughter Morna away.

She took up her sword to fight them. She broke her oath to live in peace.

Ysarene was thrown down defeated. Fled. Geiamnyn died beneath Kanda's black sword, death took him at last and there was no escaping even for him. That third one, *empty*, *nameless*, Kanda trapped and imprisoned in the waters of a great mere high on the mountain, for ten times a thousand years she cursed him to lie there buried.

She saved Dellet even after that empty one her first husband had killed him. "Get up, Dellet!" she shouted in her great war cry. "Your family needs you! Stop lying there dead!"

Calian her fierce eagle daughter did not need saving.

Sal, Kanda saved but did not save.

Morna, Kanda could not save.

For her sister Morna's sake, Sal went willingly into the dark to marry Geiamnyn. No one, not even Kanda's shining eldest daughter, could come through those dark halls unchanged. Sal returned to her mother as an old woman, white-haired, bent-backed. But Sal brought Morna back from the dark as a wedding gift from Geiamnyn.

But for all Sal's sacrifice, Morna, Kanda's youngest, the family's *golden* one, a little child still – Morna was dead and dead and dead.

For Morna in her child's innocence had befriended Geiamnyn and sought to protect him. When the great last battle had been fought on the slopes of the mountain Mal Anwen between Kanda and Sal and Calian and those three *Burning* and *Hunger* and *Empty*, in that battle, three blades had struck Morna down. But those three blades had not belonged to the monsters. Those three killing blades had belonged to Kanda and Sal and Calian.

Their home stood now rebuilt, better even than it had been, the cattle in the byre, the sheep in the field, hams and cheeses in the rafters, honey and meal in stone crocks. But they could not go back there and so they must go onward, they must pretend and believe that there was somewhere they could go to find some victory and peace. Three women great and terrible and glorious in their power; and a good man who loved the three of them with all his good kind heart; and a ghost that would never leave them, that all four would hear forever when the sun was in the sky and when the sun was setting and when the night had come and the sun was fled and set. We will find the ruins of the Hall Roven and rebuild it! Kanda had said. There, we can live! There I can speak the words I long one day to say – forgive me! I forgive! Thus they had followed the River Wenet downstream, toward a sea that Dellet and Sal and Calian and Morna had never seen.

For where else could they go, after all that had befallen them, but wander without purpose, in search of impossible things that could never be remade? The Hall Roven was gone, Kanda herself had destroyed it. Even her name when she was one of the Six and the greatest and the best of them, she could not remember even the name she had had then. Thus they followed the river as it ran to the sea, followed the river as it ran only to be lost.

CHAPTER SEVEN

So:

Kanda lay awake a long time that night, trying to remember how she could have forgotten, how could she have been there, in that village, talking to those people building a house for them on that earth where sometimes bones were churned up. But no memory came.

The spring did not shun me, the trees and the earth did not shun me. The houses welcomed me, kept me warm. I walked every day in the village and the sun shone, the wind blew, the snow was crisp under my feet, the snow was cold and wet and horrible if it got down the back of my dress. Nothing cursed me, spat at me, turned away from me in disgust. The birds sang in my presence, the crow chatted away to me happily by the springhead. I killed a cow and a sheep for eating and the meat was wholesome and far more tender indeed that it should have been and lasted far longer and filled far more bellies than it should by all rights possible have done. I helped birth one healthy baby, two healthy calves and three healthy lambs!

I helped to build a house on the site of the house I tried to destroy. A fine house, a good house, I was happy building it, I blessed that house and I felt it good and kind and sheltering and I felt that house bless and thank me.

I am on a quest to rebuild the Hall Roven. I will never stop feeling guilt for my past – and that is right and good. But I am not – not— She heard in her mind Del's words, such kind words of goodness and healing that he mostly truly meant. She thought: I am the same person I was then, but I am sorry for the things I did then, that guilt will always be with me. I will try to be better than I was then, and that's all anyone in this world can say. Sometimes it's not enough. Sometimes, if you're lucky, it is.

Stop thinking about it, Kanda. What do you think you can do: change what's done?

She lay in the warm darkness of the bothy and listened to her family's breathing, as she had only that morning in the warm light of the longhouse she had helped build. Rebuild, she thought, and had to stop herself laughing and crying both together in case it woke her family. The house poles had gone in good and easily, into the hole left where she had torn a house pole down with her bare hands, in red rage at a lump of wood.

Calian's breath came gently, a child's breathing in deep sleep. Calian's face and hands had the same battle scars already as her mother, her eyes flicked now always like Kanda's eyes, judging and waiting. *Where's the best place to stand here? What's a good place to put one's back to? Can they get in here? Can we get out?* Even in sleep her right hand was gripped around a dream-sword and her eyes seemed to be half-open watching. If Kanda touched her shoulder, she would leap up wide-awake wide-eyed, ready to fight. A greater warrior already perhaps than her mother. She had checked and double-checked the door to the bothy, any other possible entrances and exits, any hidden dangers, before she set to cooking. After they had eaten, she had sat a long time in the corner sharpening her already sharp bronze sword. 'Old White Nose the pony'– but her eyes were not a child's eyes. The first weak flames of a red fire sometimes in them.

Sal's breath came wheezing, an old woman's fitful, aching sleep. Sal's hair had been the same fire-red as Kanda's, her skin the same rich dark good earth. Sal had been taller than Kanda, graceful and strong as a young elm tree. Sal was ashes and dead leaves now, smaller, hollowed, dry earth where the rain has not fallen. A thing of pride, to have lived and worked her body so until it creaked with using – so Kanda told herself. Looked at herself and Dellet: I am better and happier and fairer now than I was when my world was young, and of Dellet I would say the same; in his graying hair and his face and the fat on his belly I see our past and our happiness. I am grown older, I see the spread of my own belly where it carried three children, I see myself well and heavily lived. I do not fear to grow old. It is no shame to Sal to be old and gray and bent. Indeed, the people in the village revered her for her kind gentleness. She has survived things that would have crushed many women. So Kanda lied to herself looking at Sal.

Dellet snored. Dellet alone was almost unchanged. The vastness of his grief for his daughters, the shock of discovering the truth of what his wife was: yet in a strange way they had not touched him beyond the grief in him. He moaned and cried out in his sleep for his dead daughter, often they sat, he and Kanda, sat in silence to share that vast grief. Perhaps he was quicker to anger than he had been – slow and steady and calm as an ox, my Dellet, my Del-my-heart, Kanda would say sometimes to herself as she worked on the farmstead, and it's for that in part that I married him – perhaps he was grayer, he too perhaps was older-eyed. But he was not changed as his daughters were changed, because he was only Dellet and had no magic in him. He was only a *good man*.

Kanda listened until her breath came peacefully, until she slept peacefully with those words *good man* loud in her head.

And she had a dream.

She might have thought that after Dellet's tale she would dream of her days of greatest glory, when she was Ikandera Thygethyn the terror of the world who sat in her hall on a throne of gold and skulls and all that lived cowered at her feet. She might have thought she would dream of her days of greatest happiness, when she was Kanda the farmer, seated at the table Dellet had made her, eating badly made bread, drinking a cup of her beloved cows' rich milk. But she dreamed of her days as the first of the Six Swords of Roven, when she was…she was….

She sat feasting in the Hall Roven with the rest of the Six. Roven, her first home, the seat of the Lord who had created her to be a sword held fast against the darkness. Roven, a fair hall set in fair fields and fair woodlands, its walls were made of silver, its floor was made of diamonds, its roof was made of gold. Roven, that is *Peace*. The Lord of Roven sat in the high seat on his throne Thalle, that is *Hope*; three of the Six at his right hand, three at his left. His hair was white as snowfall, his skin was black as night, he was as wrinkled and twisted as the tree that grows in the wind on a high mountain, for he was very old. His eyes were red as berries. His face was kind as the spring sun. He wore a green robe that fell open at the front of him as he stood upright. His belly and his breasts were that of a pregnant woman. He smiled, delighted his eyes looking at the six great warriors he had created.

Lord Morren, *Golden*, his hair hanging loose about him, a cup of wine in his hand, the dark wine flushing his cheeks, staining his lips. Lady Kestre, *Song*, her face had in it both the kindness of the dove and the keenness of a hawk hunting. Lord Palle, *Calm*, his hair and beard dressed with green ribbons, his skin painted with green patterns like the eddies in a cool calm sea. Lady Erenan, *Summer Harvest*, garlanded with pink roses that her beloved had gathered. Lord Gallyn, *Great Leap*, beautiful as a dragonfly.

And...Kanda. She sat at the Lord of Roven's right hand, the honor seat as the first and best of the Six. In her dream she saw herself very clearly, her red hair, her bronze skin, her white silk gown and her bronze crown.

In the dream, as in her waking hours, Kanda knew that her name then had not been Ikandera Thygethyn. But she could not remember what her name had been that her Lord and her companions had called her, nor could she remember what it had meant. *Kanda*, she could only call the woman who sat in the Hall at her Lord's right hand as the first and best of the Six companions. But *Kanda* had no meaning in any tongue she had heard.

A horn blew around the Hall. A sweet long note. The air spun with light and dancing, gold light, white light. A pillar of light rose in the center of the hall beside the hearth that always burned there. Like a tree trunk with branches spreading, it seemed, and then it was the form of a woman whose face was the face of a long-beaked bird. From her golden hair there sprouted a deer's antlers, a golden bird with the same long beak perched on her antlers while a squirrel with golden fur sat among her antlers grooming itself. Like her Lord, the Lady had no name that Kanda had ever heard spoken. But always wherever she went; in the wind in the trees in summer when the leaves are just beginning to turn toward their autumn colors; in the music of the stars on a clear winter night when the frost lies thick and the air is like cold wine; in the circling of birds at twilight, a great cloud of birds gathering so that the sky is made dark and they call to each other and the beating of their wings sounds like rain; in the light on the sea on the first day of the year when the sun is returning – always, in her heart, Kanda heard the Lady's unspoken name. All in the Hall rose from their seats and knelt to greet the Lady of Roven, joy filled their hearts to see her. And now the Lady was there for the feasting – they could feast.

In the center of the Hall a cauldron hung from a tripod above the fire. The cauldron's name was Helle, that is *Health*. It was so large that two men could not wrap their arms around it. It was patterned with birds in flight, deer running. Steam rose from the cauldron, sweetly scented with meat, wine, herbs. The Lord of Roven nodded, four servant women as fair and as richly dressed as queens served stewed venison from the cauldron.

Kanda stirred in her sleep then, licked her lips, her mouth watered. In the dream and in her sleep she felt the good ache in her legs where she had chased down the hind that was cooking in the cauldron Helle. In her dream she ate the stewed venison and it was as delicious as she could almost remember it being.

Erenan raised her cup. "To Kanda and Palle and Gallyn, who caught the meat we are eating today!"

"A mighty chase, we ran without stopping after that hind from the sun's rising until the sun was falling from its noontime height," Kanda said. "Twice it escaped us. We would not stop running until we had hunted it down."

"But Kanda and Palle and Gallyn did not cook it, it would not have tasted so good eaten raw as it does cooked by these women," Morren said. Morren raised his cup. "To the fair women who cooked and served the meat!"

They ate and drank, and it was good. The evening was coming in, the sun was sinking wounded, soon it would be time to retire to their beds to sleep. Kanda yawned after her great running, her eyes were heavy with sleep. Morren was not tired – he was eying very hopefully the women who had cooked the meat. "I will bid you good night," Kanda said, "I do not have as much stamina as Morren."

But just as she got to her feet, the doors of the Hall flew open.

A white goat came into the Hall. Two white kids followed the mother goat. They trotted down the length of the Hall, stopped in front of the Lord of Roven's throne.

"Help my kids," the goat said.

"Yes, please, help us, do," the two kids said.

Kanda blinked, and after the day's hunt she was so tired she thought she must be dreaming.

"A beast is in the fields," the goat said. "A wolf. It wants to eat my kids."

Gallyn leapt up with a roar. "I will drive off that wolf!" he shouted.

"It is in the nature of wolves and goats to eat and be eaten," Palle said. "You are eating a hind that you yourself hunted and killed, Gallyn."

"Yes," said Gallyn, "yes, but…."

"Should I have defended that hind from you?" Palle said.

Gallyn looked at his empty plate and he looked at the cauldron, he looked at the fine buskin boots he wore. "Yes, but, yes, but, yes, but…." Gallyn said.

"Please help my kids," the goat said.

"Please do," the kids said. "We don't want to be eaten."

"Oh come on," Kestre said. She leapt up. Kestre who never much liked to fight. She seized her sword from the wall where it hung behind her waiting, a shining sword with a hilt set with green gems. Anchai, Kestre's sword was called. That is *Thought Before Use*. She did not seem to think now, her sword was drawn and she was running to the door. "We can just drive it off," Kestre said. "We don't have to harm it."

"The Six of Roven, drive off a wolf?" said Morren. But then he leapt up. So eagerly, he knocked over his cup. "Come on, then. Gallyn can wave his arms and shout boo at it to drive it off."

"Morren can show it his new tunic," said Gallyn. "That will drive it off."

"What? Your husband made me this tunic, Gallyn," said Morren.

Anyway. Enough of that. Dreaming, Kanda thought: get on with it! Quickly the Six snatched up their shining swords, quickly they rushed from the Hall Roven out into the night with the goat and the two kids following behind them. "That took you long enough," the goat said. They ran out of the gates of Roven all in a jumble of warriors and goats together, past the gatekeeper Benethal, *Safe Place*, who raised his eyebrows at them. They ran through the apple orchard, through the cherry orchard, past the pigpens. They ran through the sheep field and the horse field. The goat at the front now neck and neck with Kestre, Gallyn at her heels tripping over the two kids, Erenan at the rear calling to them to wait.

Where the goats were kept, they stopped.

"What?" Kestre said.

"What?" Gallyn said.

"What?" Kanda and Morren and Palle and Erenan said.

"The wolf is the size of a bull, its hide is made of bronze, it breathes fire, its tail is a serpent spewing venom, it has three heads," said the goat. "Did I not mention that?"

Kanda leapt at the wolf. In her dream, she felt the raw joy of fighting such a monstrous creature. In her sleep, she remembered how good this fighting had felt. The beast was old and scarred. Its three heads snapped at her. Vast heavy brazen jaws. There was heaviness in it as if it was made not of flesh and blood but all of metal, bronze muscles, bronze bones. For all its fire, the smoke curling from its gaping mouths, the scorched marks of its fire on its own flanks, when its teeth closed around her arm it felt very cold. She ignored its bites, the pain of its cold being, she slammed her sword into one of its three necks.

Its teeth were like millstones grinding. Its fire swallowed her up.

Gallyn and Kestre were there beside Kanda, they set their shoulders, rooted themselves together firm as three branches growing on the same tree. Palle and Morren and Erenan joined battle against the serpent tail, green and bronze scales, as thick as Morren's waist. It cast its coils, looped itself around Erenan. Erenan dropped one of her sticks. Her left arm was pinned to her body. She hacked at the serpent tail, she shouted as the serpent sunk its fangs into her right arm. Moren and Palle both struck at it.

Kanda's sword smashed at the beast's neck, at the beast's flank. Gallyn shouted, "It's mine!" and his sword smashed at one of its three heads. Fire beat over Kanda; she and Gallyn and Kestre were swimming in cold fire. Their swords crashed and slipped on the beast's bronze hide, they gritted their teeth, struck harder; their swords almost buckled against the thick bronze.

"Oh, come on," Gallyn shouted. "Really?"

"Go for its neck!" Kanda cried to Kestre and Gallyn.

Bronze jaws held Kanda. Shook her. Cold pain in her arm, cold fire burning her face. She dropped her sword. Fell and was dragged and lifted off her feet. Stinking bronze, wolf slobber, heat now down into her bones from the grinding teeth. Kestre struck, a horrible shrieking noise as her blade tore into bronze skin. But a wound opened, blood flowed, black blood against the bronze. Kestre cheered for the first wound made. Gallyn cheered her, struck deeper where she had struck.

Kanda thrashed in its jaws, her eyes closed her teeth gritted against fire pain and cold pain and wolf stink. The snake tail squeezed tighter around Erenan.

Gallyn and Kestre each struck a wolf head. Morren and Palle struck the serpent tail. Four swords crunched through bronze and blood.

A howl. Kanda pulled her arm free.

"Yes!" Gallyn shouted.

The beast came down with a crash.

It lay stretched out with its three wolf mouths opening and closing helpless. Its serpent head cut off. Kanda staggered to hands and knees beside it. She and Erenan helped each other up. Morren wiped sweat off his face, Kestre clapped her hands, Palle looked at the creature gravely, Gallyn gave it a good hard kick.

"It's damaged my tunic," Morren said after a while when he had got his breath back.

"My husband will make you a new one exactly the same," Gallyn said. "Just as long as it's a different color, style and shape."

"I can't wait to go to bed," Kanda said.

"It's nearly morning," Erenan said. "Not much point going to bed."

"That took you longer than I thought it would," said the goat.

"But thank you anyway," said the kids.

They walked back to Roven. Six heroes, a goat, two little white kids.

A very good dream, yes. Kanda smiled in her sleep. Those had been the days of glory, the days of happiness. And innocence, yes. A monster was a monster, not a man, back then, and the thing to be rescued was something only good and weak. So long ago now she could barely remember – happiness now was *hugging her children*, glory to her now was only *killing killing killing killing*. But there had been glory and happiness and wonder then in Roven. Friendship, hope…sometimes, even, there had been what could almost be called peace.

We are on a quest to rebuild Roven, my beloveds, she had told her family, we are not going back we are going onward to find Roven and remake it better than before. So I can show it to you, my beloveds. So I can give you something of the wonder and the glory and the happiness of those days. And we will find it! *Go! Seek! Search!*

If I can help rebuild a village longhouse so that children can live happily there in the shadow of my ruins, surely I can rebuild a ruined world?

CHAPTER EIGHT

When she woke the next morning, the sun was pouring in through the open doorway of the bothy, the fire was high in the hearth, Sal was getting breakfast ready, Calian was sitting sharpening her sword.

Kanda thought: Calian the *Eagle*. Ha. Yes.

Dellet came in whistling. They had seemed almost happy in the village. Normal ordinary people. In this new morning she could feel them changing into a new fiercer happiness. The beauty of her dream of Roven hung in the air; they almost saw it also. A world to rebuild, a glorious world, and even in the shadow of death and ruin – that is a glorious thing to make us glad that even in the rubble of our old life – we still live.

"Look at this, Kanda, girls," Dellet said. He held out a bunch of green leaves, damp with rain and pungent-pleasant-smelling, crowned with white flowers. "Ramsons. There's a whole lane of it out there. Get the breakfast cooking, girls, chuck the last of that bacon into a pan with this stuff."

Outside the bothy in the droveway, yes, green banks beneath green trees, white flowers like white stars almost like snow. Cool and cleaning on her skin as bathing. Wallow in it. The smell of garlic; the smell of whitelace that was pungent like sweating bodies; the warm smell of cattle that must have come down the droveway recently. Drowsy buzz of insects in a shaft of greenish light.

Kanda said, "How long have I been sleeping?" She meant it as a joke, and she didn't, quite. Yesterday was *winter's-ending*. Today is *spring-begun*. She said, "A good sign, I hope. A good day for great things."

The sunlight pierced the trees and fell long and slanting like sword blades. Old White Nose was grazing happily, whisking his tail against flies. Better even than the sound of cows eating, the sound of a horse eating garlic leaves. Kanda stroked his ears. "I had a horse once called Henef, and she was the swiftest horse in all the world." The pony broke off his eating, snorted at her. "But you're a better more patient one for carrying my Sal, yes."

"The river should be up ahead," said Dellet. "A river, and oak trees." The droveway led east, up into the sunshafts, all was green dazzling, the girls' faces were striped and dappled like striped cats. Calian wore her sword now and the light made it molten, she looked stronger, taller wearing it. Kanda wore her sword but did not quite like to wear it. But when Calian saw her looking askance at the pack with the swords in, fidgeting between leaving her sword packed and wearing it, Calian said, "The black blade and the black scabbard – they're like the poles of the longhouse we built, Mum." "No they aren't, don't be silly, Calian." "Yes, they are, they look like the house poles." In the end, Kanda wore her sword at her hip. The sunlight looked like sword blades; the sword looked like house poles. Did did did, if Calian said it did.

Sal wore her knife on a cord around her neck. Dellet had a stick that he used to stir up the smell of the garlic. He smiled wide at the green and the scent.

They walked on for maybe an hour. The droveway turned sharply, sloped downward, and Kanda began to sense the river ahead.

When. When. When. When. Lush and green and rich as new cheeses. Overrun almost with birdsong. The scent of water, the sound of water – I can hear it, Kanda thought, it is calling, it is the Wenet that I love. If someone asked me, *what is it you love most in the world, Kanda?* I would list off without thinking, *my children, my husband, walking in wet grass to call the cows home, the sound the Wenet makes when it runs high after a summer storm, the sound the Wenet makes when it meets the stone just by the bend in the water meadow, the sound the Wenet makes when the cows drink.* Listen! I hear… I hear….

The river running. Her river! Running! Ah, the springhead in Lela's village had made a kind of music, but this, the sound of a river, her river, ah, they all fi— all four went faster, hurried the pony on, the droveway ran downhill and the trees were elm trees and birch trees and then the trees were ash trees and willow trees; the droveway turned, its high banks lowered, the river was there green and silver and black. The sunlight fell in places through the tree canopy, the sunlight looked like strands of long pale shining hair. Broke the dark water. Set it bright as flowers. The water was wide and deep, slow-running, glossy and fat as fat old horse flanks. Flies danced over the water, and a fish jumped to catch them.

Even a little beach of mud and pebbles. The riverbank tumbled where a tree had come down and a great many feet, children's feet and stained adult drovers' feet, had trampled their way down there to paddle and splash and look close up at the river's bottom as if there might be treasure there, or at the least some glorious never before discovered secret like a water vole's nest or a gaggle of yellow ducklings.

"Can we stop? Can we paddle? Can we can we?"

Thus Calian the *Eagle*, who this morning had strapped on her bronze sword that had once cut down half an army.

"We could," said Kanda. "Maybe. For a little while, maybe. I don't know. Should we stop?"

"Oh…."

"Of course we can, Cal-bird you foolish," Dellet said. "Your mother's just fooling you." Born and bred on the banks of the Wenet, father and daughter both. Wenet water poured over their heads as babies for the river to meet and bless them. Wenet water should one day have washed their corpses when they died in bed of old old old age. They were both on the beach already, barefoot with mud spatter up to Calian's kneecaps, throwing pebbles to make ripples spread.

Sal dismounted. Walked to her mother's side. "Look at them."

Two old women together watching a child with such love in them. Kanda thought suddenly: on the last day we lived in the farmhouse, Morna played on the Wenet's banks where it curved around the stone. If she'd thrown a pebble into the water, or a stick or a leaf, and the current took it – how many days would it have taken to reach the beach here?

The ghost child whispered in the water's running. Look upstream, and somewhere….

A hunting horn sounded. In the distance, a dog howled, then a dog barked.

A crash from the other side of the river. A man – a thing like a man – burst out from the trees, scrambled down the riverbank. He ran like he had all the evil of the world at his heels. He splashed into the river, stood there panting.

He saw them finally. His vast eyes, round and blank.

On the little mud beach, near to him, Calian and Dellet cried out in horror. Kanda cried out in fear for them.

It was so hard to look at him clearly. He was dressed in rags. Worse than rags – a beggar almost naked in his poverty, crude scraps of animal skins wrapped around his waist and his feet. Filthy, his hair caked with mud, his body stained with dirt. Skin and bone and nothing else, long dead long dead, a corpse in a gibbet or a corpse on the pyre half-burned.

The hunting horn sounded again. The man turned to stare back behind him. Easier to look at him when he was not looking toward Kanda. More real. So wretched. A piteous beggarman. "Help him!" she almost cried. The horn blew, triumphant. Barking, howling, of dogs. The man cowered, threw up his arms. Staggered, pushing his way through the river toward Kanda. The water so deep he was up now to his waist, now his shoulders, now his neck. The water churned around him red.

A pack of hunting dogs broke from the trees. Poured and flowed and foamed on the far riverbank. Eight of them. Six of them were small and white, collared in gold and rubies, and red blood dripped from their mouths. Two of them were huge and gray, one marked with white, one marked with brown, both with silver collars around their necks.

The white dogs milled on the riverbank baying at the man they hunted. A great clamor and ratchet; a belling and a gaggling of hounds.

The two gray dogs turned to fix their eyes on Kanda and her family. They growled. Crouched with raised hackles. Huge beasts, as big as Sal's pony, solid built with thick coats. They were so clearly alive. Unlike the wretched thing in the water they hunted.

The man wailed. His hands clawed at the water's surface. Clawed indeed, for his nails were so long they were more like claws, his hands were scarred and knotted, barely human hands. He fought his way through the river, the water beating about his mouth. All the time he was babbling sounds but with no human speech.

The gray dogs looked from Kanda to their quarry. They growled deep in their throats. The river welled up and the man was lost, hands fighting above the water that had sucked him down, that swirled over his head.

"Ward him!" Kanda cried out. At least, she tried to let out a great cry of protection. It came out weak and hesitant:…ward him…for he was worse almost than the dogs. Calian and Dellet were still down on the beach, fixed there staring. "Calian… Dellet…." The girl looked back at her mother somehow helpless. Dellet looked horrified. "Dellet!" Kanda shouted. The man resurfaced, spewing water, eyes nothing but whites. The red water beat and sucked at him. All the blood that ever was shed in battle, in this river that blood runs. Forcing itself like fingers through his lips. But his hands thrashed, and he might – might reach—

The two gray dogs growled.

Leapt from the far riverbank.

That was what saved the man they hunted: for Kanda of the Six in that moment must ward him. Her sword was in her hand black and burning. She leapt herself to meet the dogs.

The bloody river parted, the dogs rushed across together in great bounds. Bones and rubbish and all the detritus of warfare revealed in the riverbed and smashed beneath their feet. They came at Kanda with red mouths gaping, red blazing eyes as vast as millstones. Huge beasts, as big as the pony, for a moment it seemed even that warrior men were mounted on their backs. Slaver dripped from their jaws. They fell upon her, came upon her like blindness. For a moment it seemed the dogs walked upright, armed, savage, running on their hind legs like men.

"Mother!" Sal screamed. So much fear in her voice. "Mother! No! Please!"

One dog was on Kanda, bearing her down beneath its weight. The other now was at her throat. She thrust up her sword, threw up her left hand. Teeth closing on her left wrist. Slaver in her eyes that burned. Such a stink from the beasts. "Mother! No! No! Please!" Sal was screaming, even over the scrabbling of the dogs in her face Kanda could hear Sal's fear for her. She thought, dimly: help me, then, Sal. Breathing dog hair. Dog slaver. Dog stink. Her hand pressed forcing one muzzle open. The flat of her sword blade choked against the other's throat. Its teeth almost at her throat. "Mother!" she could hear Calian shouting. "No! Please!" she could hear Sal screaming. The pony snorted and kicked and tried to run in panic. "Kill them," Kanda tried to shout to Calian. "Draw your sword. Help. Me." And she couldn't speak, dog filth in her mouth and all her effort in keeping the dogs from biting her face open and her throat open, "Help. Me." And her hands were bleeding and the claws of their hind legs scrabbled at her belly to open it. Dug deep into the fat of her belly, clawed to tear her open, spill her guts out as dogs will eat the catch's guts in the hunt. Pounding on her belly, folded into the flesh there as children's feet had once clawed from the inside to be born. Her hands shredded, shredding dog mouth, her eyes rank with dog slaver, her mouth ran and gulped foam and slaver in. Teeth in her neck buried in her neck like kissing. Her sword blunted against a dog's throat. Silver collar and black sword. Dog hairs in her eyes and her mouth.

Dellet, Calian – help me. The dogs have come to gnaw my flesh. Calian mine – help me! And then a dog's jaws were worrying at her eyes and she could not see.

But Calian at last heard her, drew her own sword at last that was bronze and good, struck deep.

Struck deep. Dog blood spattered on Kanda's face in her mouth. Her sword was free. She flailed out with it, struck and met dog flesh. A great howl from one dog then the other. Her head rang with the sound they made. "No!" Sal was screaming screaming screaming. Kanda was weightless, light-stunned, breath-stunned, as they leapt back from crushing her. Like coming up from beneath a vast wave. She spat and choked. Staggered to her feet, saw the dogs' hindquarters fled. Blood poured off them. They ran into trees and the wood swallowed them. They howled and barked, until at last they had fled so far away their howling stopped.

All this time the little white dogs had been belling and ratchetting on the far bank of the river, like white foam they looked, as if the river had run so wild it had left its foam white on the green and the black of its bank. They pricked up their ears now, they bayed all together in one note. A hunting horn rang, calling them. They ran back into the woods.

Kanda turned on the man they had been chasing. Lady Kanda of the Six, Ikandera Thygethyn, almost killed rescuing a man from two dogs! He crouched at her feet huddled into himself. "Why were they chasing you?" Kanda said. Shouted. He disgusted her, fear in her, she thought: the dogs should have had him. I should have let them devour him. Why did I fight them off?

The wretch groveled at her. Tried to speak, but no words came from his dead mouth. His eyes flicked left and right, searching. He started up into a run.

"Stop! Wait!" Kanda shouted. "Come back!" Be grateful we saved you.

He ran on all fours, himself making an animal noise in the back of his throat, was gone from sight.

"Mother." Calian ran up to Kanda, clutched her tight. "Mother. I'm sorry, I…I was afraid…Mother. Please be all right."

"Just scratched and bruised. See?" A horrible bite on her left wrist, but that would heal quickly. Was already healing. The taste in her mouth was rank – dog slobber, dog hair, dog blood. She spat. Just my pride wounded, Calian mine. And maybe – certainly – annoyed with you for not helping me better.

"I thought…I…. They were just dogs," Calian said. "Just dogs. You didn't need help…against dogs."

Monsters, Calian has battled, Kanda thought. Vast armies, she and I have fought and beaten. Shadows, horrors, beasts of blood. The Six Swords of Roven woke one morning to find a dragon curled before the gates; Gallyn could not wound it; Palle could not wound it; Kestre could not wound it; with one blow of my sword, I struck off its head. These two: just dogs. A shame, a pain, to have to wound them. Sad and shameful it would be, I admit, if they lay here at my feet dead. A sad thing, to have to kill a dog. But she could not blame Calian for her fear of the beasts.

"Sal!" Calian cried. "You're not all right."

The pony had bolted. It stood trembling beneath an elm tree. Sal sat on its back staring after the dogs. She too was trembling. Kanda ran to her, Kanda and Calian and Dellet together grasped her, held her. Her hands gripped the reins so tight they were bleeding.

"Mother. The dogs."

"They're gone, Sal. It's safe. They're gone. You're safe."

"No, Mother. Mother!" A shriek. Sal almost fell from the pony's back. "Those dogs!"

"Come. Sit down. Here, sit." Her daughter was shaking so much she could not walk. Together, Kanda and Dellet carried her to sit down. "No, wait." Kanda carefully turned Sal's body so that Sal could not see the dogs' blood. "Some water. Here." Dellet held out the waterskin for Sal to take. Kanda had to hold the skin to Sal's mouth. Sal looked so old. So lost.

"The dogs."

"They're gone, Sal. Gone, I promise."

Sal turned wide eyes on her mother. "Gone? You promise?"

Sal had liked dogs, when she was y— when they'd lived in the valley of the Wenet. *Can we have a pup, Mum? Can we?* The dogs in the headman's hall had not frightened her, when they went to visit Dellet's family in Aranth. Big fierce hunting dogs to take down deer and boar – in fact, she'd made up a story to Calian that the headman's dogs were man-eaters, thought it very funny when Calian at six years old believed it. But in the dark places she had lived since then.... Dogs to hunt a man in life and pursue him onward in death, no rest for him or for the dogs that must run after his scent. No wonder she looked so afraid.

"Dogs." Sal tried to get to her feet. So old. So old. Skin and bones and nothing more herself, her face a gallows corpse. She staggered, fell; Kanda and Dellet grasped and caught her and held her and held her. So frail, like a thin baby bird. So weak and fragile, her trembling limbs like baby Devad's newborn bones flailing. Both so easily crushed. So helpless. Closer to death. Her heartbeat was fast and weak as a bird's wings in winter, her breathing fast and harsh and the shallow breath of one sick. "Gone," Sal said. "Yes." She drew three longer, deeper breaths.

"We need to get you" – Kanda looked around. Trees, and trees, and the droveway running empty on – "somewhere, Sal."

Dellet looked around them too, with a face full of loathing. "We've walked and walked," he said, "I thought we were walking somewhere good. 'Follow the droveway,' Dovei told me, 'it'll lead you safely to the river, and the river will lead you safely on.' He was a fine man. I trust what he said. Can you ride now, Sal-flower, do you think? Because I think we should best get on."

He looked at Kanda. Knew her so well, she knew him so well: "Not back, Kanda," he said gruffly. For, looking at Sal, his heart and hers must be crying the same thing. "Onward. I know...I know we...we can't go back."

"I can ride," said Sal. Indeed, she seemed eager now to get on. Calian helped her up onto the pony. Stroked the pony's nose and called it bravest of all brave things, bravest bravest best best white-nosed old beloved pony-heart, for not, uh, dropping dead of fright.

They went on down the droveway. Goose shit, and sheep shit, and once, but at the side of road, human shit. No trace of dead men or living dogs. But waiting all the time for something to come for them. The droveway led easily without danger of getting lost on it, no path branched off it, it ran sunk between high banks lush with ramsons, topped with blackthorn drenched in blossom. It curved and meandered like the river that ran close by just out of seeing or hearing, but it went on impossible to be lost on, no evil seemed present. Except that there were no birds and no sign of any creatures at all, not even insects among the green things.

Calian said, "What it is that is moving beyond the blackthorn and the high banks here?"

"Stop looking," Kanda said after the third time her daughter said it. "Whatever it is, stop looking for it, Calian."

"But—"

"If there is anything there, it is leaving us alone at the moment. So we will leave it alone, Calian."

"But—"

"What do you suggest we do otherwise, Calian? Run up the bank and burst through the hedgerow at it?"

"Yes?"

Kanda stopped, looked, looked. "The sun shining through the hedgerow: that's what I can see, Calian."

Calian found a stick; she swung it, stirred up the green scent of the leaves; she poked like a young child in the trampled earth.

"Those dogs—" Calian said. She lashed at the green banks of the droveway and broke a few leaves and stems down.

"Leave it," said Kanda. "Don't waste words on whatever happened, Calian."

"*Waste words*?" said Calian. "What does that even mean?" She dug hard at the earth with the stick. Some soil flew up and hit Kanda's legs. Then a pebble flew up and hit Dellet's leg.

"Calian!" Dellet shouted. "It means stop that!"

The droveway ran on, little low hillocks they had to stride up, little steep slopes down, oak trees now, still almost bare, holding in places last year's leaves dead and brown as dried fish. Winter leaves thick on the ground, a lovely noise to walk through, slide in drifts on the down slopes, in the hollows they had to be forded. Calian pretended sometimes to look for last year's acorns among the leaf litter. Kanda tried to look for her. These fine oak trees – someone should play among them and admire them. The ghost child was there, following, hiding, Kanda could see her very clearly, her pale fine hair the color of elderflowers; she ran endlessly through the leaf-drifts, she scooped up leaves and sticks to throw them as high as her head. She hit Calian with a well-aimed acorn, so well-aimed, right between Calian's eyes, that it must have been an accident. Calian frowned, rubbed her face, a gnat, she thought, a leaf brushing her face. And the ghost child cried because her mother scolded her, then quickly the ghost child stopped crying, wanted to dive into the leaf-drifts. The river was there, not visible but sometimes they heard it, it ran fast and wild and red. They had been walking a long time now, the bothy was a thousand years' walk away and Lela's village ten thousand years' walking. But they were neither tired nor hungry. They were neither weary nor cold. They simply walked on.

Once four had traveled like this to rescue Sal. One of those four was himself dead and back to life now, and one of those four was only dead and gone.

I wish, I wish, that I had stayed in those dark halls with Geiamnyn my husband and thus Morna had not been killed: that Sal had never said.

A dog barked in the distance. The ghost child vanished, whimpering and laughing. Sal let out a cry.

"It's nothing, Sal," said Kanda quickly. "Don't be frightened. And if it is those dogs, I fought them – Calian and I fought them, I mean – we can fight them off again."

"Yes." Sal looked around her, shivered. Her voice was low and flat. She sat hunched, slumped over Old White Nose. "Yes. Gone." She looked so old and bent.

Kanda thought then*: I wish, I wish, that I had left Morna in those dark halls and not taken her place there, so that I was a young woman still:* that also Sal had never said.

They went on a little further without speaking. The droveway turned sharply to the left, sloped downward, the river was there again before them. Danced over folds and sandbanks, it was shining, it had the muscled look of water rushing fast rejoicing. The droveway met it, led along its bank. They walked past tumbled stones that could be the remains of an old house. Then the river in turn bent sharply to the left, a tall stone stood to mark – a gate to the house? The river widened. Slowed its rushing. The droveway crossed it here at a ford. The banks were very low and sandy, a good ford no more than knee-deep. All was thick green trees delighting in the springtime, the riverbanks a vastness of willowherb and nettles and whitelace. Cowpats on the droveway earlier, and now fresh cowpats in plenty and the smell of cows themselves. A herd of them, white cows with red ears. They milled on the far bank of the river, their legs still wet from crossing.

White as milk and fine and fat.

Six little cows in the meadow sat.

But Calian stopped. Calian's hand went to her sword.

The pony stopped. It whinnied, Sal said, "Come on, Nosey," but it would not move.

Still no birdsong, no insects, no sounds of life. The river danced bright, but it made no sound as it danced.

A figure stood by the riverbank, cloaked and hooded so that its face was hidden.

Kanda wanted to say to her family, "We should go back. We must go back." A tall figure in a rich gray cloak, silver embroidery and fur trimmings, a flash of gold at the throat beneath the hood. A mass of yellow flowers alive at its feet. A yearning, in Kanda's heart, as the figure stepped forward to meet them. Such a yearning, such fear, such a grief.

Like to my old companions, those bright ones, those strong ones, whom I defeated and cast away forever. Like, and unlike, a reminder like a ghost.

You *empty* one I loved once so deeply – you are in the mire buried there under an enchantment. Ten times a thousand years, I bound you to lie buried there.

You *hungry* one, whom I loved once as a sister – you are gone and banished from this wide world that the sun shines upon, you fled my daughter Calian's sword, defeated, flew as a bird witless as a bird far far away.

You *burning* one, strong and mighty, almost my equal with the sword in battle – you are dead. No fine words will I waste on your fate. You are dead. My daughter Sal killed you.

You three whom I loved and rejoiced in loving, you three who took all I was from me and gave me in return all I had ever wanted – I lost my home, my peace, my youngest daughter, because of you, but you are gone now, you can harm me no longer. No longer can you haunt me.

Like and unlike those three her old companions.

Very like to Kanda herself as she was when she fought beside them.

"Oh, how wonderful, how fine," the figure cried joyfully in greeting. Horrible, and strange, the eager voice that came from beneath the folds of its gray hood. A woman perhaps, from the voice, nothing sinister there, Kanda tried to think, a woman cloaked and hooded against the early spring chill. A thin voice, fine as dried leaves, the cold wind would cut through such a voice's speaker as the cold wind cuts through dried leaves on a winter tree and sends them falling. "I have been waiting here for hours now," the figure said, "watching the sun rise high and sink low. I was afraid it would be night and dark before anyone came here to help me. My cows ran across the river: a horn blew and a dog barked and they were frightened. So gently bred, my cows, they've never heard a dog bark before. They ran across the river and I wanted to go after them. But the river is too deep for me. You look like kind people – and strong ones. You can help me."

"Too deep?" Dellet stepped forward, looked at the river. "There's a ford here. Ankle-high, no more, the river runs. A child could ford it."

The figure turned its cloaked head to look at the water. Profile just visible, nose and cheek and the curve of forehead and eye. An old woman, Kanda thought.

"Shin-high, maybe.... No more than knee-high...." Dellet said. "Thigh-high, perhaps...."

"It has been raining in the hills to the east and the river is running deep," the figure said. An old woman, frail and cold, yes. "Rain as hard as tears in the hills, it makes the river run high and fast and wild."

It turned its face back to Kanda. Eyes staring. Old woman's face in the shadows of the cloak – only that. She looked down into the water, to see what might be reflected. Cold water, ah, deep water, so fast it ran swollen by winter snows and winter storms. The cattle have starved this winter, the sheep have died in the field, the children hungered. Now the river is made cruel and wild from these killing snows and killing storms, so deep and fast and cruel it runs. Dark water, black water: Kanda felt the chill down to her bones looking into it. Her own figure there reflected, no woman but a thing like the shape of a sword – thus from her own reflection Kanda looked quickly away. Her daughters, her husband; the water ran fast and made their reflections all broken and hard to look at clearly. Three people like through movement in a glass. And a human figure broken so that it was hard to look at but a human figure no different to Dellet or Sal or Calian. A gloved hand, a booted foot, a rich long cloak. An old woman's face reflected in the water, if the water would only stop its game of running. Someone who was cold in the early springtime, wrapped up against the wind, afraid of the river and the dogs and many other things, lined face, tired eyes. That was all Kanda could see.

She tried to think: it is not that cold a day, and it is sheltered here, and the wind blows gently from the west. The river is shallow at the ford here.

"My cows ran across, I tried to cross – but I was too afraid I'd drown," the woman said. A pleasant, light voice, a voice to gossip by the fireside with Sal and the other old women in Lela's village, with only the weariness and fear in it that anyone would have if they'd been sitting stranded a long time by the river alone and afraid. "Help me across, do. My cows might run away lost on the droveway. Or those dogs might come back and kill them, if you don't help me." Fear of those dogs, that was quite normal, ah, yes, reason enough to be wary and keep one's face cloaked.

Sal said, "Did you see the dogs?" Both fear and almost eagerness in her voice. Sal too was cloaked against the spring cold. Sal's face too was half hidden by her cloak.

"Your dogs, are they? They frightened my poor little cows. You should keep them in better order. They should be muzzled and leashed. Whipped. It's wicked to let dogs run wild like that." The head turned, nodded, glimpse of the face of a pleasant old woman made angry and afraid. "The night will come and the cold night will kill me," the woman said, "if you don't help me across. So long I've been sitting here, waiting for someone to come and help me cross the river, the shadows fall long and sorrowful, the day is almost done." Darker and colder, yes, long old thin shadows, the sun's wound opened red. "Cold as winter," the woman said, "where is that bright morning spring?" Yes, frost on the ground, dead leaves, no flowers to blossom. Snow in the air, a great bitter midnight cold was creeping, to kill the small beasts new-woken from their winter slumber and the songbirds on their new-laid eggs.

Winter wind making the water shiver. Bleak as murrain at lambing.

"I'm so cold sitting here. So cold and frightened. If you don't help me across…."

That was too much. The voice a whine, wheedling, needing. Too desperate. "What are you?" Dellet called out. So much fear in his voice. "If you wish for our help, first show your face!"

Calian shouted, "Ysarene?" Raised her sword high. "*Hunger*? If that is who you are: show yourself. I defeated you once, I'll happily do it again." Though the way the woman moved with its hood covering its face did not make Kanda think now of Ysarene.

The woman shuddered when she saw Calian's sword out. Stepped back right to the riverbank. Cowed and humbled. "There's blood on your sword," she whispered. "Too much blood. Don't come near me, you. I only want to cross the river," she said. "I want to cross the river to join my cows, but I can't, I need help to cross and I'm cold and weary and I'm frightened."

"You can walk across, can't you?" Calian shouted.

But Kanda said carefully, "If we help you to cross the river here, will you…will you leave us in peace?"

Such a strange great fear in her, looking at this cloaked woman. In my nightmares, she thought, it will haunt me.

"Leave us in peace?" Calian said with scorn. "If she can't cross the river, if she's too helpless to get her feet wet, let her, we can cross and then she'll have to leave us in peace. Freeze to death here, may those dogs catch her and eat her!" Calian said. She stepped down into the river, began to splash across. The water was only as high as her ankles. The light sparkled in it. She stamped her feet to make the water splash up. "See? Walk across," she said. She kicked the water as she had loved to do as a child. "There're some minnows here swimming – oh I'm frightened! Oh I'm frightened, what danger – I've put my foot on a bit of water weeds! Help me! Save me!"

The cows on the far bank lowed.

The cows all turned together, moved to stand like a wall on the riverbank before Calian. Six little white cows, fat and fine with greenstuff in their mouths. They looked at Calian.

The river swirled around Calian's knees. Around her thighs.

"Make your cows get away from the riverbank." Calian sounded angry. Disdainful. "Make them get away." Now she sounded very frightened. The cows pressed so close to the bank, bent their heads toward Cailan. The river swirled around her waist. It had the muscled look of water rushing fast. Strong and fierce and storm-fatted.

"A man should have died in the river this very morning," the woman said. Sad, angry voice. Voice of cold water and of deep water, of a long lonely death. "He didn't die because some foolish person saved him. A bad man, a murderer; the river should have taken his blood. So now the river is angry. You shouldn't mock running water, girl. Didn't your mother ever teach you that?"

Calian pushed her way downriver trying to find a place to climb out. Clutching at plant stems to hold herself safe against the current. The banks rose very steep, slippery with mud. The cows moved with her. Blocked her from climbing out. Their black eyes looked almost like human eyes. The water rushed around her shoulders, pulling at her. Kanda almost saw the river's hands pulling.

"Make your cows get away from the bank," Kanda cried. "Please."

The woman only laughed. Tossed her cloaked head. Face hidden away. Shimmer of gold at her throat. "You think I have some magic power over my cows? They're frightened of that stupid girl's shouting. She can walk back across the river if she says it's so easy."

"Please," Kanda cried.

"I asked you for help, and got nothing. I sat here asking for help and that girl – she shook her bloody sword at me. You're her mother: what a badly brought up child she must be. Tell me she doesn't deserve to drown?"

The water swirled dark and heavy. Up around Calian's mouth. She was clutching a few scraps of willowherb to keep her from being swept away in the boiling current; the stems snapped off in her hands; she was clutching at nettles and blackthorn sprigs. And now in the distance a dog was barking.

"I'll help you," Kanda shouted. "I'll carry you across."

"That's all I wanted you to do. Just for one of you strong people to help me." The woman called to the cows, "Stop that, you sillies. My fine girls, you stop that."

The cows lowed. Stepped neatly back all together from the riverbank, went back to eating grass and whitelace as if nothing had happened. One of them had a piss, long and yellow, one of them made a big fresh cowpat. They chewed the plants on the riverbank with stems and leaves and flowers hanging out of their mouths, their red ears and their white tails flicked.

The river sighed. Shouted, rushed, relented just a little. Just enough. Calian fought her way back to her family's side of the river. Slipped. Almost went under. Splashed and gasped, cried her way quickly across, scrambled up. Dellet caught her. Held her. Blood on her hands. Weeds wrapped around her boots.

Kanda looked at the deep fast water. It moved like a man's shoulder muscles flexing in battle as he hefts up his sword to strike. The woman stepped forward. Flash of green cloth beneath the gray cloak. Leather gloves. A glint of gold at the wrists. Close up, she smelled of flowers. A rich old farmer woman, not used to such rudeness and ill-treatment.

"Put down your hood," Kanda said. "I want to see your face. Please," Kanda said.

"That wasn't part of the bargain. You'll carry me across, you said." A glimpse of silvery hair, perhaps, beneath the gray cloak.

"Do you want me to carry you like…like a…a baby…?" Yes. Say yes. Please.

A laugh. "You can carry me on your back like a horse."

Once Ysarene, *Hunger*, had made the hagride on Kanda's back. Kanda bent, waited, took the weight as strong thin arms wrapped around her neck like a harness, thin legs wrapped around Kanda's waist. Breath came in her ears. Loud and rasping, and it stank.

She shuddered. Staggered. No strength in her limbs to bear the weight.

"Hup!" her rider shouted. "Or do you need a whip?"

Reeled on the bank, trying to get her balance. On her back her rider was shrieking. Legs wrapped around her waist, squeezed tight. Long arms around her throat. Boney heels dug down into her belly, as only a little while ago the dogs had dug and sunk their feet. Squeezed so tight she couldn't breathe. Squeezing all her life out. Tear her apart from the inside outward, cleave her open, worry at her flesh until she bled and ripped.

"You're going the wrong way!" A gloved hand was over Kanda's eyes. She reeled and staggered. Always hated playing this game. Glimpsed the river, gasped a great breath, stepped one two three to the riverbank. Teetered, thought she would fall with her burden vast on her back. Drown you. Drown you. Blind you. Choke you to death. Slithered half falling down the bank into the water, a roar at how cold the water was. It was up to her waist. Her shoulders. The terrible burden on her back would be washed away. Arms and legs dug in tighter. Like ropes. Like wires cutting. Frightened. The water was rushing on. Pulling. Kanda's feet slipped. Sank into deep black mud. The water was pulling at her hips. "I'll drown!" her rider screamed. Tried to climb Kanda's shoulders, hold itself up. "Hold me up!" Like heavy armor strapped too tight. Burial by water: we wrap the corpse in sackcloth, bind it tight with ropes, weigh it down with rocks. The sick, the starved, those who must be punished for great cruelty, we hide their corpses like that.

Three steps across the river. Four steps. We'll never make it. The water was up to Kanda's mouth.

So heavy. So much weight on her.

Breathing water. Five steps.

"Hurry up! You need a whipping! What a useless horse you are!"

Things like hands around Kanda's ankles. Trying to pull her down. The weight she carried tore her back like claws. She grasped out blindly. Her right arm struck churning water. Sank with hands pulling it. Her left hand thrashed at her rider. Push it off, throw it down to be washed away. "I'll drown!" her rider screamed. "I'm drowning! Hold me up! Hold me tight! We're not yet halfway across!"

Then drown! Kanda thought. Like drowning lice, washing them off in a pot. She groped at the thing's face to shove it backward, tip it off her shoulders, drown it. Many monsters she destroyed, but not yet one by drowning it. Felt skin beneath her hand. A face. Hot and dripping with sweat. So alive she gasped, astonished, let her hand fall back. Thin arms loosed their grip around her throat. Kanda thrashed out and her left hand met nettles. Gripped, held, pulled with gritted teeth. The weight of worlds and lifetimes piled in her shoulders kicking and screaming and laughing, digging in.

The woman leapt from Kanda's back, landed neatly on the dry land on the far bank. Spun and danced in a whirl of gray and green skirts and stamping boots. Yellow flowers grew up where she trod until the bank was covered with them. Her hood flew back. Long silvery hair, dressed and shining; a stately, lovely, queenly face, fine-cast in weathered bronze; as lovely as an autumn day when the sky is blue and the sun still gives heat.

Kanda sank down exhausted on the riverbank.

"What a good horse you are!" the woman shouted. Exalted, singing and dancing a jig. "How strong you are to have carried me across that river. Very few are strong enough to have done that. We could ride farther, you and I, ride on to find all kinds of good things."

Kanda looked up. A noble, stately lady, strong and wise, full of a life's great knowledge. We could ride away forever. Find together all kinds of wondrous things.

The woman clapped her hands, delighted. Radiant smile like Lela's grandmother smiling. An old woman dancing the luck at a wedding feast.

"Cattle, spears, bronze swords for raiding; woolen cloaks and leather boots and gowns of silk; ribbons and beads and bells sweetly pealing. Arm rings for a warrior born, neck rings for a great king. All the heart desires or could desire. Charms and spells and rarey things. You the horse and I the rider, on and on across the world, visiting all the great cities, visiting all the lords' halls, demanding gifts!

"Such things we could find and win, if you only let me ride you away. Helmets made of gold and silver set with human hair for their plumes, and that hair from the heads of murdered queens. Jesses to tame a gyrfalcon. A box of sweetmeats. A box of pearls. A box with a dead man's heart inside it, where his true loved locked it away safe.

"Such things we could find, you and I, horse! The finest and the best of everything! All the heart could ever desire. Riches. Wonders. Joyful things. Will you come with me to these adventures, horse? Carry me?"

"I've carried you across the river," Kanda said. "I think that's far enough."

"Too far," the woman laughed. "Too far, you've carried me, horse. Look how far away those others with you are."

A raging torrent for a river. Three tiny figures on the far side. A river of blood. A river of liquid metal. A river of fire.

"So you'd better come with me, horse," the woman said. "If you don't want to be left alone. Lonely and sad, you'll be, all alone, if you don't come with me."

She skipped, her cloak swirled. Green skirt thick with needlework. Good boots with silver buckles.

"I agreed to carry you across the river. That's all. I've done that."

"A shame! All those things we might have found together – and some of them you could have kept, and some of those things you might have needed.

"But now I'm across the river safely, I suppose I can walk if I must…. Oh, my poor old bones! My poor old weary legs! But I can walk…. Such a shame, think of the fine places you could see if only you would come with me. Kings' halls and kings' cities, I will be visiting; you could have visited them too. I know a great city, a fine city, rich in fine good things; we could ride there as fast as thinking, you and I, if you but let me set a bridle on you with a sharp spiked bit to drive you on. A golden bit, and a golden bridle, and a saddlecloth of red silk, I'll fit you with, if you only agree to come with me."

"What about your cows?" Kanda said. "I thought you needed to cross the river to join them?"

"Oh! Oh, yes! Do you know, I forgot about them? But they're well and fine. No, to tell the truth now, that's a lie! They're dead, those cows are. Poor cows! Poor things! But, dead as they are, they still give good milk. I'll ride on your back, horse, and they'll run before you, kings' halls and kings' cities they'll delight with their good milk. A box of pearls, a box of sweetmeats, a box with a dead man's heart inside it where his true loved locked it away safe – and his true love will trade it happily for a cup of these cows' milk."

She clapped her gloved hands. The six cows, that looked so alive, fine and fat, one pissing, one shitting, all chewing green stuff, the cows began to walk slowly, cow speed, down the droveway between the green spring trees.

The old woman shook out her silver hair, pulled the hood of her cloak over her head. "I'll go, then, if you're sure you won't come with me? Thank you for helping me. A pity, truly: a fine horse you would have made. I would have fitted you with head trappings of bronze and red enamel. All this good milk you could have drunk to keep you strong."

The cows went on up the droveway. The woman followed. Green-gray light of the spring woods with the light falling. She walked old and stiff, stately, cow speed, then she and the cows began to run.

Kanda had to dig her nails into her palms to stop herself from running after them.

CHAPTER NINE

So now Kanda stood on the far bank of the River Wend and her family stood on the near bank. Wait, no, that's not right. Kanda stood on the near bank, her family stood far off across rivers of blood and fire and liquid metal and crushing ice.

No, wait, that's wrong completely. Her family stood on the far bank of a river in spring spate after the winter snows are melted. Too afraid to cross. Not a big river, as the rivers of this great huge wide world go, unless you'd not seen very much at all of the world beyond your own little river valley. A ford here, the river ran, oh, ankle-deep. Shin-deep. Knee-deep, maybe, where it ran deep deeper deepest. Couldn't even in a hole be thigh-deep.

"I can't," Calian shouted across. "I can't step in that water again. I almost drowned."

Sal sat on her pony very straight-backed looking at the sky. Far into the horizon, far above where the woman – the monster, the – where the woman had gone, up into the pale milky blue of the sky where the stars were hidden, her eyes looked as if they could look forever farther on until they saw the stars hiding and looked beyond them to see what no one can see. But she said gently, "The water will be fine to walk through, Calian. Don't be foolish." She nudged the pony forward, crossed, in four five six seven steps the pony stood on the far bank, it had barely got its feet wet. "You see?" she called. "It's fine, you see?" All the time she was staring high above their heads into the sky, and her voice sounded as far away as the stars. "Fine, fine, all fine, come and cross," she said. "Come on. Come on."

Dellet crossed very slowly and carefully, not as though the water was deep but as though it was boiling burning hot. Calian crossed, her face screwed up, walking this absurd tiptoe like she was walking through human shit.

"Good girl, Calian," Dellet said.

When Calian stood on the far bank, the yellow flowers withered.

"What was that? Monster! Witch! We should have killed it. I wish, I wish that I had killed it. Cut off its head. It looked like.... It felt like...."

Dellet said, more fiercely than Kanda had heard him speak for a long time, "Leave it, Calian. Don't even speak of it." He said, sadly, painfully, "Don't wish death even on evil things."

Kanda thought: it felt like the evil thing I once was. And she knew, somehow, because she knew Dellet so well and he knew her so well, that Dellet somehow knew this.

"You must be soaking, Kanda," said Dellet, to change the subject.

Kanda looked down at herself. No. She was quite dry, although her clothes felt stiff and vile as if she'd got soaked hours ago and dried off while walking. Calian's clothes were dry too, only they had a crumpled look to them, discolored in places, like they'd got soaked and been dried by a hot fire in a heap then put back on. Kanda's left and Calian's right hand matched. Both puffed up and lumpy with nettle stings.

"I would like a drink of water," Kanda said. She washed the water around her mouth, spat. Mud and duckweed. Grit crunched between her teeth.

Calian took off her right boot, shook it, pulled a face when a worm fell out. Kanda had a brief panic that would be the breaking point for Calian – or Sal – a worm lying wriggling in the mud would make one or both of them shriek. It almost made her shriek, to be fair to her daughters, after everything, thinking of the worm in Calian's boot. She shook her hair upside down in a frenzy. Sheer horror to think of worms and creeping water things in her hair.

"Hold still there." Dellet pulled some duckweed and some nettle leaves out. He stopped, looked. "There's a mark on your neck, Kanda, wife. Like a rope burn."

He bent tenderly, kissed it better.

Grimaced. "Urgh. Pass the waterskin. You might have just got dry but you need a wash."

They went on. No sign of fat white cows, no old woman in a gray cloak. No hunting horn, no dogs. Kanda and Dellet walked close to Sal on her pony; after a while Sal said, "I want to walk," slid down from the saddle. Sal walked close to her mother. After a time, Sal put her hand into her mother's hand. That was a rare thing. Should be a joyful thing!

Dellet saw his wife and his daughter walking hand in hand, he picked up his pace just slightly, barely noticeable if you didn't know him as Kanda did, in a while and a while he and Calian were a good way ahead of them up the path.

Not a clever man, Dellet – but a very wise one.

But so now he expected Kanda would talk to Sal. Her belly and her bones still aching from the battle with the dogs and from carrying that… that burden, and now she must talk. A wise man, Kanda thought, but ah, he had laid a heavy task on her in his wisdom, and she was so tired already, her mouth clogged still with river water, her throat too bruised to speak. But so now Sal wanted to speak and not speak a word, but so now Kanda wanted to say, "It's fine, Sal, tell me or don't tell me," and couldn't speak. And so now the whole day would be gone and the right time for talking about something would be lost, and neither of them wanted to speak.

"Mother…. Those dogs," Sal said at last. "They—"

The *dogs?*

Silence.

Fathomless, are the ways of children. Easier it is by far to riddle in the dark with dragons, than to talk to one's own child about important things. They walked on without speaking, soon and sooner and soonest the time to speak would be past and lost. Kanda thought: good! I don't want to speak. My throat and my bowels ache too much.

"Sal," Kanda said. She thought: your father, good honest wise man that he is, he waited one whole day to tell me something he didn't need to tell me that I didn't want to know. Now there are things we must all say to each other, all four of us need and want and fear to say these things, it would be better – easier – if you – would say – something.

"Mother. That—"

The stone is in your mouth, Sal. And mine. How heavy it is. Speak, Sal-flower! I, your mother, beseech it.

"I mean—"

Don't speak, Sal! I, Ikandera Thygethyn, Lady Kanda of the Six of Roven, command it.

"I mean…Mum, I mean…. That—"

Don't. Please. My bowels ache, I think I will be sick.

"Mum.

"Mother.

"I….

"Mum…."

Sal said at last: "Mum, those dogs, they—"

"Those *dogs?*"

Sal shook her head, the stone clicked against her teeth. But then she said, "Nothing. Never mind." Then she said, "I'd like to ride again now. I'm tired, Mum. You must be tired, too tired to talk about me being foolish."

So thus Kanda had ruined it all. Again again again. Friends and loves and great cities, Kanda in her wisdom or her folly or mere thoughtlessness had smashed to pieces thrown down broken to bits; so thus with two words greater than any war cry she had shattered this moment with Sal who needed to speak.

But: those *dogs?* You can't blame her for saying that in such a voice, Sal-flower, I'm sorry, Sal, but you can't. Mothers know their daughters' hearts, Sal, but their daughters' words are too mysterious to make sense.

"Wait – Sal – Tell me—"

"I want to ride again, Mum."

They called to Dellet and Calian to stop for them so Sal could get back on the pony. Had to call several times; in the end Kanda had to run ahead to flag them down. Typical Calian. Typical Dellet. But when she caught up with them, she had a sense that Dellet had been not talking to Calian, and Calian had been not talking back: *that creature. It— We— Stop, don't speak.* She could see the stone shut fast behind Dellet's teeth when Dellet smiled sadly at her and shook his head. She could only shake her head.

They went on into the afternoon spring sun. Listening for dogs and cows and a woman laughing. Hearing nothing.

After a long time Kanda realized she could hear the wind in the trees, the leaves murmuring secrets, the birds singing.

CHAPTER TEN

"Ah," said Dellet. "And here, see?" A place on the droveway bank where someone had sat down in the wet green, their stout behind and their big booted feet and a dropped crust of black bread and a load of green goose shit. It rained a little while. Raindrops jeweled Calian's dark hair and Sal's white hair. Kanda sucked the damp rain air in deep. The pony sneezed.

This walking was drawing to an end.

Evening was coming on now. Long shadows fell behind them into the darkening east. Stars already visible, if they had turned to look back behind them. The twin stars Irulth, one red, one bronze, the red star old and fading. The sky before them burned gold. Kanda could sense the trees becoming tamer, soon there would be fields, houses, people. The smell of them, almost now the sounds of people living. The droveway turned to the left to avoid a great dead oak tree. A crow sat on the lowest branch and looked at Kanda. At the tree's base a fox lay still and dead. The crow cawed. Flew off down the droveway. Black against the sun's golden wound.

There were people on the droveway now ahead of them, a boy and a dog driving two old gray wethers, a man hefting a heavy pack and bent forward with the weight he carried, a handcart with three barrels strapped to it and the carter puffing, a girl with a gaggle of white geese. Kanda looked carefully at them all. The sheepdog was gray, as many dogs are gray, high and long and wolflike, but from the shape of its head, the way its flanks moved as it trotted beside the boy, it could not be one of those dogs. The goosegirl had pretty hair and red flowers on her kirtle; the shepherd boy looked at her, Kanda looked hard at her and him. The goosegirl frowned and tossed her hair at the shepherd boy. She had goose shit on her bare feet, her kirtle was fine but old and patched. She saw Kanda, cocked her head at the shepherd boy like *look at that old woman staring at me*, the two scowled at Kanda with all the comic petulance of the free and young around the old and muddy. Failed in their petulance to notice they had trodden in sheep shit and goose shit.

"Excuse me," Dellet called. "If you don't mind my asking: I'd guess there's a…a village up ahead?"

The shepherd boy and the goosegirl both burst out laughing.

"What?"

"A village?" The shepherd rolled his eyes at these ignorant ones. "There's the king's city yonder with his feast hall raised in splendor there. That's where we're going, taking this tribute in to our king."

"The city of King Amraen!" the goosegirl said between giggles.

"That woman…she did say…." Sal whispered.

"That woman? That witch! She was lying. These two are lying too. Or what if – she's there?" said Calian. "That witch?"

"Hush, Calian," Kanda said. The words came out more harshly than she meant; that – of course – set the goosegirl and the shepherd boy off sniggering. Calian gave her a look of murder; that made the two snigger worse. Calian almost drew her sword on them, the sheepdog barked, the geese hissed. Oh, oh, for goodness' sake….

"Lela and Dovei didn't say anything about a city or a kingdom," said Dellet. He looked uncomfortable. Even frightened. He'd never seen a city, or a king, Kanda thought then. Never thought of that. As distant and unreal as the Hall Roven, or more distant, these words *city* and *king*. *Tribute. Render. Market. Rarey things.*

"They didn't, no," said Kanda. "But we've traveled a long way since then."

"We've traveled for…two days?" said Calian. But she frowned, and Dellet frowned also.

Cue what could only be called snickering from the goosegirl and the shepherd boy and the sheepdog and the geese.

"The city of King Amraen," the goosegirl said. "It's famous." She rolled her eyes at Kanda. "A. Ci. Ty."

Many cities, Kanda had seen in the course of her long life. Kydana in the dry wastes, city of the wise, whose towers are built of dragon bones; Erelene, bride of cities, in the far north where the snow lies piled waist-high in midsummer beneath a cheerless frozen sun; Tyren of the Five Hillsides, once beautiful beyond human imagining, now the haunt of gods and bloody monsters; Inakanassos in the Forever Morning, that never had fallen in war to any till Ikandera Thygethyn came down upon it with her army of dead men. Temples, tombs, libraries, graveyards. Bath houses, pleasure gardens, palaces, loggias, domes, archways, workhouses, slave pits. Courts of kings great and vast and old and long-bearded. Shaded courtyards for a lady to sit quiet in while her pet monkey chatters and her servants sprinkle perfume and paint her long fingernails beetle-red. Cities that were filled with joy. Cities that were bleak with toil. Cities that were built on narrow piety to a dull harsh god. She strained her eyes now to look over the treetops. Strained her eyes into the evening light.

Gold on gold on gold on gold where the sun was sinking in its bleeding, and the crooked lines of black branches drawn like scars across. A bird – the crow? – circling high, plunging, rising. Blink. Stare. Stare into the sunset.

There!

Buildings. Towers rising. Banners fluttering, black against the gold. A city. See…its towers are islands in the evening light…. The bird that circles there, plunges, rises…that is no bird I see…. I see…. And fires. Flames rising. Smoke – not towers! Black towers of black stinking smoke! Or – no – stare, eyes watering – the smoke is sweet and fragrant as it rises – it rises from – a hall – high earthworks surrounding – and the light shines on a palisade and an open gateway, on silver walls and a golden roof. A hall set in rich fields and rich orchards and sweet meadows, many herds of cattle, many flocks of sheep.

There – before her – the droveway opening, two stones on either side of the droveway as a gate to rush through, and beyond rose the earthworks that surrounded Roven, topped with the triple palisade of painted wood. The gates of Roven stood open. The Lady beside the gates Kanda could now almost see. And Benethal the gatekeeper, ever watchful, standing waiting. *Safe Place*, his name is. Even as Kanda saw him his head turned, he saw her.

His expression changed. Half joy, half vast fear.

It's me, Kanda! Not that monster Ikandera Thygethyn! Don't be afraid, Benethal! For the last time Kanda had stood before the gates of Roven she had come to kill and burn and slaughter, such a great destruction she had wrought. More blood she had shed that day than all the wine that ever had been drunk in Roven, enough to turn not a river but the endless bottomless ocean red. Fires she had raised higher than the silver walls of Roven, higher than any tower built by men or gods or monsters or by the earth itself. The fear thus gripped Benethal, gnawed his innards as the dogs had gnawed his innards after Ikandera Thygethyn killed him. "Don't be afraid! I've not come again to kill you!" Kanda cried. But she could not remember the name she had then, before she was Kanda and Ikandera Thygethyn, that Benethal had used so easily. Thus the fear grew vast in Benethal's face, terror and horror not joy in him to see her coming, and he ran as he had that day she came indeed in blood and fire, he ran to close and bar the open gates.

They shut black.

All was gone, faded, fallen. As the fires in the fields at last are quenched and all the harvest's golden promise is only ash. All things end. The sun set and it was cold evening and the fire in the sky was turned to sorrow-blue.

No. Come back. Then the horror: don't come back. I can't bear to see again those closing gates.

How can I bear it? she thought then. To see the rubble I made? I turned my face from it the day I brought it all to ruin. Could not bear to see what my own hands did that day. I laughed until my tears flowed – to hide from my eyes the sight of Roven burned and broken, my Lord of Roven lying maimed and dead.

Rebuild it? My hands would tremble so I could not hold one stone to raise it. My eyes would fail.

As a mother stretched on her child's corpse, so I shall be, if ever we reach the end of this quest.

And a dog barked loud and angry, savage, and the ghost child spat and hissed at that.

"What's she staring at like that? Oi, you, what you staring at? Someone died or something?"

"It's the sun. Setting. That's a thing it does around these parts."

"It'll come back again tomorrow and everything."

"If you're good."

What?

Someone died....

The sun set....

The goosegirl and the shepherd boy. Laughed and laughed at Kanda. Such innocent youthful cruelty in them. Ah, you two so young, so foolish, never stop being innocent and cruel about the dark places that others must walk in. Kanda shook her head. Wiped away her tears.

And: I'm covered in mud, Kanda thought, what would they say, my old companions, if I walked into the feast hall of Roven dressed like this?

"How far is it? To this...city? How do we get there?" Dellet asked. He was trying hard to ignore both the laughter at his wife and whatever had caused it.

"Yonder," the shepherd boy said. "The road leads there. You know: the road? You walk down it. It takes you to the city."

"Does it? My goodness, the wisdom. These newfangled things. And there was me thinking there might be, I don't know, more than one road. More than one city, even." Dellet said, "Thanking you kindly for your help." He looked at Kanda. Shrugged. You ready to walk on, woman? Before Calian punches this girl in the mouth or something? Kicks the boy in the nuts? Delightful though I'll admit that would be.

"Let us go in," Kanda said. "Let's see what this city holds for us, then."

They walked on, past the two stones that stood on either side of the droveway like a gate. For a moment, as they stepped between them, Kanda thought she saw on the horizon the lights of high shining towers.

Heard the ringing of trumpets. The roar of fire. Screams. The rasp of a drawn blade.

All the heart could desire….

If – when – we find Roven….

CHAPTER ELEVEN

Many cities, Kanda had seen in the course of her long life. Kydana in the dry wastes, city of the wise whose towers were built of dragon bones; Erelene, bride of cities, in the far north where the snow lies piled waist-high in midsummer beneath a cheerless frozen sun; Tyren of the Five Hillsides, once beautiful beyond human imagining and now the haunt of gods and bloody monsters; Inakanassos in the Forever Morning, that never had fallen in war to any till Ikandera Thygethyn came down upon it with her army of dead men. So many cities – and of all of them, the city of King Amraen was poorest and the meanest and the smallest city she had yet seen.

Perhaps forty houses, small and humble, huddled inside crude wooden walls. A central house trying to be a headman's hall like that at Aranth and failing miserably. A single bake oven; a few vegetable gardens with not much growing; a muddy orchard; a few small store barns.

The droveway led in through the open gateway. The carter pushed his cart; the man went in with his heavy pack. The goosegirl and the shepherd boy went through the gate together still giggling with what they must think was true malice at Kanda. May they marry and live to be a hundred with as many fat grandchildren as they have dog and sheep and geese. Or may they have a lovely day and a lovelier night together, never see each other again. Either is fine and good. A single guard stood on duty watching all of this apart from the barrels with little interest. He was armed with spear and sword, wore a helmet set with boars' tusks. But there was nothing fearful in him, somehow. He didn't stand like a warrior or hold his spear like he would use it without a second thought. A third, a fourth, a sixth, a tenth thought and he'd still be too scared to use it, from the look of him.

"Are we going in?" Calian said doubtfully. "This can't be right…."

The guard started at the sound of her voice. Not a warrior indeed, if he was too focused on a girl's pretty hair and a cart carrying possibly ale to watch the road. His eyes went from Dellet to Kanda to Kanda's sword to Calian's sword to Kanda's sword, got wider and more frightened each time.

"Who goes? What's your business here, you?"

He was talking to Dellet. Saw two women with swords, went green with fear, talked to the man standing next to them.

"We're travelers looking for a hot meal and a bed for the night," Dellet said. "We were told there was a…a city here, hoped we could maybe find a welcoming hearth?"

The guard stared at them. Put his right hand on his sword hilt.

Blood and blood and blood and killing. Kanda felt her own right hand itch.

Ah, no – the guard heard Dellet's words, saw old Sal on her pony with the night coming on around her, Kanda and Calian who might wear swords but who were also both covered in mud; he felt ashamed, felt pity for them. He was a man like any other: most people are kind, deep down and on the surface.

"I don't know…." he muttered. Bowed his head. "Wait here," he said roughly. "I'll send to the king." He gestured to a bench set against the wall, a well beside it, an ash tree to shade it from sun and rain and wind. He looked around, confused still. "Wyn. Ylil. One of you…. Run to the hall, Ylil, tell them there's visitors here to see the king. Wyn, you take care of this lady's horse. Get on with you, boys. Hurry!"

Two boys were squatting at a puddle by the wellhead, playing the old great game of *pointlessly throwing stones until they splash their own legs.* The younger of the boys, white and skinny as a birch sapling, gave the guardsman a glare then ran off at his bidding. The older, brown and gold and green and lanky as a willow sapling, came up to help Sal dismount, then led off the pony. Kanda sat awkwardly to wait. Sal sat beside her.

A horn cup hung by the well. The water smelled cool and sweet. Kanda washed her hands clean, filled the cup, drank, passed it to Dellet.

"Is it safe?" Calian asked, remembering a cup of water Kanda had once drunk that had bound her worse than chains.

"It's safe," Kanda said.

"I'm not thirsty." But then Calian took the cup and drank. She smiled. "It's good. Much nicer than the water in Lela's village."

"Calian!"

"It is!"

Kanda poured a few drops in offering into the boys' puddle. A kind welcome. A good sign, let's hope. "It is nicer-tasting, yes," she said to Calian. "The water in Lela's village tasted like mud." Given the springhead in Lela's village was charmed against me, that shouldn't be surprising, she thought. May I never have destroyed this village in blood and fire, either at sword point or with the strength of my bare hands.

A small request, surely, that?

The place was poor and ragged, the boys Wyn and Ylil had been dirty and thin. Rubbish piled between the houses – the water might taste good but Kanda now looked regretfully from the well to a nearby midden heap. But a dog was asleep in a warm place near the bake oven, from which drifted a good smell of almost-ready-to-eat bread. The goosegirl and the shepherd boy argued with someone about where to take the geese and the sheep; Kanda was ignobly pleased to see they lost. Bustle around the big man's house, renders brought, beer poured, meat roasted, both beer and meat also smelled very good. Some chickens strutted about. Three brown, one white. The dog got up, trotted over to sniff at the chickens. It was fat and spotted. Old and stiff. The chickens squawked at it.

After a while, a woman came hurrying toward them. She wore a blue dress, her hair was brilliant red. The guard at the gate bowed his head to her, saluted. "You're to come up to the hall, my ladies, my lord," the woman said. "My lord king will hear your story, pass judgment on you." She looked rather taken aback at the state of them, two swords, wild eyes, and a lot of mud. Before leading them the ten short steps from the gate to the hall, she stopped to see what Wyn and Ylil, who had both run back at her heels to return to playing, were doing with the stones and the puddle.

The hall was so small and mean compared to Kanda's dream of Roven. Not gold and silver, barely carved and painted wood. Rather like the headman's hall in Aranth, the settlement Dellet's family had lived in, if the headman's hall in Aranth had shrunk to half the size. Perhaps had a flood and a fire and a couple of bad winters ranged against it. The headman in Aranth had kept a warband, but he had not claimed to be a king. If anyone had described Aranth as his city, he would have laughed till his piss stained his breeches. The lord of this hall sat on a carved chair with a wolfskin hung on the wall behind him, his cloak was dyed scarlet, his beard was scarlet to match, he wore a gold arm ring on his right arm, a bronze circlet on his head. *My hall*, his face said, staring at the wall above Kanda, not deigning to look at the strangers who knelt as supplicants before him. *My city, my law, my kingdom. King-throned, glorious my rule. You will not deny it.*

The woman in blue bowed low with her eyes averted, announced: "Travelers from afar, who seek an audience with you, my lord king."

The king shifted himself on his chair to indicate he had heard her. His hands gripped the wolf heads carved on the chair's arms. He said slowly, "It is not often the custom of this hall to welcome strangers without good cause. They may approach and do homage."

Kanda wanted to roar with laughter. Heard Dellet snort with laughter and Calian hiss angrily between her teeth. Six warriors sat on the benches at their lord's pleasure, they heard Dellet and Kanda laugh and Calian hiss. Kanda touched Dellet's arm. This is serious, Dellet. He touched her hand back. I'm laughing, Kanda, because it's absurd but also because I'm frightened. The four of them stepped forward from the doorway, walked the five short steps from the threshold to the audience place before the throne.

"You are strangers here," the king said. His voice was very cold. "Warriors, two of you, I am told. I am gathering my tithes today, did not wish to be disturbed by strangers. Least of all by strangers who dare come before me armed. King, I am, and as king and guard to my people I place this binding on you: that neither you nor your kin may do harm to me or to my kin or to anything of mine."

A shiver ran across Kanda's skin where the king's binding words tried to hold her. She saw Calian wince, jerk her fingers. Look down, puzzled, at her right hand.

A king? Yes. Laughable, pitiable, Kanda might think his claim, his city little more than a village, his throne crudely carved wood – but the people saw him as their king, did him homage, thus in the naming of it there was a power in him and in his words.

And that power working for good here now, provided Kanda would agree with him that the people here were merely their king's possessions.

Kanda took one more step forward, right up to the dais and the throne. "My lord king. We are grateful indeed that you have permitted us to step within the threshold of your hall. We are travelers. Warriors, yes, but only two of us indeed, and one of those two is – a child." (Forgive me, Calian mine.) (Don't, just don't, say anything, Calian mine, please.) "And in total we are only four, and one of us old and weary at that." (Forgive me, Sal.) (You can hear in my voice, both you girls, I hope, that I'm embarrassed saying this.) "We hope only for a bed for the night in this vil— this city of yours, would be grateful if you would grant us only this kindness. A king's hall is a place of power and strength, a king holds in his hand the lives of those who dare to cross its threshold, and we come as humble supplicants. For I have always heard it said that a king's hall is a place of hospitality and welcome, far above the hospitality of other men as a king is above the least of his subjects." (These honeyed words I would use to charm when I was Ikandera Thygethyn, and often indeed they would work great magic to let me and my black sword and my armies in. So don't you dare laugh, Dellet, Calian.) (I am ashamed to use them now, obviously, Dellet, Sal, Calian. But needs must, a mother's sharp elbows, I would like a warm bed tonight for Sal.)

The man on the throne – the king – blinked at Kanda's words. Lowered his eyes to look at her. Had she gone too far? Did he think – know – that she mocked him?

The man's eyes widened. He stirred on his throne. His mouth opened.

Kanda thought: oh, please no, has Calian…sniggered? Made a stupid face?

Most unkingly, the great king leapt from his kingly throne on his high kingly dais to his kingly booted feet.

Knelt.

At Kanda's feet.

"My lady queen," he whispered.

He knew Kanda.

Kanda knew him.

A thousand years ago she had fled her life as Ikandera Thygethyn. Left an army behind her, as well as a husband. A soldier in that army it seemed had settled in this village, set himself up as a king.

His name, Amraen, was: *Wanting.*

Kanda's hand went to her sword, her head now dizzy with all that had happened this day. She thought: this is too much! Ah, it was better when Geiamnyn was hunting me through the valley of the Wenet! Her heart cried to strike him down where he stood. Geiamnyn, Ysarene, that *empty, nothing* one my first husband, often I told my children we must kill those monsters. More important than our own lives, I told my children, is the necessity of killing such things. Better we all die in the killing of such monsters, than we live but such monsters live. Eagerly, this man Amraen had served in Ikandera Thygethyn's army. Proudly, he had brought victory tokens to heap at Ikandera Thygethyn's feet. This man is evil. Kill him.

The warriors in the hall knelt. Baffled, they looked. But they saw their king kneel. They saw their king – crying. White and terrified, their king's face.

Six warriors, each armed for battle. She could kill them without drawing breath. Thin children playing in a dirty puddle, and this man demanded they toil for him, give up their hard-earned food for him while he lolled on his absurd wooden throne. *I will kill you, if you do not give over to me all that you own, I am your king now who holds in my hands your life and your death*, he says. Words he had learned from Ikandera Thygethyn. The people in the village cower in the muck, turn over their lives to him. A gift to the world, her duty, to kill him. He had set bindings to hold her hand from her sword; she moved the little finger of her right hand one hairsbreadth to dismiss them.

Amraen said, "My lady Ikandera Thygethyn. *Great Warrior.* Greatest queen. My hall is yours. My warriors are yours." His voice shook, like the call of wild birds in the marsh, his voice was. He said, breathless, trembling, "You left us, and it was to me as if the world was cold and dead. But I have ever kept faith. I knew you would return."

His voice rose stronger, believing, gasping, joyful. "You do me honor beyond words, to grace my hall." His voice was like the song of a bird in a fruit tree.

Eyes watched her: Dellet's dark with shock; Sal's wary, remembering another lord's hall with its swords and warriors; Calian's torn between rage – and eagerness at this hall with its warriors and its swords and its king doing homage.

"Honor…?" Kanda whispered. She must say something….

"A feast is prepared here," King Amraen went on. Not hearing her, not seeing her doubt. "Today the first spring renders have been brought in. The meat is already roasting, the bread baked: it is as if I knew, somehow, without knowing, that a mighty guest would come to my hall this day! You do me honors beyond honors, my lady queen. You shall sit in the throne here, I myself will serve your ale and your meat."

I could kill them all. I should, I will. Hand on her sword hilt, ready. What else can I do but kill him? Calian itched and stared, thinking the same in dull confusion: *I thought they were unfriendly here, I asked about the water, "Is it safe?" I said – now look – another monster, we should kill them.*

Amraen took off his crown, held it out to Kanda. "Honor my hall with your presence. I beg you, my lady queen. Many years, so many years, I have longed for this, to welcome you again, hail you again. The first thought in my mind, on the day I set the first house post of my hall, the words I said that day as the post was raised: 'May Ikandera Thygethyn herself one day but set one foot in my hall. May Ikandera Thygethyn but stand on the threshold looking in. The greatest, the only true queen and warrior! May this hall be worthy of her glance, her footstep, her shadow as she passes unseeing.'"

Tears in his eyes, remembering. He cannot have said that, Kanda thought, he lies – but – the light in his face, the rapture in his voice as he spoke. He had truly said these things.

"Bless my hall, my lady queen Ikandera Thygethyn."

His hand trembled as he held out his crown. Fear and joy both poured off him. And she had misjudged Calian, she saw now, the girl had no righteous death lust in her, rather, she smiled, itched and stared with delight. Cruel sneering words, Calian had heard thrown at Kanda by her enemies, and the cruel sneering words a family tends to throw at each other very often had been thrown. Now: her mother a great lady welcomed as a queen, the honeyed words flowing thicker and sweeter and sweeter yet. A lord's hall, a king kneeling, armed men in the warband not enemies to be fought but supplicants. Oh, most wonderful! Calian's face said.

"Bless this hall. Bring the luck here. I beg you," Amraen said. And his fear was outgrowing his joy now, he trembled, Kanda saw him glance at the woman in blue with a true look of concern. And that perhaps was what saved him.

She said slowly and carefully, "I thank you for your welcome, King Amraen. This promise I give you: that neither you nor your kin nor anything in your household will do harm to me or my kin or anything I own, and in return I will do no harm to you nor your kin nor anything in your household."

Dismayed at her own words, and fearful, for she had made such a promise before and been deceived. The man's face lighted as she spoke these words, and a shadow seemed to lift from him. But his voice trembled when he replied, his words were full of fear: "I would never dare do you harm, my lady queen Ikandera Thygethyn." And Kanda thought, no, but these are words also that must be spoken – even to Lela I said such words. And that is the world we two made, when I was Ikandera Thygethyn and you my sworn warrior, where there is no trust but only fear of strangers that they come to steal and kill.

She took the crown, touched it to her own forehead, gave it back to Amraen. Said, "You do me honor. Without fear for myself or for my kin or for anything I own, without threat to you, without condition – I accept your gift of a seat at the feast."

She thought: never did Amraen shine with spear or sword, he was boastful of his killing but, in truth, few men fell to him. *Rarely seen in the thick of battle, that man Amraen, he holds back cautiously, it's almost amusing the excuses he makes* – and he was younger and fitter then. Said, with more warmth, "I grant you luck and honor in return, my lord king."

Amraen raised his head, truly he was weeping for the joy of it! "I thank you," he whispered. A sigh ran around the hall. Warmer there, and grander, high walls, rich hangings, a bright fire in the hearth; the faces there less pinched and thin. A long time since the warriors in the hall had last drawn their swords for any purpose beyond playing, great relief now that the swords could remain sheathed. It was like a draft of good wine to Kanda – or, no, not like wine but like the clean water of the well. Words she had spoken many times long ago came back to her. Her voice grew stronger, the words flowed from her lips and they tasted truly sweet. Lady Kanda the greatest of the Six Swords of Roven, who had so often accepted honor, brought blessings and peace.

"A fine feast is laid here: may every feast in this hall be as fine. Many people are gathered here in homage to me: may this hall always be filled with people, may the living always outnumber here the dead. May the roof of this hall always give shelter from rain and snowfall, may the walls of this hall always stand strong against the wind. May all I drink here tonight be given back to you twice over. May all I eat here tonight be given back to you three times over. As you offer me honor, so may there always be luck here!"

Not honeyed, lying words, these. Like apples, the words rolled from her mouth across the hall. The tension was broken. The woman in blue let out an almost filthy laugh. In the corner of her eye, Kanda saw Calian mouthing those beautiful words.

Still trembling, his face soaked with sweat, Amraen rose to his feet. He staggered. Finally he croaked out, "Thank you, my lady queen Ikandera Thygethyn." His words too were like apples. Like flowers blooming after a bleak winter, like rain in the desert, his words were so filled with hope and relief. Ah, Kanda, great lady who can give blessings that delight even kings!

But a pause then, a mighty heavy awkwardness in King Amraen's hall. Such magic words as never in this hall had before been spoken.... What next? Such high magic, such power! Like flowers in spring, merely, like mere rain in the desert and the flowers bloom and the life comes? No, far, far greater was the power of Kanda's words! Like the crystal bells that ring in the highest heavens, like a pillar of light, like dragons fighting! Where can we go from such high mighty things?

"Thank you," Amraen whispered. "Thank you, my lady queen. Thank you. Thank you. Thank you. Thank you."

"My family are weary," Kanda said before the man went hoarse from saying it over, "we have traveled all day, as you see we are hardly dressed for a feast. Before we think of feasting we need to wash, change our clothes, rest." Where can we go from here? To the important things.

King Amraen blinked. "Yes...of course.... Of course, yes. I will see to it. My servants will see to it." The spell was fading a little, he was a kind host receiving a guest. He had done this before, if not for one so exalted. Well-practiced in it, as a good king must be. Drew kingly comfort from that. *A king's hall is a place of hospitality and welcome, far above the hospitality of other men as a king is above the least of his subjects*: not mere lies and honeyed words; there was a truth in them. Fear, suspicion, the doors kept barred, cold faces and spearpoints receive a visitor at first. But no blame can be made against him, for the world is a bitter place for living, violence and cruelty walk the land and worse things walk, as you well know, Ikandera Thygethyn, he must protect his people behind a cold face and a spear held in a trembling fist. But a king's hall is a place of hospitality: the guest comes in now welcome, food shall be prepared in plenty, the cups will brim with strong drink. A guesthouse waits with soft beds and fine-combed wool clothing, his servants smooth the blankets, open the windows, check all is as it should be: this is part of what makes a man a king.

And if Kanda had shrunk just a little in Amraen's eyes toward *guest* and *someone needing a hot meal but definitely needing a hot bath first*, because of that he could see beyond her – finally he seemed to notice her husband and her children. Not a guest but guests who needed welcoming.

"Your…family, my lady queen?" he said.

"This lady is my daughter Sal," Kanda said, "and this my daughter Calian, and this…my husband, Dellet."

Amraen blinked again. Truly, the spell was faded, he was a king on his throne receiving lesser-ranked guests. In Sal and in Calian he saw at least some semblance of Ikandera Thygethyn. A great lady and a warrior, he saw standing there before him. But in poor Dellet, he saw….

…burst of bitter laughter…

…in Dellet he saw…

…nothing.

Dellet must have noticed Amraen's astonishment also, for Kanda heard Dellet cough, the creak of his knees as he shifted from foot to foot. Very far away indeed were the words of her spell now. She said hurriedly, hoping these words also would have some magic (that is, that Dellet would forget the king's "your *husband?*" silent earth-shattering shout), "I thank you for your hospitality, my lord king Amraen. We are all four grateful. A fine welcome we have found here indeed. If we could go now to the guesthouse to rest?"

King Amraen shook himself. Shouted orders, rose to escort them himself to the guesthouse. Such luck: he wiped his brow, a cold sweat had come upon him thinking of the luck he'd had: if they had come but the day before when the renders had not been brought in…. Beer, fruit, meat, honey, cheeses – reckon up the very best of all the render, throw open his treasure hoard for a suitable gift.

CHAPTER TWELVE

And the guesthouse was clean, comfortable, well-furnished. A bed with clean wool coverlets and a carved headboard, prettily painted bowls of (cold) water for washing, rushes scattered on the well-scrubbed floor, hangings on the walls, the hearth neat. The family washed and dressed quickly in their best clothes (crumpled from being in their backpacks; "What's this?" Sal said, seeing the streaks of marsh mud on her left sleeve). A short rest, dozing to the good sounds of food being prepared drifting in through the windows, then Amraen himself returned to escort them back to his hall where the feast was waiting. The hall had been dressed with green stuff, the tables spread with richly embroidered cloths. Clay jugs gleamed with strong ale. Wooden platters held wheat bread, fresh meat. Amraen wore a red robe to match his beard, gold rings on both his arms and all his fingers as well as the bronze circlet on his head. His warriors wore fine robes also, fur-trimmed; they wore each a bronze arm ring.

Kanda saw Dellet's confusion. The well-furnished guesthouse, the feast, the wealth of the king. A kingdom of one village! This should not be possible – or, if it were possible, only because the people of the village were starved and slaves. And no, they were not rich, these villagers (no, wait, city dwellers, remember?) but they were not so very starving poor. The sheep and geese, the carts of tribute rumbling in through the gateway, that should not be possible in the lean months of spring.

"He is a king," Kanda whispered to Dellet. "Thus…he lives…as a king. He has made himself a king here. Made these things for himself. Warriors, tribute, wealth. A city. A kingdom." Ikandera Thygethyn had shown him the wonders that lie in power and glory. Named this…*want* in him. Truly, deeply, vastly, with all the power his kingship gave him – he *wanted*. So much work, for him and for his subjects, to make it real. The tension almost visible in his face, from clinging on to all he had made. The village was bigger now, richer now, nearly a kingdom, really a kingdom, from Kanda's hailing Amraen as a king.

Dellet frowned, did not understand.

Kanda had the king's seat, the king's plate, the king's cup. As he had promised, King Amraen waited on her as a servant, poured her drink, served her food, held the bowl and the towel for her to wash her hands. Ylil's mother, who was called Jeha, served Calian and Sal; she was one of the king's warriors, high in his favor, the best of the swords that hung on the walls was hers. Jeha reminded Kanda of Lela, despite looking nothing like Lela who would have cowered at the sight of a sword blade. Amraen could not be such a very bad king, Kanda thought, if Jeha had sworn her sword to him. The hall was full of laughter, singing, no cup or plate was not filled and refilled. The boys Ylil and Wyn were there, too young really for the feast but Kanda spied them hiding in a corner, asked Amraen to let them stay.

Dellet was awkward at first. A farmer, son and grandson of farmers, be a guest in a king's hall? He had not, perhaps, quite forgotten or forgiven Amraen's start at him; that was something even Ikandera Thygethyn could not magic away. And beyond, again, the same as with Geiamnyn in that other life last summer: this man, a stranger to me, a *king*, if that's not too absurd for thinking, this *king* knew my wife when she was…when she was…*not-my-wife*, his mind could only say. But the ale went round, jugs and jugs of it, more platters of wheat bread, more platters of fresh meat, songs, laughter, Ylil and Wyn performed something that even after several cups of ale could never be called a *tune*. The songs they sang were harvest songs, plowing songs, songs with a rhythm that might serve when raising the poles of a longhouse. Dellet smiled a little, felt it not much different in truth to feast days at home in the valley of the River Wenet, just people finding reason to be happy, drink, eat.

Sal ate bread and meat, drank a cup of ale, watched the two boys' fooling. Calian beamed at everything. A hall, warriors, honor, feasting: all her mother's stories here laid before her almost real. She had fought and defeated monsters, rescued her sister from the dark, she had returned to her childhood innocence in Lela's village, eased herself back a little to her farmer's childhood – now she was feasted as a warrior and the daughter of a queen! And a simpler, older pleasure, an old itch at last scratched – often she had seen the lord's hall in Aranth, heard the feasting, watched the warriors coming and going, never been allowed even a peep inside. A mysterious, impossibly glamorous place. Her eyes shone, she laughed with the children and laughed with the adult warriors, both child and warrior at once and as both delighted with herself. Whatever evil my mother once did (which in my child's mind I cannot truly believe in, for my mother is my mother and it cannot have happened long before I was born for the world did not truly exist before I was born and my mother certainly could not truly have existed as something that is not my mother before I was born and thus it did not really not-happen at all) whatever evil there has been, I have fought it and again and again I will fight it, and with this sword I will make a better world and I am all that I knew I should be. Waited on and attended by a warrior woman, no less!

Kanda thought sadly: don't be proud, Calian, that your mother is feasted for what she once was. No feast, no cheers, should greet that name Ikandera Thygethyn. Curse those memories. Curse this man for his pride in them. And yet...so fine, Calian's face looked, so good it was to Kanda to see her daughter's laughter, the happiness in Calian, and – yes – the proud glances Calian gave her mother when she thought Kanda was not looking. Rarey and rarer and rarest as dragon eggs, is a child showing pride in a parent being praised.

"Are you pleased, my lady queen?" Amraen asked Kanda. "It is small and poor, I know, but I have ordered my storerooms emptied for you." He alone seemed anxious and on edge, his voice was weak as if he expected Kanda to be angry with him. "A small mean place, nothing, compared to your deeds, your hall, my lady queen, I know. Not worth a glance, I know, not worth anything, I'm sure, such a poor place this is, my lady queen."

"It is a fine feast, my lord king," Kanda said truthfully. "Look at your people feasting. It is all fine and good." It is, she thought. The poor thinness of the village children, the dirty houses, they also were changed and faded by her words hailing Amraen as a good king. I see him, call him – a good king. Thus he is – a good king. As changed as I myself have changed from those days.

But Amraen paled. "You should not call me 'king', my lady queen. You are the greatest queen in all the world. I am nothing compared to you."

Dellet twitched at that. Kanda said, "I am no longer a queen, Amraen. How far does your rule stretch?" she asked hastily to cover three people's embarrassment and two people's shame. (And a genuine question she would have asked at some point: in Lela's village only two days' walk away, there had been no talk of *lords* and *cities* and *kings*.)

Amraen gave a dry awkward laugh. (And the awkwardness was why Kanda had not asked it until it had burst out to cover the greater awkwardness-without-laughing.) "My rule stretches from the deepest depths of the River Wend even unto the highest peaks of Mal Ealia, my lady queen; all who venture between the Wend and the slopes of Mal Ealia must do homage and fealty to me. Fewer people than I once commanded in your war host, my lady queen. The River Wend where it makes my kingdom's border can be forded knee-high after a winter flood. Mal Ealia is a hillock that lies two hours' walk west if a man walks slowly. Barely worth raiding, I would have thought this kingdom of mine in those days. Not worth the sweat it would have raised on my brow."

The shadows deepened over his face, he paused as if waiting for Kanda to say something. Often, serving her meat or refilling her cup, shadows would grow dark over him, he would go to speak or pause waiting for Kanda to speak. The fear grew in her that he wanted her to talk of the old days when he marched in her train to war. Let us boast of our deeds, sing of our deeds, pound our cups on the tabletop. Let us drink to blood spilled, heads taken, let us raise our cups as if they were filled with blood, tell great stories of the butchery of kings. Loudly we will raise the paean. Sing the praise song that was a raven song, a wolf song, a song only of death.

Do you remember – you won't remember, so trivial it was compared to many of your deeds – but do you know, Ikandera Thygethyn, I stood beside you in the battlelines once for red slaughter; you swung your sword, I swung my sword beside you. Never have I forgotten it: I stood once in battle at your right hand when red slaughter, such slaughter, was had!

The lines moved, you were gone across the battlefield, leading the army onward to victory; so many thousands that day you killed. I was left behind where the battle ebbed and the fighting was over; my sword took no more lives that day. Nothing, compared to many of the stories they tell of you, far greater memories you must have of those days. But that day you shed more blood than all the ale that will ever be brewed in my kingdom, lady, and I shed blood at your right hand.

A famine, a pestilence, you were, in my memory you stand upon a pile of corpses so high your head is above the circuit of the stars; so many corpses that the sun and the moon are at your feet. And I once briefly fought beside you. Briefly, once, I stood at your right hand.

Kanda waited, terrible her fear; Amraen poured her ale, heaped her plate with food; he went to speak, fell silent, drank his ale; seemed to wait for her to speak. "My kingdom is so small, so poor, you would not think it worth the effort of drawing your sword from its scabbard, but it is…." Yearning for her to speak. Ah, she thought, you and Sal both of you – spit out the stone in your mouths, speak! "I won this kingdom with my sword, my lady queen," Amraen said. "Not worth your while, this kingdom, nothing, compared to your glory, but I won it with my sword. I stood before the people here, bade them kneel to me, ordered them to render wealth as befits a king."

He dared dart a glance to meet Kanda's eyes, looked away quickly when she forced herself to smile. Raised his cup, shouted very loud, "A health, hail, to the great lady queen Ikandera Thygethyn!"

Ylil's pipe burst out, far better played by someone who was not Ylil or Wyn. Tal, the man who had been on guard at the gates. He played one-handed to wave to the feasters that they should start dancing. Jeha got up to dance, her blue dress was like a kingfisher's feathers. She was a good dancer. She danced with her son Ylil, who was not a good dancer (unfair, Kanda, he's not yet ten!); she raised her eyebrows at Dellet, inviting; the dance was not unlike one they would dance in their lost valley of the River Wenet; after some encouragement from Calian, Dellet joined in.

Soon half the hall was dancing in honor of their guest this great lady, bright robes and kirtles like the wind in a flower garden.

Wyn, triumphant, escorted in a platter of the yellow apples, "The last left until autumn!" he announced with a huge grin. "Apples!" Calian crowed, the child who had flung muck at Kanda. "If you cut them open right, they look like stars!" Wyn said. He was younger than Calian, but Calian seemed happy to chat and play with him. Kanda had shown that magic to Calian more times than she could remember; even the first time, Calian had yawned. Calian beamed when Wyn showed her. "They're not actually that nice," he said conspiratorially. "All bruisy and dried. But the last apples until autumn, and usually our lord king keeps the apples for himself."

Another dance, some kind of end-of-the-feast-luck-dance, involving four of the king's warriors waving burning torches while leaping around the hall. Jeha was the leader, she had a trick of making the flames of her torch flow almost like liquid. Circles and plumes of yellow flames. Rings, crowns, of yellow flames.

Often, after the Six had returned from battle, often their victory had been celebrated in halls such as these. Poor, low places, compared to Roven's silver walls and golden roof. But more than the feast days in Roven she had loved these simple country feasts. Lady Erenan would sneer sometimes, *rustics, badly cooked food, call this music?* Lord Palle might shake his head, *they'll need this food come winter, the last of the apples they've given us, in the lean months what will they eat?* Lord Morren and Lord Gallyn and Lady Kestre and Lady Kanda would throw themselves joyfully into it, *our duty, Palle! Every cup we drink, they'll get two back! So drink up!*

She leapt up herself now to join the dancing, perhaps a little unsteady on her feet. Jeha grabbed her hand, led her spinning and circling, somehow Jeha made a circle of yellow flame like a crown above Kanda's head. Calian was dancing, Dellet had been dancing so long his hair was soaked with sweat. Young Wyn carefully helped Sal dance. "The luck be on this hall!" Kanda shouted. "My blessing be on this hall! Joy and all that is good!" Magic words the Six had often shouted. She danced close to Dellet, caught his hands, kissed him. He kissed her back. She had felt some unhappiness, some fear about something. His hair was sweaty from dancing, it stuck to her face. She shouted, "Luck to you!" Kissed him again.

She thought: a world to rebuild? Yes! A world that will be bright and joyous and good! Queen, Amraen calls me. Sets this kingdom at my feet. Already formed, already made, simply here for me, waiting. There will never be hunger here. No sickness, no grief. The crops will never fail. Every cow will have twin calves. This gift I give.

I am Lady Kanda the first, the greatest, of the Six Swords of Roven. I am Ikandera Thygethyn, the world bows down to me. So easily I give this gift.

"A health! All hail!" Someone thrust a cup of ale into her hands to drink deep. She raised it to gulp it down. "Luck!" Kanda shouted.

Dellet went to grab her into the dance at the same moment she raised the cup. The ale spilled down her, lay in a dark pool at her feet. The music changed, a new dance began fiercer and wilder. Kanda spun, leapt, pressed close to Dellet. He learned closer still, hands tight around her. Said in her ear making her shiver with pleasure, "That would be my wife, yes, greatest warrior, strongest and toughest, mind you don't piss her off. That's my wife, and to be honest I'd have done a lot less of the hard graft around our farm if I'd known the half of what she can do. If this baby grows up to have one tenth of her strength and courage, it'll be the bravest strongest man that ever lived. That's what I should have said to Lela's grandmother. That's my beloved wife."

The torch flames rose high. The hearth fire blazed up red. Someone began to strike two swords together. Clash and clash of bronze. The hall stank from the packed bodies. Sweat smell. Blood smell. The swords beat and beat and beat and beat. Bodies pushed closer, wrestling together, thigh to thigh, cheek to cheek. Pushing, shoving. Hold the line! Steady there! Hold! Push forward, make the enemy break! The music of bronze, the music of grunting gasping panting warrior men. Voices rose singing the paean. Raven song. Wolf song. Sword song.

See it. Hear it. Marvel. Such a little way we have come from Lela's village, and so far. Walk following the River Wend the River Wenet, come so quickly from winter snows to a glorious rebirth of spring.

"Bless this hall! Bless this kingdom! All the gifts I can give, I will give!"

Wheat and fruit and flowers bursting up beneath Kanda's feet in the dark stain where the ale was spilled. Dancing and dancing. All is fine and fair and bright and good.

CHAPTER THIRTEEN

Kanda had a dream that night. A good dream, as it must be after such a night's feasting, for again she dreamed that she was Kanda of the Six. A feast, indeed, was what she dreamed of. A great kingly feast at Roven. She sat with her companions in the Hall Roven; the Lord of Roven sat in the high seat on his throne.

All of the Six Swords were gathered in the hall, three sat at their Lord's right hand, three sat at his left. Lord Morren, his hair hanging loose about him, a cup of wine in his hand, the dark wine flushing his cheeks, staining his lips. Lady Kestre, her face had in it both the kindness of the dove and the keenness of a hawk hunting. Lord Palle, his hair and beard dressed with green ribbons, his skin painted with green patterns like the eddies in a cool calm sea. Lady Erenan, garlanded with pink roses that her beloved had gathered. Lord Gallyn, beautiful as a dragonfly and as restless.

Lady…Lady…her mind groped, almost in her dream she heard her companions speak her name and she knew what it meant…but Dellet snored or Calian snored, Kanda half woke from her dream, the name and its meaning was lost. Lady Kanda, she could only call the woman who sat in the Hall Roven at her Lord's right hand as the first and best of the Six.

The horn blew around the Hall with its sweet long note. All in the Hall knelt joyful, for the horn sang and the Lady of Roven came forth shining. And now the Lady was there for the feasting – they could set knives to meat, they could feast.

Servant women fair as queens served meat from the cauldron. The cauldron boiled, the steam rose, a woman dipped in a flesh hook. The woman served up the food: fresh venison stewed with wine and herbs, fragrant and savory.

Palle raised his cup. "To Erenan, who hunted the hart we are about to eat."

"I stood on the highest point of a mountain, so high there were clouds beneath me," Erenan said. "At the foot of the mountain was a wide plain, in the middle of the plain a river ran. On the other side of the river another mountain rose, on its slopes there were deer running. Small as ants, they looked! I loosed a single arrow, struck down this hart we are about to eat." She smiled and said, "Then I had to ride down the mountain, cross the river, ride up the mountain, find the hart's body, heft it up onto the horn of my saddle, bring it back to Roven. I hope it tastes good."

They ate: it did taste good.

"It's all in the cooking," Erenan said. "Before Morren reminds me of that."

"Not today, today it's all in the hunting," Morren said. The servant women had not after all been interested in him.

They ate and drank, they laughed, they danced. The evening was coming in, the sun was sinking wounded, soon it would be time to retire to their beds to sleep. The dream was only a memory of this day's feasting, dancing, laughter in King Amraen's hall. Dreaming, Kanda smiled. I gave the people of Amraen's village such a feast as this!

The doors of the Hall Roven flew open. A woman ran into the Hall.

No stranger, she; she was one of the women who had cooked the meat. She had gone out to fetch something. To brush her hair, perhaps, or to have a piss. Her face was filled with concern.

"A man stands at the gates of Roven," she cried. "He will not come in through the gates, but he is begging for the Six to come out to him."

"Why will he not come in?" said Palle. A reasonable question, Kanda thought now in her sleep. But Kanda and Morren and Gallyn were already on their way out of the Hall, and the rest of the Six were following them.

The gatekeeper Benethal met them at the gates of Roven. The gates of Roven stood always open day and night, that any who sought the aid of the Six Swords might enter in. Only once, on the day that Roven was destroyed, were the gates of Roven pulled shut. Benethal was the only person in the world who had the power to shut the gates. He closed them in Kanda's face on the last day of Roven, he did not live to open them again. Kanda dreaming remembered this, frowned and thrashed in her sleep. A nightmare, a terror, her dream was a dark memory stirred in her by the vision she had that day. The sweat on her forehead: wake up, Kanda! Wake up! But in the dream Roven's fall was a long time in the future and the gates of Roven stood open as always, Benethal the gatekeep stood on the threshold waiting for the Six to meet him, Benethal saw Kanda coming and greeted her with joy. And Kanda dreaming smiled, eased, sank deeper into her sleep.

"He is outside the gates," Benethal said. "A man of middle years, strong and tall and plump. But he stands somehow as if there is no hope in him, and the tears run freely down his cheeks. He will not tell me what troubles him. But I fear it is not something easily mended. For he will say only that is something so vast and so terrible that he cannot bear to step within the bright circuit of the walls."

"Why will he not come inside where the *peace* of Roven will bring him comfort?" Kestre said. A reasonable question indeed, it seemed now to Kanda, dreaming, and she tried in her sleep to ask it herself. But: "Let us go out to speak with him, then," Lady Kanda said.

It was full evening. Almost midsummer, so the night that drew in would be fair and brief. The sky still had the last light in it, blue on the western horizon at the very edge of all the world, but the first stars were clear as eyes in the sky to the east. The twin stars Irulth, the red star and the bronze star, burned brilliant those midsummer nights. They formed a gateway indeed, for the man who sought the Six's aid stood between them. As Benethal had said, he was strong and tall and plump in the stomach, his hair hanging to his shoulders, a wide, honest face. Simply dressed but not poorly dressed; from the cut of his tunic and his heavy boots, Kanda would have said he was a prosperous farmer. He almost smiled when he saw the Six there come to help him. But, as Benethal had said, his tears streamed unchecked and there was a terrible pain and an emptiness to him.

Kanda had seen many dead men on the battlefield. Dead men at peace in their beds. Only last year, on the first day of winter, a dead man had ridden in through the gates of Roven to beg the Six to help him. But if someone was to ask her then what death looked like, she would have pointed at the man before her here with his panting breath and ruddy cheeks.

"Will you help me?" he said. A kind, good, honest voice. "Will you come with me?" And Palle cried out, "No, stay back from him!" and Kestre cried out, and Erenan cried out. But Kanda took one step forward to stand with the man outside the gate's threshold. And Morren followed her, and Gallyn.

"Stop!" Palle shouted. He reached out, grabbed at Gallyn's shoulder to pull him back.

And Gallyn turned with anger in his face. Struck Palle so hard that he fell to the ground.

The man began to walk away into the dark evening fields. Kanda and Morren and Gallyn followed him. Their feet trampled the summer wheat. The man was ahead of them. A man, or the figure of a man, a shadow in the dark, he was not running, he walked slowly as any man taking an evening stroll in the summer fields, but the three ran until their breath came sobbing and they could not catch up with him. A spear's length, almost sometimes as little as a sword's length, between them. They went on, the man walking, the three running following.

"Stop! Wait!" Kanda shouted.

"Wait!" Morren shouted.

"Come back!" Kanda thought she heard Palle and Kestre and Erenan calling, but she ignored them. Their voices faded behind her like little chattering birds.

They ran on and on, it grew darker, always the man was ahead of them so very near, almost they could catch him if they ran but a little farther. The red star and the bronze star Irulth were always above his head now, as if they too might almost catch him. Almost be caught in his hair.

They came to the edge of the fields. Four horses were waiting there. Three gray horses. One beautiful black horse. Gold ribbons on its mane and tail, gold trappings on its head. Bronze on its hooves.

"How beautiful." With all her heart, Kanda longed to ride that black horse. But the man was already mounted on its back. The horse began to walk: Kanda and Morren and Gallyn leapt up to mount the three gray horses, kicked them to run after him. And again, the black horse walked at a gentle pace and the three gray horses ran like the wind and they could not catch the black horse or even draw level with it.

"Wait! Please!" Kanda shouted.

"Wait!" shouted Morren and Gallyn. All that mattered to them in all the world was to catch up with the man and talk with him.

They went on. The black horse was so swift in the black night that they quickly lost sight of it, though it went always slowly at a walk. They heard the soft slow tread of its hooves ahead of them. On and on, and then it stopped.

A house there, with the black horse standing outside it. A strange house. As they drew closer, Kanda saw that its walls were made of sword blades stacked together, its roof was made of spear shafts.

The door of the house stood open. Kanda dismounted, walked to the threshold, looked in. A fire burned in the hearth. The man stood by the fire, holding his hands over the flames for warmth.

Gallyn came to stand beside her. "What place is this?" he said. "There is something vile here. Yet – my heart longs only to go in."

"It is because it is vile," said Morren. "It would be cowardly now not to go in."

The swords that made up the four walls were all bent and broken. Flaws in the casting, swords raised to save a man from dying but they had shattered uselessly, swords that were thrown down in bitter death. The spear shafts that made up the roof were rotten, soaked with dank water, fungi crumbled through them, grubs eating the wood. Weapons from the charnel house, dug up from lying long-buried beside the bones of dead cruel men.

Dreaming, Kanda choked with revulsion, thrashed, tried to wake. But also dreaming she called to herself to step inside the house and greet the man who lived there, for as she stood hesitating in the doorway his mouth opened to speak her old name. "Come in, come in," he was about to say, and he would call her by her old name.

"I am not a coward," Morren said. "Whatever horror this is, yet the longing is so great in me that I would rather throw away my sword than walk away from this house without going in." He stepped forward.

"I will be the first to go in!" Gallyn shouted. "The doorway is too narrow for two to enter together. I will not let you be the first to go in!"

"Curse you!" shouted Morren.

The two began to fight. They struck each other with their fists; then they drew their swords. They hacked at each other, no beauty in their fighting. They cut and stabbed and hit, each striving to go in through the open doorway, each striving to stop the other entering.

Kanda stood and watched. It seemed to her that there was no interest in watching her companions fighting. She did not care whether both or either of them were killed. She also longed to go into the house and talk to the man who waited there. Yet it seemed to her that it would be more fitted to wait until blood had been spilled. Such a house as this, and such a man inside – better, surely, to go into the house trampling blood when one or both of her companions lay dead.

A great feast was laid in the house, which was a huge house now, a kingly house, the weapons of a great army had been used to make its walls and its roof. They sat to their meat on tables made of their own bones, the meat was their own flesh. A cauldron hung above the hearth, gleaming bronze, the feasters fought and killed each other, threw the dead bodies into the cauldron and fished them out boiled and tasty, and when they had eaten their fill they threw the bones and the scraps back into the cauldron and out of the cauldron stepped living hungry men. The man they followed sat at the head of the table. He did not eat or drink. He beckoned Kanda to come in. A place was set at his right hand with a golden plate and a golden cup and a gray stone knife. A silver crown hung above the chair set for Kanda. A serving man stood by waiting to carve Kanda's meat and pour her wine – and it seemed to Kanda dreaming and Kanda in the dream both that she knew the serving man's face.

But she could not go into the house because Morren and Gallyn were still fighting. A well-matched pair, well used to sparring, those two: neither was winning, neither was losing, neither would give way. Matched in strength and skill – and pride. Stubborn as two old donkeys. "Come on, come on," the war host shouted from the hall, "time's passing, we can't wait like this all day!" "Three times already, I've been killed and eaten and boiled up to life again," a voice shouted, "the meat will spoil soon if you don't come in." "Let her in, let her in," the war host shouted, "get on with killing each other, you stubborn ones you, so that she can come in!" Stubborn as donkeys, Gallyn and Morren. They had been fighting for the honor of being first into the house; now, when they saw what was happening in the house, they fought each other harder, fiercer, for the honor of being the first to kill the men inside it. Their swords were almost blunted, they had fought so long, they cast around to snatch up better swords from the walls of the house. "I'll go in first and kill them, that honor will be mine!" "No, no, I will have that honor, I alone will kill them all, curse you, Gallyn!" And: this is boring, Kanda thought. Watching and waiting for one of them to win. Her hands itched and her heart ached, she longed to go inside the house but she could not go in until her companions had stopped fighting, only when her companions' blood had been shed would it be fitting to go inside. She thought: it's cold out here. Get on with it! I'm tired of standing around waiting.

Kanda dreaming moaned and thrashed in her nightmare, but she smiled at that thought. Less patience, perhaps, Lady Kanda not-yet-a-mother had had then.

That stubbornness, that boredom, was what saved them.

Great power, the *empty* one they had followed must have in him, to be able to lead them to such a place. His sorrow and his pain gave him great power indeed. But a cold and empty power, as he was cold and empty and dead. Kanda stood looking into the house waiting for her companions to kill each other, the cold and the dark grew, she shivered, stamped her feet; she was bored, and the power that held her faded. Angry, tired of waiting, she shrugged his power off. She blinked. She started. Like someone – Kanda dreaming laughed here – like someone waking from a fevered sleep. "What are you doing?" she shouted to Morren and Gallyn. "What is this that has happened to you? Stop!" she shouted.

"What has happened to me, what am I doing?" she shouted.

Morren stopped. Gallyn stopped. They stared at each other, at the wounds they had made on each other's bodies. They did not need to think further: they turned together to strike down the evil in the house. With a roar, those three of the Six of Roven threw off the last dregs of their enchantment, stood shoulder to shoulder with drawn swords to fight not each other but the monstrous thing that had enchanted them. The doorway to the house yawned wide, they rushed to strike down that *empty* one. Such anger, that they had been trapped in his coils. What fools, each thought in their heart, he had made of them. One who was wounded; one who was wounded; one who was cold and bored. That was a far more bitter blow to each's heart than any enemy's sword could deal.

Three of the Six of Roven: that *empty* one, that *nothing* one, now the enchantment was broken he could not, dared not, face them. The house shook and fell, the war host vanished, and the cauldron, the *empty* one stood alone. He bowed to Gallyn and Morren. "Fooled you both a while," he said. He bowed to Kanda, and he smiled, "And you," he said, "one day," he said, "I hope, you'll be a guest at my feast."

Kanda stared back at him with loathing. The dead eyes widened. Not eyes, only empty holes where his eyes had been pecked out by crows. Yet they grew wide and filled with wonder in his dead ruined face.

"Oh!" the *empty* one whispered.

"What are you? Curse you! Get back from me, monster." She drew away. Revulsion. A desire to vomit.

His hand reached, trembling.

A dead hand, not a human hand. All bent and broken.

He was gone. A pool of black liquid spread at Kanda's feet. The filth that stains the battlefield as men's flesh rots away.

Horrors. She shuddered. Retched. But his voice echoed in her ears. His strange sad whisper: "Oh!"

And silence. The dark of midnight in a thick close wild wood. Three people there cold and alone.

Kanda and Morren and Gallyn embraced.

"What was he?" Morren asked finally when he could speak and not simply cry into Kanda's shoulder. For that was the first time that Morren or Gallyn had met that *empty* one.

"He was a man once," Kanda said. "What he is now I do not know." For she had met him once before, at a distance. This was the first time that she had met him face to face. "He was dead and now he is alive," she said.

"Alive?" said Gallyn, with a look of horror on him. He spat on the ground to get the taste of what had happened out of his mouth.

The beautiful black horse had vanished with its master. Three old gray nags, fit only for the knacker's yard, stood where they had left them beneath a tree. They were very far from Roven, dressed still in their feasting finery, Morren's and Gallyn's clothes all tattered and torn. Little choice but to mount the horses, ride them slowly and painfully home.

It took a long time to get home.

Morren said, "If we meet him again, I will kill him. I swear it. He will lie with the dust covering him."

Gallyn said, "If we meet him again, I will kill him. I swear it. There will be no joy and no light for him."

Kanda said, "When we meet him again, I will kill him. I swear it." She said sadly, "But I think that already there is little joy and little light for him."

And all the time they rode, a shadow seemed to be beside them, a man riding beside them that they could not clearly see. All the time they rode, they felt sick and weary and their bodies ached, they wept and groaned as they rode. It was not until they had reached the very gates of Roven that the shadow left them.

And one day soon Kanda did not kill him, and Morren did not kill him, and Gallyn did not kill him. But one day soon Morren lay with the dust covering him, and Gallyn lay in the dust and there was no joy and no light for him.

And dreaming Kanda smiled, sank warm and deeper in her good sleep. A good dream indeed, for she remembered killing Morren and she remembered standing beside that *empty one* her first husband with Gallyn's body at her feet.

She sank deeper into her sleep filled with pleasure at her dreaming, and the dream faded away.

CHAPTER FOURTEEN

Headaches all around the next morning, and plants withering across the hall floor, grapes and apples and rose petals trampled sticky and crushed. Kanda's voice was hoarse and her feet ached. Bread and milk and honey for breakfast. Not that anyone apart from Calian wanted to eat much. "My mouth still tastes of apples." "My mouth still tastes of ale." "Lucky you: my mouth still tastes of vomit." That last was Dellet, in bed refusing, verily unable, to get up. Calian laughing at him. Cruel as the goosegirl this morning, that one.

Wyn and Ylil came to see if Calian wanted to play with them. They peeped at Kanda in nervous wonder, looked terrified-hopeful she'd work more magic. Calian gave them the side-eye, *me, a queen's daughter who has fought monsters, play with little boys?* while honey dripped down her chin. *Go away, little boys.* Her leggings somehow had honey on them.

"Stop looking like that, Calian," Sal said crossly. "Go and play, why don't you?" Sal watched the two boys fidgeting. They looked very small and young indeed, newborn calves beneath Calian's disdainful eagle gaze.

"You have a milk mustache, Calian," Sal said. "Now go and be friendly to these people who've been so friendly to us."

A deep loud sigh from Calian. "Go on, Calian," Sal said. Calian looked at her sister, sighed her deepest sigh, went off with Wyn and Ylil very superior because older but still a child with other children. "I'll show you how to skip stones," Calian said. "But only because your mother's a warrior too."

"Well done, Calian," Sal said. Sal and Kanda sat side by side in the guesthouse. "Such sweet boys," Sal said. Somewhere outside a woman was singing at her work. A dog barked, the woman broke off from her singing, called to the dog, began to sing again. After a little the song broke off, there came instead the sound of wood cutting, bronze ringing against wood.

Kanda winced. "Nice thing to do this morning." She was half listening for an argument between Calian and the two boys. Or someone shouting angrily at all three of them.

"They'll be waiting on her every word, doing everything she tells them," Sal said. "Don't worry. They've set Calian up as their Great Queen overnight. She'll beat them every time at skipping stones and be delighted." There was another brief thunder of the woodchopping, then a deep silence fell over the village. The sun moved, throwing a beam of light over Sal's face.

Once, twice, three times, Kanda thought Sal was going to say something. "Mother," Sal got as far as saying, once, twice, three times. "Mother: I—" Kanda thought: I can cause flowers to grow from the floor (drunk, I can cause flowers to grow from the floor!); a river in spate and a landslide falling I have turned back with a wave of my hand; I have brought mountains down, tumbled fortress walls; I have saved from ruin many a king and many a kingdom. Ten thousand times harder: to speak to my child.

The sunlight played on Sal's mouth, teasing, then the sun went in behind a cloud. Sal said, "We need to get on, Mum. You know we can't stay here."

Kanda looked over to the curtained sleeping area. Heard Dellet groan. "It would be good to leave today, you're right. But it would be rude, after the welcome they gave us, to go any earlier than tomorrow, don't you think?"

"I suppose it would be rude," Sal said, also looking over to the curtained sleeping area, and they smiled at each other the way they had begun to share a wry smile even before Sal was made old. Not mother and child but two adults. They looked at each other in the same way, sharing knowledge; Calian had started giving them both the same eye roll and deep fake sigh. And Kanda realized suddenly how fine that was, a new way of being with her eldest daughter, that she had just begun to grope her way toward when their little world was first broken. Shared bodies, shared hopes and fears. *I never understood why you got so cross about it...but it is so much easier this way, yes...and Calian's refusal to do it this way is infuriating, yes. I was a right brat about it, wasn't I? After fifteen years of being a right pain about it: sorry, Mum.* Then Morna howls or Cal roars or Dellet curses, and two pairs of blue eyes meet and speak without saying a word and want themselves to howl roar curse and silently laugh. Not only mother and daughter but two adult friends.

It had felt good, then. Fresh, exciting, long-anticipated thing. What do I see, when I feel my child here still in my belly kicking? I see her growing with a great rich life stretched.

Kanda thought suddenly: I spent years dreaming of the future with my daughters, looking at Sal so grown compared to her sisters, treating her as grown – forcing her to be grown. *Help your sisters, Sal; come and help me, Sal; it's time you learned, Sal; come on, Sal, how old are you now?* In three days she grew from child to older than I am, and it eats at me like a wound.

Sal my eldest I wanted to grow up quickly, and Morna my baby I never wanted to grow up at all. And here we are. Bitter magic.

She could not remember Sal's face as a child.

She could not remember Morna's face.

She'll grow out of it soon, it seems forever, but, honest – in a blink of an eye they grow out of it, and you think, could the blink of an eye hurry up? And it seems forever for ever, and then—

"I'm just going out for a piss," Kanda said quickly.

Sal might have been going to speak then. Kanda thought later that she might. Sensed it, guessed it, made it up to burden herself. Rare and rarer, the child opening her mouth to ask for help from her mother, tell her mother some terrible secret thing of shame that the mother already might deep in her heart somewhere fear she half knew. Goading, hoping – tell me, Sal! Speak it! I'm your mother! I'll always be here to help you to listen to you. Nothing you say can be too awful for me to hear. Nothing can harm my love for you. Whatever it is – I think, Sal, I can't shape the words but yet I know them – whatever you have done or suffered, nothing is too terrible for me to try to make it better, and nothing can be worse than the things I your mother have myself thought and done. Sal was about to speak so that all this and more Kanda could pour out to her meant truly; Sal's mouth opening, the words like the first stuttering drops of rain breaking out; I can help you, mother to child, friend to friend, Kanda about to speak. But Kanda fled the guesthouse without guessing without seeing, made up later to herself that Sal had been about to speak. "It's a nice morning," Sal had only been going to say, or, "Do you want some more milk?" But Kanda would never know and Sal would never know if she would have spoken.

Outside the king's hall two men were chucking armloads of green stems, crushed wheat ears and bruised fruit into a handcart. "Sure the pigs should eat this stuff? Better to burn it. It being—" They broke off and bowed to Kanda, terror in their faces. Kanda went past them, trying not to feel that they were terrified of her. Their downcast eyes watched her footsteps almost expectant. No flowers and fruit and ripe wheat bursting up this morning, friends, I'm sorry. Or are you relieved, she thought, that there's not another mess to clear up? Yesterday you weren't afraid of me. But even good magic is a fearful thing to remember the next morning, when you're no longer dancing and drunk.

She had never done such tricks for the people in Lela's village. She wondered now for the first time: why not? But it would have been different, if they'd known. *My lady,* Lela's kind voice saying, with a tremble in it. *Will you honor us? Bless us, please, we beg? We are not worthy to look upon you, my lady. Merely nod your head to us in blessing.* No! Not that! And it was always like that, for Ikandera Thygethyn and for…for… she groped, tried to remember Lady…Lady…no. A void where that name had once been. For Kanda of the Six.

The story Dellet had told her: if I'd known that about Lela's village, Kanda thought, whatever would I have done? She remembered the boggy, soft taste of the spring water, the way it had trickled dancing through her cupped hands. The good soil she had dug a hole for a house post in.

I must have known? How could I not know? In my heart, somewhere, surely…. But then she thought: it would be a comfort, if I remembered, if I could say I'd known all the time in my heart. But Ikandera Thygethyn destroyed so many villages, how can I remember one of them? Nothing, insignificant, I forgot it within a few days, I expect.

Do you remember a village with a longhouse, Amraen?

I remember a city with walls of white marble, my lady queen Ikandera Thygethyn, I remember what we did there, marvelous, wondrous things. I remember a forest, my lady queen Ikandera Thygethyn, every tree had leaves of diamonds, the birds in the forest had red wings; you burned down the forest, caged the birds. I remember—

So many villages we destroyed, like asking me do I remember the whetstone I used sharpening my sword before a particular battle, what I ate for breakfast one morning, do I remember what sword stroke I used, my lady queen. A village? With a longhouse? A thousand villages we destroyed, and a thousand more, and a thousand more again, and most of them, I suppose, had houses of one kind or another in them.

A little girl came out of a house, stared at Kanda. "More flowers?" she said. Kanda wished so much she could stamp her foot now to make flowers spring up. But I can only do that when I'm…drunk? Sorry. Look, there's some pigweed growing beside your house, is that good enough? A woman came out of the house after the child, saw Kanda, gasped, "Oh, I'm sorry, my lady! Please! Out of the way, Gya, come here!" Pulling her child back into the doorway, hiding her from Kanda's sight. "You need to put your cloak on, come on, now, and your shoes, I told you, hurry!" the woman's voice came as the door slammed shut.

"It's nothing," Kanda said, but the door was closed, from inside she heard the mother shout and the child wailing. Ikandera Thygethyn and Lady Kanda of the Six both had known this, yes, the eyes that stared in fear mixed with fascination, looked quickly away to settle on anything else. The people who bowed and praised and barred their doors, cowering. *Don't harm me! Don't see me!* The power in her hands and words, for good or ill, that she had forgotten: if Amraen can conjure up bronze arm rings and embroidered wall cloths to fit his *wanting*, I can leave a man in mortal fear without being aware he's near me, all I need do is sit or stand or exist. My shadow falls on the earth near him, my face is glimpsed through a crack in a door, and a man weeps for fear. I don't need to exert myself to speak or move my hand. I don't need to think.

Great magic, that.

And she thought: and I remember Erenan complaining sometimes that to do great magic was a hard thing.

The smith was working; she could hear the rasp of a whetstone polishing the bronze, smell charcoal burning. Fine smell. She breathed it in deep. A horse neighed, a man hushed it. A group of men were busy behind the king's hall, fussing over something; another burst of someone chopping wood. Strong constitutions, King Amraen's subjects had: she and Dellet seemed to be the only people with sore heads. A woman was walking fast toward the hall, a basket in her hands. The woman saw Kanda, started, almost dropped the basket, ran off behind the hall. "I'm sorry, my lady queen," she called as she fled. Kanda thought wearily: yes. And I wondered sometimes why I found it hard being one of the Six of Roven. At least, she thought, when I was terrible and feared across the world, the worst of monsters...at least there was a reason for people to run from me like that.

At the king's hall the doors stood open. A man came out, Tal, the piper and the guard from the gates yesterday. His face was gray and drawn, worse state this morning from the look of him than Dellet, poor man. I'm sorry, Kanda wanted to say to him. I can't help it, some blessing I was given by my Lord of Roven, *for every cup she drinks, she will give two back....* My Lord of Roven, he didn't really drink ale, you see.... The hall was almost empty, still in something of a state itself with scraps of food and a broken cup scattered on the floor. Amraen stood talking to Jeha. Oh, Kanda thought, good! My daughter's playing with your son, Jeha, he's a fine boy, it's good for her to play with him. She's, um, teaching him a new way of throwing stones. I hope that's okay? Jeha was dressed as a warrior today, her red hair curling over her brown leather tunic. She and Amraen stood in the farthest corner of the hall with their backs to Kanda.

"– do?" Jeha was saying.

"I remember how it was. If you go now, if you take them...." Amraen made a sweeping gesture that seemed to Kanda very sad and helpless. The very opposite gesture to drawing a sword. "Somewhere. I don't know. I don't know. Just get them away. Mal Ealia," he said. "There. Go." A crack, his voice dropped broken. "I'll try…." Something inaudible that made Kanda shiver, crawling feeling down the back of her neck. Then, in lower voices:

"…don't understand…?"

"…necessary. What else can—?"

"…the hilltop…?"

Kanda made a noise with her foot. They broke off, realizing someone was there.

"My lady Ikandera Thygethyn!" Amraen's voice was loud and bright. "I hope you slept well, my lady queen? My best furs and coverlets, I sent to your bedchamber. Your daughters, your, your husband, they slept well?" His hands waved at nothing, at the hall. "The food this morning – the feast last night – I hope they— Not what you are used to, I know, my lady, but I hope – I hope – You will perhaps, would you care – I could show you the extent of my lands, my lady queen? We could walk out together this morning?" His hands moved in empty gestures toward Jeha. The woman's head was bowed, eyes downcast staring at Kanda's feet. Yes, there, the flowers grew in the tread of these rough boots, Jeha, Kanda thought. Why don't you look at me?

"You have…some things to…to attend to, Jeha?" Amraen said.

"If that— That is, if— Excuse me, my lady queen, excuse me, but I—"

"Jeha?" Kanda said.

"Forgive me, my lady queen," Jeha said. She too was gone in a heartbeat, fleeing from Kanda. But you are a mother and a warrior, Jeha, so like me…. Forgive you all for what? Enjoying last night's feast?

Amraen fretted, fidgeted, toyed with his robe. "My lady queen…." He bent his head foolishly. "I…." Looked up, met her eyes. Desperate. Fear on him. "May I—? That is— Will you walk with me a little, my lady queen? I would like – I would like, I offered, did I not, to show you my kingdom? Poor and small though it is…."

He, too, seemed desperate. His mouth too closed on the words like barred gates. Kanda could only nod. Yes, yes, of course I will walk with you, Amraen. You can walk at my right hand, even, as you have boasted you once did. It seems only fitting: this kingdom and this power and this mighty roaring glory of yours, a few muddy fields, a few thin children, all this you have raised because once by chance you stood a little time in battle at my right hand. You would make me a queen here, all I was and more remade in splendor, you as a king groveling at my feet. So hard you worked to raise this, and you offer it out to me. It is only fair, Kanda thought, that I do you some little honor, walk with you through fields you toiled over to be acknowledged king, speak kindly of them. A shriveled gift. Patronizing. But pleasing to us both in its mean way. (She thought then: *I love it, how beautiful it is, just what I wanted*, my eyes meet Sal's eyes over Dellet/Calian/Morna's head. But too much dignity here, and this strange tension, and pity for poor *wanting* Amraen, to run off away.)

The king's hall was low and gloomy. Yet, outside, Kanda blinked at how gray and gloomy the sky had become. Where is the sunshine? she thought, I saw the sun this morning bathing my daughter's face so that her hair was like silver and her skin was like gold. They walked past the pigpen. A sow and new piglets. Someone had decided in the end not to risk feeding them Kanda's green stuff. Grow fat and strong, you piglets, no runts you but all good porkers, in the winter snows may you be the finest ham. Past the apple trees with the bee skeps beside them, trees and bees both still sleeping, first green ghosts on the trees where the leaves and the flowers stirred and dreamed. Burst up and give so many apples they have to be left rotting on the ground, you trees, you, so Wyn can eat apples every day. Thrive and do not sting, you bees, you, give honey dripping from the comb as water flows from a spring, so Ylil can eat honey cakes. Past the dovecote, white doves for peace and fat living and fine to eat, and their soft cooing, like babies, thus as many fat babies as fat white doves I grant this village.

Past chickens scratching for worms, and Kanda-with-a-hangover had not the strength left in her to bless them to lay countless as the very stars eggs. And besides now her fear grew like evening shadows, and she feared her blessings now fell on dead burned ground.

"I swore I would do you no harm, Amraen. I will swear it again now."

He only nodded.

"What do you want, Amraen?"

He only shook his head. "Nothing."

Past the gate, outside the village. They stood with their feet sinking in the mud of a new-plowed field. The sky was low and gray and heavy, breaking into rain. Spring rain is a fine thing. Make the wheat grow up in the field, Kanda! Touch the earth with your right hand, the earth is soft and damp as if it has been washed with blood! The smell of it, the good smell of wet earth that smells almost, sometimes, like rent flesh and spilled blood! Make the wheat thrust up now through the earth like sword blades! Like spears! Like ranks of killing men! Crows and starlings and blackbirds picked in the field for insects, but the birds flew up as Kanda came close, they made a dance that was hands opening stark black against the gray sky. At the edge of the field by the hedgerow a fox sat; it turned its head toward Kanda, tail like a helmet plume. It ran: not away, frightened: it ran toward Kanda, fast running, tracing a spiral on the raw earth. Like a horse running, she thought. The hedge it ran from was starred with blackthorn.

White trees. How she loved white blossoming spring trees. Look at this here, she thought, be calmed, Kanda, look at the beauty in this place. Well, no, I grant, not beauty, the land is nothing special, just muddy fields, trees, squalid village. But—

But the birds drew a spiral in the air, flew away. The fox ran away on its long legs. So the world was cold and still as the dead.

She said, "I swore it, Amraen," just as he said, like a child vomiting, "My lady Ikandera Thygethyn…I must tell you…."

CHAPTER FIFTEEN

"I was a soldier in your army, my lady queen. A very long time ago. I fought in your army, it pleased me to fight. I led men into battle. Encouraged and urged them on. At night around the campfires, I sang songs of your glory. I did not stint to praise you, and when I stood in the ranks before the battle I recited your deeds to myself and they gave me strength. I was never the last to draw my sword when the fighting came. I was never the first to break off from the fighting. If my name was never foremost in the praise when the cup went round and the feast-fires burned low – neither was my name spoken in the shame-song. I gave my share, and joyfully. An arm ring I once received from your own hand! I do not boast, I think, if I say of myself then that none would have dared to call me coward.

"Years, I marched beneath your banner. So many years. You were good to us, my lady queen, always you were generous with gifts and with praise. Boldly you led us. No campfire general you: fiercely you fought always in the front ranks. Your first concern and your last was for your warriors; when you returned from the battlefield, bloody, aching, mouth dry as dust, you would not rest, wash, you would not drink a cup of water, until you had seen that your warriors were well-tended. We grew rich and fat on the wealth you gifted us, proud in our many glories, we walked always with our heads held high. Each of us seemed to wear the garlands of the victory on our head.

"But one day, without explanation, you left us, my lady queen.

"An hour, a day, a night passed, and you were gone and your tent stood empty, there no trace of even your footsteps. You had given no hint that you would leave us. We did not know what to do.

"Many days we sat in our tents, waiting for you to return.

"And that one your husband, he....

"We asked to the east, to the south, to the north, to the west. We asked the sun, we asked the moon; we asked the day, we asked the night. No word was there of you. We set up offerings, raised stones, raised bones, raised carved wood. Swords and spears we cast into the water. Our blood, we cast on the water. We sang the paean, begged you to return to us. There was no light without you. Our food had no taste.

"Some threw themselves on their swords in despair, for they could not live without you. Some lay down on the cold earth and did not eat or drink, more slowly and painfully death claimed them. 'There is no praise in dying of thirst,' we said. 'There is no praise in living without Ikandera Thygethyn,' they said. Not easy to argue with, those words. I was tempted to join them.

"That one your husband.... Never, I hope, will I feel the grief we saw in him in those days. He begged the wind, the river, the earth, the trees, to tell him if they had seen you. Though he knew the wind, the river, the earth, the trees, the sun and the moon – he knew such would never speak to him. He sent out the fastest riders and the best hunters to search for you, 'Every leaf, every blade of grass, every pebble, you will turn over in search of her,' he bade them. 'The one who brings me word of her,' your husband said, 'I will honor as my brother for all the days of the world. The one who brings me one word of her whom I love, until the day the sun dies and is not healed, I will do him such honor that I will wait on him at my table as a servant to a lord, pour his wine with my own hand, carve his meat with my own knife. Should he but bring me one word of her whom I love, one trace of her shadow where it fell on stone or soil or water, thus I will reward him.'

"I was one of those who went in search of you. Not the fastest rider or the best hunter, I, but, ah, so much that glory that one your husband promised, so much I longed for that glory. I knew he lied, would never keep such promises. Merely drunk on grief. 'I will do anything, my own life I will give up, only let my child live,' I have heard people in the village say, and with him it was the same.

"But still, so much I longed for that glory. So much I *wanted*.

"I set out, far I traveled searching. Not one trace of you could be found. Not a place where your shadow had fallen could be found. The wind did not whisper your name. A house I found where all the occupants were sick to dying, they lay in their blood and their shit – I hoped, my heart grew bright – but you had not done that. A house I found burned, the cattle burned bone, the stored crops burned to ash – I hoped, my heart sang – but you had not done that.

"Despair began to overtake me. Winter came, it grew cold, the wind gnawed at my bones, colder yet was the knowledge that you could not be found. My food was as dust to me. My drink was as dust. I returned in despair to that one your husband.

"He was gone. Your army was gone. Nothing remained.

"I did not know what to do.

"I wandered. I wept. So long it had been since I was anything but a soldier in your army. I did not know what to be without that. I searched for that one your husband as I had searched for you, and as pointlessly. I did not find one blade of grass he had set his foot upon.

"I stayed a whole year at that place, waiting for someone to come back. No one came. Not a fly did I see in that place in a whole year. The grass stretched green to the horizon, the sky was gray above me. The grass grew very lush and dark green, the wind was dry as the wind that blows from desert places. I began to fear that all your great army was not merely gone but dead.

"I left that place at last. A year it took me to walk from the place my tent had once been set to the edge of your camp. Another year it took me to walk through the forest that had grown up around your camp. On the other side of the forest I saw people again, tilled fields, flocks and herds, houses made of wood and houses made of stone. Why have these houses not been cast down? I asked myself. I felt that I should do it. But I was only one man, so I walked away leaving the houses unharmed, the fields green, the beasts living. I crested a hill, I turned to look back and saw the place behind me with no trace of my passing. How strange that was to see!

"I wandered a long time through fields and forests. I should be killing, I should be destroying, I thought each day. Today I will kill and destroy!

Great shall be the ruin! But each evening as the wound of the sun tore open the sky – the world was unharmed with no trace of my passing. I did not feel like I was alive, I felt like a ghost.

"One morning I came to a village, and I was resolved to be alive again. 'Today,' I said to myself, 'there will be a destruction.' I walked into the village, drew my sword, and I started killing.

"I felt alive that day, oh I did! Such ruin as never before I had managed.

"The people fell on their knees before me. They had never seen a sword before. They could not understand how I was able to kill them so easily. They prostrated themselves at my feet and begged for mercy. They spoke to me as a man speaks to fever or flood or famine.

"I had killed perhaps ten people. There were many more in the village, the houses were as packed tight with people as a war tent. The easiest killing I had ever had, they lay beneath my blade to be slaughtered.

"A great destruction…."

He was silent. Bent, pressed his head into the cold earth. "If you wish to kill me, my lady queen Ikandera Thygethyn, do it now! Before I reach the end of my story. Before I am further shamed before you."

The birds had flown, the fox had gone, the heavy sky and the dark raw earth made all gray and joyless. Even the blackthorn in the hedgerow only stark black and white. The rain dripped down Kanda's back and off the tip of Amraen's nose. It made the red dye in Amraen's white beard run. Kanda looked down and there was a fat pink worm writhing about in coils, throwing itself about in the earth. She kicked soil over it to hide it from birds and creeping beasts.

Said in confusion, "Why would you be shamed, Amraen? You have welcomed me here, feasted me in your hall. It was a fine feast. Your village is a fine place."

Said, trying to find a way to sound joking and cheerful, to make him laugh, as she might with Dellet or the children when she had shouted at them for no reason and hurt them, "I have to leave tomorrow, yes, if my poor husband was up to it I'd leave today. But that's proof of your hospitality, Amraen. If you're offended that I'm running away…. Should

I blame you that my husband has the worst hangover I've seen on him for years? I would accept your apology I suppose for that. I—"

Babbling. Babbling.

"Just tell me…the rest of your story, Amraen," Kanda said.

Tell me! Speak! These words of yours, they must be said.

"I…. One morning I came to a village, my lady queen, as I said, and I was resolved to be alive again. I walked into the village, drew my sword, and I started killing. The easiest killing I had ever had, they lay beneath my blade to be slaughtered. A great destruction, yes. I thought of you, I saw there beside me, my lady queen, each stroke of my sword was a blessing and a song to you.

"A great destruction. But….

"But….

"My lady queen Ikandera Thygethyn…something stayed my hand that day.

"I am greatly ashamed telling you this story, my lady Ikandera Thygethyn. How little you will think of me. *Is this what I taught my servant Amraen, whom I honored enough to make a captain in my army?* you will think. *Faint praise, he deserves, this man before me, no praise for him. He stinted his arm, his sword was still thirsty for blood when he sheathed it. No songs will we raise for him.* Wanting, *his name is, but he did not* want, *rather was he found* wanting. That is what you will say.

"For I….

"I spared them.

"I put down my sword, told them I would not harm them further, provided they made me their king."

Somewhere far off a crow called but it was hidden. Amraen bent his head. "And that is the tale of my shame, my lady queen Ikandera Thygethyn, that I have lived with all these years fearing and hoping you would return."

The crow called, louder. Amraen raised his head. A faint hope in his face.

"But…perhaps…

"They did not know that word, *king*, my lady queen. They had never heard of *kings* and *lords* and *orders* until I taught them.

"I taught them *obedience*, and *power*, and *fear-of-other-men*. I taught them *toil* and *work harder* and *not enough*.

"*Render*, that must be brought even in the leanest months, a tenth of all they have and more than a tenth, if what they have is lacking, more than enough for the king's house, no matter how little might be left for old women and young children.

"*Hunger*, thus, I taught them. *Greed*, and *envy*, and *poor*, and *rich*: those words I taught them."

He held out his arm to her, so that the gold arm rings he wore clinked. "You see here, their *toil*, their *fear*, that I have molded into these fine arm rings."

He tried to smile at Kanda. "Perhaps…perhaps you will praise me a little for that, my lady queen Ikandera Thygethyn?

"Raiders came that first winter, I led my men out and I fought them. I killed the raiders, set their heads over the gates of my new walls as a warning. The men I led had been afraid, cowered, some of them wanted to hide rather than fight. Four of them, also, I killed, set their heads also over the gates."

He tried to smile at Kanda. "Surely, you will praise me just a little for that, my lady queen Ikandera Thygethyn?"

CHAPTER SIXTEEN

I—

But—

Praise you, Amraen?

A tiny yellow flower lay crumpled beneath her foot in the mud. Kanda shuddered looking down at it. Its beauty, and that it had been crushed so. Trampled yellow flowers, and a woman's grief and a man's grief.... She shook her head violently to try to clear it of something she could not remember. Just a dream she had once dreamed.

I'm sorry, rather, I should say to you. That I did this to you.

CHAPTER SEVENTEEN

Kanda and Amraen stood together in silence then a long time. Kanda waited, thinking the man must say more. About something. He looked about him once or twice, stared once quickly over toward the village then away far off toward a hill that rose ghostly in the rain in the northern distance. She thought he seemed to be listening for something. She raised her head to listen too. He blinked, frowned, strained to listen further; Kanda in her confusion tried to watch and listen too.

Praise you, Amraen?

She shivered. A cold wind, and the rain blowing in her face, and perhaps the water on Amraen's face was only the rain. *Yes, I was…happy is not the right word at all. I agreed to see your kingdom with you because it seemed important to you, seemed to bring you happiness, Amraen, but it's raining, I still have something of a hangover, I have seen some pigs and some doves and some mud and I think I can safely say I've seen most of your kingdom and it is good. Let's go back to the guesthouse. Also I genuinely do now need a piss.* But she was not the monster she had been then. She said, "Thank you for telling me your story, Amraen. You have made a fine kingdom here, I see that, yes." Her family sat in the village (Dellet still lay groaning in bed in the village?), if Amraen wanted to hear praise in that, let him. Kanda turned toward the village.

"No!" Amraen was suddenly between her and the trackway, huge, his face pressed close. "No! That is…I mean…I haven't shown you everything yet, my lady queen Ikandera Thygethyn. There's a farm a little farther yonder, up on that ridge where the field curves upward, a good farm I'd like to show you, the richest of the farms in my kingdom. Jeha's brother works it. That's what we defended from the raiders in my first winter here, my lady queen, it would please me greatly to show you."

"Yes, but…." A kind of grief, to walk to see a farmhouse standing proud and alone on a ridge and once defended against raiders.

"Or there's a fine bull I have in a field yonder, down there where the river runs, a white bull, the best of my herd, all the best of the milch cows and the strongest of the oxen, he's sired."

"Yes…."

"Or…a tree, the tallest tree in my kingdom…the best hay field…the pool that's best for catching fish…."

Kanda shouted, "Just. Tell. Me. What's. Wrong. Amraen!" Like a child, she thought. What. Is. Bothering. You. So. Badly. Amraen? You once stood beside me briefly in a battle, man, I only remember you at all because you were fairly useless even back then. I have my own troubles, my daughter farting out words then blushing crimson and pretending she's not spoken – not you, little more than a stranger, to worry about as well.

The man stared at his feet in the mud. Bent his head to bare the back of his neck. Kanda saw there a flash of red a moment, as if…then Amraen raised his head and his eyes were bright and shining. "There is…." He paused, licked his lips. Thoughts moved across his face like clouds that run before the wind. "My lady queen Ikandera Thygethyn…I fought off raiders when first I made myself king of this place. Several times, they have returned over the years, they or others like them – sometimes, indeed, it seems I should recognize a man's face among a raiding party, greet him as an old companion of the spear – and the usual troubles besides, wolves, once a huge boar…but…."

Get. On. With. It. Amraen. Easier is it by far to fail to talk to Sal about what troubles her, than to listen to this nonsense.

Like a child vomiting, his words came? More like a child learning to use the pot.

"A boar…a snake once…but there is…is…." The man drew a great breath and said: "This village my kingdom: it is cursed.

"Down by the river, my lady queen Ikandera Thygethyn. Why we keep the bull in a field there, where no one will dare go to try to steal it, where the children – the adults, no one – will dare go…. The droveway runs on to reach the river south, yonder, crosses the river at a ford. You must have come that way yourself, I think. But…at the ford—"

Ah. Kanda shuddered. Yes.

"There is a curse there by the river, my lady queen Ikandera Thygethyn.

"A monster."

The man closed his eyes. His voice came low, filled with real dread. "The ghost of a man. Running. Hunted."

CHAPTER EIGHTEEN

Kanda said after a long time, "You would like me to…to kill it? Kill a…a ghost?"

Amraen bowed his head. "I tried once. As I am the king…." He broke off, looked away. "It has the form of something like a man. It is not alive, my lady queen. It is too horrible to look at. Naked, ragged, covered in wounds. Some say it has been flayed. It runs through the woods when the moon is waning thin, running as if all the evil of the world is at its heels."

Kanda said carefully, "It could have been…a traveler? Running because he was…frightened of something? A man, pursued by…by wolves?"

"No, my lady queen. It haunts the droveway up from the river. Night and day, it runs there, but only when the moon is old and dying, never when there is a new moon or a full moon. Its eyes shine white. Its mouth foams and bleeds and shines red. Many have seen it, or heard it running through the trees, sometimes it cries. Sometimes it comes up close behind you in the dark. It cannot speak but it cries like a beast sometimes. If you see it twice, you will surely die.

"Jeha has seen it once. I am afraid to see it, in case…."

"Are there dogs pursuing it?" Kanda said. "A hunting horn blowing? An old woman in a gray cloak?"

"Dogs? A horn?" Amraen shook his head. "No. At least, not that I have heard. Only – only! – the shape of a man, running. No one knows where it came from or why it is here. I had them dig at the ford once, there's a stone there I thought might be…I don't know, its grave perhaps. If we could find its bones to give it decent burial and let it rest…. But: nothing."

"A man running through the woods," Kanda said again carefully.

Amraen misunderstood, perhaps. Or perhaps not. "I…I admit I was….

embarrassed to speak of it to you, my lady queen. Standing here in the daylight it sounds absurd, I know. Jeha and I were speaking of it when you came into my hall, I wanted to tell you then, but seeing you there, it seemed…."

Kanda thought of the scene in the hall that she had overheard that morning between Amraen and Jeha. 'Embarrassed' was not the word she would have used.

"A man came to my hall early this morning, my lady queen. Dall, his name is, he lives in the woods beyond the river, his house is outside the bounds of my kingdom but he has bound himself in homage to me. He should have been here yesterday for the render-feast, he should have brought gifts of honey and venison. I have been expecting him these three days, his absence surprised me.

"He is a strong man in his thirties. Helped me drive off the raiders I told you of. He was not afraid to fight that day, was not found wanting then or since. I was surprised he was not at the render-feast, but I had no fear that any danger could have come to him.

"He was standing outside the gates this morning, pushing something away from him that was not there. The only way we could stop him pushing like that was to bind his arms. He can say only that he saw the man running close to him."

Amraen said, "We had to gag him, to stop him speaking of it."

The strangeness this morning was explained, then. The tension and fear in the village and in Jeha. But…the man was a monster to be feared? Kanda thought instead of the dogs, the hunting horn. The woman in the gray cloak.

"I have tried to get up my courage enough to face it. But I— Where would this – this village of mine be if I was to die, my lady queen Ikandera Thygethyn? And how does a man kill a ghost? But now you are here.

"You can kill it. You alone. I know this."

"This is what you are so ashamed of? Afraid of? This is why you cringe from me and the cold sweat drips from your brow? Because of a ghost?"

Amraen nodded, wretched. Would not meet her gaze.

You marched in my armies, Amraen. Claim I once did you the honor of letting you stand near me. All we saw in those days! And you are afraid of a…a ghost? A man who is running away?

I turn up, I shower them with blessings, cakes and ale and roast meat and fresh flowers, *oh my lady Ikandera Thygethyn, could you do something for us, just a small thing?* Kanda of the Six Swords, Ikandera Thygethyn, scare off a ghost!

Kanda thought: it had better not turn out to breathe fire. Or have three heads.

A memory of something caught her, a dream, she thought, I dreamed…last night? of dead things and ghost things. What did I dream? I saw something dead and terrible. A fear and a shadow. A memory of a memory of a dream.

A long time since I felt as afraid as I was seeing those dogs. This man whom the dogs were hunting. The woman in the gray cloak. There is some horror here that I don't want to think on. From a gentle sleep in Lela's village I have woken to something like madness. This is an evil place for me. I dreamed last night of something evil. There is danger here, I feel it, I hear it. She moved slightly, shifted her feet, and her hand brushed her sword hilt. Closed comforted on her sword. Cold metal. Good to hold. Amraen made a noise of something…fear? He blinked, his eyes fixed on her hand on the sword. Kanda thought in sudden wonder: why am I wearing my sword? In all those months in Lela's village it had lain hidden and barely thought of. A cheer, a roar of praise for Ikandera Thygethyn, and she had put it on, walked with the swordsman's swagger through the village streets.

Amraen's face was haggard. He looked a ghost himself. The rain was washing the dye from his beard, red water ran like blood down his neck.

The sooner we leave this place the better it will be for all of us, Kanda thought wearily. If Dellet hadn't drunk so much beer…if she hadn't magicked up so much beer…they'd be on their way down the spring green droveway already, walking away from all this. Roven is waiting for us! Every day, every hour we linger, its ruins crumble farther into dust beyond all repairing, in my mind the memory fades a little further until at last it will be gone beyond recall like so many memories of precious things. I forget Sal's face when she was young and innocent of the world's cruelty. I forget Morna's face. The Hall Roven will be lost and I will not remember to recognize it or to rebuild it. It had…walls, and a roof, and a door, I will say. Just as Morna had…a child's face. We wasted all the winter in Lela's village, sleeping. Why did we stay so long there, what foolishness possessed me to think we should stay? Truly, that village put a curse on me. (But: no, Kanda, only a dream of going back to something else you fear you will forget, her heart said.)

Worse now, if I stay here. Every moment I stay here in this absurd kingdom…. A dream of going back to something else again, Kanda, something else you loved so deeply and fear that you will forget, her heart said. And she shuddered as even her hand gripped tight on her sword hilt. We must leave as quickly as we can, tomorrow we will be gone at first light down the droveway following the River Wend that we can pretend is our own River Wenet, into the rush of the green spring. That will be good – and she thought, remembering Amraen's face in the hall last night and that morning, that it would be a relief to Amraen when they were gone, also. How she herself had despaired when she found her former companions returned to her. A hard thing for a mere man like Amraen, having Ikandera Thygethyn under his roof!

"I cannot help you," she said. "I cannot do this thing, Amraen. It's raining, look, you're soaked. Let us return to the village."

Amraen let out a groan at her words. As great a groan as any war cry of Ikandera Thygethyn. So terrible his groan that a crow burst up from the trees in fear and a starling fell from the sky dead. So great that the earth shook as if in an earthquake. So full of grief that blood burst from his lips. His face was terrible, his eyes bulged and his tongue lolled from his mouth as if he had been strangled, his neck swelled and his golden neck ring almost broke. For ten heartbeats he could not speak, he could not breathe. Then he fell to his knees before her in the wet mud. "Please," he cried at last. "Please, my lady queen. Please go to the ford. Kill the ghost."

Ah, Kanda. Like a mother giving in to a child's pleading, as a mother, rather, for Amraen like all her soldiers was to her as her child, as a mother sighing, shaking her head, weary, defeated, won over, helpless, hapless.

"Please. Go there now, please, please, only you can do this thing, my lady queen. I beg you."

"I will go to the ford, Amraen," Kanda said. "Help you. Free you of this curse, if I can. Fight this…ghost."

The relief in Amraen's face was like another feast day. Like people dancing.

CHAPTER NINETEEN

Amraen's village, however, was strangely empty when Kanda and Amraen returned. All the noise and bustle of the morning, clang of hammers, crack of axe on wood, but now the place was half-deserted, a lone woman hurrying into her house with a bundle in her arms, a heavy hanging silence.

"Where is everyone gone?" Kanda asked Amraen. He only said wearily, "Busy. Working. Frightened."

"Can I see the man who saw the ghost that I must fight?"

Amraen frowned. "He.... He would be sick with shame if – when – he is sane again, if he learned you had seen him as he is now, my lady queen."

In the guesthouse Dellet had got up at last, was sitting with Sal and with Calian who looked cross and bored.

"Hello. Stopped playing with Wyn and Ylil, then?"

"Wyn and Ylil had to go and do something else." By which she probably meant she'd managed to upset both of them by being older and better than them. "Where have you been, anyway?"

"Talking with King Amraen."

"About what?"

Spare us from children who've not slept enough and husbands who've drunk too much. "Things."

Calian said, "Ylil says there's a ghost that haunts the village."

"Yes. That was one of the things we were talking about."

"I told them not to be so stupid." Ah, Calian who had fought a dead man and a monster made of wood and bones!

Kanda opened her pack, took out her helmet and her armor. Strapped her sword at her waist.

"They seemed really scared, though, Wyn and Ylil. Ylil said his mum had seen it." Then the girl said with great surprise, "What are you doing?"

"What does it look like I'm doing?"

"You're going to…?" Calian leapt up. "I'm coming with you." She said, "Wyn and Ylil were really scared when they talked about the ghost. This is like…this is what you did when you were one of the Six of Roven! Coming to a place that needed help and helping them!"

Kanda tried to smile. "It is, yes, Calian."

"I thought they were talking about that…that woman, at first. Or the dogs…. Oh! The ghost of a man, running…?"

Dellet said, "And you said Ylil was being stupid?"

Kanda looked at Dellet, saw his face strange and frightened. Saw him look at Sal, the fear in Sal's eyes. Something passed between Sal and Dellet. *Those dogs, Dad…. That woman….*

"It's nothing. A beggar man out in the woods. Thin and hungry and afraid. You'd be scaring people, if you were homeless and hungry out in the cold…."

"Come on then!" Calian said. "Hurry up!" Calian already had her sword at her hip also. Don't tell me, Kanda thought, she had it on when she was playing with Wyn and Ylil? No wonder Jeha was awkward around me this morning….

"Are you sure your mother wants you to go with her, Calian?" said Dellet. By which he meant: if you have any care for any one of us, Kanda, wife, you'll tell Calian she's not going one footstep outside that door.

"I'm sure I want to go," Calian said. "I've faced far worse than ghosts." Her face at her father would make even a ghost laugh. She can come to lend me her courage, Kanda thought. Or her heedlessness, at least.

"I want to come, Mother," Sal said then. And Kanda thought: oh, come on! Dellet, are you coming? A family outing? With picnic? Shall we put on our best clothes?

Never was Lady Kanda of the Six asked to do such a deed, and never would any have dared ask it of Ikandera Thygethyn (…wait…). But never did Lady Kanda of the Six have children tagging along behind her (she thought of Gallyn and Morren…wait…). *Are we nearly there yet? It's hot, can you carry my jacket? I'm bored and hungry, can we stop for a snack?* Ah, that's unfair to Calian, she's nearly old enough to have grown out of behaving like that. That's the ghost child, Kanda. Anything and everything since the making of the world, you'd give, to have her whinging on I need a wee I need a poo I'm bored I'm hungry Mum Mum Mum.

A ghost man. A ghost child. The ghost of Ikandera Thygethyn the Great War Leader. The ghost of Sal's life. We can go and play together all of us ghosts, and oh how happy we'll be!

Tried to think and tried to think: there is nothing to fear, just another monster to kill. I have killed so many monsters. A wolf with three heads; a dragon; an old friend. A ghost will simply be another thing to kill. A new thing I've never before had to meet in battle, and it's not often Ikandera Thygethyn can say that of something – a new thing I've never yet killed! I've killed more men than walk the earth now; as the dead outnumber the living so the men I've killed. I'm bored of killing men! Indeed, I'm bored of killing dragons! The whetstone on the blade, the fires in the fields, the cries of slaughtered children – familiar to me as my children's coughs and farts. So boring! So commonplace! Bring on a ghost that runs away!

Tried to think: it will be well. There is nothing to fear. I am being foolish in my old age and after a heavy night.

Tried not to think of the old woman at the ford. Or the dogs. Or the ringing of that hunting horn. The beast from which that horn came, she once had hunted.

A woman brought them a meal of bread and cheese and cold meat left from the night before. Milk and ale and water (Dellet groaned loudly at the ale: "take it away, away, away"). Five yellow apples, mottled with brown stars. Kanda looked at the five apples a long time, and Sal looked at them.

After they had eaten they were ready. A strange party for a hero's quest. Dellet, wise man, was not coming, knew what he was and where he would be best placed in a fight, and that was ten miles away behind a barred door. Kanda said, "Stay with your father, Sal, stay to look after him," but Sal said flatly, "No."

"You're an old woman, Sal, you shouldn't be fighting monsters."

"Look at yourself again, Mother. Find a mirror. The blade of your sword, that's polished, look at yourself there, what do you see?"

Sal had a stone knife on a cord around her neck. Sal had the gift of healing in her hands. "The ghost might know the way to Roven, Mother. You never know a thing unless you go along and ask."

True, that: you don't. Kanda wearing a golden bit and a golden bridle and a red silk saddlecloth might have been halfway to Roven now herself.

"Ready, Sal? Ready, Calian?" Say goodbye to your father, everyone got their cloaks on, had a wee? And they had been into battle before, a mother and her daughters, click of Kanda's knee joints, Calian sulking, genuine worry (genuine moans) about aching feet and going too fast and too slow and one of the others stopping to piss; a mighty stand by a fussing old woman and her daughters, three women all of great power armed and fierce, too few winters the one and too many winters the two and the three; and it had felt the best joy of Kanda's life and the strangest weirdest worst thing she could ever have imagined; and it felt more joyful and worse now even than it had then.

That had been to fight the darkness to bring back Sal and Morna.

This was....

This was....

A king has sought my aid as a great warrior against a monster, that's what this is, Kanda tried and tried to think.

They packed up the last of the bread and the cheese and a waterskin. Kanda and Calian put their right hands on their sword hilts so to show their swords were hanging there ready at their hips. Sal smiled at that, as did Dellet. Went out into the village, which was still strangely quiet and empty. The woman who had brought them their food went hurrying past with her cloak wrapped tight. The smith was still working at the crucible. The axe was still chopping wood.

Someone had screwed up their courage: the piglets were eating Kanda's green stuff. That made her smile. They looked bigger than they had that morning. There seemed to be more doves in the dovecote. The chickens all sat on new-laid eggs.

"I was hoping to see Wyn and Ylil," said Calian, looking around the strange emptiness.

"Show off your sword and your adventuring?" said Sal.

"No!"

Grin.

"Yes."

Kanda had herself thought that Amraen at least, or Jeha at least, would have come to see her off on this quest. The people they had come to save usually did see the Six off on their quest. Only polite, as Erenan had said once when someone else hadn't bothered. No one was about, not even children. Usually in a village like this you'd hear a baby's yells, someone's song as they worked the loom, someone singing and groaning as they ground the quern, someone shouting curses at someone or something. A fearful, strange silence apart from the woodcutter and the bronzesmith's work. Kanda began to feel dread on her. What is this here? What has happened? At the gate Tal the guardsman stood looking into the village not out. He stood up straighter when he saw them.

For a moment Kanda thought she saw something red at his throat. A mark. And his face looked so pale and gray.... She blinked. The man smiled nervously at her. "My lord king Amraen, he said...he couldn't be here to wish you luck, but he said...."

"Have you seen the ghost?" Calian said eagerly.

A pause. The man shifted from foot to foot. "My father said he heard it once."

"Well...."

"Well...."

"We'll be back when we've killed it," Calian said. "Wish us luck!"

Tal shifted. Smiled his frightened smile. "Good luck to us all."

The trees looked taller and stronger, thick with budding flowers and budding leaves. The wheat in the fields stood brilliant green as high as Kanda's hips. Fat ducks and geese in plenty on a pond. White lambs with black feet and black noses, which could only be described as gamboling.

Primroses blossomed on the banks of the droveway. It looked like butter had been spread on the green banks. Drizzle in the air but a thousand birds singing, all with new-laid eggs in their nests like the hens. Kanda glimpsed the fox slinking through the hedgerow, its belly swollen with cubs. The sun was warm. A warm wind blew from the south. The damp green banks of the droveway almost steamed. Bees and flies were waking and drowsing.

Kanda thought: did I do this?

She thought: I think I did.

She saw Sal smiling at the fox.

She thought: we did this.

She thought briefly and happily: a king has sought my aid against a monster, and I have answered him. My comrades are beside me and I trust them to fight this monster at my side and win. Instead of Gallyn, *Great Leap*, there is Calian, *Eagle*; instead of Erenan, *Summer Harvest*, there is Sal, *Shining*. This is my heart's desire. My quest to find Roven is – for this. Rebuild Roven? It is here rebuilt already in my sword and in my daughters. A quest and a beast and three brave companions and I hope a happy outcome. Thus no different in its way from the greatest of the deeds of Roven.

They walked back down the droveway until they came back to the River Wend and the ford. It was not good or right to walk back. Once, Kanda looked behind her and thought she saw towers rising, the sunlight flashing on domes and glass windows, banners fluttering black against the gold. Things like birds circling, rising up to dance in the sky higher than the sun. Ah, Amraen, she thought – is that your kingdom as you see it sometimes? Such kingdoms such cities such worlds you and I saw once. Wyn and Ylil dressed in silk, Jeha's sword studded with diamonds, your hall a palace with crystal fountains and a golden throne. These things we both once made and dreamed. They walked on, past the two stones that flanked the droveway. Kanda did not look behind her again.

A longer walk than Kanda had thought it – it had seemed long when she came this way, true, but that had been fleeing from the old woman at the ford, it should have been a far shorter walk, surely, to go back? They had to stop so Sal could rest herself, they ate bread and cheese, drank from the waterskin. Already it seemed to be turning toward midafternoon, thus too soon it would be turning toward evening and then toward night. They walked east so the light was behind them. If they went on long enough they might come back to the bothy, the marshes, Lela's village.... Or they might not.

If they walked on long enough, Kanda thought, they might reach their old home. Or not.

Not. Not. Not.

Did I tell you recently that Morna was dead and they could never return to that house?

A crow called in the trees to Kanda's left, shouted angry at something, and a fox barked. Kanda thought: thank you, crow, thank you, fox.

You did tell me recently that Morna was dead and they could never return to that house, yes, but you haven't told me that for, oh, ten heartbeats.

Call again, crow. Call again, fox. Make a noise in the darkening woods. If they walked on long enough they might reach....

"Is the moon new or old? Waxing or waning?"

Kanda said, "What?"

"The moon. Waxing? Or waning?"

The fox barked. The crow called. Kanda said, "...I have no idea, Calian...?"

Calian said, "Only, the ghost only comes out when the moon is waning thin, Ylil said."

"Yes?"

"So: is the moon tonight waning thin?"

The crow called. The fox barked. The wind stirred the leaves in the trees.

"Oh. Yes." Kanda tried to think. "I don't know." Tried to think of the moon the previous night walking the whole twenty paces from the feast hall to the guesthouse. A hazy moon, you might say. "Amraen asked me to go today. 'Now,' he said. As soon as I could. So I suppose...."

She thought: I think of these things all the time when it comes to my family. Is Calian's period likely to come in the next few days so she'll need clout clothes? What's in the cupboard that needs eating up next? Does – did Morna need her nails cut? I never stop thinking about such things.

A quest, a quest, a fine quest: to sit by the river in peace under a beautiful fat waxing moon. Twiddle our thumbs for days.

This, also, she thought, had not often before – not ever before – happened to either Ikandera Thygethyn or the Six of Roven. These things that must be right sometimes for the magic – *on the third day after the first full moon of winter; at just the moment the sun's rays first strike the ash tree in the field beyond the stream; when the first leaf falls from the oak and the thrush sings in the holly: only then may you do this thing*. We knew. "Come, hurry," Erenan would shout, "come on quickly before the right time is gone!" Kestre fought a giant once that could only be killed when the tide on the beach beneath his castle was at its lowest ebb and the last wave of the ebbing tide had just broken. She was in a cave deep underground when she fought that giant. The cave was thirty miles from the sea. She struck one stroke. Killed him. The phases of the moon; the rising of the sun and moon and stars; the neap tide and the spring tide; the courses of the wind: we knew: in our bones.

Forgotten now. Replaced with reckoning up the urgent intimacy of Sal and Calian and Dellet.

"It will come for us," she said loudly, firmly. "We will go to the ford to wait; it will come." I'll have to trust that Amraen—

He has no idea whether it's a waxing or a waning moon, she thought. In his mind is only: it will be there when Ikandera Thygethyn goes to meet it, because it is his want that I fight it and thus it will be there for me to fight. If it isn't there – that will be my fault or its fault. Not his fault.

Some magic in that, I suppose. Sal and Calian use that magic often also.

Then she said suddenly with a laugh, "Oh I'm being stupid! We saw it yesterday, and Amraen said a man saw it."

I'm sorry, Amraen, she thought. Most uncharitable (true) thoughts about you (and Sal, and Calian). But, to be fair, it was all so much easier then. Fewer worries. (These worries are themselves another kind of magic.)

CHAPTER TWENTY

They reached the ford. The bank with its green stuff rushing, trampled down by Calian's feet and cows' feet. A last few dregs of withered yellow flowers, and Calian and Sal both seemed to see for the first time that last night Kanda had made flowers grow and the cloaked woman had made flowers grow. Kanda looked around; there in a nettle patch was a big flat-topped whiteish stone. It could be a grave mark, she thought. The sky was clear and pale, the light was fading to evening in a sorrowing call of birds. Thin clouds that ran fast. Kanda pushed away the nettles, laid her right hand on the stone. Very cold. A tree by the stone, a tall tree with thick branches; a hundred years ago and more it could easily have taken a hanging man's weight. She stood flexing her hand to wish away the nettle stings. The birds called and called in such sweet sorrow. In the west the sun was red. Then the birds were silent and the river was still and silent and there was no wind.

A quest, a beast, a danger, the right moment. Kanda shouted, "Come out!"

The birds were silent and the river ceased its running, there was no wind and the evening sun was held still.

"Come out!" Her voice was wrong, shouting, calling. In cold silence we must wait and wait.

"It's not here, Mum," said Calian. Ah, that was poetry in this silent waiting! Such poetry that the birds burst out singing their sorrow, the river ran, the wind blew in the trees. The sun sank into its wounding. Kanda looked behind them down the droveway, there were shadows falling there but nothing to fear. She looked ahead of them across the river, the droveway ran on leading perhaps still to Lela's village, there were shadows on the droveway on the other side of the river falling but they also were nothing to be feared.

"I know it's not here, Calian," Kanda said. "There's this thing, you see…where you wait?" They stood all three close together. Sal pulled her cloak tight around her, put up the hood – then Sal made a noise that was a laugh or a groan. Put down her hood. Kanda pressed to her elder daughter. Sal's hand groped for her mother's hand. Kanda squeezed it, held it tight. She could feel Sal's fast heartbeat.

"It's all right, Sal." Whispered. Mouthed, barely speaking. Sal did not hear her. Stared out into the onrush of the evening. Her mouth was parted. Her eyes were very bright.

"Sal?"

Sal squeezed her mother's hand back.

The evening too suddenly galloping. In the distance a dog barked. Two dogs. In the blue evening there would not yet be ghosts. But a shape moved on the riverbank beside the stone. A whiteness, ill-formed, spreading like river mist across the ground. And a reflection was cast on the river, the dark river ran deep and cold where rain had fallen on the hills of Kanda's dreaming, the currents moved like a body moving, the water was black like eyes. A whiteness, a reflection, the sun held still, the river rushing fast. Fast as tears are shed, the river ran. The sky marked by the sun's wound beyond all powers of healing. The sun dies in the gape of blood. The birds called their sorrow, as grief-filled as the sky. The evening gloom fading blue away to blackness, and the river was cold and almost as solid as a sword. Water moving as the light is caught and moving on a drawn sword.

Dark now. Dark of *cloudy-night-in-heavy-woodland.* Yet the river gleamed darkly. The whiteness on the riverbank was very clear to see. A shadow or a reflection on the water, of something or nothing.

Kanda whispered to Sal and Calian. "So. Now, I think, we will see."

A bird called that was not quite a bird. A beating of birds' wings.

Fearful. Fleeing.

The man burst out from the trees. Dark now: Kanda should not have been able to see him as anything more than a man's blurred shape. The scene was as clear as their first encounter in bright daylight. His eyes were mad and huge. Nothing left in them. He was naked. Flayed – that is, *skinless*, yes. See the muscles of his body move as Kanda had so poetically seen the rush of water as muscles. Blood dripping, dripping, dripping from his every part. Blood dripping like sweat.

Red as the sunset. Dripping like a man after a hot bath. Ripped up, ripped open in his legs and arms and belly by biting eating teeth.

Calian cried out in horror. Sal cried out. Revulsion filled Kanda, she felt herself wanting to vomit. This wretched man…the fear and the horror in him at what he had suffered. He ran past them toward the river to throw himself into the water as he had done the first time they saw him. Sal turned her head to stare in the direction he had come from; Kanda waited for the dogs to come bounding out in pursuit. But this time when he reached the riverbank the man's hands flew up as if some invisible beast was there before him. He made no sound. He did not seem to see Kanda, Sal and Calian so close to him. He looked back once, his mouth shaped a scream. He stumbled. Fell forward onto his hands and knees. He crawled thus a few desperate steps along the river's edge. Collapsed. Where he had fallen the earth churned. His blood eating away the damp earth.

He lay still. Dead? He looked as if he had been dead a long time. A ghost, yes. A thin, wretched, lonely ghost.

The hunting horn sounded. The horn of a black bull, bound in gold, set with two diamonds. Great cities such as Amraen dreamed of ruling had trembled once to the music of that horn. Once, twice, three times, beloved lips would set that horn ringing to call an army to march. On a white horse with red saddlecloth and golden bit and gilded hooves, a queen would lead the charge when once, twice, three times that horn was rung. And when a city was fallen, beloved lips would set it joyfully ringing again. (And Amraen would have been there somewhere. Guarding her camp or such, perhaps. At the very back of the back ranks.)

She thought: so, a ghost hunting horn?

The undergrowth at the edge of the droveway stirred. Two huge gray dogs burst out from trees. They rushed together to the man's body. Began to tear at it.

That noise, so familiar, of teeth rending human bone and muscle. The smell of a body being torn open. The smell of raw fresh man-meat.

No, no, Kanda, that's the smell familiar from butchering cattle. Jointing a sheep for the pot. The smell when it's your monthly bleed and you get the shits.

That's where you remember these smells from. These sounds from.

"Get off him," Calian said weakly. "Get them off him, Mum." She stood frozen, horrified; she had drawn her sword but it hung useless at her side. "Make them go away, Mum," she said like a tiny child. "I don't like them. . . ."

Kanda thought: I should drive them off. Rush at them, kill them. They are what Amraen truly meant me to kill. Her body was raw where the dogs had mauled her, she felt their claws digging into her belly, ripping her open. She felt afraid.

Sal took one shaking step forward toward the dogs.

One of the dogs raised its head. Growled, bared its teeth. The dog with the white markings. It had a wound on its face. The dog with the brown markings too growled, stood over the dead man staring at Sal and Kanda and Calian. It had a wound on its left foreleg.

The dog with the white markings took one step toward Sal.

Kanda tried to put her hand on her sword hilt. The dog crouched. Ready to spring.

The dog with the white markings barked at Sal.

Sal stood frozen.

Kanda wrestling to put her hand on her sword hilt.

The dog with the brown markings tossed its head.

The hunting horn sounded.

The dogs pricked up their ears.

Whined.

Relaxed.

The woman in the gray cloak stepped out from the trees. Walked over to stand looking carefully down at the dead man.

"Oh you good boys," she said sweetly. "Oh you good good clever boys. You've caught him finally. Well done."

The dog with the brown markings yapped at the woman.

The woman pretended to notice Kanda and Sal and Calian for the first time. She clapped her hands. No gloves now: slender fingers that glittered with gold rings.

Sweet happy voice. Eager voice. Like singing.

"Oh, you've come back! Do you want to come with me after all? How fine! I've been walking this way and that, I was just thinking to myself how nice it would be to have a horse to ride on. Rest my weary creaking legs."

Calian's sword flashed out. "Shut up! Be silent! You…you witch!"

Poor thin words, Kanda thought.

But the woman drew back with a hiss. "That sword reeks of blood. Put that sword away. You terrified my poor cows. Now you want to frighten these poor dogs too? And what about the corpse lying here? You're frightening him, poor thing."

"He's dead!" Calian shouted.

"So were my cows. They were still frightened."

"Put your sword down, Calian," Kanda said gently.

Calian brandished her sword. Thrust high, thrust low, jabbed out toward the woman's heart. "No!"

"Calian: put your sword down."

Sal said, "Put it down, Calian. Do as Mum tells you."

The woman snorted. Laughing. Kanda said, "Come on, Calian."

Calian lowered her sword. Shook with anger. Kanda sighed. "Good girl, thank you, Calian." The woman snorted laughing.

A great quest to fight evil, three companions striding out at a king's pleading, almost like the glory days. All bitter and spoiled already, look what you made me do, Calian, why do you have to spoil things, oh stop sulking, grow up, can't you, Calian? Look what I did, ruined it with my first words, turned all Calian's fierceness from warrior's joy to child's shame, what a waste I've made.

The woman turned her cloaked head to Kanda. "You did," she said. Sad voice. Pitying voice. "You ruined it," she said. "Destroyed it." Kanda was certain she said these words. The woman turned her cloaked head to Calian, "That's better, thank you. But really! Do you ever think of anything except slaughter and killing?"

Calian made a noise like a croak. Kanda held her tight. Felt her daughter's rage so hot it made even Kanda wince.

"Some things need to be killed," Sal said.

"Do they?"

A silence.

"Yes," Sal said.

The woman turned. Her hidden face looked straight at Sal. Count one two three four five long breaths. Almost awkward. Almost waiting. The woman laughed. Almost nervously. The river made a rushing rain-fed song.

The woman pushed back her hood to show her face.

Kanda had been wrong before to think her an old woman. Her face was that of a woman perhaps a little younger than Kanda herself. And a woman more beautiful than Kanda had ever been or could ever dream of being. Her hair was white and silver, shining like the sun after rainfall when its beams are pale and liquid, shining like the high clouds when the sun sets them blazing. Her skin was bronze, the color of the river flowing over rocks and deep pools where the trout lie in stealthy wait. She looked like a summer meadow when the pasture is rich and lush and green, the grass is filled with buttercups, the hedgerows are clotted with lace-flower, the soil is almost black. The sky is blue, as blue almost as the woman's blue eyes, high clouds white without hint of rain but bringing only welcome shade in the midday heat. The river runs over the deep pools, the smooth stones. Grass so rich the cows give pure cream, warm sun, sweet breeze. Laughing children play on the riverbanks, splash in the clear water, so safe a place their mother does not need to watch them. On the good milk and the silver trout the girls grow strong and plump. A shrine is there for blessings; flowers that are thick with drowsing bees. The river sings and the birds sing and the bees drowse only of peace. So fair! So fair, so rich, so splendid a place! And this woman was as fair – no, this woman was fairer even than the summertime meadows of the River Wenet. Her gown was yellow silk, she wore gold bracelets and silver bracelets and gold and silver rings. Silver ribbons in her lovely hair. A necklace of amber beads around her lovely throat. She stepped two dainty footsteps away from the dead man, and yellow flowers grew up where she set her feet. The night was dark and the forest darker, a thin moon in a clouded sky, but Kanda could see her so fair and fine and stately, because she was so fair and fine and filled with light.

"Oh!" All that Kanda had longed to be, when Kanda had been the greatest of the Six of Roven, and better, and fairer and finer and more queenly, and stronger and wiser in her arm and in her face.

"Who are you?" Calian shouted. "What's your name? Tell me!"

The dogs growled. "Camryth," the woman said sharply. "Mannan. Stop that." She put her hands on the dogs' shoulders. "People you don't care for, Camryth, Mannan, my fine dogs? Don't worry, I won't let those wicked swords hurt you again. Bloody to the hilt, those swords, I know, I can see the blood and smell it. But they won't hurt you again, I promise.

"Look what you did to these dogs," the woman said. "Wounded them. Why should I tell you my name, you failed butcherer of innocent dogs?"

All this time, Sal had been staring, staring. But now she gave a cry of horror, the tears ran down her cheeks.

Calian shouted, "I thought you were so frightened of these dogs, Mum had to carry you across the river away from them?"

"Ah, but that was then," the woman said. "Now she's carried me across the river, all's safe and well. A great hunt, these dogs were making, I was eager to join it. 'What's the sport?' I asked the man they were hunting, 'Why are they chasing you?' 'Because I am a murderer,' he said. 'I've killed people, I'm a wicked man, they want to punish me.' 'Well!' I said, 'that's a good reason!' So I joined in."

Calian's hand itching on her sword hilt. Holding Calian from drawing her sword was like trying to hold back the wind. "Those dogs attacked my mother," Calian shouted. "Tried to kill her!"

"Well but they didn't kill her, did they? Some things are dead and still walk and talk, it's true. But you can't fool me that easily: I can see she's not yet dead."

Calian let out a roar. Her sword was out and up, and she was running.

The woman stood poised. Watched Calian run. Like a storm coming: the farmer stands in the field, sees the sky grow black and the rain come down on the hills like a wall, he stands waiting in the cloud shadow, the wind blows his hair, the rain is on the next field he hears it beating the crops down, then the rain strikes him. Thus Calian ran and struck at the woman.

The woman leapt. A sword in her hand also. A sword of gold. It blazed like all the fires of morning. A hearth fire cooking food on a winter day when the snow lies heavy; a bronzesmith's fire working to smelt the precious killing metal; a city as it burns all its towers falling in ash – brighter, clearer, more beautiful, as beautiful as the woman who held it, as beautiful as the hearth fires and the bronzesmith's fires and the killing fire when it burned Roven, that sword burned. A golden sword for a woman splendid with gold and splendid as gold and golden light.

Calian's sword and the woman's sword met.

A swirl of bodies. The two so different: gangly, dark Calian in her mud-spattered leggings and tunic, her bronze sword a simple thing. Shorter, lighter, weaker, younger. Girl and sword both.

Kanda's hand flashed to her own blade. Rush in to join the battle! Two against one, mother and daughter together, sword on sword, pressing and pushing their enemy back! They had stood together once against an army. Evil made manifest, darkness a thousand-armed thousand-bladed thing. Together now they would stand against one woman weighted down in silks and jewelry. One woman and two dogs. But something held her, stopped her. A voice in her heart or her head. *Don't spoil it for Calian. This is her fight. Don't spoil it by charging in.* When I fought with Geiamnyn or with Ysarene, or with a dragon, or with a mere idiot pompous warrior youth…if anyone, Palle who was nearly my equal in battle, a farm boy thinking to help save his friends, if any had tried to help me, come between me and my enemy, thought I needed *helping*.... Don't spoil it, don't ruin it for Calian.

Calian's sword was brushed aside. Elegantly, as this splendid woman must do everything with elegance. Calian howled, roared, the two swords bronze and gold met and met and met and met. Stepping, lunging, pushing in, throwing out. They spiraled together, leapt apart, met. Kanda thought, oddly, of the way she and Calian or Calian and Sal were together – sudden anger, a burst of furious bitter words, then as suddenly a tight embrace. Calian pressed close, she had speed to her, her opponent hampered – slightly, barely – by her fine clothes. Calian leapt backward, dived to one side then the other; each time, the woman met her stroke for stroke, caught Calian's sword with the golden sword.

The dogs watched. Crouched on the riverbank, teeth bared. Growled.

If they jump at Calian, Kanda thought, they are taller and heavier than she is.

They are taller and heavier than I am, she thought, never mind Calian. I had trouble enough with them before, and then I'm sure they were not as big. And the woman.... Calian moved back, panting, her eyes fixed on her enemy's face. The woman stood almost on the riverbank. She is perhaps a better swordswoman than I am, Kanda thought. She is winning.

I mean Calian, she tried to think. Hand on sword hilt, own hand red and hot. Cut the enemy down, throw her body into the river, kill the dogs. *(Don't spoil it don't spoil it for Calian this is her fight don't spoil it.)*

Sal grasped Kanda's right arm. Kanda saw her daughter flinch as if her right arm was truly burning hot. "No, Mother!"

"To help Calian." Pulling herself away from Sal, trying to shake off Sal's grasp tight on her arm, while Calian now was fighting defensively, Calian, not her enemy, was pressed against the riverbank now, thrashing artless with her sword, panting.

"No, Mother! No! You can't—"

"Calian!" Kanda cried out in fury. Pain in Sal's face as Kanda grasped Sal's hand. Ripping at Sal's fingers: "Get off. Stop holding me. Stop stopping me. We have to help Calian!"

"No!" Sal was screaming and choking the word out: no no no no no.

"What are you doing, Sal?" You want Calian to die? Kanda tore her daughter's hand from her arm. Old thin hand, age-spotted, wrinkled as cold-meat skin. Pushed her daughter away from her. Sal's thin body – falling. Still the sobs came: no, don't, please.

Kanda's heart screaming with hate at her elder daughter.

You think Calian can win this?

You want Calian to die, is that it?

You're killing my child, Sal.

Calian howled. A child's cry of fear, not a warrior's cry. Ikandera Thygethyn cried her war cry, drew her sword.

Calian fell. Her sword fell.

"Calian!"

Rolled, staggered to her knees. Groped for her sword. Her enemy was on her, struck out what must be the killing stroke. Calian caught the blade as it came for her, blocked it with her arms.

Screamed as she bled.

"Calian!" Kanda threw herself forward. Hunger. Desire. Cut her daughter's enemy down.

The dogs rose vast before Kanda. There was fire in their eyes, they were terrible and strange. Kanda saw there a moment before her an army of warrior men.

Teeth closed on her right arm.

Teeth closed on her left arm.

The golden sword at Calian's silent screaming throat.

All was still and silent.

CHAPTER TWENTY-ONE

"Oh dear." The woman's voice, sweet and singing. "Oh dear, deary dear. You should have come with me," the woman said. "Carried me on your back as my horse. You should, you should. How foolish you are! If only you'd listened. Now look what's happened instead."

The dogs holding Kanda like two men holding a prisoner between them, two sets of white teeth drawing Kanda's blood. Calian slumped on her knees, her blood running fast down her arms as she herself had been so recently running, the woman's golden sword pressed to her throat. Sal standing sick, looking from her mother to her sister to the dogs and back and back.

This is what had happened. Kanda looked at it indeed. Couldn't stop her looking. Would never stop her looking, not when this night was a thousand years and a thousand years and a thousand years more away.

"A fine horse you'd have been, too," the woman said. "How strong you were when you carried me across the river."

Kanda said slowly, "And if I agreed now to be your horse?"

"Oh, it's too late now!" A pretty laugh, a ringing laugh – almost a sad laugh.

"I told you to put that nasty sword away," the woman said. Her voice sounded older and tired now. More like it had on the other side of the ford when she was old. "I told these poor dogs you wouldn't hurt them again. I promised these poor dogs that, in fact. So you won't, you won't, you won't."

She lifted her sword from Calian's throat. A single drop of blood on Calian's skin. Red jewel at her neck to match the red jewels on the woman's arms.

Calian did not move or speak. Only her eyes darted wildly from side to side. Looking for her sword.

"If you move, she'll drop dead," the woman said to Kanda and Sal. "But if you speak, you'll drop dead."

Kanda wanted to shout to her in fury, shout her war cry that rang so loud it broke men's armor, broke men's skulls to spill out their brains to leave them dead. The lofty walls of many fair cities her war cry had shattered; Erelene, bride of cities, in the far north where the snow lies piled in summer and in winter, Kydana in the dry wastes, city of the wise whose towers were once built of dragon bone, Inakanassos in the Forever Morning, that never had fallen in war to any till Ikandera Thygethyn cried her war cry to break its gates. Less furious then, her voice lower and quieter then than it would be now if she dared to shout. Louder, louder, louder, Kanda wanted to shout in rage and fury and grief. And humiliation: I am Ikandera Thygethyn! I am the greatest warrior who ever lived!

She stood with the dogs beside her, flanking her. Sal stood. Calian knelt.

The woman walked over to the dead man on the riverbank. In the dark the yellow flowers that grew in her footsteps seemed to glow.

She raised her dainty foot.

Kicked the dead man.

"Get up, you, you laze. Stop lying there dead. I need a horse to carry me. I've walked all day and I'm tired of walking. This woman didn't want the honor. She's too stupid, yes, I know. Get up and be my horse, and I will give you a red saddlecloth and a golden bit and a golden bridle. I will give you sweet milk to drink each morning. You'll make a fine horse for me."

The dead man got up slowly. Dead and torn open. No skin on him. His head hung down where his neck was broken. Flopped down horribly, and his tongue lolled out half torn away. His entrails hung tangled about his legs.

He bent forward onto all fours. Crack and crunch of bones. Creak of bones. Grinding bones. Ripping rippling rushing running blurring flowing forming flesh.

A horrible gobbling neigh came from his lips.

Red saddlecloth, head trappings of bronze and red enamel. Gold bridle. Gold bit.

Sharp spikes on the bit: cut deep into the bloodied mouth.

Saddle sores open oozing.

"That's better. That's better than better: that's best. Now I think it, a dead horse is far better than a living horse. Far less work."

The woman pulled her hood up to shadow her face. And Kanda almost wanted to cry out to her not to hide such beauty from their eyes. Too fearful to shout her rage – but how dark the night was without sight of that lovely queen's face.

"You see what could have been? Think how fine you would have looked! But it's too late now; I've found a better horse than you, I'm afraid. How fine he is! A stallion!"

The woman pulled herself up lightly into the saddle. The raw flesh of the dead beast stained her hands and her cloak red. The horse stamped gilded hooves. Yellow flowers grew up thick. "Such a pity," the woman said to Kanda. "There's a city not far from here we could have visited together, fine and fair, a great city filled with good fine things. Anything the heart might desire you can admire there, in fact! Many fine good rarey things. Cups and plates and bowls and blankets, everything a family might need. Cakes and capes and bedcovers and knives for butchering meat. A crown made for a king who never wore it. A sword that killed a dragon – but the sword's useless, just a lump of metal, that sword is. A ship made of gold, too heavy to sail in. A ship made of silver that will never sink. A broken pot, a broken heart, a broken wind. So many rarey things! Babies' clothes and babies' bottles. Babies' shrouds and babies' coffins. Love philters to catch a husband so he'll love you forever. Potions to grant eternal youth.

"So many fine things."

She waved. Kicked the horse to walk. It moved stiffly, its body cracked and tore until it was used to walking on all fours. "Well, goodbye then."

The dogs slunk off behind her. She took the horn from her belt, blew it, kicked the horse to a gallop. The dogs howled, ran at the horse's heels. The horse galloped faster, trying to escape them.

Calian fell to the ground. Bleeding from both arms and from her throat. Kanda let out a breath and roared. Sal sank to the ground weeping.

Dark and cold, a thin waning moon, a starving moon, showing through thin ragged clouds. Beginning to rain. The river rushing bleak.

They got up at last, helped each other up. Walked back down the droveway toward Amraen's village, all three of them silent. It was coming on to dawn when at last they reached the village gates. Pink softness just touching the east and hidden, only the scent in the air, the sense of it, a bird calling because it knew the dawn was near. The village walls loomed up vast in the dark, it might be a city there with great towers and bastions. Movement in the field near the wall, something white there. Calian whimpered.

"It's all right, Calian mine, it's just...just cows."

Calian whimpered worse, and Sal made a noise like the bird.

"No, it's sheep. That boy's sheep."

All three had been shaking. All three trembled and laughed. The sheep, insulted in the way sheep often can be, bleated at them.

"You wait, sheep, you'll be mutton soon, you can stop trying to scare my poor children," Kanda said. "Concentrate on getting fat."

The sheep bleated again and a friend joined in. Kanda had a sudden panic they'd wake the geese and then there'd be a chorus.

Which might have meant someone woke up to open the gate. Because the gate was closed and barred from the inside, and no one heard when Kanda knocked at it.

This, also, had rarely happened to Lady Kanda of the Six of Roven. Or to Ikandera Thygethyn.

They knocked again. It was properly raining now. Heavily raining. Might be coming on for dawn but it didn't seem exactly a rapid coming.

Did you kill the ghost then?

Umm...not quite.... I mean.... It's gone. I think. So there's that.

She felt – honestly, she felt ready to lie down in the droveway and cry. The days of glory, the days of wonder, of power, of happiness, of towering, awesome strength. Days of joy. Days of bliss.

Find Roven? Rebuild…anything?

And no one came and no one came, and they had to sit in the mud outside the gates with water dripping down the back of their necks and off their noses. With the sheep and the horrible goosegirl's geese.

And that was the quest of the ghost at the ford, the first quest that Kanda and Calian the *Eagle* and Sal the *Shining* set out on.

CHAPTER TWENTY-TWO

So, at last, when you'd guess from the lightening of the sky a little that the sun had risen and the rain had soaked through three cloaks and three tunics and three undershirts and Kanda and Calian had run out of curse words and Sal had started to look frankly alarmingly cold and ill – someone noticed them outside the gate. It wasn't like they'd been knocking and hoping and shouting for someone to open the gate, oh no. Like a bloody siege, Kanda thought. Be quicker and less painful to construct a battering ram against this wretched gate! You'd think, maybe, girls, your father might be wondering where we've got to, be hanging about waiting for us.

Easier than some other things to think about. Praise this cursed gate!

So, at last, the gate was opened. Tal the guardsman and Dellet all apologies, *we didn't hear you, you should have shouted, we bar the gates every night, we thought you'd be back later, we thought you'd be back earlier, we didn't think.*

Did you kill it? Did you kill it?

Did you see it, at least?

"It won't be a trouble to you any longer," Kanda said carefully. The wait had given her time to think of what to say to various people, at least.

"You killed it?" said Tal, awed. "The ghost?"

"It's gone," Kanda said. She half expected Calian to start up telling everything, but even Calian closed her mouth on the words. Even Calian – Calian was like a drowned rat with shadows big as mountains under her eyes. Need. To. Go. To. Bed. Need. To. Sleep. Mum. Sleepwalking to the guesthouse, pulling off wet dog-slobber mud-slobber bloodied clothes. Wrap Sal in blankets, then wrap Sal in more blankets, then watch her drink something hot. Dellet beginning to ask what had happened. Kanda saying, "Not now, Dellet." Then the girls were tucked up sleeping.

Kanda sat and stroked Calian's muddy hair and stroked Sal's white hair.

Calian whispered in her sleep, "Don't do that, Mum. It's annoying."

"You should be sleeping too, Kanda," Dellet said. He said after a moment, "Was it…as bad as you look like it was?"

"I have to talk to Amraen first," Kanda said. "Tell him. His kingdom – he has that right."

Dellet said in a low voice, "They barred the door here last night, Kanda. I sat up all night watching for you. But they must have thought I was sleeping. And they—" He shook his head. "They barred the guesthouse door from the outside."

He said after a moment, "So I barred the door from the inside." He looked at Kanda, they looked at each other, and there was a new kind of wisdom in Dellet's eyes that Kanda had not seen there before and wished she did not have to see. "The village is almost empty, Kanda. The children and the older people are all gone. There are new-made spears piled in Amraen's hall."

Rain-soaked. Dog-bitten. Bone-tired. Heart-broken. Thus crowned, thus hung with garlands, thus rang the praise song with voices raised. Thus Ikandera Thygethyn, wroth and raging, strode like flood and fire and famine into King Amraen's mighty kingly well-made hall. The throne there on its dais, behold that kingly seat of power! The wolfskin, sign of strength and cunning, such a mighty sword arm, with one killing stroke our king so kingly killed that killing beast! They trembled, throne and dais and wolfskin, the timbers of hall and throne and dais shook like young gale-uprooted saplings. The wolfskin howled. A fearful howl! Scrabbled; tried, dead and motheaten even before Amraen found it, to scramble down from the wall. No swords hanging there on the walls beside that wolfskin, no spears, no shields; hastily cleaned, repaired, resharpened, they hung at men's hips, a new, unfamiliar, frightening weight. The swords trembled with fear in their scabbards, the spears and the shields rattled with fear like knocking knee bones. Six warriors stood in the hall at their king's pleasure. Near cacked themselves with fear when Ikandera Thygethyn threw open the door, marched in.

Limped in. Squelched in.

"My lady queen Ikandera Thygethyn...." Amraen, white with terror, the look in his eyes howling and scrabbling to get away worse than the wolfskin.

Kanda shouted, "You thought a ghost could kill me? A ghost?"

Kanda said, her voice cracking, "You wanted me to die?"

Fire ran across the walls, leapt the hall's rafters. Fire and blood, running, pouring, dancing across floor and roof and walls. The warriors stood cut open into pieces, their guts and their brains and their blood pouring out.

Amraen fell to his knees before Kanda. His face grinding against the beaten floor.

"Kill me now, my lady queen. I am ready now. Kill me. Kill us all. I should have known there was no escaping."

The wound opening on his neck where her black sword cut deep.

What—?

Amraen—?

Why—?

What—?

Babbling.

Nothing that makes sense.

"Kill me. Kill us. Please. Please."

Be still! Be silent! Not another word will you speak! If you say – another word—

Amraen—?

I—

What—?

She saw it then. At last.

What should have been the most obvious thing in the world.

Do you remember a village with a spring, Amraen? He knew what she would do here: the same destruction she had dealt so often in those years when he was one of her captains. Kill all who lived here. Delight in the killing.

A tiny bitter cold laugh: use her bare hands to tear down the houses.

Not honor, Amraen offered her. He feasted and praised and groveled to her out of blind fear. *Walk with me, my lady queen, honor me, let me show you my kingdom, the fields and the trees will be honored for you to look at them.* Meanwhile in the village behind her all was chaos, spears readied, shields readied, defenses prepared, *get the children out to safety, Jeha. Flee, anywhere, I don't know where, just go, we will hold here, die here, you try to get the children a little more time to live.*

There's a ghost down by the river, my lady queen, only you can kill it, save us, help us, please, I beg! They watch me go, hope against hope that it will kill me, kneel beseeching all the powers of the world that it will. *Another few hours it will grant us at least, while she's walking there, we can get the children and the vulnerable away, even one more hour is one more hour to live, if we're lucky she might come back tired and wounded…bar the gate, pile high the weapons, be ready, a few more hours we can look at the stars and the clouds and each other's faces…just get the children and the old people away from here and hidden before she returns.*

Kanda drew breath to let out a great howl. The sky rang with her grief, the sun was made black. Like ripples from a stone thrown, like a bronze bell that sounds to warn of great danger, so her grief rang on and on. When the echoes of her cry had faded at last long and cold like the brilliance of a winter sunset, Kanda held out her right hand to Amraen.

"You do not need to fear me, you do not need to flee with your children, you do not need to ready your weapons, Amraen! I swear it! See my right hand here, my war hand, I hold it out to you. Take it, Amraen, you who were once my companion in red slaughter. May my hand wither dead and useless, should I raise but my little finger against any who dwell in this kingdom. May my hand fall from my wrist."

She unbuckled her sword belt, threw belt and sword down onto the floor before him.

Amraen cowered away, crawled on his belly away from the sword as if it would leap of its own accord to strike him.

"Yes, yes, as you said, as you wish it, my lady queen, yes! I will proclaim it, my lady queen, my lady Ikandera Thygethyn, I will proclaim to all my people, that no one is to think of danger, all are safe, all is well. Today will be another day of feasting in honor of the lady queen Ikandera Thygethyn not only for my warriors but for everyone in the village. All the children in the village especially, all the children in the village, in my kingdom, will come to the feast. They will be lined up before you, sing your praise." Croaked it out, poured out all he had to try to placate her, crouched already dead and bloodied in the raw mud. As a man offers all that he has and more before a shrine-stone, when the harvest has failed and his child taken sick. "Whatever you want, whatever, anything, everything, yes, yes!"

"No! I swore it! The first thing I said to you when you knew me and greeted me – that I would not harm you or anything of yours. A supplicant, I called myself, begging for your kindness; if you had not recognized me, that is all I would have been to you." She shouted, "I swore it, Amraen!"

Amraen said, very slowly and very quietly, he was terrified and sick and did not want to speak but it ran out of him vile like piss and shit and vomit, "I thought you lied, my lady queen."

CHAPTER TWENTY-THREE

Always indeed Ikandera Thygethyn is lying and breaking her promises. Not one promise she makes, it seems, is she able in the end to keep.

She did lie, Amraen, when she promised that she would not harm you.

For did she not say also, Amraen, that you would do her no harm in return?

CHAPTER TWENTY-FOUR

Thus word was sent to Jeha to bring the children back from wherever she had smuggled them away to; the sick and the old and the weak came creeping back; Jeha took off her armor, put on her blue kirtle, rolled up her sleeves to help bake and cook. "Mum packed us loads of food, and clothes, and Gya's doll," Wyn said, "she said we had to go away with Aunty Jeha, we had to go away into the woods…." He groped for it, old enough to know exactly why they were to be sent to hide in the wild wood, young enough to say it straight out except that…Kanda thought, hoped, that it was except that he liked her and had never imagined she could do him harm. "Anyway, we went but – we came back again," he said. "Which is lucky, because Calian said she'd teach us how to juggle. And Mum said Calian was too old to go to the woods."

"I didn't know Calian could juggle," Kanda said.

"Calian can juggle two pinecones." And then his face closed up in terror and he backed away from her, as if she would kill him for disagreeing about Calian's juggling skills.

Thus in the king's hall knives were set into the food, drink was poured into the cups, the floor was strewn with sweet rushes, the benches were crowded with more people than ever sat to food and drink there before, so crowded was the hall of King Amraen that four people sat in each place, four people ate from each plate, drank from each cup, and each was in the finest clothes and the finest jewels from the king's treasure house. A feast, to celebrate Ikandera Thygethyn the hero, who had driven away the ghost! A victory feast! Praise her! Glory! Raise a poem, a paean, chant her name! But the people in the hall all watched Kanda without looking at her, and the fear was on them, and they were gray and thin as shadows as they ate. Kanda's sword hung on the wall beside the wolfskin, above the king's throne that Kanda sat upon. She had not picked her sword up from the floor where she had dropped it.

The servants had gone to the storeroom to find it filled with twice and three times as much as before the first feast. The goosegirl and the shepherd boy were almost in despair trying to manage the number of geese and sheep. "More apples!" Calian sang. "With no bruises on them!" "Twice as much ale?" Dellet groaned. "Why, Kanda? Please, no." And honey in the crock that was scented with pine and heather, some already brewed into strong mead; and cobnuts with shells brown as cows' backs and flesh white as cows' milk; and fruits such as no one in that hall had before seen; and salt meat, and smoked meat, and fresh meat, for some like salt meat, and some like smoked meat, and some like fresh meat, and some like fish and some like cheese and some like eggs, and all must have their preferences at such a blessed feast. But the people in the hall sat like warriors sit on the night before a slaughter. But the people in the hall sat like captives when the city has fallen. But the people in the hall sat as a man sits when the harvest has failed and his child has died and there is nothing left. They ate, they crammed the food down for fear Kanda would be angry if they left it. They poured the drink down for fear. Hot fat ran greasy down their fingers, stained their faces; honey made their lips gleam gold. The mead was sweet with no bitter aftertaste. But the drink did not bring them joy, and the food did not give them strength. No songs, no laughter, no flirting and foolery. No speech. Kanda sat on the king's chair and he waited on her, he was gray and bent and too attentive. Kanda longed to dance, lift her cup in homage to king and kingdom: *I drove out the ghost! Blessings, luck, many feasts!* Instead she sat still and sorrowing, held her cup without drinking from it.

Look at me, she wanted to shout, the scab here on my wrist where a bramble scratched me, the thin white line of a burn on my thumb from a cook pot I put on the fire then forgot somehow was hot. Mud under my nails, dung under my nails, dry skin on my elbows like warts. A farmer's wife, a mother, stinking of cow shit! Look at me with my sagging breasts and my gray hair! Amusing! Disgusting! Thus Geiamnyn and Ysarene had once taunted her, for they had seen her for what she longed to be. But no one else would ever again see her as she longed to be.

Sal sat to eat with a face Kanda recognized, for it was the face Sal had worn at her wedding to Geiamnyn. Calian sat to eat as in a nightmare, tears ran down her face. She stared around her. "I don't understand, Mum...." Dellet sat hunched with the face he had worn when she told him the truth of her past. He understood.

A good spring time for questing, she had thought when she woke in the bothy to green wild-garlic stinking sunbeams. All the lushness of the spring all damp and green and growing, the onrushed overrun unfurling that the spring sun brings. Plunged into the greenness, snorted and wallowed and near-drowned in growing green stink.

Kanda, who helped build a house for a baby! Wheat, fruit, flowers, blessings, luck, she had granted, she who trampled out magic with her dancing feet!

If I returned to Lela's village now, Kanda thought, Lela would kneel at my feet in the cold mud and her throat would open red. She had felt the air and the earth and herself change, the light change, the world change, when she stepped out of the circuit of Lela's village, for Lela's kind village had held a magic as powerful as any magic of Kanda's, for it had let her pretend that she was not Ikandera Thygethyn. If she returned – but she could never return to Lela's village, if she tried it would be better for her if the marsh were to swallow her up.

Ah, Kanda, the clouds gather, the storm builds thicker and darker in the west. The sun is thin, weak, defeated. *I will drive the sun down from the sky! I will drive the moon down! I will hobble them with ropes!* That is what Ikandera Thygethyn would sometimes say. *Such a great destruction I will work that there will be only a scar where the sun should be!*

The people at the feast sat and walked and ate and drank, and the marks of their death were upon them. Their bodies were rent with their death wounds, they stepped over their own corpses as they served the meat and the drink. Jeha who had whisked Dellet into the dance in a swirl of blue like a kingfisher: her face was ashen. Jeha who wore a sword and good leather armor, strong and bright: Jeha was too afraid to look at Kanda, the blood where Kanda would kill her ran from her heart, stained her blue dress. Ylil and Wyn, sweet bull-calf boys almost ready to be warriors, even they cowered with the other children, cried, were too afraid to eat but too afraid she would kill them in anger if they did not eat, they could not eat for they were both slain with gaping throats.

A whole barrel of apples I made for you, Ylil, Wyn!

Kanda called to Jeha. "Come here, Jeha. Look at me." Looked long at Jeha as the woman stood before her trembling. "You can't think I would harm your son, Jeha?"

The woman only stared at the ground. You see him already dead at your hand, Lady Ikandera Thygethyn, and I see him, we both know that you have killed children before.

"I wished you luck and a bountiful harvest, Jeha! We drank together, clashed cups. Jeha: yesterday my daughter spent the morning playing with your son! You laughed with me only yesterday about my husband's aching head."

Finally, Jeha spoke. Her voice was a whisper, a withered horrid thing. "That was before my lord king told me what you are, my lady queen." A long silence. Jeha, Kanda thought, but Jeha, you are everything I long to be. And perhaps then Jeha felt those unspoken words, for she raised her head, her eyes were warrior's eyes, as fierce as Calian's eyes, even, almost, were Jeha's eyes then as she spoke. Loud, slow, clear, her voice ringing around the hall rich as music, she spoke.

"Better the crops fail, the cattle die in the fields, now I know what you are, Ikandera Thygethyn," Jeha said. "My son was playing yesterday with your daughter because I was too afraid of what you would do if I stopped him. He was playing with your daughter to keep her occupied and keep you occupied and unwary while we readied our swords to defend ourselves from you. Greatly I long to kill you, Ikandera Thygethyn, monster, accursed, enemy of all that lives. If I did not fear for my son, I would fight you now, knowing as I do that you would surely defeat me.

"But I fear too much for my son. So I serve your children meat and bread and ale, and wait for you to kill us all." She raised the jug of ale she held. "Let us all drink a health to the glory of the great warrior Ikandera Thygethyn! Let us rejoice that she has so blessed and honored us – that she has chosen to kill us!"

All raised their cups, drank deep. The cups were filled with their own blood, the meat on the table was their own flesh. The hall was burning around them. They waited only for the blow itself to be dealt. The hall was the killing ground when the battle is over – before every battle the warriors see it, see the dead already piled there, see their own wounds and pain and death. The wolfskin howled on the wall. There was no sun, there was no moon, there was no sky and no earth and no wind and nothing outside the hall. "Kill us. Kill us. Kill us," the people begged Kanda. "Kill us. Kill us. Kill us. End this." Fire and blood ran through the hall, the walls burned, the roof burned.

Kanda thought: there is no blood here, no wildfire burns. A heath, low-banked for warmth, fresh rushes on a clean floor. But all the tears that ever I shed for my children, all the tears in the world that every parent has ever shed, could not wash away that blood, or put that killing fire out.

Calian gave a cry. Threw down her plate and her cup. Leapt to her feet. "Enough of this!"

Calian's eyes were wide as huge round shields; in her eyes eagles were flying. "Enough!" Calian cried. "You are all cowards and ungrateful and mockers. Why do you hate us so much? What have we done to you?

"We are great warriors! We killed the monsters!" Calian shouted.

The people in the hall drew back in terror, sobbed, the stink came where some of the children wet themselves. A howl of fear rose. Like a great wave, it broke over Calian. Kanda saw it as a real thing crashing down over Calian.

Calian's sword crashed down on the table, smashing plate, cup, wood. Her hair stood out from her head like eagles' feathers, or like an eagle's spread wings. Her skin was bronze, and it was made of bronze, nothing could harm Calian. Her hands were clenched like eagle's claws; in those claws she held her sword.

"We kill the monsters!" Calian shouted.

The droveway and the dogs and the dead man and the witch woman: *what's that hiding in the shadows? What's that there following us? I'll kill her, Mum. Kill her, Mum!* Fear, and wonder at her mother's powers, the fierceness in her, she who had battled monsters – and such anger in her, women, dogs, ghosts, wonders, confused, angry, disbelieving, frightened. She had slept, in Lela's village, been made a child again merely, her right hand, her war hand, ah, through that long dull winter peace her right hand too like her mother's must have burned and itched. In the dark of the night, terrified, she had fought a monster and been defeated, the shock in her, the horror, that she had lost so easily, come so close to death at the hands of such a monstrous thing. *That woman! Who is she?* She wore a sword at her hip, so beautiful that sword, so strong that sword that had indeed cut down evil monsters; always a sword hungers, begs to be drawn, to be used.

And Calian was a child, overwhelmed, frightened, stuffed full of sweets, exhausted, fed up with people ruining things.

"I'll kill you all!" Calian screamed.

Screams. Panic. Running, shoving. But the doors were choked with dead bodies. The doors were closed and barred. Fire licked at the doors where the hall burned after this great destruction. There were no doors to get out of the hall. Amraen screamed his grief, then he cried in a great voice like a trumpet, "Warriors! To me!" The power shone in his face also. For all that his kingdom was one village it was a kingdom and he was a king, thus the power was in him now to defend his people. "To me!" he shouted, his voice was the war song that gives men courage in the darkness, that urges men joyfully to stand and fight. His power was reflected in all his people's faces. They drew out swords and spears and helmets from where they were heaped about the hall. Ten, twenty, thirty warriors, and more, and more – all turned on Calian.

Calian raised her sword to meet them.

With a howl, Kanda caught up her own sword. It sang in her hand. It had fought dragons, killed monsters, never was her sword sated, always the joy ran in the sword at the wonder of killing. She shouted, "Sal! Dellet! Get out, get away!" Tried to fight without killing, shelter her husband and daughter, push her way to Calian. Calian was so close to her. They had been seated side by side. But the crush of people pushed closer and closer around Kanda, striking her with swords and spears and knives. She had to strike back, harder, harder, until she too like her daughter was killing. Fear, now. Anger. Trying, failing, to reach Calian. Harder, faster, without thinking. The blood flew around her. Bodies began to pile at her feet. Slaughter choked her breath.

"Calian!"

Couldn't see her daughter.

"Calian!" Kanda shouted.

All warriors here, men, women, children, all armed. Swords, spears, knives, woodworking axes, hands, teeth. Two nights and two days, they had been preparing themselves to fight the monster Ikandera Thygethyn. The red rage was there in the hall. They had cowered, readied themselves, waited knowing Kanda would be their death. She was here in the hall trapped with them: they would not stop killing. They fought Kanda, threw themselves at Kanda, rejoiced in fighting her. Even as they died they rejoiced in fighting that monster Ikandera Thygethyn.

A woman came against her with her knife very bloody. Calian's blood? The woman stabbed at Kanda. Kanda had no choice but to strike the woman. Tried, so hard, not to strike the killing blow. But she was Ikandera Thygethyn, fifty warriors and fifty camp followers and fifty horses had fallen once to one blow from her sword, and that not the strongest blow she had in her life struck. A youth came against her with their fists grazed from hitting. Calian's face, he had struck? The youth punched at Kanda. Kanda had no choice but to punch him. Tried, so hard, not to strike the killing blow – but she was Ikandera Thygethyn, a man's head had leapt from his neck and flown three miles into the sky once when she punched him. And even that not the strongest blow she had in her life struck. Thus she stepped over two corpses, trying to find Calian.

She saw Calian. Dead heaped around her. Back to a wall. Very bloody. Wounded. Four mighty warriors came at Calian all together, a sword aimed at her heart, a sword aimed at her bowels, a spear and a knife aimed at her throat. Calian struck just as all four warriors struck her. Twisted, ducked, stabbed, slashed. Four bodies fell. One had no head left on it. One had its right arm cut off. Two swords and a spear and a knife lay at Calian's feet and four warriors lay ruined at Calian's feet. One for the weapon, one for wielder, one for her anger, one for her fear. She howled somewhere between joy and horror, attacked a woman before the woman could move to use her blade. The sword in Calian's hand was alive, so beautiful.

The joy that ran in Kanda. To see her daughter madly slaughtering. Such a mighty warrior, Calian my child! A greater warrior even than I was, Calian is!

"Calian!" Shoved her way through toward the girl. Pushing, shoving, killing; to get people out of her way; to reach her daughter to stop her daughter from killing.

"To me! Calian!"

Through the red rage in her mind, the girl heard her. Kanda saw her hesitate, lower her sword a hairsbreadth. Eyes opened wide. With a roar, Jeha threw herself at Calian. Her sword was alive as Calian's sword was alive. The most trusted of Amraen's warriors: yes: Kanda saw in the woman's stance, the woman's blade, the woman's bitter eyes, that Jeha too was a great warrior.

I'm sorry, Kanda wanted to say to Jeha. But Jeha's sword came down, struck, was stained with Calian's blood. Calian reeled, slumped down against the wall. Because her mother had called to her and she had listened, she had lowered her guard enough for Jeha to strike. Again, Jeha raised her sword high to come down on Calian.

Kanda shouted in her war voice: "Stop!"

"She does not mean it!" Kanda shouted.

Jeha's sword came down on Calian. Kanda leapt, met it, struck and struck and struck and struck. Jeha fell back and she was red and opened, a great warrior she was but she was nothing compared to Ikandera Thygethyn. She was but dead meat to Ikandera Thygethyn.

"Calian!" Kanda cried. The girl struggled. To fall wounded into the joy of *no longer killing*. To stand more brilliant in the wonders of *yet more I can kill*. "Stop, Calian!" The girl spun away from her, her face turned away, she was lost again in the mass of the fighting. A wall of swords pressed about Kanda.

She fought back. She did not try now to spare them. Swung about her left and right, with every stroke she killed at least one person. She killed so many her arms ached. Corpses tripping her feet. Her mouth was filled with blood. A long time since she had felt this grim pleasure in simple killing. She found herself beside Calian – there were so few people left in the hall that she could leap easily to stand beside Calian. Shoulder to shoulder the two warriors raised a final great destruction in the hall.

Amraen came at the two warriors. Once a warrior himself in Ikandera Thygethyn's own army. Not the best warrior, that man; but a thing he had learned well in Ikandera Thygethyn's army: the value of hanging back to see the best of his comrades kill the best of the enemy. Not the worst of things to learn. A king, and a king hangs back, does not hurl himself into the front ranks madly, a victory with a dead king at its head is worse than a defeat when the king lives. But a king, and thus he must defend his people, not for nothing should a king's sword be the best sword in his kingdom, not for nothing should a king's sword hang in pride of place in his hall. He grasped it from where it was hidden, leapt to face these two warriors now. His hand was weary on the sword hilt, long he had rested with his sword only hanging splendid in its dust in the hall. But he did not spare himself, gathered all his power to him, in this world of Ikandera Thygethyn's making a king has some true power in him, his sword too had a fire on its blade, his face too had the fire on it. He cried out as he struck. A great blow, a strong blow, a killing blow, he struck. Not only to hang back, he had learned in Ikandera Thygethyn's army: one death for the weapon and one death for the wielder, that blow was worth against any other than Ikandera Thygethyn, that blow would have cut out one man's heart and cut off another man's head. It opened a wound in Calian's shoulder. It cut a scratch as bad as a scratch from a bramble bush on Kanda's wrist.

The words he cried out as he struck were: "Stop! I beg you! Please!"

Red rage was in Kanda's head, she heard his words like the buzzing of a fly. She thrust her sword, Calian thrust her sword, such music their breathing and the sigh of the good metal, such music Amraen made as he cried out again as they struck, cried out his death cry! He was down beneath them, his blood spilled red. His blood spilled black and clotted, his blood hissed against their swords' flames.

Calian snorted, pleased.

Ah, that was good killing!

They moved together almost as one. Kanda had forgotten this also, the delight in fighting beside one she loved almost matched to her in strength and skill. They cast around the hall for more people to slaughter, it was a sorrow to them that there were few people left.

Another voice cried, "Stop! Please!"

Kanda heard it but did not understand what the words might mean. Not a fly buzzing, less than a fly.

The voice cried, "Stop this madness!"

Kanda heard it, but it was nothing.

The voice cried without words.

That, Kanda heard.

Hands of light, reaching – they grasped at Kanda's sword, tore it away. Enemies packed around her. Black light broke over her eyes.

She fell. Calian beside her screamed as Calian too was falling. Calian's sword – hands of black light grasped Calian's sword.

Everything stopped in the hall.

The dying stopped dying. The living stopped hiding and cowering.

Kanda stopped. Could not move.

Calian stood against a wall with her sword still raised. Calian was bruised and wounded, cut hands, cut shoulder, cut face.

Sal stood in the center of the hall. The black light blazed around her, shone from her hands and face. Dellet like a child held safe in her arms, pressed close in her protection. She turned great eyes on her sister Calian.

Calian's face had the wonder in it. I have seen…. I have fought…. Ah, wondrous things! Better even than fighting the monsters, this killing! So many I have killed. The same bright tremor as after the birth of Lela's baby. Did you see? What deeds I have done! Kanda was frozen and rooted, but Calian moved her right arm, struggled to raise the sword. Stared about her looking for more to kill.

"Calian," Sal said. "Stop."

Calian stared at her hand around her sword hilt.

Then she threw the sword down, fell to her knees, slumped over the bodies of her victims, let out a scream.

The four of them alone in the rubble of Amraen's hall. Dead bodies heaped around them. Calian soaked in blood from her hair to the soles of her feet, her face masked in blood. Sal with her arms protectively around her father, holding her father like there was no beginning and no end to them. Sal with the black light slowly fading away from her hands and her face. Dellet hidden. Refusing. Kanda looking from one child to the other, her eyes flicked from Sal to Calian to Sal to Calian. She could not move at all beyond the darting of her eyes, so powerful was Sal's magic. A sweet relief, that she could not move, for there was nothing she could do.

But she looked from one to the other of her daughters and she thought: ever since my daughters were born, I have hoped somewhere in the depths of my heart that they would do such things.

CHAPTER TWENTY-FIVE

But at last Sal's binding magic must fade. Enough at least for Kanda to move her arms and legs. Kanda stepped one two long vast steps to Calian. Like two steps over the edge of a cliff. Bent, pulled her daughter Calian to her feet. Harshly, roughly, dragged her daughter to her feet. Blind eyes turned to her: I don't understand. What happened, Mum? I had a dream I was killing.... And: we can fix it, Mum, Calian's eyes said. Kanda remembered well that feeling. Like smashing a plate, and you didn't mean to throw the plate, and suddenly it's broken, and you think, you think, I didn't mean to, and you think, well, but, we can, I mean, we must be able to fix the plate.... When they built the longhouse a pole had split in half just as they got it steady. Everyone had roared with disappointment, then started work on a replacement pole. Calian's eyes turned just so to Kanda. You can fix it, Mum. You can fix it, Mum?

"Sal...." Kanda said. Her elder daughter tried to come toward them, but Dellet clutched her and whimpered in terror, Sal could not move.

"Sal," Kanda said again, and it took all her strength to say it. To ask her daughter to mend this thing that she, Kanda, had done.

"Sit down, Dad," Sal said to Dellet. Eased him down gently, loving as a mother with a child; he sat in the rubble of the hall with corpses knee-high around him. Looked at the dead without seeing.

"Sal," Kanda said, she looked at her daughter with the hope somehow.... You can make this better, Sal, you are a healer and a power, the light in your face is so brilliant it blinds me like black night.

You can...you must....

Sal shook her head.

Ylil's body and Wyn's body, and Jeha, and Tal, and poor wretched Amraen, and so many whose names Kanda had never known. The goosegirl and the shepherd boy, look, there – they had died hand in hand. Two lovely days, two lovelier nights, they had had before they died. Better for them if they had had two sad nights and two sadder days, and still been alive. Beneath the blood, the hall floor was still stained with the fruits of Ikandera Thygethyn's blessings. And she thought then – it is well known the grass grows greener, richer, in a place where blood has been shed.

I was only trying to protect Calian! Kanda wanted to shout to the world, and to Sal. They were hurting her. I had to fight them.

Together, we can fix this, three women of great power, Kanda thought, we can, surely. Such power we had, Calian and I, to do this!

Don't look like that, Sal. Like it's hopeless.

It's so hard, Kanda wanted to say to Sal. So, so hard, Sal, being Ikandera Thygethyn. And so easy, too, Sal. Being Ikandera Thygethyn. You saw, just now, how rich and joyful it is, how easy it is.

And Sal had been married to Geiamnyn. She understood. A little, as much understanding as could be fitted into a mote of dust and less than that, Sal understood; even that was a comfort to Kanda.

Outside the hall, a dog barked.

Two dogs.

The doors of the hall flew open. Two dogs ran in. Huge beasts, bigger than warhorses, solid built with thick gray coats. One was marked with white, one was marked with brown. Each had a silver collar around their neck.

They ran around and around the hall barking and whining, sniffing at the blood. They ran together, shoulder to shoulder. They stopped at the throne, sat flanking it.

They looked at Sal and whined. They looked at Calian and growled.

A woman walked in through the open doors of the hall. Slowly, she walked down the length of the hall. She looked about her with interest. Stopped to look at some of the bodies, walked on. She held her skirts raised to stop the blood staining them, stepped carefully to avoid getting blood on her shoes. She did not look at the four people in the hall.

She was tall and slender, as lovely as blossom. Young as any maiden in the halls of Roven, young and fair like the dawn sun. Her skin was the rich dark bronze of stones-in-water, her hair hung loose and pale like a cloud to her slender waist. She looked like a spring meadow when the flowers are bursting up through the dark earth that shines rain-jeweled, the grass hisses silver in the wind of first morning and the light falls in silver beams. The children wake early, slip out into the wondrous newborn world to play, they run through the long grass making tracks behind them, silver tracks in the damp grass; they gamble like lambs and like moon-calves and like young hares, and then the lambs and the calves come up to play with them, they dance through the grass that grows as high as children's waists, children's shoulders, in the new spring the grass and the whitelace grows so quickly they can see it growing, they hide themselves green and playing away. Earlier still the lovers have woken bathed in the morning, made their kisses, drunk their love and kisses deep with the dawn on their lips. The mist rises from the river, blurs the meadows; the birds sing. A thousand colored flowers, ten times a thousand, yet in the pale light the flowers are pale and silver as the fading stars. First butterflies and bees to sip the new flowers' nectar, the drowsy bees are waking to make their honey to be smeared on newborn babies' lips. So fair! So fair, so delicate, so lovely a place! And this woman was as fair – no, this woman was fairer even than the spring meadows of the River Wenet. Her gown was white silk embroidered with birds and flowers, she wore bracelets of gold at both of her wrists and rings of gold on each of her fingers, a necklace of silver and red rubies hung close around her slender throat. The air was silver around her, as the air is made silver and sweet in the meadow as the dew rises in the dawn sun. Where she walked, yellow flowers grew up in her footsteps and spread across the floor of the hall. Over the dead, over the blood, her flowers grew until the dead were hidden and all was only beauty and yellow blossom and cool silver mist and light.

One slight mark in her beauty: a long scar ran across her forehead.

When the woman reached the throne, she sat down on it, carefully arranged her skirts. Finally she looked at the four people in the hall, and her eyes flashed one moment with hatred. Her fingers curled with hatred, her nostrils flared. The dogs growled, raised their hackles.

"Camryth," the woman said in her sweet voice. "Mannan. Stop growling. You are frightened, I know. Look what these people have done: you are right to be frightened. All they want to do is kill, these horrible ones! All they ever think of. But I told you, my dear good dogs, I promised you: I won't let them hurt you like they killed these poor people here."

A long time, not Kanda nor Sal nor Calian nor Dellet could speak. Not one word from the mouths of those four. The woman sat on the throne with her dogs one at her right hand one at her left.

"Like they killed me," the woman said.

"Stop this," Kanda said at last.

"Morna, my daughter, my love, my flower. Stop this. Please."

CHAPTER TWENTY-SIX

"You've finally recognized me, then?" Morna said.

"I've known who you are since I first saw you at the ford, Morna," Kanda said.

"Oh, that's a lie, Mother!" Morna said.

"I knew you, Morna. In my heart, I knew you."

"Oh, that's two lies!"

"I…." Kanda said in despair, "I killed you, Morna my love. You were dead and gone. Not even a body to bury was left to me, I could not raise a grave over you to mourn you, Morna my own love. How could I think to see you again? In every child and every young woman I have seen since I lost you, I have seen your face, Morna my love. But you were dead and gone."

Morna laughed. "And you, Sal? You, Calian? And you?"

Calian said nothing. Her head was still bent, she saw only her own bloody hands. Dellet said nothing. He clutched Sal as an infant clutches a parent, his face hidden in the folds of her dress.

Sal's eyes met Morna's. Sal who had gone down into the dark to marry that monster Geiamnyn; willingly, happily, Sal had gone into the dark as Geiamnyn's bride in exchange for Morna, but Morna had refused to be rescued, *I like it here with Uncle Geiamnyn*, Morna had said. Sal's eyes met Morna's, and Morna should have turned her eyes away for shame at what Sal had done for her sake. But it was Sal who turned her eyes away, Sal who wept for shame at what she had done.

"I…." Sal said, and there was nothing she could say beyond that. "I…. I…."

"Oh, shut your stupid croaking," Morna said. "I wish your mouth was still sewn up with thread." Sal opened her mouth, no words came out, and then she could not open her mouth at all, she could only stare at Morna with the tears running down her cheeks and blood on her lips where her husband Geiamnyn had once sewn them shut with gold thread.

"So much for you," said Morna. She said in her sweet voice, "I look around this hall, I look to the east, to the north, to the south, to the west, I look in the darkest corners, in the eaves, in the high rafters, in the space beneath the threshold where nothing is buried. I see four here who did not know their own Morna when she stood before them and spoke to them."

Her lovely hands gripped the dogs at the nape of their necks, her lovely nails dug in, made the dogs growl. "I look at the east, I look to the north, I look to the south, I look to the west, I sit in death and in ruin, I see four who have lived happily despite their Morna being dead. I look all around me and I see four who could have been in a city full of wonders and treasures as I told them, but instead I see—

"Look what you did, Mother, sisters. And *that woman*, and *evil*, and *curse her* – you call me?"

That's true, Morna, Kanda tried to say.

"You were dead!" Dellet cried out. He could not be accused of being anything but a *good man*; Kanda thought with a bitter laugh: truly indeed he is only…*nothing*, and that is a good thing for him to be.

"I saw you die, Morna," Dellet said. "I saw you lying dead, and then when I looked for you your body was gone." He said in a terrible voice that Kanda had never heard before or since that day Morna died, a voice she had not known that good man Dellet had in him, "I thought you were dead, I have mourned you every moment since that day, and all that time I should have known that you – you—"

"You should, yes," Morna said. She got to her feet, smoothed out her beautiful dress. The gold at her wrists and on her fingers glittered, flashed in the hall's dim light. She shook out her lovely hair, pale as elderflowers, fine as cobwebs, a great cloud of hair that fell to her slender waist. She was the fairest creature that Kanda had ever seen, far more beautiful than Kanda had ever imagined her child would be.

"None of you knew. Not one of you cared to see or look. But my father," Morna said, "he knew. He brought me back to life."

A light in Dellet's face, a smile, but then – confusion.

"Not you, stupid," Morna said. "The father I wish had been my father since I was born, the father who loves me far more than any of you here ever did – because he truly loves me, he brought me back to life."

"He?" Kanda said.

And then Dellet roared and howled and screamed and bit his hands and struck his head until the blood ran from his head and from his mouth.

Greatly it had pained that *empty* one her first husband that he could not have a child with his beloved wife Ikandera Thygethyn. Greatly it had pained Kanda that she could not give him the child he longed for. And that *empty* one her first husband, he had been hanged from a tree and drowned in the mire and dragged himself back to something like life.

But he's gone, Morna. I cut him down with my black sword, I cut him to rubble. I turned him into a toad, I scooped him up in a leather purse. A gray pebble soaked in my red blood, I put beside him, his own finger bone I put beside him. I sealed the purse tight with a hair from my own head. I threw the purse into a stream, the stream carried it away quickly into the waters of the lake Elelan Mere. The blood went to the stone and the stone went to the stream and the stream went to the lake. I set a binding upon the waters, that they would hold that *empty* one my first husband prisoner for a thousand years. Have a thousand years passed without my noticing? I am growing old and time passes quickly, quicker it seems the seasons come around one after the other rushing and my hair grows grayer and my children grow, a thousand years and a blink of an eye it might seem since you were last alive, Morna, and Sal is grown old and old in the blink of an eye until I do not remember her child face – but I do not think a thousand years have passed since that day.

But she had seen – try to remember – in the terrible blindness of grief that day she had seen – bloodied earth where Morna had fallen beneath her mother's sword, and a dried-up thing like a toad, clawing and mouthing at the earth, trying to grasp hold of something…?

And she had picked the toad up, disgusted, imprisoned it in a leather purse.

"You were there in my hands with him, Morna!" Kanda cried out. "I held you in my hands with him, and I cast you away into the lake with him!"

Morna said, "You did, Mother. Your hands held me – mother's cradling hands, often they had held me. Your hands shook with disgust, threw me away. I was weak and frightened, a killing wound to my body, a worse wound by far to my heart. You struck me down with your sword and killed me. You threw me into the lake and the waters of the lake drowned me.

"Such pain. I was so frightened. I was dead and dying. I was dying and dead.

"But my father saved me.

"Poor thing, he too was drowned and wounded. His heart too was broken by what you had done to him. But he held me in his arms to comfort me. He could not speak – that was Calian's doing! But he talked to me even so. He told me stories, told me how deeply he had longed for a child with you.

"'My daughter!' he said. 'My daughter Morna, my child, my love. I will be your father now, I will care for you as my own. You will want for nothing. Nothing, I promise, nothing will ever harm you again.' He showed me how to live again. Mother and father both, he is to me, for he took me from death back to new life.

"I was not bound by your magic, mother. A weak magic – it held my poor father, but it could not hold me. Three days and three nights I worked to free myself from that prison. As the sun rose on the fourth day, I stood on the dry earth on the shore of the lake Elelan Mere.

"I looked for you, Mother. I looked to the east, to the south, to the north, to the west. I saw many things. A squirrel in a tree, a gyrfalcon circling overhead, a white hind and a white hart and a white calf. A woman and a child living peacefully on a rich farm, and woman and child both were contented. But I could not see you. I called for you. When there was no answer, I called to you in the voices of birds and beasts and the voice of the autumn wind. You never heard me calling.

"I knew then that my father had spoken the truth.

"I reached down into the waters of the lake. A deep lake – but my hand reached easily to the bottom, touched your leather purse. The waters of the lake rose up then, your curse holding my poor father prisoner. I fought the water. I gathered myself, I drew up all my strength and power. I was only a little girl – four years old! All day I fought your curse on the shores of Elelan Mere. Your curse on my poor father was very strong. The water ran in steam over the mountain from the highest peak to the roots. All day I wrestled with your curse. Wrestled with the water. I could not break it to set him free.

"So I returned to him. Together we lived in a house I wrought at the bottom of the lake. He was a toad, tiny and weak, broken, hurting: I cradled him in my hands to give him comfort. I was a child, frightened, sorrowing: he held me to comfort me as any father might. I made a house for us, a fine house there in the dark inside your leather purse. Its walls were pebbles and fish bones and frog bones, its roof was water weeds. Pebbles and bones and rotten weeds were our beds, our chairs, our cups, our plates. Pebbles and bones and rotten weeds our food and our drink.

"'Thank you, my daughter,' my father said when he saw what I had done for him.

"In that house inside your purse at the bottom of the lake Elelan Mere – we lived. Happily, together, we lived. Though my father was weak and broken. These many years I have tended him and nursed him. He cannot speak still. He cannot walk, or eat, or drink, he cannot piss, without my help, poor wretch, after what you have done to him. But he taught me all that he knows. Beautiful things and wise things and sad things and secret things. And we were happy together for many years, in our house of bones inside your leather purse at the bottom of the lake.

"Time passed. I grew. A tall young woman, lovely with youthful freshness, I grew. 'You cannot live here forever, Morna my daughter,' my father said one day. 'This is no life for one such as you.' But he was my father, and he needed me, and I refused to leave him. Time passed, time passed, he begged me to leave him and make my way in the world, I refused to go. 'I will care for you, I cannot leave you here alone,' I said to him. 'A thousand years, your mother bound me here,' he said to me. 'I will not let you stay here a thousand years, you who are so fine and grown.'

"So I left him. Many tears we both shed that day. Easily, I freed myself from that prison. Three heartbeats, and I stood on the dry earth on the shore of the lake Elelan Mere.

"I looked for you, Mother. I looked to the east, to the south, the north, to the west – and I saw you. You and my-father-that-was and Sal and Calian. You too were building a house. You too were leaving that house with tears in your eyes at the parting. I called for you. I called and called, in the voices of birds and beasts and the voice of the spring wind.

"But you never heard me calling.

"And then I knew and I knew, and I knew yet again. He is not my father by blood, no – but he is my true loving father who gave me back my life after you had abandoned me.

"You were my father and mother in my first childhood, and I do not forget that. But now he is my father, and I love him as deeply as any child loves their parent."

CHAPTER TWENTY-SEVEN

Such silence as never should be heard. Be silent. Be still. Be still as the dead.

She doesn't mean it, Del-my-heart. Of course you're her father and she knows that. I was always jealous that she loved you more than me. She's just angry with us, you know how children are. Lash out, say these awful things they don't mean. When she says, she says you were her father in her first childhood, she says— She doesn't mean it, Del.

So still.

Such silence.

But I always thought, in my heart, that Calian was like his child. Not you, Morna.

Still as the dead are still. Silent as the dead.

CHAPTER TWENTY-EIGHT

"So now I've found you! All's well!" Morna said. But Morna looked around the hall and sniffed in disgust. "What a mess you have made here, Mother. And you, Calian. What a horrible stinking mess." There was a splash of blood on one dainty little green leather boot. "Ugh," Morna said, "look at that! You keep saying you don't like killing, Mother, but, oh, for someone who doesn't like killing – what a lot of things you seem to have killed."

One of the dogs was nosing something crumpled beneath a bench in the hall. "Camryth, don't do that!" Morna said. She looked closer at whatever it was that the dog was interested in. "Oh, Camryth, oh, look, not things, *people*, oh, not people, *children*, what a lot of children my mother and my sister have killed. And look how upset Calian is at what she's done."

Calian had not moved, she had not noticed Morna, she only stared at her bloody hands. "Stupid Calian," Morna said. "Doing such a thing and wanting her mother to make it right. And your husband, Mother: how sad he looks at what you and Calian have done. Broken his stupid heart, I think. Yet again.

"I did tell you. You should have listened to me. I said you'd find wonderful things if you came with me. Fine cities, fine halls – you know what hall I'm talking about – and I waited at the ford to lead you on! Beautiful things, all you are seeking and all your hearts long for. I told you! But look at this place you found instead!"

Morna walked down to the center of the hall. The dogs whined and milled around her. She frowned. "You'll get in the way. Outside with you, dogs. Go and mind my cows, guard my horse, that's what I brought you with me for. Those cows and that horse both – they wander and fall down dead if nobody watches them."

The dogs whined, she pointed, they growled at her but slunk away out of the hall.

"Right," said Morna. "Let's sort out this mess my mother and my sister have made."

Morna clapped her hands. The fire in the hearth had sunk low, been kicked and scattered by trampling desperate feet. Now when Morna clapped her hands the fire blazed up. The smoke was sweet-scented – applewood and pinewood. The firedogs had been knocked over; they righted themselves; they had been shaped like longhorned cattle; now they were shaped like dragons. The food for the feast had been cooking outside in the kitchens; now a huge bronze cauldron hung from a tripod above the fire. It boiled, steam rose from it, a savory smell of meat, but it was so huge and high, the tripod reaching almost to the rafters, the cauldron as tall as a man, it was so huge and high that its contents were hidden. "That's better," Morna said. "That's good and needed."

Again Morna clapped her hands. The tables in the hall righted themselves. Where they had been broken, they were mended. They were made of fine golden wood, well-polished, their legs were carved in the shape of men holding the tabletops above their heads. Shining white cloths covered the tables, worked with gold and silver embroidery, flowers, birds, leaves, in the patterns there were hidden curious peeping faces. The benches righted themselves, they were set with soft cushions. Bright hangings on the walls, green and blue and yellow and red. Fresh rushes and sweet herbs scattered on the floor. Wooden plates on the tables, running beasts and dancing people carved around their rims. Bronze cups for the lower tables, silver cups for the higher tables, gold cups for the king's table. Beautiful work: the bronze cups showed people fighting a battle, the silver cups showed people hunting wild birds, the gold cups showed people dancing. Jugs of dark wine, baskets of apples, platters of roast meat and wheat bread.

"That's good," Morna said. Then she seemed to think. "Wait. That's not right." Where Kanda had been seated, there was a horn cup of milk and a gold platter of roast meat and a silver platter of bread. "That's it, isn't it, Mother?" Morna said. "Or were the gold and silver platters the other way round? Can you remember?" She said with a smile, "That was a good day. I've never forgotten that day."

She looked at the bodies piled around the hall. Prodded one gently with her dainty foot. "Oh dear oh dear oh dear," said Morna. "All these poor dead things."

As she had said to the dead man at the ford, and as Kanda had once said to Dellet, Morna said sweetly and softly, "Get up, you people. How foolish you are, letting my mother and my sister kill you. Get up, come back to life, stop being dead, get back to your feasting.

"It's too fine a day to be dead, when you could be feasting."

The bodies in the hall stirred. Slowly, painfully, they began to sit up. Stand up. Their wounds healed. Blood ran up from the floor, ran back into their veins. Broken bones healed, rent flesh closed. Smooth clean skin, clean shining hair. No tears, no bloodstains on their clothing – and they were dressed in silks and furs. A gold arm ring on every man's right arm, a silver necklace or a gold necklace around every woman's throat. Even the children wore silk, precious metals, gems. Jeha wore a gown of blue more brilliant than any kingfisher, every shade of blue the eye could see was there in the skirts of her queenly dress. Ylil and Wyn were as brilliant as two young drakes in springtime, red tunics, blue leggings, green cloaks with silver clasps in the shape of leaves.

Amraen sat on his throne at the center of the feasting. His throne was made of gold, studded with red rubies and black pearls. His robe was cloth of gold, his mantel over it cloth of silver with black bear fur trim and gold embroidery a handspan deep. His crimson-dyed beard fell in two plaits to his waist. His boots were made of kidskin, they were as crimson as his beard, with buckles of gold. His belt was gold with a gold buckle in the shape of a boar's head, his cloak pin was set with a huge red stone. Five gold arm rings on his right arm. Five gold arm rings on his left. Rings on all his fingers. A silver crown on his head, a neck ring of gold thicker than a man's wrist at his throat. He looked ten years younger than he had been. His sword hung on the wall above his head, it was so big it would take four ordinary men to lift it and another four to draw it from the scabbard.

But Amraen was a king in his king's hall, with one hand easily (his left hand, easily!) he could draw his sword.

The piper Tal struck up a tune. The servants, dressed more finely than many lords and ladies in other kingdoms, went up and down the hall serving food and drink. The knives were set into the meat, the wine was drunk from the beautiful cups. Kanda sat at Amraen's right hand, Dellet sat at Amraen's left. Calian sat beside Kanda. Sal sat beside Dellet. Morna sat in the farthest end of the hall where the servants were sitting. The two dogs came back into the hall, and they lay at Morna's feet.

Wonders! A blackbird flew in through the open doors of the hall. A branch in its beak; the branch was made of diamonds. It flew three times around the hall, dropped the branch before Sal. It settled on the back of Dellet's seat. It sang. *Henket, henket, mare, mare, henket*, its song was: no one in that hall save Kanda could understand what it meant. A thrush flew in through the open doors of the hall. A branch in its beak; the branch was made of rubies. It flew three times around the hall, dropped the branch before Calian. It settled on the back of Kanda's seat. It sang. Nonsense, its song was: Kanda thought, almost, almost, that she understood its song but she could not understand it. The two birds flew out of the hall together, still singing and calling.

Wonders! A deer ran in through the open doors of the hall. Its eyes shot sparks. A wolf ran in through the open doors of the hall. Its tail was bright flame. Deer and wolf fought in the center of the hall by the hearth fire: the wolf snapped at the deer with its jaws, the deer kicked at the wolf. Where the deer was wounded – roses! Where the wolf was wounded – violets! Neither could conquer the other. They fought until the hall was knee-deep in flowers. They ran together out of the hall.

Wonders! The people in the hall ate and drank and talked and laughed, the platters were refilled with food, the jugs were refilled with drink. They had no memory of their fear of Ikandera Thygethyn. That fear had died with them. They cheered her for her greatness. They cheered themselves for being happy and well-feasted. They cheered the simple kindness-no-kindness of people welcoming weary travelers. A space was made for dancing, Jeha danced and her blue gown was dazzling to look at. She danced with Wyn, she danced with Ylil, she danced with Amraen the King. They made a fine matched pair, Jeha and Amraen. Amraen looked so happy when Jeha asked if she could dance with him.

Wonder of wonder of all wonders! Dellet and Calian ate and drank and laughed. Clicked cups with Sal and Kanda to drink a health, chatted with Sal and Kanda and with the people in the hall. Calian danced a foolish dance with Wyn then a yet more foolish dance with Ylil, then Dellet danced with her after he had sulked because Kanda said that she did not want to dance. Dellet and Calian had no memory of what had happened. In their memory, they were simply enjoying this good feast. They did not see Morna watching from the end of the hall. They did not see how happy Morna looked to see them laugh and dance and feast. They had no memory at all that every person there save Morna and Sal and Dellet had died that day beneath Kanda and Calian's swords. They saw the people in the hall as if they were still alive. Calian's hands were clean of blood; her sword was sheathed and clean of blood. They did not remember the terrible words that Morna had spoken.

"Oh that was a fine feast, Kanda, wife," Dellet said that night in bed. "Don't, please, let them feast you again tomorrow. Drunk two nights in three days! Have pity on me, wife! But, ah, that was a feast, even better than the first night."

"It was," Kanda said.

"I thought this was a cold place, compared to Lela's village," Dellet said. "But I see I was wrong. A fine place, this, also."

He yawned hugely. "Ah, drunk two nights in three days, Kanda! So stuffed full of good food. Such dancing. Don't wake me tomorrow until the sun is almost set."

CHAPTER TWENTY-NINE

Headaches all around the next morning. Dellet lay in bed, refused to open his eyes let alone get up. Calian snored with food stains around her mouth. Kanda tried to lie quiet next to Dellet, pretending she too was tired and her head ached. "What a feast," Dellet muttered. "Never again." Ah, there I can nod agreement, Dellet, Kanda thought. She got up, went to the window, stared out. A great fear – or not quite a fear, fear and hope both at once, that the people in the village would be—

would be—

would be—

I don't know which would be the better thing, she thought.

"A few days before another feast like that, at least, Kanda, wife, please…." Dellet said. "Such a good feast!"

CHAPTER THIRTY

And a fine early spring day that morning. Those who had to be up and working were set to with great reluctance. Those that could snatch a moment more sleep, slept. Kanda watched them working, watched their bodies move, their faces move, their shadows on the earth. Felt and saw them sleeping, alive and safe in their beds. The old dog wandered through the village looking for scraps, the geese were awake hissing at the dog. A woman came into the guesthouse with bread and honey and milk. She smiled: she was pretty and plump and rosy, her eyes were bright with shadows under them from lack of sleep. She had an unwashed smell, dancing sweat and too-much-food sweat. So obviously alive.

"Do you want anything else?" she asked Kanda. Her voice was bright and tired both at once like her eyes.

No fear in her, of Kanda or of anything. *This is a good world and I am a good woman within it,* her voice said. *The sun is weakly shining, come smell this new-baked bread.*

"No, thank you." The woman smiled again, greatly relieved, went out possibly back to bed. There was a jug of water already on the table. Kanda poured water, washed her face. Ate a little bread and honey, drank a cup of milk. Rich, creamy milk.

"What are you looking around for?" said Calian. "Is there a cat about or something?"

"No, no, nothing, I'm not looking for anything. Just looking at the village."

"Well stop it. It's irritating. Isn't it, Dad?"

"I'm saying nothing. I'm lying here trying to remember how to sit up."

"Well, it is. Really really irritating."

Kanda sat with her head absolutely still looking exactly straight ahead.

Counted one two three four five six.

"Sal!" Calian shouted. "Stop looking around! It's driving me crazy you twisting your neck around like that!"

"I'd like to think I'm allowed to move my own neck, Calian. I'm sorry, I'll stop moving my own neck in case it upsets you. Can I maybe move my foot, or will that upset you too?"

"Girls, please! Please.... What are you two looking for, anyway?"

"We're not looking for anything, Dad."

"Could have fooled me. Then your sister is right, for once, you two are being extremely irritating."

"There! Wait – what do you mean 'for once'?"

Keep talking, Dellet, Calian, my beloveds, keep bickering. Dellet: please fart again like – please fart again not quite as stinkily. Calian: curl your nose and roll your eyes again like that. Calian: please snap at me again.

She didn't mean it. Didn't mean it. Didn't. Didn't. Did—

Kanda twisted her neck and looked again out of the window of the guesthouse, and Morna was there at last standing waiting.

Even brighter than before was Morna the *Golden* in morning sunlight seen and with eyes washed clear of sister's bloodshed. All that is good and fair, so Morna in that morning, ripe fruit and rivers' running, fresh flowers, the summer sky made liquid after longed-for healing rainfall in the dry dust. Everything Kanda might have dreamed, bent over her daughter sleeping as a baby, crooning to the infant held to her breast. She too was watching the people of the village, smiling at the groans of those who must be up and doing, smiling at the warm fug of those who still could sleep. I did this! her face said, wondering. I brought them back to life! A man half-asleep backed into the dog which in turn leapt backward into the geese which ran about honking around the man's legs. I did that! Morna's laugh said. Kanda thought: you did that, Morna, yes! You gave joy and life here, while Calian and I brought only death.

Kanda looked around at her family and perhaps she worked a little unfair magic. For after a little while Calian went off to find Wyn and Ylil, Dellet fell asleep again, Sal dozed by the hearth (pretended to doze, snored too loudly, as Calian once also had done). So this time Kanda didn't need to pretend she needed to go out for a piss.

"Hello Mother," Morna said.

"Hello, Morna." *Hello Morn-Morn, hello Morna-bird, hello Morna-lamb, good morning good Morna my littlest babiest.* "You vanished away. Last night. I thought—" I thought you'd come home with us, back with us to the guesthouse, I mean, bed down between Sal and Calian. Three little heads on the pillow, three locks of hair tangled up. Well I remember that.

"You all looked tired," Morna said. "You needed to go and sleep. It was very late." Less bitter now. Got the anger out. A young woman talking, slightly hesitant, to the mother she had not seen for many years. Trying to remember – recreate – how they spoke. "And I – I wanted to see – my father."

How is he? Kanda wanted to ask. Is he well? Has he recovered – you said he cannot speak or walk? Does he think of me at all? She had fought that one her first husband, cut him down to pieces, left him a shriveled dried dead toad thing, and before that Calian had cut him down also, Calian had not been able to kill him but she had wounded him.

The joy in him, when he and Kanda had fought together that last time over Morna's corpse. So deeply he had loved Kanda, and she had loved him deeply back. How good the life they had made, their fine house, their marriage bed. How they had longed to have children together. And now here she was. Her child and his. More power in her than Kanda could have dreamed.

You didn't mean it. Of course you didn't you— Your father— Your real father – Dellet—

Kanda thought: eagerly rather would I wrestle in the dark with dragons, than speak these things now I should say to any of my three children.

"You'll come with us now, though. Come back to us? Won't you? Won't you, now you are…you are…."

"I went back to my home and my father last night," Morna said. "Don't you ever listen to me?"

Yes, yes, but…no, I confess, I didn't really hear you say that like it was meant and real…and anyway, surely, you went back to see him last night to say goodbye to him…. "Yes, but…."

Morna's voice grew bitter. "But when I went to the shore of the lake Elelan Mere, the water was dark and closed to me. I called to him. He could not answer. I reached down into the water. Only cold water, and a cold wind blowing. A thousand years until we are together again and I can next see my father's face." A sad smile: "You don't need to fear you will have to fight him again."

That smile was worse, somehow. "Dellet is your father! That…that… he is not even a man, Morna! Not even truly alive! Even before, he was not a man, he was not alive! He stole you away! Every day since then we have longed for you to come back to us."

Morna turned away. "I won't listen to this."

All angry and spoiled already, look what I did, ruined it with my first words. Look what you made me do, Morna, why do you have to spoil things?

"You left me," Morna said. "He cared for me. He gave me life when I was dead and dying. How can you say he is not my father? How can you say that?"

"He cares for nothing, Morna. He cannot. I don't believe that. I can't – believe that."

But Kanda thought: lying, lying. So deeply, so truly, he cared once for me.

"But you came to find us, Morna," Kanda said.

"I did." The harsh, mocking tone back in the woman's voice: "I wanted to see you, the people who abandoned me. The people who so badly hurt my father. The people who—" She shrugged. "I thought I could help you, even despite everything. You ignored me."

"I don't understand…." Kanda said.

"Look around you! I told you that you could find your heart's desire. But you didn't listen, you came here instead. And look what happened because of that. If you'd listened to me…understood….

"If you'd recognized me," Morna said.

"Morna—" A pause. Hopeless. Useless. "Morna, last night, you did… wonders, glorious good things. If not for you—" Helpless. Thankless. "If not for you, Morna," Kanda said, "I cannot think how it would be this morning for any of us."

The lovely eyes widened. "Can you not? You would be celebrating for having killed the monsters. Was it not the highest of high deeds?"

"No!" Almost her hands raised to strike her child.

"You feasted for three days, after you destroyed Roven, didn't you?" Morna said. Sweet and gentle and innocent, questioning voice.

"No!" Almost struck her, as a warrior striking down a vile beast. "No!"

They faced each other, and both had their hands on their sword hilts.

"What you did last night for Calian was a wonder, Morna," Kanda said at last. "Thank you, Morna my love."

They faced each other, and Morna's hand never moved from her sword hilt and her eyes never left Kanda's face.

"I told you to bring her up better," Morna said. She held and held and held and held her mother's gaze. Then she lowered her eyes. She shouted at the earth, "You never listened, you never heard a word I said to you about anything!"

"You were a tiny child!" Kanda shouted. "Then you were dead!

"Then I killed you," Kanda whispered. "I thought I'd killed you, Morna my love."

Silence.

Then Morna said, "But now look at me, Mother."

Yes.

My heart's desire I see.

What have you been doing? Tell me about yourself, what you like, what you do, what you know. I don't know anything about you now. You have two gray dogs and six white cows and a dead horse with a golden bridle. That's all I know. The last summer had just started fading from the leaves when Kanda had last seen Morna, and Morna had been a child of four. The next summer had not yet been born, the same leaves still clung to the trees with the last of the light clasped in them, and

Morna like Sal had grown and grown. So much Kanda had missed of her daughters' lives. So short a time, and they were changed and gone in her mind beyond recall.

What had Morna looked like as a child? Like…a little girl. Any little girl. Pale hair. A smiling face. But I never wanted you to grow up, Morna, my littlest one, my baby one, my smallest.

"Morna." Kanda held out her arms. Should have done this last night, clutched her, held her, should still be holding her from that first embrace. Never let you go, never stop holding you loving you. Clutched her, yes, and Morna was fighting her off, shoving, and Morna was clutched tight in her mother's arms. "We thought you were dead," Kanda was sobbing. "We saw you there, you were dead and gone. But the monsters were there – and Calian and Sal…and your father…they were alive."

Wrong words. Morna had stilled. Rested into her mother's arms. Was held and was holding tight. Now she pulled away. Her face was bitter again and her eyes were full of hate.

"Dellet, I mean…." Kanda tried to say.

"You don't understand anything," Morna said. "Look what you did last night, Mother. Look what you've turned Calian into.

"I wanted to give you—

"I wanted—

"Dead? You killed me, Mother! You. Killed. Me. You—

"Never mind," Morna said. "Nothing." She cast her hands around her, like she was fighting, or trying to hold or shape the air and the world. "He's not bitter toward you, Mother. Well…not…. Well…. Anyway," she said, and Kanda could hear and see…herself? Sal? that *empty* one her first husband? in Morna's sigh and shrug and turning away. "Anyway. You could stay here, you know, Mother. You could have stayed in that last village. You could have gone back to the farm and stayed there, you know that. Not one of us will harm you now, you know that. Not him, or me, or…." A dog barked. The old fat thing from the village – but Morna frowned. "Anyway.

"You look well, Mother. And Calian. And – Sal – looks—

"Anyway. If you'd listened to me when we first met, Mother, come with me – you'd have found—" So sad: like the one she claimed was her father now could look and sound when he spoke of his life. Then she shook her lovely hair, her lovely blue eyes flashed. "Instead you found a dunghill," she said. "A dunghill with an idiot crowing over it. A captain in your armies! You know what this man Amraen was. I came to find you, Mother. To help you. Why did I bother? Why did I care?

"I gave you a chance. I hoped you'd know me. You should have known me. Your daughter, and you didn't recognize me. Now if you want to see me again, Mother, you'll have to come to me. Find me.

"Anyway.

"Anyway." And if Kanda had said one word, if she had said the word that must be spoken, if she had said – or done—

"Anyway.

"Anyway."

And Morna was gone. Yellow flowers grew up where her feet had stepped.

Yellow flowers, Kanda thought. Yellow flowers, and a mother's grief, and waste.

She didn't mean it. She didn't. Didn't. Did—

CHAPTER THIRTY-ONE

One battle she remembered. Thought she remembered. Amraen's face she thought she could remember in the ranks. Didn't remember whom she fought now, or why she fought them; to kill them, that was why she fought them, she could only suppose. But she remembered that the sky was red with the sun's fire, it made the earth red, the men's faces, everything was red in that red light. The enemy came on and they were beautiful. Tall men, clad in armor of silver and gold. There was a calmness in their faces as they marched toward her. When they came close, she saw that they were not men but manlike beasts. Their faces were human faces, but their bodies were like some wild creatures she could not name, walking on their hind legs. And when she killed them, they did not bleed, but light poured out of them. When the light had faded, they died. The ground beneath them was stained with light. The battlefield had been red from the sun's wounding, but by the end of the battle it was golden with spilled light. Light dripped off her sword. Soaked her hands. Her face was stained with light. And then the light faded away and was gone.

CHAPTER THIRTY-TWO

When Kanda returned to the guesthouse, her family were packing up their things to leave. Dellet groaned as he worked: "I'd beg for us to stay another day, except then they'd only go and feast us again."

"The more Mum eats and drinks, the more they have," said Calian. "So we should stay another day…." She began to count on her fingers. "If we stayed another ten days, and every night they get twice as much and three times as much as Mum eats and drinks back…."

Dellet threw up his hands. "Please, Calian."

Kanda said, trying to laugh, "I'm not sure it quite works like that."

"Here's your bag, Kanda love," said Dellet. "I tried to pack it, did a bit, but…your armor and things…. But we're all pretty much ready to go. Even Calian."

"Even Calian? When did you get so rude, Dad?"

"Since you got so fierce, Calian. I'm an old farmhand with a warrior for a daughter: what am I supposed to do except be rude? Pass me that shirt, will you? Thanks."

Kanda said carefully, "So…we're leaving today, then?"

"I thought that was the plan," Dellet said. "That we left today. We just stopped for a night for a bed and a hot meal. Weren't exactly planning to stay beyond one or two nights, were we? Then get up and get off?"

"No. Yes."

"Been so generous to us, they have. And you – driving off a ghost for them! Kindness all round, I'd say. But now we need to get on. Before they offer to feast us again," he said to Calian. "That was the plan, yes, to get going as quick as possible this morning?"

"It…was." Kanda looked at Sal. Sal looked away.

"I'll go and check they've got Nosey saddled properly," said Calian. "I bet they won't have." Never saddled a horse in her life before White Nose. Not warhorse, not cart horse, not lame donkey. A dead horse, Kanda thought, she's never saddled that. Calian said, "That's the last thing to be done, then we can get moving." Eager to go, despite her words about staying and feasting. The fever in both Calian and Dellet, they both knew deep inside that something was terribly wrong here they must flee from, that something terrible and wonderful both was waiting for them.

"You do that, Cal-bird." Dellet watched the girl go tripping and dancing, and he looked around the room and almost he seemed about to say, "And Morna? Is she ready?"

Run away from here and try to blot it from my mind, Kanda thought, try to forget. She threw her own clothes into her pack, stuffed them down to get it done as quick as possible. In the folds of cloth she saw Calian shrieking as she killed Wyn. Calian's sword cutting into Ylil's chest.

Dellet's face when Morna said—

They know, she thought. They've forgotten, but they know deep down inside what happened here. They can't stay here any more than I can. All of us are running away as if all the evil in the world is at our heels.

She thought: as if all the evil in the world is at our heels?

"Be good to be on the road." Dellet was whistling as he packed. Alternately groaning and whistling and groaning at himself for whistling. He noticed his wife's packing. "Woah, Kanda, that's fierce packing. You…don't like that skirt? That's how great warriors on campaign pack?"

Dellet's face when—

She tried to laugh and say, "Oh yes. This is how we great war leaders always pack our things," and he said, "Well, us hungover old farmhands don't and our clothes look the better for it, in my opinion," and he seemed genuinely happy and eager to be going, excited to get on with the journey, looking forward to the adventures to be met.

"This is a good place," he said. "Be sad to leave it too, just like Lela's village. But – onward! Before they find any more ghosts for you to fight!" *We could have stayed here. Easily. More easily even than Lela's village. You could have been their queen, Kanda, wife, and I could have had the run of any farm I wanted. But no. We go on, on some mad quest, because you and Sal and Calian—*

But she was being unfair on Dellet, Kanda thought, (but life's unfair, she thought, parents and husbands and wives especially) he was genuinely happy and eager to get on. A kingly hall with silver walls and a roof of gold, whose very name is *Peace*: who doesn't want to hurry on to find that?

"Well, you've got it done quicker than me, certainly," said Dellet. He pulled the thongs on his pack tight, knotted them. "There. Now that's good and well tied, let's see, what have I forgotten to pack? More to the point, what's Calian forgotten to pack that I'll have to pack? You ready, Cal-bird?" he called toward the door. "You got that horse sorted out? You ready to go, Sal-flower? You—?" He seemed to twist his neck to look around the room, as if he too almost saw Morna, she would walk in any moment in her yellow dress, so beautiful. "Dad!" she would say and he would catch her up in his arms to swing her round to make her shriek with delight. "I'll go and see she doesn't manage to start a fight over Nosey's saddle straps," he said. Kanda had to make herself remember he was talking about Calian.

Like Lela and Dovei before him, Amraen looked truly sad to hear they were leaving. "You could stay longer. A few days. You drove away the ghost that has been a nuisance to us for so long, and for that alone we owe you more than I can say. I'd like very much to show you—" A puzzled look: "I was going to show you my kingdom." *I thought…I remember….* Then a shrug, a wry smile. "That would take all of half a day, at least. If we walked slowly. If I showed you every cow byre and oak tree and pigpen."

Kanda felt a terrible laugh building inside her: what do I say to a man I've killed? *I'd be delighted, Amraen, my old companion-in-arms, only – the funniest thing, Amraen – one, you've already shown me every cow byre and oak tree and pigpen in your kingdom, and, two, you're dead and a ghost now yourself.* You're easier and happier in yourself, Amraen, you're so much better at living – now you're dead. Most people are kind indeed, want to offer hospitality, enjoy seeing people relaxing with food and drink. And you're a kind man, Amraen, now you're dead and not so desperate to be wanting things.

"If you're sure you must leave…I'll get you supplies."

"That's very kind, thank you," Kanda said.

Kind, kind, kind, she thought. Stop thinking it! As if by thinking it I can…. Like I'm daring myself to keep thinking it. Ah, tell me, how does one measure guilt, Ikandera Thygethyn? And more – how does one stop feeling guilt? Shout at it like a naughty child and shoo it away? Stop tugging at my skirts, guilt, can't you see I'm busy? Go and find something to do by yourself for a bit.

Calian's face, killing. Dellet's face, when—

She didn't mean it. Didn't mean it. Did—

"I would like to stay longer, Amraen, truly." More lies, Kanda? More false words? No? Yes? "But we must get on with our journey. We are following the River Wenet, going west and north, we must go on." A blank look from Amraen: *I have never heard of a river called the Wenet, my lady queen. No, of course not, my lord king Amraen, like Roven, like so many things, the River Wenet no longer exists. As far away and lost as my daughters' childhoods: I'm looking for my daughters' faces when they were babies, their first words, the smell of their hair, do you know where to look for them?*

Ah, stop, she thought. The people here are happy today!

"I would have given up my throne to you, my lady queen. Gladly, happily, I would have done it. I won't offer to feast you goodbye. I think perhaps your husband would cry if I did. But we will escort you to the bounds of my kingdom, if it pleases you?"

"That would be…kind, Amraen. Thank you."

He laughed. No fear in him, no awe toward the great Ikandera Thygethyn. A king in the comfort of his kingdom, greeting and feasting and bidding fond farewell to an old companion of wilder days long ago and half-forgotten, embarrassed, a little, to meet now, wiser and more real, and have to look back. *We fought, we did great deeds together, you and I, my lady; I served you well and loyally, if not always perhaps in the very front ranks. We talk of it as great slaughter, great destruction, cities and armies and kingdoms uprooted, corpses piled to the sunless sky, no mercy, no kindness in us only bloodlust running red – but we know, both of us, in our aging hearts we know those are but the memories of youth, overeager, overweening, self-aggrandizing, a tale filled with sound and fury and poetic license. We raided, looted, yes we killed, but we did not do – those terrible romantic things we pretend we did. A war leader and her captain, two comrades of the sword, fighting our ragged little warband battles, that's all we were then.* And he was indeed a happier better easier man, now he was dead.

All the people gathered at the gate to see them off. How alive and bright they looked. How smiling they looked. Their clothes glittered, they were plump and clean and smiled and waved. Like a child's story, Kanda thought. All happy and smiling all the time. Never felt cold or hungry, never suffered war or famine or disease. It wasn't warm, the spring wind blew in their faces to remind them of winter hardships, their bright living faces smiled and smiled and smiled.

Let them go now, Morna, Kanda thought for a moment. This is not right. I saw them dead, I saw what Calian and I did to them; this is false. They will never be truly alive now, Morna. The Six had great power in us to heal; this is not healing, Morna. This is an evil thing you have done.

But it was hard, looking at the smiling wind-blown faces, it was hard not to feel it was the killing that had been an illusion. These people were alive. They did not know they had died and been brought back to something almost like life. The wind was blowing in their faces, they said goodbye to this family about whom their memories were hazy but whom they had enjoyed feasting, a child was bored and started moaning, they would quite like this family to get on with leaving before it started to rain harder, one of them was desperate for this family to leave because she needed a crap. Their deaths were something that had once happened here, terrible but gone without trace. Like so many things.

They shouted: "Goodbye! Good luck! Come back one day! Thank you for banishing the ghost!!!"

As they were leaving, Kanda said, "Amraen: did you ever hear tell of a king's hall near here? A great high feast hall with silver walls and a golden roof?"

He shook his head. "I dream sometimes of such a place.... Go out to the bounds of my kingdom, screw up my eyes to look to the horizon, if the sun is shining on it to light the walls and the thatch of the roof, with my weak eyes I sometimes see my hall raised in silver and gold. But no, there is only forest and wilds and small places for many days' walk in any direction. Follow the River Wend west and north and west and you'll come to the sea at last, there is nothing like the hall you describe between here and the sea. They say there was a city here once. A fine city, a great city. I…." He frowned, turned away. "That is just a story. And no one has ever spoken of a king's hall."

As he had insisted, Amraen, Jeha, Tal and another of Amraen's warriors, Gaten, accompanied the family. They went on foot – it occurred to Kanda that, because Amraen was a king, her mind had furnished his hall with stables, grooms, horses in plumed headdresses. He walked beside Kanda leading White Nose; far from arguing with grown men skilled in the breaking of horses, Calian had had to show his servants how to saddle the pony, how to check its hooves.

They went out through the one gate they had come in through. As they crossed the threshold, Kanda held her breath, her body so tense her shoulders hurt her, her hands clenched until her nails dug into her palms. White Nose snorted, for Sal had clenched her hands on the reins, dug her knees into its flanks. Waiting, fearing – they'll all fall down dead, Amraen, Jeha, Tal, all of them. Calian will remember killing them. Dellet will remember us killing them. A smattering of rain blew in Kanda's face. She walked on, Amraen was beside her, Jeha was beside her, she could hear Wyn behind her bellowing "Goodbye! Goodbye!" like the bullock he was. She walked on, the pony trotted on, Amraen was alive, Jeha was alive, Wyn and Ylil were shouting. She twisted to look back, which made Calian tread on her left heel and her right toes (a wolf, a flame, a dancer, thus Calian in battle – how can anyone be so clumsy out of it?), the village was there with smoke rising from its hearth fires, soggy people waving in the gateway, going back into the shelter of their houses. Wyn's father having to restrain him from running after them to say more goodbyes. So alive, she thought.

"It is a fine place, Amraen," Kanda said. "A very good and fine place. You are right to be proud of it. May you have many more years here in peace."

"It—" The man smiled. "It is a fine place, yes. Thank you, my lady Ikandera Thygethyn."

Two villages, Kanda thought, that I have butchered, that no one knows what I did there, two villages I have been kindly welcomed in. Ah, she could see Dellet's eyes wander south following the droveway back to Lela's village. Ah, he wanted to walk where his eyes led. We could have stayed here in this hall, Kanda, that Amraen offered you as a gift. We could have built a hall in Lela's village, Kanda, if the building part is so important to you. Built a hall and called it Roven that is *Peace*. We built a house there, after all, that's nearly the same thing. A better thing, Kanda, wife, a house for people to live together, not a hall for lords and warriors and servants. We built a house and we could have called that house *Just About Bearable Despite Everything*, and I think it could have been, Kanda, wife, my love. Still could be. Except—

He smiled ruefully at Kanda; shrugged.

CHAPTER THIRTY-THREE

The sun was high and pale and beginning to sink down slowly toward its dying. They turned west and the sun was running before them hidden, rain blew in their faces, the sky was gray. Rich country, to Kanda, thick trees dripping water down the back of her neck, old trees with heavy trunks, knots of roots and stagged branches, this year's leaves not quite fully born yet and unfurling in the rain like baby's fingers, last year's leaves a slime beneath their feet. A squirrel ran in the trees, chattered *ratatusk ratatusk*, there would be bluebells here soon enough, see the green stems of them everywhere here, Jeha said as she pointed. Starflowers and lace-flowers and the stink of the ramsons all frothed together, the road a narrow weak tracing that struggled its way through the nuzzling green. A dog barked far off and Kanda knew they were followed. She felt blue eyes on her back. Calian jerked to look left and right and right again, there's something there, something there, what's that? Even Amraen felt it – or, Kanda thought, especially Amraen and Jeha and the others, for they felt the power that had brought them back to life.

She thought herself a moment of standing before her Lord of Roven, knowing he had called her into life. No easy thing, that.

The fear was still great in her that Amraen and Jeha, Tal and Gaten would fall away dead in the road, maimed corpses on the green stuff. A funny game to Morna, to let them drop in a pretty place or a stupid place. The road crossed a stream, they had to splash through with running water around their legs ("It's the rain, my lady queen," Amraen said, embarrassed, "it's not usually this deep, there must be heavier rain up in the hills. A well-made road, this, usually, I promise you"); it would be funny-horrible in just the way children delight at, Kanda thought, if Morna let them drop there into the stream. Splash! Splash! Splash! Splash!

Or a lovely glade just off the roadway, a little space where a tree had come down and the light flooded, whitelace had sprung up rampant and they could sink dead into the froth of the flowers, flop flop flop flop, oh how Morna would laugh.

The rain began to slacken. Faded away. The road rose ahead steeply through bracken, cut brown against sodden spring greenness; two trees stood together on the skyline and the road ran between them and was gone where the land dropped away at the hilltop. The sky was paling; the sky was gray, the sky was white, the sky was blue. The road ran with water; the water sang as it was running down, there were rainbows in the water there; shallow streamlets that poured away to find and form a stream and then a river and then a great sea; when Kanda looked down the water was fathoms deep and filled with beasts, merfolk, serpents; a beetle was washed by, and a red flower, and a green budding twig. When she looked up the sky was the deep blue of eyes, still gleaming with dampness, rain-freshness, the sunlight was fresh from being washed. Sunlight shone and leapt back skyward from the wet road, from the wet bracken, from the travelers' sodden clothes. A swirl of birds rushed from where they had been sheltering out of the rain, the light danced also from their wings. The light was like the birds. The birds were like the sudden rain and the sudden brilliant light. The road led through the jewel-green bracken, the bracken reached out so eager that Kanda could see and smell its young growth. The two trees the road ran through were rowan trees. They were richly black with only the sky behind them where the world fell away. The sun was above the trees. The sun was pale: Kanda could look at it with her eyes wide open. The birds came rushing, rainwater shimmered on their feathers, they drove against the sun, they dived and circled, they rested in the branches of the two rowan trees.

Mal Ealia.

That is, *Truth Hill.*

Kanda stopped. Well before she reached the slope of the road that led up to the trees. Turned to look back the way they had come – bracken gave way to scrub and blackthorn, then the tideline of the oakwood, smudges of hearth smoke from Amraen's village, all that lay beyond veiled away in rain. She had not realized they had climbed so high or come so far.

She remembered then Amraen's pleading instruction to Jeha: *take the children to Mal Ealia.* And Jeha in response: *the hilltop?* Yes, she thought. This would be the safest best place to keep a child safe. But it was brave of Amraen to come here, where his kingdom ended.

Calian was walking at the front, heading on up the road toward the rowan trees. "Come back, Calian!" Kanda shouted.

"What? Why?" Calian's face shouted her eagerness. *We stop, Mum, when we get to the summit. When we see what's beyond. That's the rules.*

"We'll be saying goodbye to Amraen and his warriors here," said Kanda. "Thanking them. They won't be coming farther with us," she said. "Will you, Amraen?"

The man shook his head. "No, my lady queen." They had walked to the farthest edges of the little world he had made for himself. He knew, if he could not say and did not understand, what would happen to him if he walked to the hilltop, followed the road through the rowan trees and down and away. Kanda glanced at him to see if his arm rings were still there gleaming golden. Yes. Just.

"We should eat a crust of bread together here before you walk on, my lady Ikandera Thygethyn," Amraen said. "That would be fitting. A way to wish you well on your journey, and to wish us well in our village."

Calian pouted. The rules! Can't I at least go to the top and come back? But Kanda said firmly, "Come back here now, sit down and join us," and she wanted to go on herself and Sal wanted to get on and Sal was the one who had taught the walking-to-the-top rule to Calian.

But there were other rules here to follow, as there had been when taking leave of Lela's village, when Kanda had had to kiss the trembling dry skin of an old old woman's hands.

Kanda looked around her. Only a little way off the road, half-buried in the bracken, she found a wide flat stone. It too was gleaming wet, a great number of small red-and-white snails had crept out from beneath it, traced a silver pattern across its surface. There seemed an order in their trails: a slow stately snail dance, she thought, snail ladies and snail lords tracing out the motions, exchanging wisdom and news. The stone had a lovely smell to it, wet stone drying quickly in the sunlight while the bracken around it held the raindrops clutched. It was a lovely color also, dark gray to show off both the snails' bright shells and the silver of their paths. By moving only a few of the snails she was able to clear enough space on the stone to set out three things that she had not used for a while. A wooden bowl, small as a child's food bowl so that she could hold it in her two clasped hands, carved of blackthorn wood; a lump of white stone no bigger than a pebble, a piece from a quern long broken; a cup of ill-fired clay, patterned with Kanda's fingerprints.

She had to rootle around in her pack before she found them. Throw out: a shirt of Calian's, her spare leggings, her old apron that Calian had made her, a shirt of Calian's that must despite all appearance be a different shirt, a tangle of leather ties that might be useful for something, the shirt of Calian's yet again (oh, what, how, Calian?).

Someone – it might have been Tal – sniggered. To be fair, Kanda thought, this probably does look a bit stupid.

Amraen was watching her very gravely.

Albeit – in bafflement.

The shirt appeared for the third or fourth time. Something caught up in the sleeve – wait, ah ha, the bit of broken quern stone! Oh, typical, Calian! And now three things, carefully placed on the flat gray rock.

Kanda drew her sword. Cut her finger enough to draw blood there. The middle finger of her left hand. It hurt. She let three drops of her blood fall onto the flat gray stone.

In her mind, a trumpet blared.

In her mind, she said the words that must be said.

And lo! The wooden bowl was a gold platter, piled high with roast meat. The quern was a silver platter, piled high with fresh bread. The cup was a horn of sweet milk.

She thought, in Morna's voice: that's the right way round, isn't it?

Gaten said, "Oh! My lady queen!" Tal said, "But how—?" as if he had not seen any of her other wonders. Jeha only laughed in delight.

A magical feast to eat in a magical place in a company of four living people and four dead people. They sat down on the bracken to eat.

When he had eaten his fill (which was a good amount for a dead man, Kanda noted) Amraen said, "My lady queen…will you do me the honor of walking a little with me?"

"Of course." Although Kanda's heart sank. Amraen looked hesitantly toward the upward slope of the hillside, set off walking east and south downhill. The bracken grew chest-high, they shoved their way through it following an animal track. The smell was wonderful, strong and cleaning, the curled fronds of the bracken made Kanda think of caterpillars. Brown dusting of spores on her skin and her clothes.

Amraen walked until he was out of earshot. Then, still walking, not looking at Kanda, he began to speak.

How he spoke, once he had begun to speak! Sweet as fresh water. Pouring like good milk.

"I told you my story, my lady queen. That I was a part of your war host, so happy, so proud to fight beneath your banner, and then one day you left us, and I did not know what to do. That I searched for you, and I could not find you. That I waited for you in the mustering field, when all the rest of your army had despaired and fled away. That I wandered the world alone and grieving, and at last I found a village where I could settle, and I made myself king.

"I told you all this, did I not?"

"You did," Kanda said.

"Cattle thieves came that first winter. I led a warband to drive them off. It seemed…. It was no different to any fighting, killing men before they killed me. Indeed, I was glad of it, my heart rejoiced in the killing. A long time since I had fought and killed warrior men! I pretended to myself that you were there leading me; almost I saw you there at the head of my warriors, it was your sword I imagined cutting the raiders down. I think perhaps that is how we won the fight. When I returned to the hall I had made the villagers build me, they thanked me for aiding them. Praised me. That too felt good and my heart rejoiced."

He broke off a sprig of bracken, picked at the furled leaf tips.

"It is good," Kanda said, "that you helped them. I have driven off raiders many times myself. Be glad that you had the skills to defend them."

"Yes. Perhaps." He threw the sprig away. Picked another, began to unfurl that. "Perhaps. Yes. It's true, I have fought off raiders since then, although fewer come now…not for a long time, now I think of it, as though my little kingdom has since then been kept safe and hidden. But when I sat on my throne that day after our victory, it came to me, my lady queen Ikandera Thygethyn, that there had been a sound in my head all the years I fought for you. A sound like a millstone in my head. As if all my life was being ground away."

Silence. No birds, no droning insects.

"And now?" Kanda said.

He'll say: *it has gone, only peace in my head*— No*: children's laughter, I hear in my head*, he'll say, *a happy ending for me.*

Amraen said, "I used to think to ask Jeha to marry me. I would have liked – I tried, once, to imagine Ylil was my son and I was his father. She would say yes, of course – Jeha, I mean – she would marry me if I asked her. But only because she would feel she must say yes…. But I fear sometimes…." He frowned. "It would be worse, I think, this fear, if I had a wife and a son, perhaps other children….

"For I think sometimes…. I think…. It seems to me now when I look back on my memories that I was…. I think, sometimes, that I was not a good fighter. Not good at waging war. Yet it seems to me still, my lady queen, that it was a fine life while we had it. A beautiful life."

A blue sky and this green hillside, so rich in color and scent. The sun was pale above the rowan trees, almost it might be mistaken for the moon when it shows itself weak in the day. Clouds were building on the northern horizon, thin line of rain cloud that was like a blade – when we marched, you and I, or rather, I should say, when you marched to my order beneath my banner, unknowing often where you marched or why save that I had ordered it – when we marched, we were like the storm building, on the far horizon people would see the darkness of our coming, see on the horizon in the clouds our army fighting, killing. In my dreams, Kanda thought, yes, it is still beautiful, Amraen.

The man shook his head. Trying to shake away the noise that ground still in his head.

Ah, Kanda thought, but you are lucky, Amraen, I hear it, or something like, the whetstone on the blade, I hear, it is to me sweeter music than ever was played on pipe or flute, but it is far off and I can barely hear it, as in the night when I think I hear one of my children as a baby still crying. I wish I heard it as you do. Close, ringing in my head.

Amraen said, "Old men, in their last years…sometimes they forget the present. Return in their minds to the dreams they had in their youth. I am so afraid of that."

He looked at Kanda full in the face, daring to look at her. Begging her, with the courage of a man desperate past any caring. "Tell me, my lady queen Ikandera Thygethyn. It would it be good to hear it from your lips, my lady. My queen. Tell me truly – that I was never any good at war and killing."

His arm ring was old and worn, bronze, not gold, and a crude, badly made thing. His kingly robe was threadbare and patched and tattered, a soldier's loot long past its best long before it was looted. An old man with weak eyes and old scars that pained him but he could no longer remember in what distant battle he had come by them.

Kanda looked back straight into Amraen's eyes, and if she did not tell the truth entirely, she did not entirely lie to him.

"You were the worst warrior who ever served in my armies, Amraen."

We talk of it as great slaughter, great destruction, cities and armies and kingdoms uprooted, corpses piled to the sunless sky, no mercy, no kindness in us only bloodlust running red – but we know, both of us, in our aging hearts we know those are but the memories of youth, overeager, overweening, self-aggrandizing, a tale filled with sound and fury and poetic license. And of all the men who made these empty boasts with me, you were the worst of all, you did the least.

His face! Ah, it was a gift to see it, as wondrous in its way as flowers and fruits and birdsong and horns of rich creamy milk.

"Thank you, my lady queen," he whispered. He had known she lied when she promised she would not do him harm: but she saw now that he believed this, clutched the words treasure-tight to his breast. In the night he would wake, stare into the dark with the terror rising, grope for those words. In the calling of swifts, in the running of water, in the bark of a fox on a frosty morning when all is stripped clean, he would hear those words and hold them close.

If there was any true kindness in him, Kanda thought, he would say such words back to her. *You were never so great a great warrior, my lady queen, for all the years of my life I followed you, I knew deep in my heart and I will dare say it now at last: the stories they tell of you are absurdly exaggerated, you rewarded the poets the more they exaggerated their songs. I say to you now truly, I will swear it: you are far better at milking cows and scolding children than ever you were at killing.*

But this man, for all his newfound happiness, his name was only *wanting*. Greatly and deeply and ardently with all his heart he *wanted* to be kind. "Thank you, my lady queen," he only said again.

Kanda turned to go back to her family. Lead them off on their quest now she had given Amraen this final gift. Morna, she thought. Morna, my dearest love – wait! We're coming now. We will find you as you found us. One last kindness I had to do, and now we're coming! Soon we will be with you and never again will we be parted. Amraen caught her hand and she thought with anger: storerooms filled with food, barrels of good ale, flocks and herds, health to your children, joy to your village, geese until you're knee-deep in goose shit, now this gift of a kind lie too I give – what more can you want from me, Amraen? My hand hurts where I cut it to conjure up bread and meat and milk for you, you grab my hand now like one of my children, needing, needing, wanting, when I have something so precious waiting for me.

"Wait, my lady queen. Kanda. Please – tell me – one more thing—"

His face very grave, his face too was tired. Feel guilt, Kanda! He does not know the weight the last days have been to you. In his memory you have feasted, laughed, danced. He had walked with her in the rain to this green hillside. A good enough man, now. A good enough king.

"Ask," Kanda said.

Amraen paused, frowned. Kanda knew what he would ask, then. Felt things far beyond guilt.

He said, "I look at myself and I think I'm alive, but I'm not, am I, my lady queen?"

He said, "All of us in the village, Jeha, Tal, Ylil, Wyn: we're all dead. Aren't we, my lady queen? Something happened, yesterday, or last night, I don't know when, I don't know what it was that happened, but a fear has been growing in my heart since we left the village, when I sat down to eat with you here I knew."

One can tell many lies because the lie is better. Parents and lovers and great leaders of the war host, they are well-practiced in the art of good lies. Grownups, sometimes, when they say things….

Death cannot be lied about. "You are dead, Amraen," Kanda said simply. "You and Jeha and everyone in your village. My daughter Calian and I killed you all."

She thought that Amraen…. She had no idea what he might do or say. What could anyone say? But when he looked down at his hand and then at her hand, said simply, "Yes," she had not thought it would be that.

He said after a little while, "What will happen to us when you walk away over the hilltop?"

Kanda was silent.

"Tell me! Tell me, please, my lady Ikandera Thygethyn."

Kanda said at last, "Nothing. I don't know. Nothing, I think. You will go back to your village, carry on your lives. You will know. But no one else will know. And you will all live good lives, quiet lives, in peace." She spoke loudly, as if Morna was hiding nearby and would hear and grant it. But, like Sal talking about Lela's baby, she was quite certain she spoke the truth.

Amraen only stared down at his hands, turned them over and over, looking for some sign of his life or his death.

"What would you prefer to happen, Amraen? I could break the enchantment. You could all fall dead now." She said, cruelly, to stop him wishing it, "We would bury you here on the hill. You would never have to worry about growing old and returning to the dreams of your past."

Hands turning, turning. These aging, living hands…how can they be dead? So many times, in wonder, Kanda thought, have I looked down at my killing, healing hands. She strained, and he strained, to see through the enchantment. See his hands dead and beginning to rot. That *empty* one's dead broken hands…that was what Amraen would always now see.

He said, "No. Don't." He laughed. "I like being alive."

"Well, then? You were a good enough king in your way, Amraen. Now, knowing this, you could be a good king.

"Or better yet – you could stop being a king."

He laughed again. "Stop being a king, and be only a man at last after all I have done?"

They walked back then through the bracken, following the animal track, breaking yet more bracken stems. "It makes good bedding, bracken," Kanda said for the need to say something. "Even when it's dried, that lovely smell…." No insects still, no birds, but there had been animals here recently, she realized, since they were following an animal's path. Her family were waiting politely at the flat gray stone. If Calian leapt up and mouthed "finally" when she saw her mother, that was just her being Calian.

"Goodbye then, Amraen." Oh, she thought, I am so very good at farewells. "Gaten. Tal. Thank you, be safe, farewell." She embraced Jeha with all the awkwardness of two women who were not entirely comfortable doing such things. "Jeha. My blessings to you and your son." Again she was waving goodbye, again she was watching people she could have been content to live beside walk away from her. Again she felt their sadness that she would not stay, and the relief that she was leaving taking her killing power away from them.

Unlike their departure from Lela's village, however, there was no sign of regret in Dellet or Sal or Calian. "Come on!" Calian shouted, she ran on ahead of her family, up the steep slope of the hillside following the brown road that stood out clear against the sweet green bracken. To the south and the north the ridge ran along very sheer before sinking away at last into scrubland and woodland and shadows. In the south the sky was blue as in midsummer, the woods went on thicker and yet thicker, far beyond the eye's reach there were great mountains to the south that Calian did not know existed, could not conceive of, mountains so high not even a gyrfalcon could fly above their peaks for all that a gyrfalcon can fly beyond the stars and the moon. In the north the storm clouds mounted the horizon, men fighting without mercy and without fear of dying, the sea was there somewhere in the far north cold and gray and endless, the edge of the world finally where sea and sky and starlight met. To the east, behind them, Amraen's absurd village kingdom, and Lela's village where Lela sat nursing her baby, she had never heard the word *kingdom* or the word *king*, and somewhere only perhaps ten, twelve days' steady walking eastward was the farmstead that Kanda and Dellet had built to raise their children in. To the east behind them the sky was gray and full of spring shadowlight.

To the west ahead of them the road ran steeply upward, to end suddenly in a pale strange sky. The two rowan trees were black and stood as a gateway, the sun hung above them. To the west, again, they were walking out of one world into another, again the earth changed, they were changed and they were made new. Calian ran on up the hill until she was almost at the trees. Then she stopped. Waited. White Nose the pony toiled up the hill, Dellet toiled up, Kanda toiled up. "Come on!" Calian shouted.

She didn't mean it. Of course Dellet's her father and she knows that. I was always jealous that she loved him more than me. She's just angry with us, you know how children are. Lash out, say these awful things they don't mean.

She's waiting. She's near.

Soon, you'll know. She'll tell you.

"Hurry up! Come on!"

CHAPTER THIRTY-FOUR

The trees framed the sky, the sky was pale, the trees were very black. Beyond, birds circled, they were so far and so high, they too were black, they swam up in the white light. A sunbeam caught them, they glittered and flashed. To stand and look down into deep water, choppy, wind-ruffled, a beam of sunlight spills down upon the water and a thousand thousand sparks of light are there and they rise and dance. Thus the birds and the white sky beyond the rowan trees, and it was to Kanda as if she walked upward into deep water, she was falling upward into the dance of sunlight on waves. As the spring in Lela's village had poured out water and she had bathed her hands in it, caught up the water to run through her cupped hands beneath the bird-spell-carving, so she held out her hands now to catch up the sky and the birds' sparkling light. The hill fell away almost sheer before her, green turf and patches of bare steep rock. At its foot, low green hills running like clouds onward, richly wooded. Looking north, a line of silver cut the greenness: she thought joyfully: the Wenet! To the north and the west, all ended in the farthest distance in a line of darker silver, barely visible, that must be the sea.

She had come so short a distance and so very far, to find the river and the sea; she had found it.

Once, she might have leapt from the hillside. Plunged into the strange white light. Rushed like a bird herself, fearless, hair and arms stretched out as wings. Fallen to earth like a falling star or like a raindrop. *Gallyn,* Great Leap, *will you leap with me?* Her shout would ring from the hilltop, she would land with a puff of breath and a laugh and a shake of her head. The grass would be soft to catch her, barely crushed by her feet; her sword belt and the necklace she might be wearing would jingle like bells. A magic in the leaping, the rushing, the laughter, the wildness, as much as in the careful step between the two black rowan trees. Her companions would follow, themselves laughing, leaping or running or setting their horses to fly and plunge, *I'm a hawk! I'm a dragon! Watch me!* Gallyn would shout as he leapt. She would look back, see the slope rising steep and sheer, the animal paths that more cautious feet (Lord Palle's) would be taking. "We leapt that!" she would shout. A magic in the joy of it, as much as in the two black trees. "'A star falling!'" she would shout, "'a firedrake!' That is what the people around will be saying of my leap!" And, ah, not – barely – winded, she would run on or ride on or fight on, a monster to slay, innocents to rescue, a city to break.

Instead, now, she fretted about how Old White Nose the pony would manage, getting Sal down the steep slope.

"Oh, see! See!" Calian shouted. "See it!"

"I see."

Calian's eyes were bright as Kanda's would once have been. She was thinking of the leap.

"I'll take the rein, Sal, help you with Nosey."

Sal said with great relief, "Thank you, Calian."

Kanda said, "So we must walk down between the trees." She said, "Don't look back." She thought: will they all die now? She thought: Lela's village, Amraen's kingdom, will they ever have existed?

She thought: Morna is waiting for me on the other side of these trees.

She stepped, and behind her Calian stepped, and Dellet stepped, and Old White Nose the pony with Sal on his back stepped.

Steep and sheer and slippery to walk down (run down, roll down, slide down, flow down laughing as the rainwater laughs and flows), following pathways that were made by creeping timid surer-footed tiny beasts. It ended in a dip of nettles and a stream and a bog. Calian of course did run it, whooping, arms out, hair flying, very very very nearly but at the last moment pulling back from going arse over tit. She had at least thought enough to drop the pony's rein that she had only just taken up. So Dellet led the pony, Kanda walked at its side reassuring it. When Kanda looked back the ridge was a long hump of bracken in the scrub and the woods about it, a curiosity perhaps, certainly a local landmark, nothing more. The two rowan trees crowned it, dark against the sky but a warmth in the color of their slender trunks. The patch of sky between them was sinking down into twilight; the birds were circling and twisting, flashed where the evening sunlight struck their wings. The sun was low and red on the horizon; if they had only seen it from the hilltop, it would be setting the far-distant sea gleaming gold and red. It was in their eyes, for they had walked down into the wound of the sun.

Kanda waited to hear the crash of walls falling, the shriek of people falling back into death. A thin cry, high-pitched, like a bird's sad evening cry that the day was ended. *A bird, that's all,* she was ready to say to Calian.

No cry came. Though the wind blew from the east. No smell of blood or smoke.

"What's up, Mum?" Calian said.

Kanda shrugged and said, "Nothing." And now, she thought, now we will meet Morna, and Calian will have to know.

They walked on into the green evening. Oakwoods, the tree trunks cushioned with moss until they looked like the stone wall in the northern corner of Kanda's farmhouse. Moss underfoot, and more bracken. Cool and damp and still, the trees too thick for a wind to cut through, but deeply alive with birds and beasts and insects. To Kanda the sky was too small and hidden. A low, pressing sky. A bush of holly stood out dark and hard as burnished metal. The stream they had splashed across, which must be only the rain running down Mal Ealia, trickled along laced with tree roots, glimpsed and met, glimpsed and met. The joy of running, leaping, rolling, down the hillside, the wonder of the white sky and the white sun and the birds in their thousands wheeling star-sparked, that joy was faded, though the woods were beautiful and rich with life.

"It's getting dark," Dellet said fretfully. "We should make some kind of camp." He was an upland farmer, his father and his father's father before him. Liked woods well enough at a distance, beautiful to look at from a moorland hilltop, but....

"We'll find somewhere to stop soon," Kanda said. She looked at Sal, sitting very attentive on the pony, looking and listening all about her.

Droveways run across the high hills, paths made by men to lead their cattle. Henket paths run in the high hills, made by warriors marching to die and to kill, the paths of the dead where the dead might wait. Wilder paths made by beasts, wolf path, deer path, fox path; paths made by the dead walking who cannot rest and are not buried, traced in the sky above by the cries of the wild geese. None of these different paths ran through these oakwoods. No human paths, no animal paths. Yet they followed a path invisible, as long as they followed it they felt no fear. Once four had traveled like this, onward through the night into the dawn, dreaming, through the night into the dawn to rescue Sal. One of those four was dead himself and back to life now, and one of those four was dead and back to life and waiting for them.

We should be hungry, Kanda thought, and thirsty, and tired, and Dellet should certainly have needed to stop to piss. Bracken ran against her legs, she stepped carefully to avoid a patch of celandines waiting to burst into flower. Old White Nose will stop immovable soon, she thought.

A fox trotted ahead of them. Gave them a long stare of fear and wonder, never seen people in this wild wood, trotted away. Old White Nose snorted.

Calian will speak soon, or Dellet will speak, Kanda thought. Calian to moan, Dellet to yawn and sigh. *Old Nosey's getting tired*, Calian will say hopefully. *Dad's tired, look, Sal's tired, needs to stop.* But no one spoke, no one spoke, no one spoke.

A dog barked in the distance. The air began to change. The trees began to change. The trees were great and tall and spreading, but they were strange, empty trees. Two dogs barked. One to the left, one to the right. One to the north, one to the south. On the left side of the path-no-path, a fox with a deer's antlers walked on its hind legs. On the right side of the path-no-path, a crow walked and it had the head of a wolf. Both fled away when Kanda saw them. *Can't see, can't see, can't see*, the crow shouted. Rain came down soft and gray, splashed and sang where it pitted the surface of the stream. The trees were great and tall and spreading, but they were made of bones. The earth was made of bones. The fox hung dead from a bone tree. The crow pecked at its black eyes.

Both turned their heads to watch the family go past. It was hard to walk, for bones crunched and slipped and caught beneath their feet. So they stopped walking.

Sal got down from the pony. Her eyes were very bright, as if she was fevered. She looked around her searching for the two dogs.

Soon they would come to what they were seeking. Kanda felt it, shivered. "I think we should stop for a rest here," she said.

"In these bones?" Calian looked sick. Ah, Kanda thought, you remember deep inside what you did in the village, Calian. And once before that Calian had fought a great battle standing at her mother's right hand, against all the power the darkness could summon, every man in Geiamnyn's army, in Ysarene's army, in the army that was sworn to that one *empty* and *nothing*, who had once been sworn to Ikandera Thygethyn as her war host. A thousand men, and ten times a thousand, and unseen things that crawled and crept and slithered on bloody legs. No fear had been in Calian when she fought that battle, only the joy of killing that which must be killed; she had cut down her enemies until their bodies lay as deep as the ocean, their blood ran like storms when the earth is dry and parched. That had been great killing – and needful. As many men had fallen that day to Calian as there were men's bodies around her now making up this hill of bones and forest of bones.

"In these bones," Kanda said.

Sal sighed. Out of eagerness, or fear, or – something else. She raised her hands, moved her fingers like weaving. The bones began to click and move.

No no no, it was like the dead horse, it was like the dead in Amraen's hall, it was like the dead armies that Ikandera Thygethyn had raised up. *These bones I sow, these bones I scatter, dead children killed in senseless war – and I raise you, I grant you vengeance, you will rise from your deaths each full grown to serve me, each with the strength of twenty men.* Kanda moaned no no no no no no no no no stop it. The bones moved, rose, a little hut, a shelter, stood woven together out of bones. As warm and welcoming as the longhouse in Lela's village.

A good place.

Sal went to the tree where the crow sat and the fox was hanging. "I'm sorry, oh crow," she said, "you are hungry, but we are cold, tired, we need this warm fox pelt."

The crow sat in the tree and looked at Sal, thinking, then it nodded. It flew away, there was a music to the beat of its wings.

"I'm sorry, oh fox," Sal said, "it is a great thing I ask of you. But we are cold, tired, I want to rest a while before…." She frowned. Sighed – and Kanda heard in her daughter's sigh both fear and longing, felt a stab of pain in her own heart, saw Dellet hear and feel the same. "Before what will come will come," Sal said.

The fox hung from the bone tree. It turned its ruined head to Sal. It did not need to think, it only nodded. Sal took the stone knife that she wore on a leather thong around her neck, cut the fox down from the tree.

"You get a fire going, Dad," Sal said. "You tend to the pony, Calian. I want – to rest."

"Tend the pony then, Calian," Kanda said, as if all was quite dull and normal. "Come on, then."

"Tend it how? With what?"

"Use your…initiative, Calian? Umm…?" Umm…. A little while back there was rich good green stuff for a pony to grow fat on.

Calian took off the saddle, rubbed Nosey's flanks. She grimaced, but she looped the reins around a bone branch. In the packs there were apples from Amraen's stores, Kanda's magicked-up apples, Calian scattered some on the bone ground. The pony whinnied appreciatively.

"Yes, you eat them. Enjoy them. And have this to keep you warm, you dear thing." Calian put her cloak over the pony as a blanket.

That was well done. Now Kanda nerved herself to go into the bone hut. "Come on, Del," she said. "Come on, Calian. Now the pony's tended, you can come in and stop dawdling." She stopped on the threshold. As if there would be and should be words that should be said. I'm sorry, she should say to the bone walls, the bone floor. I'm sorry, I'm so very sorry, for killing you.

"What's this?" Dellet said. Inside the hut there were fox furs to sit on, bones stacked to make a hearth.

"A fire," said Sal. "I'm cold." She seemed different suddenly, Kanda thought. Harder, stronger. Strapping armor about herself, perhaps. *You know, Dad, and now I have to tell you…what Calian did and Mum did, and what Morna did, and what Morna said.*

"A fire?" To Kanda the hut felt safe, welcoming indeed, but Dellet, and she herself, frowned at the bone hearth, disgusted. "You can't burn bones like that, Sal," Dellet said. "They won't burn. Like trying to light stones. Pointless." He said, "I won't try. If you want a fire, you or your mother'll have to magic a fire up."

"Just try, Dad," Sal said. "That fire kit Dovei gave you. Try it."

Dellet snorted like the pony at gadflies. "You being lazy, Sal girl? Not like you." He watched the stacked bones in the hearth like they were dangerous and might leap up and bite him. Which seemed fair enough. He was circling them with his hackles up. Which also seemed fair enough. "You can't burn bone like this," he said again. "You can't. It won't work." He squatted down, investigated the hearth as he would a bit of damage to a wall he needed to fix. "If it did, the whole place would burn down, hut and trees and all," he said. "If it did, which it won't, think of the stink." He moved a few bones around in the pile, moved one two three four. He put: bone two where bone one had been, bone one where bone three had been, bone three where bone one had been, bone four back where it had been before. He took bone five away completely, then he put bone five back too. "Won't work, won't work," he muttered all the while. He got out Dovei's fire kit. "I'm sorry," he said to the strike stone. "If you could see me now you'd laugh, Dovei," he said. "'What are you doing, Dellet?' you'd say. 'Just what?'"

The fire took, of course, in but one two three strikes.

Rushed up so fast, such a good fire, that it scorched Dellet's hair and burned his eyebrows off.

That stank. But the bones burned with a white smokeless fire that smelled sweet.

There was a very long silence from Dellet. Crispy bits of his graying hair on his hands where he rubbed his face. "Told you you'd laugh," he said. Sal was smiling smiling smiling, "A very good firestone, this," Dellet said, "thank you, Dovei, my friend. I hope you and yours are well."

CHAPTER THIRTY-FIVE

The Six of Roven had burned their dead, and mourned, and forgotten. Too many dead even for those Six created by the Lord of Roven to stand as lights against the darkness – too many dead even for such as those great ones to bury, to remember every (any) name or face. Ikandera Thygethyn had left her enemies' bodies where they lay, let them rot there, let the dogs and the flies eat them. Her own dead, uncaring, she had left to rot. The people around the valley of the River Wenet where Kanda's farm had stood, they had buried the dead near their houses to keep them close, remembered, part of life still; like the people of Lela and Dovei's village they buried a skull in the walls or beneath the floor of a new house as a charm for luck and health. A long life well-lived would delight in sharing that good fortune with others. A life cut short would strive to give to others what it had never known and had lost. When Kanda had lived in the farm one of her favorite places had been a little ruined grave house on the riverbank where she grazed her cattle, where a man had been buried so long ago that no one could remember his name. She had gone there often to leave a sprig of flowers or a few leaves or pebbles; someone else, she thought it was the young woman from the next farm, went there often and left flowers also. A good place, because of the man buried there, whoever he was, whatever he had been or done.

The shelter Sal had raised looked very much like that grave house must have looked when it was new, round and domed like a bee skep. Felt as good and safe. The bones that made up the shelter…as unknown as the man buried on the bank of the Wenet. Kanda's war dead and Calian's war dead. Somewhere far off a parent or a lover or a child had (perhaps) mourned them. They raised up a shelter now for travelers to rest and find some little comfort. They saw the good gift of fire that one kind man had given another, leapt to receive that fire and give it yet stronger back. Warmth, peace, rest, laughter: the cold dry bones of Kanda's dead and Calian's dead rejoiced to see at last such things. Thus the shelter was as warm and as strong and as welcoming as the houses in Lela's village. The dogs barked in the distance, one to the north, one to the south, not as distant as they had been, soon they would be drawing close. *I have to tell you, Dellet, Calian, I have to tell you what Calian did, and what I did, and what Morna did, and what Morna said.* These words – more words! – that must be spoken were a weight in Kanda's mouth. For a little while, though, she sat quiet among the bones with her hands resting peaceful, rejoiced in the fire's warmth.

CHAPTER THIRTY-SIX

The dogs barked. One to the north, one to the south. They were almost upon them. They were very close. Sal said, "Mother. Mum. I—" The dogs barked and they were not to the north and the south, they were outside the hut.

"It's time we spoke, Mum," Sal said, just as Kanda said, "It's time and past time we spoke, Sal my love. If we don't speak now, it will be too late."

I know what you will say, Sal, Kanda thought. I wish you never need say it. But more: I wish you had told me long ago. Do you think so little of me, Sal, not to be able to tell me?

Ah, a bitter pain in Ikandera Thygethyn's heart now, what do you think I will say or do to you, Sal? Do you think I will be angry with you? I mean, I'll try, Sal, not to be angry with you, and I won't, I mean, not really be angry with you, not for long. I'll yell, you'll yell, I'll weep. Then it'll be said and done. So knowing this I don't understand, Sal, why you don't speak and I don't speak.

"I need to speak, Mum."

They went out of the hut together. "The dogs?" Kanda said, but Sal said, "They're near, but they won't show themselves yet." A bone moon had risen. It lit white the bone trees. The crow hung, poor wretch, where the fox had been hanging. Antlers on its head. The twin stars Irulth shone right overhead. The *Gate.* Words and secrets came running now like a frightened child through that gate.

"Those dogs…." Sal said. "Morna, I mean…."

"Yes?" Kanda said. She thought: like a baby birthing, or a fever rising, or a storm: it's coming and I can't make it stop. It's coming rushing now like the day ending, like the summer ending and the winter coming on. Like a man dying, it's coming now and I cannot stop it. Sal: stop speaking, Sal:

swallow the words down. I beg you, Sal. Have pity on me. She could hear the waters of a great river churning in the dark so near them. The Wenet, the river she loved that had flowed through the farmland on which she had raised her three children. Wild and terrible, the river sounded. Running to drown a man.

"I was a girl of sixteen when I went down into the dark to marry Geiamnyn," Sal said. "I came out of those dark halls an old woman. Dad and Calian think this aging– they think it was some cruel magic of Geiamnyn's. But you know, don't you Mother?

"For you at home it was three days, but for me – I spent a lifetime in the dark wedded to Geiamnyn."

"Your father thinks it is a spell Geiamnyn worked on you," said Kanda. Dellet's mind.... Some things no parent can endure to know unless it is said openly, and even then.... *Three days, and she kept him away from her with her knife*, his heart can only think. "I don't know about Calian."

"I told you I kept him off me," Sal said. "And I did."

"I know you did." She thought of Geiamnyn in his golden beauty, young and strong. How much, once, Kanda herself had enjoyed looking at him.

Don't speak it, Sal. Please don't speak. Put the stone back in your mouth. Stop, Sal! I command it! If you have any love for me, Sal, don't speak another word, for the pain will cause my heart to break.

"He was very beautiful," Sal said. "My husband."

And your father, Sal, think of him and be merciful and don't speak. I know what you want to say, Sal, if you dare say it, I will be so angry I am afraid I will kill you.

"He was my friend for many years," Kanda said. "He was like a brother to me. I cared deeply for him." And that was the bravest thing she might ever have said.

Sal said, "I held him off with my knife and would not let him come near me, because he was a murderer and a monster, a bloody beast.

"But I wanted to make something of my life beyond waiting in that darkness.

"So one night, I put down my knife."

Ah. Yes. Stop speaking, Sal! I command it: close your mouth! Bind your lips shut with gold thread! That sound you hear, Kanda, that is the last of all your world shattering. But the twin stars Irulth shone as bright as sunshine, Sal's words ran on and on unstoppable through that open gate.

"I had a daughter," Sal said. "A beautiful daughter, with golden curls on her head just like his. Her eyes were green as the green grass and her skin was golden. She was strong and healthy and I felt no pain when I labored with her. Her skin smelled like new-baked bread.

"One night, she lived.

"Geiamnyn wept over her body beside me. Wept until I thought he had a heart to break.

"Six daughters I bore to Geiamnyn. Six daughters died before they had lived a night and a day. Six graves Geiamnyn dug for them.

"I took up my knife then, because I knew it was him, Geiamnyn, he was so vile he could never father a child that lived. I warded him off, I cursed him, I spat at him.

"But I wanted a living child. My arms ached, my heart ached!

"So, after many years had passed, I put down my knife, I opened my arms to him.

"I bore him a son.

"A splendid son, he was as big at two days old as most children are after a year, at three days old he was walking. His hair was golden curls like his father, his eyes were green as the green grass, his skin was white and gold as his father's skin. He smelled of honey in the comb and new milk and wet earth in spring.

"'My son! My fine son!' Geiamnyn said of him. 'He will not die, this boy! He will live and live and live!'

"And he lived!

"Such joy I had in him, my baby boy, my child! Such joy…and so after a little while had passed again I put down my knife and I opened my arms to Geiamnyn.

"I bore a second son. A splendid son, he was as clever at two days old as most children are after a year, at three days old he was talking. His hair was silver curls, his eyes were blue as the evening sky, his skin was silver-gray.

He smelled of may blossom and starlight on cold waters and autumn mist.

"'My son! My fine son!' Geiamnyn said of him. 'He will not die, this boy! He will live and live and live!'

"He did live!

"Geiamnyn raised them both as great warriors. By the time my elder son was ten years old he could kill a boar with his bare hands, tame a wild stallion to ride into battle, with one stroke of his sword he could take off a grown man's head. By the time my younger son was ten years old he could outrun a hind with the hounds behind it, he could shoot an arrow from one shore of the sea to the other, he could command an army.

"'My fine sons!' Geiamnyn said of them. 'Look at them!' I could not disagree with him. When they were grown to manhood Geiamnyn took them away in a silver ship with crimson sails, and when they returned my sons were dressed in gold armor, on their heads were gold helmets plumed in burning fire, in their hands were swords with blades of black fire and spears with points of white fire, each rode a red horse that could run faster than the storm winds.

"They loved each other like brothers should. Delighted in each other's company. There was never any rivalry between them.

"They loved their father. And they loved me, Mother. I loved them, my sons, my strong terrible monstrous sons, and they loved me! They returned from their wars with gold and jewels and cattle and slaves beyond any counting, they offered it all up to me because they loved me. I took it all from them joyfully, because I loved them."

She said, her voice tiny and ashamed and filled with happiness: "I had done so much more with my life in that dark place than only waiting. I raised them to be warriors, and I was so proud of them.

"I am – so proud of them."

She said, "I left them behind me when I fled with you. I am glad I fled with you, Mum. Of course I am. Never, not for one moment, would I go back, not for anything.

"But for all that they are like to their father, monsters, killers, warlords – I do so greatly miss my sons."

She said, "My sons' names are Mannan and Camryth."

CHAPTER THIRTY-SEVEN

What shall I tell your father? And Calian. What will she say?

Why didn't you tell me you had children? Why didn't you tell me? I'm your mother, Sal. How could you not have told me?

I should have known without being told. How can I not know my own daughter has children? But I remember Dellet looking up at Morna, the cry he gave then. I'm your father, Morna, he said, I should have known that you were still alive. But he didn't know. I didn't know.

How can someone not know? About their own children?

Darkness came over Kanda's eyes. Night fell over her heart. She shook. She moaned in grief. I too, I thought – I lied— Three days, you spent as Geiamnyn's wife, Sal. You were there less time than it takes to reap the barley in the south field; less time than it takes to brew a vat of ale, to fire a cook pot. You cannot—

My daughter bore children, and I was not there to help her. I was not there to see them.

In the dark, alone, my daughter labored, gave birth, raised her children.

She looked at Sal's old face that had lived a lifetime, she held Sal's beautiful hard-worked hands with the stains of a life on them. She thought: I must be strong now, I must not grieve. I must not be a weight to my child after all she has suffered. I must not feel anger or pain or grief.

And Sal says sadly, "I love my children by him. What does it mean, that I – with him – that I reared – his sons? That I love – his sons? What does that mean about me? Mum?"

And Kanda says brightly, "What it means, Sal, is that you chose to live your life as best you were able. It means that even in that darkness you found something good."

But she thinks: lying, lying.

CHAPTER THIRTY-EIGHT

And they must tell Dellet and Calian.

Kanda must tell them. Muster all the strength of Ikandera Thygethyn and of the Six of Roven.

Calian did not at first see it meant something good.

"What are you? How could you? With him? I would have stabbed him in the heart and cut off his manhood. I would have cut my own throat, rather than…with him." Calian was still very young.

Dellet closed his eyes, when Sal told him his face was that of a man who has lived too long. He sat with his eyes closed, he clenched unclenched clenched his kind fists. Two tears ran down his face, one from each of his closed eyes. Screwed up face and eyes to stop himself crying. Or to make himself weep. He got up from the hearth where he had been sitting so pleased and enchanted by the bone fire. "I lit that," he had been saying to himself, so pleased, when they came in to tell him. "Me." His body trembled. He opened his arms to Sal, held her as tight as she had held him to protect him from the slaughter in the feast hall. He ran out of the shelter and struck his own head with his hands and tore at his hair. He bit his own hand. He came back inside to Sal and there was white spittle on his lips. He held Sal tight. He said, wondering: "So, I have two grandsons."

"That monster," Calian said then. Her voice was so fierce and angry that Kanda drew back from her in fear. "That woman. I knew she was one of them. Worse than Ysarene, worse than Geiamnyn, worse than that *empty* one, even, that woman! Why does she—? What does she want, mocking Sal like that, calling her dogs after Sal's – Sal's sons?"

Ah, soon, soon, the worst words of all must now be spoken, worse words by far than Sal's words. Nothing good, no pretense at joy, in those words she must say to Calian and to Dellet. "I don't know why she had done this," Kanda said to Calian. "To hurt. Only that. Because it amuses her."

She did not say what she thought was true, that – that Morna had thought her mocking words would tear the family apart in hate. No need for swords or monsters: the four of them would fight, rage, all would be broken by the news of Sal's children by Geiamnyn. *"Whore, bitch, shameless,"* Dellet would shout, *"no daughter of mine. Disgusting." "How could you, I would never have done such a thing, you should have fought him harder,"* Calian would scream. *"My sickness repeated in you,"* Kanda would weep, *"and worse"*; then Dellet would turn on her also, *"Yes, yes, your daughter, vile as you are, corrupt, filthy, both of you, go, get away from here, both of you, better that Geiamnyn had killed you."* And that was how it was, yes, for a little while, yelling, screaming, vile words, curses, gnashing and baring of teeth, and they would not have been people if they had not said and thought those things.

And perhaps they might always sometimes with and without meaning think such things. But they were not broken apart by them.

CHAPTER THIRTY-NINE

Long and hard that night, and hard to sleep, when sleep was such a great thing for healing. So: my Sal is a mother. So: I have two grandsons. The words ran together round and round and over and over in Kanda's head and so loud she could hear them in Dellet's head. Morning came at last and far too quickly. So: my Sal is a mother. So: I have two grandsons. So: Sal, and Geiamnyn. Calian's eyes were red and weary and so angry, Dellet's eyes were red with grief. But so: morning. But so: they must set out again. So close to something now. So far from where they had started, days and days and days.

To a child, that's a very long way away. To a king or a warlord or a great lady, that's but a little way down the road.

They walked through the bone forest. Bones crunched and shifted beneath their feet. It was still dark, the bone sun had not yet risen to shine its white light down on the bone leaves. The family walked in silence, it did not seem right to speak in this place. Only when they had first left the hut that morning they had thanked the dead ones whose bones had sheltered them, and the bones had whispered as they fell away back into the earth.

No barking of dogs. But the dogs were very close behind, Kanda could almost hear their panting, the scuff of their feet on the bones. Sal sat on the pony's back with her head raised, stared straight ahead of her. Her face was very calm. A smile on her lips. She seemed to look not at the world they walked through but at something far off and hidden that only she could see. Once, Kanda saw, her right hand went to her throat where her stone knife hung. Once, twice, her left hand went to her stomach.

"Tell me about them," Kanda wanted to say to her. "Tell me about my grandsons." But this was not the place.

The trees were made of bone, still, the ground beneath Kanda's feet bones a mile deep. But life coming in the shadowless, soundless light of first morning. Birds beginning their sun-songs, calling the sun, urging it on to rise, to live. Bloody discharge – the sun's birthing. The tops of the bone trees gilded red. Kanda could hear water running. A great river. The Wenet. Wide and huge. She could hear it but not see it.

Ah, Kanda thought, we are back on the right track. We are leaving the dead behind us. We are coming to the end.

So now, now, Morna was coming.

They stopped for a rest and a meal, in a place where a bone oak tree bent its branches over a thicket of bone plants. Calian looked it up and down, thought long, said, "We can stop here, can't we?"

Kanda said, "Yes. I want to stop and rest."

"I saw a deer," Dellet said, "on the other bank. A fox's tail, just a flash." He pointed up. "There's a nest up in the tree above us. A bird on her eggs." He said, "So look out where you sit, to warn you. Trust Calian to stop where a bird shits."

Calian and Sal were fussing over Old White Nose. He was chomping an apple, they were petting him. Calian's voice came drifting: "Oh, you good deary thing!" Calian was trying very hard to be a girl with her sister. See Sal as not…not….

Dellet looked at Kanda like he expected her to say something. What do you want me to say, Dellet? She thought it, then she said it: "What do you want me to say?"

"I don't know, Kanda," Dellet said. The bird in the nest did shit in the bush just next to Kanda.

Dellet said, "So, Kanda, we're grandparents, then." He laughed, "You're a grandmother, Kanda, and I'm an old grandpa. Listen to my creaking knees and bad jokes."

He said, "From what I understand, we've rather skipped over the helping out with screaming and wet clout cloths eight times a night bit. I know you'd have helped Sal gladly with all of that. But I can't say I'm entirely sorry." Held out his hand. Strong and heavy in the bone-white dapple, aging like Kanda's hand was aging, but strong and able, calloused with work. Not an old man's hand, in the strange light it looked indeed no older than it had when they joined hands in marriage, so Kanda was not surprised when he said, "I don't feel old enough to be a grandpa. And my wife a grandma! But I suppose that's what grandpas all say. Seems like only yesterday Sal was a child herself in clout cloths. But that's not a funny thing to say." He squeezed Kanda's hand tight. Dry rough skin that was not entirely pleasant to hold. "Ah, Kanda, wife, how has it come to this for us? Our Calian, our Sal.... Me a grandpa, you a grandma. That doesn't suit you the way a sword does, I'll tell you that.

"There's that fox barking," Dellet said. "Ah, that's a sound." He shook his head. "But 'Grandpa Dellet': I suppose there are far worse things a man could be."

Kanda said carefully, "Their father was a monster. They may – will – be monsters too."

"Their father's dead and gone, and good riddance. My daughter killed him. Whatever they are, they're Sal's children, until we meet them that's all there is anyone can say. That's all there is to say now. So that's all I'm saying."

A long silence. They both looked at the dappled light in the bone trees and at the bird shit.

"I will tear the birds from the sky! I will trample the trees beneath my feet! I will burn the world and break the world and piss on the ruins I have left!" That is what Geiamnyn would say sometimes. *"There will be only a scar where the world is."*

"They might live in the dark, but they are – Sal's children," Dellet said. "They will be—Just because—

"Whatever their lives, they must be—"

"I will piss on the sun to put it out!" Geiamnyn would say.

"They're Sal's children," Dellet said.

They got up, began to walk on. One, two, three, four, five, six steps. Seven steps. Eight steps. They had counted steps when Sal and Calian and Morna were little, such a game it had been by the time Morna was ready to play it, one two three four of them teaching Morna to count one two three four five six steps. Seven steps. Eight steps. There were twenty steps on Morna-sized legs from the front door of the farmhouse to the apple tree. There were forty steps from the apple tree round to the cow byre behind the house, but by then everyone but Calian had got bored of playing. "One two three," Morna had said whenever she walked anywhere, for months she had done that when she was first talking, because they did it so often she thought it was a necessary part of this thing *to walk*. So nine steps, ten steps, did you count like this with your sons, Sal my *Shining*, did Geiamnyn count with them like this? eleven steps, twelve steps. All the woods were alive with small shy creatures, insects, birds, plants, flowers, all around them in the white bones things were alive and things were dying and things were being born. Thirteen steps, fourteen, only Calian would have the patience to count soon. There was the crow, and the squirrel and his wife and his rival for his wife's affections, they ran and chased in the trees *ratatatusk*. There was the fox. It ran from the woods onto the path and it was filled with fear of the family and it fled away.

The dogs barked, one to right, one to the left, one to the north, one to the south.

From the west before them came a blaze of sunlight. Kanda's heart leapt. The dogs barked as loud as thunder. *Come on*, they seemed to say. Like hunting dogs who have found their quarry, calling their master on.

"I'm coming, Morna my love," Kanda almost cried aloud. And Sal, too, seemed to cry something as she urged the pony on.

The green trees ended very suddenly. The land fell away sheer. A gorge, a crack in the earth, very deep. A river flowed far below. The River Wenet, Kanda thought. It was grown wide, a mighty river such as even she had rarely seen, a river such as forms the boundary between kingdoms. The gorge was so deep and so wide that the river seemed only a stream. A bridge, beautiful, carved of black stone, spanned the gorge, so high above the water it cast no reflection in the river's depths. On the other side of the gorge rose the walls of a great city, with open gates. Beyond the city, in the farthest purple distance, a flash of light merely, a sense of light and dark at the farthest end of all things, was the sea.

The dogs sat on the bridge waiting. One marked with white, one marked with brown, silver collars about their necks. They leapt up joyfully when they saw the family, bayed, skipped, ran on across the bridge.

Many great cities, Ikandera Thygethyn had seen in the course of her long life. Kydana in the dry wastes, city of the wise; Erelene, bride of cities; Tyren of the Five Hillsides; Inakanassos in the Forever Morning. Temples, tombs, libraries, graveyards. Bath houses, pleasure gardens, palaces, colonnades, loggias, archways, shaded courtyards for a lady to sit quiet in while her pet monkey chatters and her servants sprinkle perfume and paint her long fingernails beetle-red. Cities that were filled with joy. Cities that were bleak with toil. Cities that were built on narrow piety to a dull harsh god.

This city with its spires of pearl and silver, this city with its marble walls, this city with its gardens, its domes, its towers – this city was the fairest and the greatest city that Kanda had ever seen.

All our hearts' desires, she thought. Yes! She looked across at her daughters, saw the hunger, the wonder, on both their faces. And Dellet also, astonished, mouth gaping – what is this, Kanda? These last days, so much, too much, I am an old man now, a grandfather, my daughter Morna I know in my heart yet lives – yet all of the wonders and the horrors, wife, Kanda, for a moment here it seems – it seems – this city is the most terrible, the strangest, the most wondrous.

Dellet shook his head. "What's that, Kanda, wife?" He said, "I thought we were looking for…for a hall, Kanda, not…not…."

For Kanda had seen such places before, and Sal perhaps had when she was Geiamnyn's queen in those dark halls beneath the mountain, and Calian had seen such places perhaps in her warrior's dreams. But Dellet had never seen or dreamed of such places. He trembled to look at the city. He could not comprehend what he was seeing. Battles he had seen – briefly, before he was killed in one; feasts and a king's throne and magic he had seen. Not a city like this.

The dogs barked. They had run to the open gates of the city, waited there eagerly for the family to follow them. By some trick or spell or something stranger, they seemed big and near so that Kanda could see the eagerness in them, although the bridge was long and the city vast. They barked and called for the family to come to them. Sal seemed to start forward, her face bright as a child's, *come on! come on!*

The dogs growled. Crouched, hackles raised. Bared their teeth.

War dogs, hunting dogs, fierce and well able to kill.

Kanda's hand went to her sword, she thought: kill these beasts!

Sal shouted, "No! Mother.... They can't...."

Calian shouted, "Look!"

Dark shapes and pale shapes. Behind them. Rising out of the bone woods. Rushing, riding. Warriors on horseback, but they were not horses, they were monsters, savage, fangs tearing from their mouths, fire flashing from their hooves. The horses were white and their riders were white. White clothes, white skin, white hair, white swords.

They came down the path the family had followed. A narrow path, fit only for walkers and cattle, they came down it all six together with a wide space between each. Like a waterfall bursting and rushing hungry and fair and all-devouring, pouring down in rain-sodden flood-bearing ruin and nurturing spate. The horses' hooves like the wave caps rushing, the horses' manes and their wide wild eyes. Liquid, they came, like their own eyes, wide and mad and rolling with fear. Like the wave caps white and churned in sea-storm, like the foam and wave of the waterfall pouring. They rose and broke and crushed all down beneath to fall and break. Hooves and swords and the roar of harsh voices.

"Stay back! Go back! Turn back!" the riders shouted. And they were on Kanda so fast that she could not but meet them with her sword and with a shout. As a wave breaks and there is no time to breathe or think but only to gasp and flap in the cold water, as the shock of falling and being struck and fearing and there are no words. Her sword struck without need of thinking, her feet already braced, her body fixed and clenched to meet.

And Calian beside her with her sword held high, waiting, waiting, and the killing light again in Calian's eagle eyes.

Horses and riders and heavy blades. A whirl and a crush, the roar of hooves and metal. Horse stink, skin stink, bronze stink.

Kanda struck, her black sword heavy against a sword that was bigger and longer reaching. White horse, white clothing, white blade – hard it was to tell where to strike. Ring of metal, sword-song, as her enemy's blade and her blade met. The horse ran on, unstoppable as water. Kanda spun and braced to meet another rider, again she struck, again the blades met singing. Again horse and rider rushed on unwounded past. A third, white brightness dazzling to her eyes. She struck. Deeper. Harder. Felt her sword meet flesh, not metal, felt it wound, cut deep. Her enemy unscathed, uncaring, rode on.

Through, as water breaks the dam and rushes onward, nothing can stop it, halt it. Six riders on the bridge between Kanda and the city. At the far end of the bridge, before the open gates, the two dogs howled in grief.

"I got one," said Calian. Her sword was stained with blood. There, yes, one was injured. Both horse and rider cut and soaked in red blood.

"Well done, Calian." Did I hurt one? Kanda thought. No? How did my daughter wound one, but not me?

"Will they come again?" Calian whispered. She stared at the enemy with longing. The horses snorted, pawed the ground. Smoke curled from their fanged mouths. The riders sat silent. Six faces fixed, looking at nothing. They might be one face, drawn out on a cliff face six times in the chalk.

"Go back!" the riders shouted in one voice. "Stay back. Turn back."

"Never!" Calian shouted. Kanda's heart sank. Of all the words in any language that ever had or would be spoken, those were the worst words that could be said to Calian. Six times a hundred warriors she would kill now if she had to, rather than not cross that marble bridge.

A thought, then. Kanda looked behind her. The woods stood dark, the trees densely packed together, branches entwined. Scrub and brambles and low branches, humps and hollows and tangled roots. An impenetrable wild wood.

No path. No way back.

"Turn back!" the riders cried. Their horses champed their bloody teeth, stamped their hooves until the bridge shook. "Go back!"

Kanda thought then: they sound almost afraid, this time, as if they fear that we will go in.

Calian shook her sword at the riders. "What is there inside this city that you would keep from me?" The two dogs howled at her words. "I will cross into this city or die for it," Calian shouted.

Alas, indeed, for a stubborn young girl with a sword. Kanda's heart said wearily: Oh Calian. You will shout any moment those most terrible of young girl words: You. Do. Not. Tell. Me. What. To. Do.

"There is nowhere else to go, Mother," Sal said. "We have to go past them." That shook Kanda: Calian the fierce one would fight to the death now to go past and not turn back, but Sal, wise and gentle – surely Sal would see sense? *We can go back into the woods, find the droveway, walk through green trees with the stink of ramsons and the drifts of lush spring flowers. Follow the path onward like any family walking, never know what was in this city we have found. Her heart lightened, a healing warmth in her, at that thought.*

"We must go in!" Sal cried. "These.... These.... I will not let them stop me!" Real anger in Sal's voice.

"Will you charge at them on your pony, Sal?" Gray hair flapping like a flag in the wind....

"If I must." Sal's voice was distant. Not hearing the absurd and bitter humor in her mother's voice.

"Sal?"

The dream of this city, Kanda thought. All the longing in the world, to cross into this city where their hearts' desire waited. She had promised them a quest to find the Hall Roven, *Peace*, with its golden roof and silver walls. *Health* was housed there, and *Hope*, and beauty, splendor, joy, grace. Great lords, fair ladies, feasts, silks. What had they found so far on this great questing? Two crude villages of wooden huts. A city rose here more splendid even than Roven. The Lord of Roven, the Lady of Roven herself, would stand in awe before the walls of this city. The Lord and Lady of Roven, the Six in their shining armor, would look mean, like beggars, before these city walls.

"Turn back!" the riders cried. Kanda thought she heard in their one voice a note like: *please.*

"I will cross this bridge and enter this city as I chose," Calian shouted. "You cannot stop me. You will not stop me. For my mother is the war leader Ikandera Thygethyn!" Calian shouted.

"No, Calian!" Kanda screamed.

Never. Never. Never have I boasted of that. Not in your hearing, Calian, at least. Or...if I did...when I did...I didn't mean.... Not like that, Calian, not as something for...for you to claim. And she thought of Amraen's hall, her joy there, the pleasure his fawning had raised in her – but that was because...because...that was not...he was an old comrade from the past, Calian, that was but nostalgia for long-vanished never-to-return days. So old men return to the stories of their childhoods, yes, but they don't expect, they don't mean— When we say, *the world was better then*, when we say, *ah, the young today...ah, it was good*— Those are but stories told to pass the time, Calian! Games! Dreams!

Lies, Calian.

But Calian cried, "I am Calian the *Eagle*, daughter of Ikandera Thygethyn, many enemies already I have killed! Men and women and children! My sister promised me that I would find my heart's desire within this city. Even were this city of no interest to me, mere rubble, another village merely of cowering craven men – I am Calian the daughter of Ikandera Thygethyn. I go where I choose."

Calian remembered all that had passed in Amraen's feast hall. She had lied to Kanda and to Sal, pretended that the magic (Morna's magic? Sal's? Kanda's?) had worked. Days, she had gone on deceiving them, proud all the time of the slaughter she had wrought. Rejoicing in the memory of the slaughter she and Kanda had wrought.

Kanda knew this, every part of it – perfect, clear truth. For in her secret soul Kanda knew that she too had lied. That Calian's pride in her mother as Queen Ikandera Thygethyn was a glorious thing and a wondrous thing. That it was because of Calian's joy and pride in her mother as Queen Ikandera Thygethyn that Kanda had blessed King Amraen. That it was because of Calian's joy and pride at the people's fear of her mother as Queen Ikandera Thygethyn that Kanda had killed them all and let them all be brought back to life.

Passing fine to stand shoulder to shoulder with her daughter, killing, each delighted by the other's power and strength. Long years, yes, Ikandera Thygethyn had yearned for this. In Amraen's feast hall – ah, that had been the best of days, the day she had dreamed of since she first knew she was pregnant. Two against a hundred, and neither mother nor daughter had been found wanting.

A true test of a warrior now: to stand on foot against a horse charge. So, please, now, may this girl, my daughter, may she be like me, first in glory, first in bloodshed. Strong and brave and dauntless, a better warrior even than I. When these enemy riders charge, let her make me proud when she kills them. Let us stand together side by side, and let me rejoice in her strength. So Kanda's heart begged.

Calian cried, "I too am a *great warrior*! Meet my sword! Come on! If you do not come to us now, I will rush at you! Cowards! I will enter this city trampling on your corpses! I will kill you all! I will cross into this city on a river of your blood!"

The dogs let out a howl, they bayed and bayed like hounds when they scent the kill. The horses champed and stamped, smoke came from their mouths, blood welled beneath their feet. The riders raised their swords, kicked their horses forward, horses and riders charged. Across the bridge that shook beneath the thunder of their hooves, together as one warrior and one horse straight at Kanda and Calian. Kanda braced herself, sword out, waiting. Calian laughed, gritted her teeth, shook her sword. Sal and Dellet cowered, arms clutched around each other behind Kanda, as if Kanda could shelter them from the oncoming storm.

The white swords all together met and struck Kanda and Calian.

CHAPTER FORTY

Whirl and rush and spin of killing. Like dragging currents, a riptide – there is no use in fighting it. White water rapids spinning a body, knocking head and limb against the rocks – and there is no use in fighting, the water drags the body on, throws it, drowns it. And the currents drive the body onward, sink it down, thrust it up. And there is no use in fighting these strong currents, and the body is hurled and flung and torn and twisted, drowned and drowned again again again. Thus it was to be two on foot before a charge of six great mounted warriors, two with short swords against six spears and long blades. Spun and thrown in a current of horses' movements, smashed against horse flesh and human flesh while the blades bit deep. Gasping, breath coming faintly, blinded by the bulk, like mountains, of these vast things. Roar of noise – horse breath, human breath, hooves in your head in your heart thundering out. No faces. No wild white rolling horse eyes. Roar and crash and stink and nothing in your own wild eyes but bronze and horses and six great spears and six great blades that fall. Your sword so small, jabbed at horse flesh, human flesh. Your sword is red. Horse blood and human blood runs. Your blood runs.

Kanda: you are gasping, panting, falling. The horses and the riders grow around you huge as worlds. You are failing, Kanda, as the light from a star fades at last as the dawn comes. The swords beat down, you cannot ward them. Horses' hooves stamp and break the earth. Human sweat drips, stings your wounds. A white sword blade cuts your hand. You let go of your sword. A hoof crashes down. Your sword is lost beneath churning horses' hooves. You are an old woman, Kanda, a grandmother, gray-haired, gray-boned. Of wildfire and sown earth, and red autumn berries, the Lord of Roven made you – you are the sun as it sinks tired and wounded, the autumn as it gives in to winter death. You are too old and weak. Long ago, you threw away your sword *Kind Strength.*

You cry out.

Cry out.

The riders break.

Thunder of hooves, and shouting. Fearful. Kanda's eyes swam dark, she could see nothing, hear nothing but these distant cries of warriors and horses. So much pain in her. Running like horses through her body and her head. She blinked. Tried, failed, tried to raise her head.

The riders were gone. Kanda strained, flailed to get her head up. Like a baby flailing and straining. The earth around her was trampled and bloody. She could see the riders at the very edge of her vision, drawn up again in a line before the city's open gates.

Calian stood, sword lowered now, only watching, between her mother and the riders.

Kanda: Calian is the dawn. Her sword is the sun rising to banish the star's light. On foot, alone, she fought six mounted warriors until they broke. Not *kind strength,* your daughter Calian, but *burning strength.*

You are weak and spent, Kanda, old, gray as winter trees. But: Kanda: be proud! Your daughter is a great warrior now. See how fierce and strong she is! Fierce strength! Burning strength!

Kanda: your daughter is a greater warrior than you are, just as you always hoped.

CHAPTER FORTY-ONE

Painfully, slowly, Kanda got to her feet.

Sal and Dellet came toward her. They too moved slowly. They looked like cranes picking their way across a marsh. It seemed to take a lifetime for her husband and her daughter to reach her. Three lifetimes she had lived, and this walk to meet her was as long. When they reached her they held her close. But that embrace was not long.

"Are you hurt?"

Kanda looked down at herself. Many wounds, the fine clothes Amraen had given her were torn and bloodstained. But already the wounds were healing.

"I'm not hurt," she said. Inevitably, she thought at once: *lying, lying*. She thought: a true test of a warrior, that battle. One I seem to have failed. You have forgotten how to fight, Ikandera Thygethyn. Or at least, to fight anything but cowards and shadows and unarmed peasant children. She bent down, winced as she did so, made a noise in her throat to try to cover her groan as she more often might try to cover an ill-timed fart, picked up her sword.

"You are hurt!" Dellet said.

"No, really. Just…shaken." (And the attempts to cover a fart were as convincing, drew more attention to the farting than the fart itself did, and she was rambling half-crazed from the battle like an old grandmother half asleep.)

"Is Old White Nose all right?" she asked Sal, because that too seemed important.

"I…I think so…." Sal said.

"Good."

Sal said, "Are you sure you're all right, Mum?"

You have two sons by that monster Geiamnyn, Sal, and I'm a grandmother, and Morna is alive and that *empty* one's daughter, and Calian and I killed every man, woman and child in a village, and for the first time in my life I have just lost a fight. I can worry about a pony if I want to. Kanda said, "I'm fine, yes."

They looked at the line of riders, drawn up on the bridge. Very still now, like statues not living things. Silent faces blank as masks. The same face, six times reflected, the same hair, the same rich clothing.

"Go back! Turn back!" six voices one voice shouted again.

They are guarding the city, Kanda thought.

They are guarding the city…from us. Me, and Calian. And they are right to do so, she thought.

"We should do as they say," Kanda said. "Turn back into the woods, find the right path that leads to the sea. We have got lost here again, always we are getting lost and being led by false hopes and false fear off our right road. These riders mean us no harm, as long as we do not try to cross into the city, they do not seek to attack us, you see? They are not our enemies." She said ruefully, "That is what happens on a quest."

"I will go into that city if it kills me," Calian said. She stood very still also, her sword lowered but bright in her hand.

"This is the right path, Mother," Sal said. "I know it." And all the time she was looking beyond Kanda at the city's gate.

"Come on!" Calian shouted. "Morna promised we would find her here! Come on! We can fight them! Kill them! Look behind you, Mother – there's no way back through the forest. Morna is waiting for us, what do you want her to think? That we turned back? That we didn't want to see her?"

"Morna is in that city," Dellet shouted. "You know she is, Kanda, wife. Those riders seek to keep us from finding her there."

Then I will thank those riders with all my heart, Dellet, as if they were old and dear friends. And then the horror struck Kanda. That her husband and her child spoke of Morna alive and waiting. Knew what she had said. Knew what Kanda and Calian had done.

And both Dellet and Calian had lied that they had forgotten that night in Amraen's feast hall. Thought Kanda and Sal had forgotten all that had happened there; in their kindness they had kept the secret just as Sal and Kanda had kept the secret from them. *Don't speak of it to Sal and your mum, Cal-bird; it's horrible I know, but look, they don't remember and...some things.... It'll kill your mum, Cal, if she knows what Morna said to me, so it's best.* Kanda thought: was Morna's magic to make us lie that we had forgotten, was that a cruel thing or a kind thing?

Or: not lied: Dellet had not spoken of it, Kanda had not spoken of it, Calian had not spoken of it, all had presumed and merely pretended. *She hasn't said, so if I don't say anything....* No magic at all. Or only more of the common ineffectual magic we use every day. Like a man coughing up blood in the morning, *everyone does it, perfectly normal, not to feared; if I can't see it I only imagined it and it was never there so close my eyes and wipe it up*. Like a child hiding a broken cup under the bedframe, *we never had a cup like that ever, no, Mum, not ever, I don't know what you're talking about, Mum, what cup?*

So now we speak too late and the battle comes.

"Morna is waiting on the other side of those riders," Dellet said. "My Morn-Morn, and she was angry with us, rightly, she was angry, but she'll forgive us now, Kanda, wife. We turned our backs on her once, left her – you left her, Kanda, you thought she was dead! She's there in that city waiting for us. You might pretend, but in your heart you know it and I know."

"But those riders will kill us," Kanda whispered. And, indeed, "Turn back! Go back!" the riders cried. If Calian and I go into that city, Kanda thought, it will be only more death.

"Never!" Calian shouted.

"Morna is there waiting inside the city," Dellet said. He said in a dry dead quiet voice, "She thinks I abandoned her. She's not wrong in that." Like a dried-up dead old toad he looked. He began to walk toward the bridge, toward the line of warriors.

Sal gave a hopeless glance at her mother. Then she nudged the pony to walk toward the bridge. Kanda knew what Sal thought waited for her there. Thought and feared and hoped.

"Turn back! Go back!" The riders drew their swords. The horses gnashed their teeth. Charging, running horses.

Calian knows – does not regret – what she and I did.

And if you heard but the outline of it – two against so many – it was in truth a mighty deed of warrior skill.

And Morna is there waiting, monster that she is, and I will not fail her and lose her again. All the blood that ever was shed in battle, may all that blood be shed, for I will not lose my child again. And thus in the end, Kanda thought, does every parent speak. What would I be, if I did not speak so?

"Do it, then, Calian," Kanda said. "Kill the warriors. Make it safe so that we can go in."

Calian stepped forward, readied herself to leap and run.

Then Calian looked at her mother with wide eyes. "With you, Mum. Not without you fighting beside me, Mum."

CHAPTER FORTY-TWO

Killing and killing until her arms ached.

Trampling the blood of warriors and horses, Kanda walked into the city through the open gates.

CHAPTER FORTY-THREE

Once, long ago, in the first morning of the world before she knew that men too could be called evil, Kanda had led the Six Swords of Roven against four vast dragons. Beasts so huge they had filled the sky. One gold, one silver, one black, one white. Six Swords of Roven, tiny, set against them. They had come against Roven with the harvest, the workers in the fields had been bringing in the wheat when they came. The workers had fled, shrieking, the harvest had been scattered, the ripe wheat and the good straw had burst up in flames. The orchards, too, the dragons had burned, the apple trees and the plum trees. The apples had been ready for eating, the plums lush and ripe. Old trees, beloved friends they seemed, that the children of Roven delighted in climbing. It is very safe and easy to climb a fruit tree. The orchards burned, the trees and the grass and the flowers beneath them, the pigs fattening half-drunk on windfall apples had squealed as they burned. All Roven had cried out in fear and outrage, never before had danger come so close, the golden roof and silver wall of Roven, even, were marked by the dragons' fires. The Six had seized their swords, rushed to battle.

Stopped rushing. Stood in the burned fields. Gazed upward at the dragons.

"They are so beautiful," Morren cried, yearning.

"The most beautiful things I have ever seen or ever will see," Kestre whispered, and the tears ran down her cheeks. Like liquid gold, her tears looked, reflecting the dragons' fires.

Palle's lips were thin, his face set with grief.

Gallyn groaned as if his heart had broken.

Only Erenan and Kanda thought of fighting – but they stared upward at the dragons, and they had had no idea how they so small and earthbound could fight such things.

Thus all six stood and stared in wonder, unable to act while the fields burned, the orchards burned. Sweet smell of apples and of applewood.

"They will destroy Roven itself," Morren said at last. The fire was in his eyes, he seemed half in love with the idea of Roven burning. The gold would run, the silver run in waves, the tables and benches were old wood polished with beeswax to feed the flames...Kanda saw it there in Morren's eyes, saw that it would be beautiful to him. His hands reached, lover's hands, yearned to touch the bright fire.

It would be beautiful. She who was made out of good sown earth and wildfire and red autumn berries, she knew.

"Nothing will touch Roven," Kanda said. "I forbid it." She spoke quietly, then she shouted it loud, started up. She ran, she climbed the golden walls of Roven, she threw herself to stand on the crest of the silver roof.

"Leap with me," Erenan said to Gallyn. "*Great Leap*, leap with me now." Gallyn leapt, like the flames, with his arms around Erenan, the two stood with Kanda on the hall's roof. Morren clambered up, and Palle, and Kestre; the Six stood proud shoulder to shoulder, back-to-back, on the Hall Roven's high roof. The dragons roared their terrible roar, opened wide their terrible jaws, belched out, spewed out, screamed out fire and smoke. Great gouts of fire, one gold, one silver, one black, one white. The spell of their beauty was ended. They were beautiful still, but they were monsters.

They were fools, for they flew low all four together, rushed reeling at the Six. Their fire poured out, waves, yes, waves and whole great oceans of molten gold and black and silver, liquid white fire that burned as cold as ice. Gallyn whispered, "Kestre?" like a tiny child. Broke in fear at last as the fire washed over him. He had fought men and monsters, but never such as this. So vast, these beasts, that they could swallow him whole. In their fires he ducked and ran, a child merely, wiser, better than if he had stood to fight. Kanda braced herself, firm-fixed as the Hall Roven. Her legs like the hall's mighty house poles as the wave of fire hit. White fire poured over her. Through her. Cold and burning both at once. She staggered, she too was sunk in fire. Held, forced herself to keep upright. She threw her sword out. Her teeth gripped shut in her mouth. All the strength of her body in her sword rising and falling. Groping to meet dragon flesh. Blind with fire. Blind with the force of her blow. Felt, not saw, that she had struck one of the beasts.

The beast shrieked. Her sword shrieked, and the joy ran in the sword at the wonder of killing such a huge beautiful thing. Kanda's arm ached with the effort of wounding it. The fire ebbed, as a wave ebbs on the shore after it has broken in white foam. Sucked and pulled at Kanda's feet.

Kestre shouted. She stood firm beside Kanda. Her yellow hair was scorched white. She looked so fearful, then a shout, the two set their shoulders, braced themselves together firm. And the dragons came again. Kanda struck and Kestre struck, claws ripped Kanda's body and she howled, another of the beasts shot up from them wounded, blood running raw over Kanda, its hind claws and its tail lashed to rip and strike her as it fled. She thought, seen through still half-blind eyes, that Palle too had struck it. It turned in the air jolting with fury that it was injured. It screamed and loosed its fire. Gold flames tore the sky open.

Another, another, another spout of flame.

The world disappeared in fire. Nothing left. As a wave breaks over a mound a child digs in the sand, sweeps it clear away. The beasts roared triumph. Kestre shrieked and Kanda shrieked. The silver roof was boiling, blazing. The golden walls were lost in smoke.

Two dragons wounded but still fighting. Two dragons still unharmed. Six Swords exhausted, battered, choking, helpless.

No hope, Kanda almost thought.

She struck, struck, struck, endless. Hacked and hacked. Sweat running to make her sword hilt slippery in her hand, and the metal so hot it burned her skin. But her hand clenched also around the hilt so tight she could not open it. She struck. Hacked. Stabbed. Beat like a child's fists. Her sword cut fire and smoke, cut dragon flesh wide open. Kestre's sword cut. Morren's sword. Erenan's sword. Palle's sword. Gallyn's sword.

Six Swords. Four dragons.

One dragon injured.

Two dragons.

Three.

Only three!

Four dragons poured out fire. White. Silver. Gold. Black. Kanda struck and Kestre struck and Morren struck and Erenan struck and Palle struck and Gallyn struck. (From the shelter of Roven's walls, far from danger, far from being able to wound any of the dragons, Gallyn struck.) And struck. And struck. And struck. And struck. And struck.

Four dragons gnashed their terrible jaws. Clawed and burned the Six. All four now were injured. Although not one of the dragons was badly injured enough not to be able to fight. Kanda struck and Kestre struck and Morren struck and Erenan struck and Palle struck and Gallyn struck. (From the shelter of Roven's walls, far from danger, far from being able to wound any of the dragons, Gallyn stuck.) And struck. And struck. And struck. And struck. And struck.

Four dragons roared together. A music, their voices made. A terrible music – grieving. They had not thought that anything, not even the Six Swords of Roven, could harm them. Beautiful monsters – and very foolish. For all their beauty and their power, the dragons began to feel fear.

The gold dragon broke from its fellows. Fled, like the sun as it sets. The silver dragon broke and fled like the moon when the clouds cover it.

Kanda struck and Kestre struck and Morren struck and Erenan struck and Palle struck and Gallyn struck. (From the roof of the Hall Roven, where he leapt when he saw the silver dragon fleeing, where he could just about do some small damage to the tip of a dragon's tail, Gallyn struck.) And struck. And struck. And struck. And struck. And struck.

A howl, and a crash of fire black and white and choked with blood. Smoke in the Six's faces, black smoke that reeked of blood. So nearly! They struck again, all six together, each putting all their strength and fear and anger into the blow. All six of their swords cut home. Fire pounded them. The dragons desperate. "Strike!" Kanda cried. "Strike!"

Fire shattered over her. Claws raked her body. Blood stung her eyes. "Strike again!"

Her companions…did not hear her, for the rage and howl of wounded dragons pounded them as hard as the dragons' fire. Through beating wings she raised her face skyward, saw reeling darkened shapes. Three of the dragons, wounded. Shrieking. Vomiting fire and blood.

And they fled.

Kanda's heart was almost broken as she watched the dragons flee. She longed to pursue them, finish what she had started, for she knew that the dragons were yet more dangerous for being defeated and wounded. She felt so helpless, useless, standing on the roof of the Hall Roven watching her enemy fly away.

A crash. A roar. No: a wail. Pain and shame in a dragon's fiery shriek. The last of the four was too badly injured to fly. Morren, or Palle, or Erenan, had wounded it at the base of its right wing. It twisted in the air, trying to pull itself upward and away. It was so raw with wounds that Kanda could not tell what color it was. It reeled, its wings seemed to clutch at the sky like hands trying to hold on to something.

Not like a star but only like a stone, it fell.

It crashed to earth in ruin. The earth beneath it wounded. Its head lay stretched out with its jaws opening and closing helpless; its blood ran out dry in a rattle of dust.

"Oh!"

Tears of grief ran down Kanda's cheeks.

Palle roared, "Come on! We must kill it!" The Six ran across the burned fields toward the dragon. (Gallyn at the front, for he had been well-placed on the very edge of the hall's roof.) Quick as quick, they were running, for already the people of Roven had begun to creep up toward the dragon, awed and wondering at it. A child got too close: the great jaws snapped. The child's mother ran to scoop up her child; a snort of fire burned her skirt, made mother and child scream.

Palle, horrified, shouted, "Keep back! We will finish it!" And Gallyn, fast runner on his young, long legs, had already reached the beast, stood, planted his foot on its neck, raised his sword to kill it.

But he did not kill it. And Palle, the next to reach it, did not kill it.

The Six stood in a circle around the dragon's head.

Erenan raised her sword. The dragon stared with the panic of any animal.

Uncertain, Erenan lowered her sword. Her sword blade cast dancing light on the dragon's skin. She whispered, "I can't…."

Kanda looked straight into the dragon's dying eyes. The dragon looked back afraid. So afraid. Kanda raised her own sword. Shouted her great war cry. In her mind, a trumpet sounded. She knew the words that must be said.

"I will not kill you," Kanda said to the dragon. "I cannot bear to kill you, beautiful as you are. It is but in your nature to burn and destroy, as it is in my nature to…to defend. But neither can I let you live."

She touched her sword Iath to the dragon's forehead. So brilliantly, the golden blade shone.

She said to the dragon: "Dragon, beast, killer: that you shall no longer be. A bird, a song thrush: that you shall now be. You will lose all your grandeur and your fury. You will go in fear of men and beasts and winter frost. From your throat will pour sweet birdsong.

"You will not die, dragon. You will live a long life. You will fly now on your new small bird's wings, into the west you will fly, into the sun, straight and sure as an arrow loosed by a master bowman you will fly, until the sun sets. The first village you find when the sun sets, there you will stop, there you will live. You will be that village's luck. Blessings, you will bring. As long as that village stands, you will haunt its bounds. As long as there are people in the village to hear you, you shall pour out your song. You will live beside them in the shape of a bird, watching over them. Only when that village lies empty and ruined, may you cease your watch and your song.

"I bind you to this fate, dragon."

She lowered the sword. Her hands were shaking from the power of the words that had poured out of her. A bright taste as of metal in her mouth.

The dragon shivered, thrashed in pain, its limbs rent at the earth, at its own body, its jaws snapped, bit at itself. It screamed. Its blood poured out of it in dry rattling streams. And lo! it was a little brown bird, a song thrush, its belly soft and white and speckled. It looked at Kanda with sad eyes. It opened its yellow beak, the song poured out of it. Long and loud, the song poured out.

It flew three times around Kanda's head. Three times around Erenan's head. It flew away across the burned fields. Singing.

More beautiful even than Kestre's songs.

Her companions looked at Kanda. Awed. She was indeed the greatest of the Six.

They walked together across the burned fields back to the Hall Roven.

Palle rolled up his burned sleeves, "We'd better get to work replanting the trees here," Palle said.

"Can't it—? No, obviously it can't wait," Morren said. Morren clapped his hands. "Plum trees! Apple trees! Fat pigs!"

And that was the joyful end of that quest.

This is what was in Kanda's mind, as she walked through the open gates of the city treading beneath her feet the blood of warriors and horses, with the blood of warriors and horses staining her hands red.

CHAPTER FORTY-FOUR

"Stay close to me. We don't know what is in this city. What dangers."

The most foolish words ever spoken by any person who lived or will live, those words, Kanda thought to herself in Dellet's voice.

But Sal shivered, her eyes wide looking at the high white walls. She gripped the pony's rein, tensed as if there was still danger here. Bit her lip, and Kanda heard her whimper to herself as she crossed the gate's threshold.

"Come on. Hurry," Sal said. "Morna is here waiting."

That's not much comfort, Sal my sweet, Kanda thought.

They passed through the white marble walls. They stood in a great square paved in white. A fountainhead poured water into a trough for travelers to refresh themselves, it was shaded by a tall tree. The fountain was made of gold, the trough was carved from a single ruby, the tree was made of diamonds and the fruits which hung from it were each a huge pearl. A bench was set beneath the tree for travelers to take their rest before they walked on into the city. The bench was carved from green stone. A songbird sat on the bench, knocking a snail shell to break it open *tock tock tock*. The bird was made of gold and ivory, the snail shell was made of gold. When the bird saw Kanda, it flew away. The square was filled with stalls, the stalls were busy with people. Like the bird and the snail, the people were made of gold. They had jewels for eyes, silk ribbons for hair. Like dolls, with pins to hold their arms and legs in place. But they traded for food and drink and clothes and toys as if they needed them. And indeed the stalls were spread with rare and lovely things. Wondrous things.

Many cities, Kanda had seen in the course of her long life. And this city was one of them. Once, as the sun sunk weary into its wounding, she had ridden into this city with Palle and Morren and Erenan after they had saved it from shadow and ruin, and it had seemed to her to be a fair city and the people who lived there had seemed kind and wise and worth saving.

She could not remember what the city was called. But as she remembered the people greeting her as she went in with Palle and Morren and Erenan, she could almost hear the name they cheered, her name when she had been one of the Six.

Be silent. Listen. Concentrate. It echoes still in these white stones....

Listen.... Listen now....

Lost. No.

"Kanda. Ikandera Thygethyn," the voices only cheered in her memory. As if that had always been her name.

For it was not only with the Six that Kanda had entered this city in triumph. "Hail Ikandera Thygethyn!" the people of this city had cheered once. Before Kanda killed them.

Do you remember a village with a longhouse, Amraen?

I remember a city with walls of white marble, my lady queen.

I remember what we did there.

Marvelous, wondrous things.

Sal squeezed her right hand tighter on the pony's rein. "Soon!" Sal whispered. Sal's left hand pressed against her open mouth.

They went on slowly and carefully. Through wide streets edged with palaces. Avenues of trees twice as tall as the tallest Wenet oak. Gardens thick with flowers. Smaller squares for daily living, where crystal fountains sprayed not water but white milk or dark wine. In the corner of her eye, glimpsed without meaning to look, Kanda could almost see the peoples' lives being played out. Two women drawing water at a wellhead, two lovers taking their ease in a shaded courtyard, a workshop where children toiled at the loom. The people were tall and beautiful, bigger than real people, she could not see them clearly but only as flickers of silver and gold.

In the center of the city rose a huge building. Amraen's village could have fitted ten times into it. It was set in a garden of fruit trees, the fruit was not to eat but only more shining jewels. The hall's roof was silver, its walls were gold.

And Kanda burst out laughing, because Morna had got the walls and the roof of Roven the wrong way round.

"As long as stood the silver walls of Roven, as long as the sun struck each morning on the roof of gold," she had told her children, the first time she told them about her past; "Again! Tell us again! The beautiful hall and the garden and the lady!" Morna had shouted, "Tell us again!" On an island beneath a rowan tree, with good magic keeping them safe all around them, a moment none of them could forget. But Morna had been so little then. A child of four. Half asleep. All these long years of her life, Morna had held her mother's words tight in her heart as treasures, and wrong.

"So…we go in there, I suppose?" said Dellet. He was looking up at the hall like it was a surprise to him to see it here, like he had not at all expected this. The doors that stood open before him were so high he would be swallowed by them, and I suppose he has never seen a building this large, Kanda thought. Cannot conceive such a place could exist.

Well and so and anywhere else but here he'd be right, Kanda thought. All the cities and palaces and king's halls I've seen over the years: this place would fall to rubble before it was a quarter-finished, however it was made. Had an army of slaves given blood for it, had a wizard raised it with a spell-word, had my Lord of Roven himself asked it to be built, yet those walls would buckle under their own weight before they stood a quarter as tall as they do. And as for the weight of the roof – so many pillars to hold it up inside, there'd be no room for a child of four to slip between them.

It's the ugliest thing I've seen since my glory days as Ikandera Thygethyn. Even Geiamnyn, Morna, even he had better taste than this. And Kanda said firmly and loudly to Dellet, "Yes, Del-my-heart, I think indeed we should go in. For if the sun breaks through the clouds that build gray above us like warriors in battle, if the light breaks and flashes upon these walls of gold, this roof of silver – we'll be blinded all by the flash. So, yes, we had better quickly go in." Then she said, "But you'd better leave the pony out here, Sal-flower. Tie him on a long rein to a golden tree. He won't come to harm here, I shouldn't think." And her feet rang on the golden floor as she went fast and heavy treading through the golden doors up diamond steps. And that was a good sound.

It was cold inside the hall. Nothing like Roven. A great fire burned in the hearth at the hall's center but it did not give off any warmth, for those who lived here did not need warmth and did not need to cook food to eat. The wall hangings were very fine, but the pictures on them were hard to see. Kanda had run up the steps and through the doors but when she had crossed the threshold she made herself stop and wait. Calian came up fast, Sal and Dellet came up. Of the three, only Dellet paused on the threshold, Kanda heard his little gasp of breath before he went in. The family walked together slowly, itched to run to meet Morna but made each other walk slowly to put it off. At the far end of the hall torches burned. A throne was set on a high daïs, above it hung a sword of shining gold.

Kanda recognized the throne, for it had once been hers. Poor Amraen had tried and failed to capture something of it in the crude chair he sat upon as a king.

The lady of the hall sat on the throne, as all these long years she must have dreamed.

Oh she was so lovely. Oh she was so beautiful and fine. Like a summer meadow when the pasture is rich and green and lush so that the cattle give the richest milk, the grass is filled with buttercups, the hedgerows are clotted with lace-flower, the soil is almost black. Like a spring meadow when the flowers are bursting up through the dark earth that shines rain-jeweled, the grass hisses silver in the wind of first morning and the light falls in silver beams. She was dressed in blue like a kingfisher. Rings on her fingers, bracelets of gold and bronze and silver at her wrists. A neck ring of bright gold at her lovely throat. A crown of silver flowers on her lovely head. Yellow flowers grew up around her feet. So Morren had composed his poems for the youth of Roven, *Her plaited hair is like the irises that grow on the banks of the river, her eyes are new-opened violets. Her cheeks are apples, her lips are cherries, like rosy dawn is the skin of her neck. Her shoulders are curved as swan's wings, her teeth are like snowflakes, sleek and smooth her arms and the long fingers of her hands.* So Morna, yet fairer and more queenly even than she had been in Amraen's feast hall, fairer than any woman Kanda had seen in Roven or on any of her travels, she could only say now of any woman she had seen in all the course of her life, *she seemed beautiful to me, yes, until I saw Morna.*

The lovely Lady of Roven. All the stories Kanda had told.

Sal said, "Hello Morna." Sal was the only one who could bring herself to speak.

"Hello Sal," Morna said. She smiled. "This is a better place to meet you."

Calian said, "Morna?" Her eyes were wide and huge and wild. Madness in her eyes and her voice. "Morna," she said. Not madness in her voice and eyes now. Eagles in her eyes, hunting. "Morna," Calian said.

"Morna," Dellet said.

For one moment – for one moment – Morna looked at her father and stepped forward toward him. For one moment – for one moment – her lips moved to say: "Dad."

She frowned, shook her lovely head. She did not spit at Dellet that he was not her father this time, Kanda thought, at least. Dellet went as if to step forward to embrace her, then he hesitated and stepped back and made a deep bow, as he had not thought to make to King Amraen.

Then silence. Four old bronze swords around one fair shining sword of gold.

"You found it," Morna said at last. "Is it as beautiful as you remember it?"

Kanda paused. "This is not the Hall Roven, Morna." She said slowly, "I destroyed Roven, Morna. It is gone. You can't bring it back."

"I know that!" Morna looked around her beautiful empty hall. "It's better and more beautiful than Roven."

Morna rose to her feet. Stepped down from the dais as light as a flower, the yellow flowers burst up thick in the tread of her feet.

Calian stepped forward fierce as any warrior. "Morna…?" Calian said. She blinked, confused, she had known all the time since the ford that this was Morna, but she did not understand and did not know. "Morna…."

"Calian," said Morna. She wrinkled her nose, frowned, pouted. "Is that more blood I smell on you? More killing?"

"Shut up!" Calian shouted. "Shut up! Go away! I'll kill you again now! Like I killed the people in Amraen's village! Monster, you! Witch woman! I'll cut off your nose, your eyelids, your lips, then I'll cut off your head. I'll kill you and kill you and kill you, I'll keep killing you every day." Then the girl whimpered, "Mum." Crept into her mother's arms. "I didn't mean that, Mum. I don't know why I said that."

Because…it's true, Calian, Kanda thought.

But those words even Ikandera Thygethyn could never say.

Sal stepped one two three steps toward Morna. The torchlight caught her hair, made it gleam as silver as Morna's crown.

"Hello Morna," Sal said.

"What do you want?" Morna said. "Are you going to be horrible to me too?"

"No, Morna, my sister," Sal said. "I am happy to see you again, and looking so fine and so well."

Sal paused and looked around her, she looked at Morna as if she thought Morna was going to say something, do something. She stared at Morna. Morna stared back at Sal.

Sal stepped one step closer toward Morna. So very close and bright.

"Morna, my sister," Sal said. "So. Here you are: a queen in your hall. And as a queen, I want to ask you for something, Morna. I want you to give me something."

She said with fear in her voice indeed, "I want you to give me a gift."

"A gift?" The flowers that grew at Morna's feet were so thick and so fair that she seemed to be rooted in the earth like a statue of beauty and love. Her eyes flashed mocking-looking at old gray Sal. But she made a little noise in the depths of her throat as if she was afraid. Took one two three steps back.

"You and Calian and that one my mother killed me. You never even gave me a grave cloth or a gravestone, Sal. Why should I give you anything? What should I give to you? All these years we've been parted, you without a backward glance, we meet finally after all this time and the first thing that happens is that my sister Calian insults me and my sister Sal asks me for a gift?

"You killed me, Sal my sister! Killed and forgot me and lived your life! You think I will give you a gift?"

But Morna took another step back away from Sal, and her voice shook. And Kanda opened her mouth to ask Sal – stop her – beg her, trembling, or to ask Morna, or to – to— And Kanda closed her mouth.

"I remember when we were all three of us only children, Morna," said Sal. "I remember, if you don't, how much Calian and I loved you. You, Morna, you begged for things Mother wouldn't give you, sweets, toys, things you shouldn't have because you could hurt yourself on them, things you couldn't have because they would break. But: 'If Mum won't give it to Morna, we'll have to get it and give it to Morna ourselves instead,' I would say to Calian, or Calian would say to me. Nine times out of ten it was me who had to get it, because I was taller and older and so better with bolts and knots and hidden things. Often you would break it. Often Mother would be angry with us. But we still got it and gave it to you if you wanted something."

Sal said in a cold clear voice: "I never gave you a grave cloth or a gravestone, no, that's true. But I gave my hand in marriage and my youth and the summer of my life for you, Morna. Willingly I gave them.

"You say that *empty* one our mother's first husband has been kind to you as you grew from a child to the woman who stands before us, and I hated him and feared him from the first moment I met him, before that, even, from the first time I saw the rotten track his feet had left on the earth where he had passed, as if the very earth was wounded by the guilt of letting him walk upon it – but, if you say he was kind to you, I will try to believe it, perhaps it is unfair of me to judge him, for I do not know him as you do.

"That he was kind to you, I will give you.

"You say you are not our father's daughter, that that *empty* one is your true father not this *good man* Dellet – that, although I do not want to believe it, I will try to believe, even, for your sake. Many children are raised by parents who did not bear them and did not sire them but whom they love and who love them, I know. Hardly a difficult thing.

"My mother may cry at it, my father may cry and howl and dash his fists against his face, but that, also, I will give you.

"So you give me now what my heart longs for. My heart's desire, as you promised that day by the ford. Two things I have just now given you. So, now, Morna, my sister, in return I ask you for two things."

Sal's hand so old and frail – she reached out to touch her sister's hand. But Morna snatched her own hand away in fear. The yellow flowers at her feet wilted away brown and crushed.

"Morna, my sister," said Sal, "give me back my two sons."

"Your sons, Sal?" said Morna. "There are far away, mourning their father Geiamnyn whom you killed."

"Lying, lying," Sal said.

A doorcurtain flapped open in the corner of the hall. The two gray dogs ran out from behind it. A lady's dogs: fine silver collars around their necks. They fawned at Morna's feet. The dog with the brown marks growled. The dog with the white marks barked. The dogs pricked up their ears and whined and whimpered. Morna whimpered like a dog herself. She tried to laugh, it came out cracked and ugly. She stared at her sister, tossed her head, looked away from her sister, looked down ashamed at her feet.

The dog with the white marks growled. The dog with the brown marks barked.

Morna touched the dog with the white marks. And lo! A man stood there, tall and handsome, his hair was gold, his eyes were green as the green grass, his skin was gold-and-white. He smelled of honey in the comb and new milk and wet earth in spring. He had a scar on his left arm where Kanda's sword had cut him.

Morna touched the dog with the brown marks. And lo! A man stood there, tall and handsome, his hair was silver, his eyes were blue as the evening sky, his skin was silver-gray. He smelled of may blossom and starlight on cold waters and autumn mist. He had a scar on his face where Calian's sword had cut him.

Sal's cry of joy was the most beautiful sound in the world. Three times only in all her life had Kanda heard a sound as wonderful as Sal's cry to see her two sons. And that had been the three times Kanda had heard her own children make their first cry at their births.

"Camryth!" Sal cried to the man with silver hair, her younger son, her *Fierce* son, the runner, the archer, the wise and cunning leader of men.

"Mannan!" Sal cried to the man with golden hair, her older son, her *Strong* son, the hunter, the breaker of horses, the taker of men's heads.

The two tall great men drew up to Sal, "Mother," they whispered, they halted before her with all the hesitance and love and uncertainty of mighty warriors before the aged mother whom they love and who so greatly loves them. Taller than Sal. Taller than Kanda or Dellet! First Camryth then Mannan embraced their mother carefully, held her close.

Strong tall men in their prime, both of them. Not green boys, not callow youths. Strong, battle-scarred, their eyes filled with knowledge – war, women, love, heartbreak, power, death, all of these things and much more besides were well known to these two strong grown men. Older than Sal had been when she had left Kanda to marry Geiamnyn. Older than Geiamnyn had been on his wedding day.

Older than Kanda had been, she realized, on the day she threw down the Hall Roven.

"Thank you, Morna," Sal said through tears. There's nothing to thank her for, Kanda thought in rage. But Morna seemed to watch with pleasure, delighted in giving the gift. Expectant, eager: Kanda imagined her working her magic to change the two men into dogs and already smiling, *she'll be so happy, oh, think of her face when I turn them back into men and she sees.*

"But I won't take off their collars, Sal," Morna said. "A fine silver collar each of your sons wears, those won't come off." Yes: both were dressed in lordly robes and fur-trimmed cloaks but a slave collar lay about each man's neck in place of a neck ring.

Again, she must ruin it, Kanda thought. She who must have dreamed all these long years of such a scene.

"You look tired, Mother," the silver-haired man, Sal's younger son, Camryth, said. "Are you well?" He looked around at last away from his mother: "Where is this place, Mother?" he said. "Who are these people?"

"You should sit down, Mother," the golden-haired man, Sal's older son, Mannan, said. "You look so tired and old. Are you sick?" He too looked around at last at anything other than his mother: "This is a cold place," he said. "Not a good place for you. How did you come here?" He gestured at Kanda. "You! Find a chair for my mother to sit down on."

"I'm fine and well, now I have you two back around me," Sal said. But she smiled at the way they fussed over her.

"We should not have left you the last time," Camryth said. He looked ashamed. "We would have returned to you sooner, but we met Aunt Morna and she promised us...promised us...." He shook his head. Still a little doglike, the way he shook himself. He looked puzzled, *methought I was, and methought I had, but....* So Kanda came hurrying with a chair for Sal to sit on (*methought there were no chairs in this empty hall, but...*), a fine folding chair of carved wood with a velvet seat, the two men had to get it properly safely unfolded, sit their mother down, wrap her in both of their cloaks.

"So all's well now," Mannan said. "We'll not leave again until we've seen you comfortably home. We have so much to tell you!" said Mannan happily. "We've done such great things!"

"You have, I'm sure," Sal said. "My strong sons." She turned to Kanda. Her face was radiant. "Mannan, Camryth," she said, "often I told you about your grandmother, how strong and fierce and wise she was. And see: here she is. Ikandera Thygethyn. Lady Kanda of the Six."

The two men cried out in amazement. Crowded around Kanda – they were huge and tall. "Grandmother! Our father's old enemy and companion! 'The greatest warrior, matchless, she'd teach you to be true warriors, ah, I wish, boys, that you could have seen her fight!' That's what Father would say, when, as they often did, he and Mother spoke of you. All my life," Mannan said, "I have longed to meet you."

"It is an honor," Camryth said, "finally to meet you, my lady grandmother."

If either thought it absurd to talk thus to a woman perhaps ten years older than they were, neither showed it. And Kanda felt a flush of pride. More than a flush. A wave of pride, a river, a sea of pride, a bottomless world-circling ocean of pride flooding her heart. How differently she had thought once of meeting her grandchildren, a vague unformed dream of holding Sal's hand through the birthing, being the first to hold the newborn squalling child. So often she had dreamed that, Sal with a heathy baby in her arms that Kanda would help care for and love. How different, I should have been there for the birthing, helped her, I should have helped her in those hard early years, but how fine, how right it seemed. These two strong warriors – impossible to imagine them shrieking in dirty clout clothes, mewling and puking, raging over being put to bed. They bowed as a man does to his leader before a battle, they greeted her with the respect a man gives to a companion who has excelled in the front lines. *You were always the first to draw your sword when the fighting came. You were always the last to break off at last, reluctant, from the fighting. Your name was ever first in the praise when the cup went round and the feast-fire burned low – never was your name spoken in the shame-song. You gave your share, and joyfully. None would dare to call you coward or lacking.* To see her grandsons meet her thus, see her thus, and she thus to first see and understand them – that also was a fine great thing.

Lady Kanda of Roven, she thought, never dreamed of children or of grandchildren. Great warriors' homage was all she dreamed of.

"And this is your grandfather!" Sal was saying, as joyfully.

"An honor, Grandfather, often has Mother spoken of your...of your kindness," silver-tongued silver-haired Camryth was saying in response. Mannan hung back, perhaps, for a moment, his face had the same nothing look for Dellet that Amraen had not tried to conceal. Little enough, Kanda could guess, had they in truth been told of Grandfather Dellet. *This, my mother's father? This, my famed grandmother's husband? Must I pretend to be pleased that I am related to him?* A toddling infant with a full clout cloth, Kanda thought sadly, might better have loved and respected Dellet. The two brothers hesitated. Trying. They clasped Dellet's hands, stammered out a fine greeting. Gave him the smiles men in a good mood in the feast hall might give to other unknown lesser men. Dellet felt it, saw it, Kanda felt and saw that. Being what he was, he took it quietly. Accepted it.

Great warriors; Geiamnyn's sons. And whatever he had said and thought of Geiamnyn, burning, monster, vile, death-bringer, accursed – Geiamnyn had been a warrior and a war leader, where Dellet had never dared take up a sword. Which was to Dellet a great and good thing – and deep in his heart, perhaps, a shameful thing before his grandsons.

"And Calian my sister!" Sal was saying, as joyfully, or even more so.

"Aunt—" Mannan began to Calian, looked appalled and she looked appalled back. They stared at her with bafflement a moment, this fierce girl child – they were used to lovely silk-clad ladies, clean-haired, blushing, swooning over them, Kanda might guess – they stared and then they greeted her as a young comrade or perhaps as a little sister, a little patronizing, perhaps, their greeting, Calian met it as patronizing, tossed it back at them. Great tales Sal must have told them of her fierce warrior sister, which they had lapped up as young green boys yet to be trusted with a sword. *So brave, so fierce, so wild and clever like an eaglet, like…like her mother's child, my sister is, she was a great warrior at twelve years old – just ask your father, no, wait, don't ask your father – but imagine that, boys, a warrior at twelve, imagine that!* The two men smiled warily, awkwardly, *this child???? We did ask our father, and he said….* Towering over her, they could pick her up like a toy, snap her like a toy, she stared back *hate you, hate you, monsters, Geiamnyn's sons, kill them,* Kanda could see Calian thinking. Calian's eyes went to the sword hanging on the wall. The two men's eyes there too, or Camryth's eyes at least.

"Cousin," Camryth said after he thought out the right word. "Good to finally meet you." The three clasped hands with some caution; together all three let out a little awkward laugh.

Whatever they are, they're Sal's children, until we meet them that's all there is anyone can say. They might live in the dark, but they are Sal's children.

Remember that. Try to. Try very hard.

Look at Sal, so happy with them. Listen to the happiness in her voice.

Try to look, try to listen.

CHAPTER FORTY-FIVE

Parents and children. Joyful! Happiness! Wonders!

"Morna," Dellet said when the greetings had all been made. "Morna....

"I....

"You...."

These fine reunions, all hugs and kisses, and Dellet hung back now and looked at Morna, and Morna looked at him. Never mind words for speaking: stop being so stupid, the pair of you, Kanda wanted to shout, to howl, to yell. Stop it, your daughter said something stupid and hurtful, Dellet, like children do; you can see how upset your father is, Morna, what happened to you was terrible, I understand you're angry; but, look, both of you, you don't have to apologize, just hug to make it up. But the two looked at each other, carefully, warily, not unkindly, but...but....

"Morna," Dellet said, "that was a...I won't say it was a kind thing you did, but...for Sal...after the unkind things you did...." He looked away at the ground, then he looked at Kanda, then he looked at Sal, then he looked at Morna's left shoulder, for he couldn't quite look at her face.

"What Sal said," he said, "she said it...she said it well, Sal did.

"I....

"Sal said it well, Morna. I can't say more than that. I'll always love and care for you, for four years I loved and cared for you, and you were my own child and I'll never forget that. I'm your father, Morna, in my heart I am, you said, I was the father of your childhood, you said that. But I know.... At least, I'm trying to understand.

"I mean....

"Like Sal said...."

Twisting and twisting and twisting his hands. "I understand. I mean, I don't understand at all, but…I mean….

"I heard your words in Amraen's feast hall, and I didn't want to believe them, but….

"I mean….

"I heard what you said…."

And Morna was a woman grown and tall and fine and golden. And Dellet was a man who had once had a child called Morna. But this woman was not that child.

"Just be happy, Morna, tell me you're happy, Morna," Dellet said.

Dellet!

You can't— You won't— I won't—

You—

She's your daughter.

Our daughter.

Morna: stop this!

Kanda shouted, "This is absurd!"

Silence.

"Our daughter was four years old, Kanda," Dellet said. "Our daughter Morna was a little babbling unformed thing. This isn't Morna as she was when she was ours, Kanda. Can't you see that? This is a woman who has lived a life.

"Look at her, Kanda! All the time she has lived, the things she's done and is: we didn't give her those things. How can you not see it?"

CHAPTER FORTY-SIX

'My mother', 'my father', 'my child', people say, and you think nothing of it. It's only the truth. That one, that…he gave her back her life, he raised her as she grew into what she is. She chose and he chose; look at her and see that it was a good choice to make. And here are the words that must be spoken: father, parent, child, love.

If it was anyone else in the world but us, Kanda thought, I would accept without question that he is Morna's father. Of course I would.

CHAPTER FORTY-SEVEN

So. So. Two great vast men still half wagging their tails still half barking. Morna looked at Dellet, Dellet looked at Kanda, Kanda looked at the floor at her feet.

Kanda thought: trying, trying.

Morna clapped her hands. Servants came running into the hall, laboring under the weight of chairs and tables. White cloths were spread on the tables. Plates and cups were set. Flowers were strewn on the floor, yellow and white and purple; greenery was hung on the walls. Dishes of food were set: fresh bread, fruits, custards, sweetmeats. Jugs of dark wine, jugs of white milk. Two men carried in between them a spit with a whole ox on it, set the spit over the hearth fire to roast. A peacock dressed back in its feathers; and a white peacock the same beside it for effect. Songbirds, larks, thrushes, blackbirds, sitting on nests made of honey cake.

The men sweated as they turned the ox. The smell of the roasting meat was wonderful. The fat ran down sizzling, made the fire spit and smoke and blaze. The flames of the fire looked like the petals of red and yellow flowers, not like a fire at all.

A harper began to play – Kanda had been waiting for this. He played very beautifully on a beautiful harp. Kanda could not see him.

"Sit down," Morna said. "A feast for family and friends."

Kanda looked around her in horror, for fear that that *empty* one her first husband would be there.

"A feast for ones long separated," Morna said. She looked at Kanda sadly. "Don't fear, Mother. A thousand years must pass, remember, before I can next sit down to a meal with my father." She said with a sad smile, "That will be a great feast for ones long separated, if I live to see that day."

Kanda remembered Sal's wedding feast to Geiamnyn, how Dellet had eaten and drunk and despaired. Raw, living flesh, he had eaten that day, "It doesn't matter now whether I eat it or not," Dellet had said. "So I might as well eat." Waited for something awful. Felt such fear, such rage. But Morna looked so joyful, setting plates of food and cups of drink. Seemed to remember from her childhood that Sal liked roast beef best while Calian (who loved pigs far more than cows or sheep or chickens) preferred roast pork. She had been so young then, Kanda had had no idea she had noticed these little things.

"Sit down, sit down," Morna said.

One of the cups on the table had a crack in it at the lip. A servant filled it to the top with dark wine, the wine began to leak out through the crack. The servant ran with napkins to mop up the spill, poured wine back into the jug until the cup was only half-full. "There's a trick to it, there, that's it," Morna said. That was what broke Kanda, made her sit at the place set for her at the table, begin to eat and drink, for when Morna was a child and they had lived on the farm above the River Wenet Kanda had once had just such a cup. *"It's a perfectly good cup, you just have to remember not to overfill it, it's not like it's broken at the bottom, it's a waste to throw it out when you can still use it." Eyes roll, Calian sniggers, "If you say so, Mum."* Dellet saw, tears came into his eyes, he sat beside his wife and began to eat. Kanda picked up the cup, held it the way she remembered, drank a sip of wine.

A family meal together, no one else present, Sal's sons quiet at the end of the table beside their mother trying not to disturb the rest. Morna smiling her wide smile, so happy, tending to her sisters' plates and cups.

Morna spoke to Dellet sometimes, carefully, she did not call him Father or Dad or Daddy, he spoke to her carefully back, called her Morna not daughter mine. Look at you two, Kanda wanted to shout at them, bang their (oh so similar) heads together, look, stop being so stupid. Calian had dark hair like Dellet's sister, Sal had had the same red hair as Kanda, Morna's fair hair was like Dellet claimed his hair had been as a child. All Dellet's roughness – he could never have been called handsome – there in Morna as perfect beauty and grace. But it seemed to Kanda that the more she looked at Morna, the more she saw in her the likeness to that *empty* one. The way Morna moved her hands, the expressions and pauses and rushes in her speech, the way she twisted her head. And Morna and Dellet were like anyone sitting at dinner with their mother's husband and their wife's daughter. A very normal commonplace thing.

If she was anyone else, Kanda's heart said.

When they had eaten their fill and the hall was warm with the smell of food and well-fed bodies, Morna said, as Kanda had known she would, "Tell us a story of Roven, Mother. Do, please." Those few days telling her children the old stories of lost heroes, Morna's innocent young eyes so vast and lit up bright, *"the beautiful lady and all the beautiful places…tell us about them, Mummy, please…."*

"I…." Kanda had to strain to think of something. Heartsick, all the tales that came into her head were of pain. She stared down at the floor, trying to find a good memory. Stories. Stories. The great deeds of long-forgotten heroes, the great stories, every story: we killed and killed and killed. Who now remembers the Hall Roven? Morna at least remembers it: badly.

"I…."

Or perhaps, she thought suddenly for the first time, like a shock – perhaps it is my memories that are wrong. Perhaps it did have a silver roof and walls of gold. I try to remember it but perhaps I don't really remember it properly…. Greater days long ago and half-forgotten. Do you remember? Do I? I talk of it as vast and shining, filled with wonder – but I know, in my aging heart I know those are but the memories of youth. Overeager, overweening, self-aggrandizing. A tale filled with dreams and beauty and poetic license.

There was a hall called Roven, and its Lord was an old man who was not even a king. And I served him, and one day I killed him. The end.

"Tell me what you have been doing, Camryth, Mannan, my sons," Sal said bright and happy and urgent. "Great deeds, I think, I hope."

"Great deeds! High deeds, Mother!" But Mannan laughed. "But what's to say? We fought and killed and fought and killed and killed and killed and fought."

"Hush with you," Camryth said to Mannan. "That is not all we did. Sometimes we destroyed before we killed and fought."

"Oh," cried Morna, clapping her hands. "The highest of high deeds, that is! Yes, tell us about that!"

"Well...." Mannan said, "well.... Let's think. Ah, yes, here: there was a great hall we came across, a fine lordly hall, kingly, rich; there was a wedding feast there, lovely the bride, happy the groom, fine the bride gifts, well-roasted the meats. We were invited in to join the guests assembled, and then—"

"There was a monster," said Camryth. "Before you think you know which way this story is headed. It came each night to the hall when the people were sleeping. It—"

"Terrible, it was, terrible, huge—" Mannan said.

"Terrible, fierce—"

"Oh," Morna said, "I've heard that story before, or something like it. That's boring."

"Boring?" Mannan said. "What?"

"I haven't heard it," Calian shouted. Her eyes were so bright and eager: you'd never think, looking at Calian now, that she should be longing to kill these monsters, had rejoiced at their father's death. "Tell the story, Cousin Camryth, please. You and Cousin Mannan and the terrible huge monster you killed."

"Well...."

"Oh, go on. Please."

"Well.... If you insist.... A vast destruction, it was," Mannan said. "The finest. And we...."

Strange and wrong. Kanda was the one with the great stories. The hero. The parent weaving wondrous words the better to charm her children to their beds. These others in the hall would sit and listen, harken to her words as those around her had always done. Ikandera Thygethyn – when she spoke, no man dared but listen. Kanda of the Six Swords of

Roven – then, also, it had been the same, no one would dare so much as cough when Kanda of the Six was speaking.

"We hacked and we smashed, and there was so much blood on our swords, we were stained with blood from the soles of our feet to our helmet crests," Mannan said. "And the bride and her ladies were all screaming."

"Everyone in that hall was wounded, and screaming and bleeding like pigs," Camryth said. "We alone were unharmed, and we hacked and we cut and we stabbed and we slashed." And Morna looked enchanted by the tale, and Sal looked enchanted by her sons' tale, and Calian looked enchanted.

Ikandera Thygethyn's three fine daughters!

Ikandera Thygethyn's two fine murderous grandsons!

She closed her eyes in pain to stop seeing them, saw Roven in the dark behind her eyes poor and broken, a white-painted daub-and-wattle building with a leaky roof of yellow dried sedge, the Lord of Roven only an old man, the Lady of Roven only a crudely carved statue. Herself at the gates of Roven breaking them down in her fury, and they were wood and yielded easily to her, and she was only a woman armed with a sword, bent on killing. And it has grown vast and splendid in my mind now only because I feel such guilt and such grief.

But: "Roven," said Kanda then. "Roven. *Peace.*" She whispered it, then she shouted it. Yelled it. The word was as music. She closed her eyes, saw it. Wattle and daub, reed roof, tattered, in need of repainting. "Roven." A fine, homely, loved place.

"Roven." She spoke and the words poured out of her of glory and beauty and wonder and happiness and hope: "A tale of Roven, then, you wanted, my loves."

She opened her eyes, her three daughters' faces were bright with the joy of listening together to her stories, and her grandsons' faces and her husband's face were bright.

Whatever might come after, whatever had been before, whatever had befallen her family, whatever Roven had been, whatever Morna and

Mannan and Camryth might be or do or have done – to tell her children and her grandchildren a tale of Roven, see their faces light with joy and wonder, to see Roven rise anew in their minds – it was as joyful as Kanda had ever hoped, and yet more joyful, and more joyful, and more joyful. Nothing mattered. No fears. No grief. No pain. Freely and easily her words burst from her mouth, flew like birds around the hall that Morna had raised whose roof was made of silver and whose walls were made of gold.

So be still. Listen.

Be silent and still.

Still as living things.

CHAPTER FORTY-EIGHT

It was a winter day in the Hall Roven. The trees had the last of their autumn leaves clutched to them silvered; the frost lay thick on the bare black earth, it showed up the ridges of the plowing so that the fields looked like the sea capped with white waves. A cold white mist covered the pale sun. One of those days when all is muffled, not by snow or ice but simply by the world stopping in the drear cold. The birds sat hunched and black in the trees and in the fields; a fox ran beside a hedgerow, even he seemed colorless. Frost lay thick too on the Lady of Roven, crusted the green stuff that had been left in offering at her feet. The gatekeeper Benethal stamped, clapped his arms against his sides, puffed out white smoke breath. He wore a leather cloak over his armor. His head was turned most often in the direction of the kitchen, waiting and hoping for someone to bring a cup of hot milk for him to drink.

Gallyn and Morren were in the stables saddling their horses. They had decided to ride out that day. No reason for it, no word had come that the Six were needed. Three days of drear frost cold with a gray sky and empty fields, and Gallyn and Morren had grown bored. "You could be on the practice field," Palle said to them, but they would rather practice by doing, and so they took each a satchel with bread and cheese and a wine flask, wrapped themselves in their warmest cloaks, set out.

"You're mad," Benethal shouted to them cheerfully as they rode out through the gates.

"We know," Morren shouted back. "Wise words, those."

They rode on through thickening mist that turned the world to dreams and shadows, made a ghost-world of Roven's lovely orchards and fields. The trees were dank and black, and there a beech hedge held its leaves close like a wall of bright blurred flame. Haws in a thorn hedge black now, dark as blood clots, half-rotted; apples left for the birds were as pale as the sun caught in the bare branches. Those few people at work were muffled thick in layers of cloaks and wrappings. Their voices carried strangely through the cold, muffled but too loud both at once. "Cold as graves," Morren said. He kicked his horse into a great fast rush and run. Beneath the frost the fields were deep mud churned by the winter plowing, the horses threw up clods of earth that spattered their legs, their riders' legs, their riders' fine warm cloaks. "Hoo!" Morren shouted. They smashed over a puddle with a skin of ice that shattered beneath their horses' hooves, over a puddle that was solid ice that creaked and groaned. "Hoo! Hoo!" "Hoo!" Gallyn shouted, "Hoo! Foo! Fool you! More fool me for following you!"

They rode south, for they remembered an innocent quest they had once ridden south on, on a fine midsummer day. A deer ran south in the fields and a flock of winter birds wheeled south, distant but keeping them friendly company. And south was as good a direction as any to ride in.

It grew slightly less cold, which was worse, for the frost that crusted the earth was turned to thick mud, and the white mist that made the sky and the trees and the bare fields strange and bleakly haunted to set Gallyn's imagination running as fast as his horse, the mist was turned only to gray cold rain. Drench and drizzle and drear, it set into the bones and the blood of men and horses both, even where it caught in Gallyn's silver curls it was not beautiful but only gray cold rain. Horses muddied to the belly, men muddied to the waist. Morren with a smear of mud on one handsome cheek.

Gallyn shouted, "What's that ahead?"

"What's what?" Then Morren shouted, "Ah! That is surely why we have ridden out on this horrible day."

Two horsemen were riding riding rising on the crest of a hill on the horizon. Far off, barely visible in the rain – and then fast as rain the horsemen were upon Morren and Gallyn. Two handsome men in fine armor, almost as handsome and well-armed and well-mounted as Morren and Gallyn. Strong and tall, men made for fighting. They were upon

Morren and Gallyn before they could think further, so fast the strangers' horses ran.

"Friend or foe?" cried the first, a brown-haired man on a black horse.

"Shall we fight for enjoyment, or out of hatred?" cried the second, a black-haired man on a brown horse.

"For enjoyment," Gallyn cried back. "I hope never to fight a man out of hatred unless he has given me great cause."

"We should certainly be friends," Morren cried back, "since you also have ventured out in the rain today."

"The gatekeeper to our hall said we were mad as we rode out," cried the black-haired man.

"I hope you told him he was right," cried Gallyn.

"What are you suggesting?" cried the brown-haired man.

"That we certainly should be friends," cried Morren. "Don't you think?"

"True, true," the black-haired man said.

"So it's settled then," cried Gallyn.

"It is," cried the brown-haired man. "Let's fight!"

The next thing was to decide whether they fought on horseback or on foot or on horseback or on foot. But I shan't bore you with the details of that. Suffice to say, they decided in the end that Morren and the brown-haired man would fight first on horseback, then Gallyn and the black-haired man would fight on foot. Three bouts each. The winners would have the glory, also the losers' saddlebags of bread and cheese and wine – because the winners needed to win something tangible to bring home as a prize to the feast.

"Right," said Morren to the brown-haired man. "Ready?"

"Right," said the brown-haired man. "Ready and waiting."

"Have at you!" Morren shouted. Which wasn't a thing anyone often got to shout, even one of the Six.

"And you!" the brown-haired man shouted back.

Their horses met with a crash.

When the mud had settled, Morren lay in the mud on his back.

Three times, Morren ended up in the mud on his back.

"You win," Morren said. He handed over his saddlebag.

"Good wine, good bread, good cheese," said the brown-haired man. "Lucky, as I'm certainly peckish after that fight."

"Right," said the black-haired man to Gallyn. "You ready? You still want to do this?"

"Right," said Gallyn. "I, yes, I'm ready and waiting."

"Have at you, then!" the black-haired man shouted.

Then Gallyn and the black-haired man ran at each other.

Then Gallyn was lying on his face in the mud.

Three times, Gallyn was lying on his face in the mud.

"Oh, come on," Gallyn said. He handed over his saddlebag to the black-haired man. "Come on. How did that happen?"

"The problem is, we weren't fighting for anything worthwhile," said Morren. "A little bit of bread and cheese and a bit of wine.... The Six don't fight for wine and bread and cheese. Never have, never will."

"Six of you, are there?" the black-haired man said with interest. "Really? Three of you each or something?"

"This saddlebag's got a leak in it," said the brown-haired man. "One of you didn't fasten the straps properly, look. This bread's gone soggy. I'm not eating this."

"I think I know how to fasten a saddlebag to stop it getting wet," said Morren.

"But do your four invisible friends?" the black-haired man said.

"Look," said the brown-haired man. "I've an idea to settle all this. How about we fight again, three bouts, Goldy and me on foot this time, the youngster and my friend on horseback? Winner of the foot battle gets the loser's sword, winner of the horse battle gets – can you guess it? – the loser's horse."

"Morren...." said Gallyn, looking with concern from his horse to Morren's sword. "I don't think...."

But: "Three bouts," said Morren eagerly at once. "Right. Ready? Have at you! Come on!"

"Morren!" shouted Gallyn.

Too late. A short sharp battle, sword on sword on sword. Morren on his face in the mud to match the mud on his backside. Three times.

"My sword…." Morren moaned as he lay in the mud.

"Right then," said the black-haired man. "You ready, young one?"

"No!" said Gallyn (for greatly the Six valued truthfulness as well as bravery and the doing of high deeds).

Horses are fast runners. That horse Gallyn rode was faster than most. You may not be astonished beyond words to hear that a very short time had passed before Gallyn was lying on his back in the mud to match his muddy face.

Three times.

"Right," said the black-haired man. "Your horse."

"Right," said the brown-haired man. "Your sword."

"Well, that was fun," said the black-haired man, when all four were mounted up and ready to ride away. "We should do this again sometime." And the black-haired man and the brown-haired man rode fast away back wherever they had come from over the brow of the hill. Faster than they had ridden to meet Gallyn and Morren, even, now the black-haired man was mounted on Gallyn's horse.

So now Morren had lost his sword that the Lady of Roven herself had given him. Belelia, that sword was called: that is *Love and True Speech*. Its hilt was gold with pearls set in it. So now Gallyn had lost his horse, Toth, that horse was called, that is *Cold Brilliant Breaking Waves of the Sea*, that was brother to Kanda's horse Henef and to Erenan's horse and was the model for the horse on Gallyn's helmet crest. The sword Morren wore in Belelia's place was a fine sword, good bronze with gold and silver on the hilt and plaques of walrus ivory carved with lovely young women dancing. The horse Gallyn rode was a beautiful stallion, its hooves gilded, its mane and tail plaited with red ribbons, a copper headdress, a saddle of red leather and copper and red leather and copper reins and bit.

Like for like, a foolish man might say of the exchange. Worse for better, he might say if he was very foolish, looking at the ivory plaques and the red leather saddle, that's a fine sword and a fine horse.

"We have never lost a battle before," said Gallyn. "Never. Only to another of the Six – to Kanda, especially! – have we ever lost. On horseback or on foot."

"That was not real fighting," said Morren. "If we had been fighting in defense of innocent lives against great peril and towering monsters, we would not have lost."

"Yes, Morren, but that doesn't bring my horse or your sword back," Gallyn said. "Or even our saddlebags of wine and bread and cheese."

They rode back to Roven. Both, like naughty children, trying to think what they could say to the Lord of Roven and their companions and anyone and everyone else in Roven they had ever met or would meet.

"We could run away as traveling musicians," Morren said after a while.

"Or bandits," said Gallyn. "That could be romantic."

The sky was clearing to pale cold clean blue, the sun was brighter, shafts of light falling into the east. The wind got up. A white thin day moon in the sky, shivering. Colder and colder; the wet mud on Gallyn's and Morren's clothes began to freeze. There in the distance, there – the fields and orchards of Roven. The flash of the falling sunlight on the Hall's golden roof. The white moon hung above Roven like a bone.

The horse Gallyn was riding stumbled.

Suddenly it was lame.

It dragged on for one two three four steps, then it stopped entirely. Stood in the cold.

"Oh, what?" said Gallyn with a kind of weary accepting exhaustion. Like he knew this was going to happen. "It's going to turn into an old beaten-up nag again, isn't it?" he said. "Fit only for the knackers' yard. Dog meat and glue. And that sword at your hip, Morren – no, don't draw it, you know as well as I it's turned into a stick by now. A rotten worm-eaten old stick with a broken end and a smear of something on it that you hope could just be mud. You know it." He dismounted and kicked at the hard frosting earth. "Curse it!" he shouted.

"You'd be wrong there," the horse said.

Then the horse said, "Well, not about the stick."

Where the horse had been – and it was lucky that Gallyn had dismounted, don't you think? – where the horse had been, a man stood. He was very tall and strong. Dressed in the robes of an enchanter.

His skin was of course brown and his hair and beard were of course black and his robes were of course red with copper trim. His boots were trimmed with gold.

He whistled.

Thunder of hooves. A neigh.

The horse Toth, *Breaking Waves*, came crashing out of the setting sun with joy in its eyes to see Gallyn again. Sunlight flashed and caught on the sword Belelia, *Love and True Speech*, that was strapped to the horse's saddle.

"Your horse," the enchanter said to Gallyn.

"Your sword," he said to Morren.

"There's cheese and bread and wine in the saddlebag," he said. "Dry, fresh, not in the least bit damp or nibbled on."

"Uh…." said Morren

"Umm…." said Gallyn.

Then Gallyn grabbed his horse's reins and threw Morren the sword and leapt up into the saddle. All in one move, quick as thinking. "Did we fight you?" Gallyn shouted. "Who are you? How did you defeat us both?"

Morren shouted, "Do you want to fight us again?"

The enchanter laughed. "I would not dare fight you, Lord Gallyn, *Great Leap*, Lord Morren, *Golden*. Rather would I face an army of monsters, than face either of you alone in battle, and I armed and in armor and with all my power, and either one of you alone and naked and unarmed and with your hands bound behind your back. Had I an army behind me, indeed, fell beasts and demons and dragons with bronze claws, and you alone and naked and unarmed, I would not dare to fight either one of you, let alone the pair of you at once."

"So how…?"

"So what…?"

"You fought yourselves," the enchanter said. "Yourselves, alone, you will and can never defeat. Be cheered, my friends. You are undefeated still!"

It took a little while, perhaps, for Gallyn and Morren to make any sense of this. I can see indeed that you now look puzzled yourselves: how did they fight…? That can't work, that doesn't make any sense. Well… those were magic days of long ago, and one was a great enchanter and two were the brightest and the wildest of the Six of Roven. So it was magic. I don't know. I can tell it in words, so it must have been able to have happened.

Wait….

"Who are you?" asked Gallyn.

"Why?" asked Morren. "What was the point of this?"

But the enchanter – as enchanters must, the enchanter only smiled, and waved his hand in a curious gesture, and he was gone in a gust of hot wind.

And Morren and Gallyn stared after him a while. Then they could only laugh.

"Let's get home then," said Morren.

"Let's not tell the others, maybe," said Gallyn. Which he did not manage to do, he told all the others each one in confidence, which is how I'm able to tell you this story now.

(In Gallyn's defense, to be fair, Morren told all the others each one in confidence a little later too.)

"Let's go home," said Morren. He caressed the sword Belelia lovingly. Took the stick out of Belelia's scabbard, pulled a face at the muck at the end of it that might just be mud, threw it away.

"Home, yes," said Gallyn. He nudged his horse. "Ah, I was frightened for you there a while, dear friend."

"Next time you ask me to ride out with you, remind me to say no thank you," said Morren.

"Next time we ride out together, remind me to ask one of the others along," Gallyn said. "Palle or Erenan, one of the sensible ones."

They rode back to Roven in the cold winter rain. And that was the end of that quest.

CHAPTER FORTY-NINE

A silence and a stillness when Kanda had finished her story.

A strange silence indeed.

Then Mannan and Camryth both threw back their heads to laugh, bellowed with laughter, and Calian joined them.

Not one of the high deeds of the Six, that story. Though it could only have happened to Morren and Gallyn in their glory days. "His face, when the horse spoke," Morren would say of Gallyn each time he told the story in strict confidence to Kanda or Kestre or Palle or Erenan. "His face, when the horse spoke," Gallyn would say of Morren each time he told the story in strict confidence to Erenan or Palle or Kestre or Kanda. Kanda longed in her heart to tell one of the high deeds of honor and bright glory, the Six as a light against the darkness, the Six as the last bright fierce hope against evil things. *The shadows came, the nightmares came to meet us, innocence was lost. We stood unmoved – unmovable. The light was upon us – the light shone from within us. We Six, alone, and all the armies of the dark came howling. We were swallowed up in gaping jaws and tearing wings. But we were without fear, we stood firm together side by side, determined, raging, we held the darkness off, we drove the darkness back. We were the Six Swords of Roven! All the gathered powers of the dark could not defeat us. There is evil in this world, my children, and some things it is in the end necessary, even right, to kill.* But this story had crept out instead like a mouse, weak and comic, as the wrong words, some little words, so often crept out of her mouth and Sal's mouth and Calian's mouth and Dellet's mouth. Yet, she thought, they all seemed to have enjoyed it. An innocent story. And she looked at Morna and at her two grandsons and wondered indeed whether her mouth had not been wiser than her mind, to sneak out a story such as this one.

"It's lucky they took the sword and the horse with them," said Mannan. "I'd have thrown the sword down in disgust. Driven the horse off in disgust. Then where would I have been?" And Calian nodded in agreement.

"An enchanter running after you in the rain shouting 'Wait! I have a metaphor to teach you'," said Camryth. "That's where you would have been." His face laughing was like Geiamnyn's – handsome, like Geiamnyn's, which was surely no bad thing – but his laugh and his face were so like Sal's, and Kanda could see Dellet too in his face when he laughed.

"That was a fine story," said Dellet. "Ah, it was."

Morna sighed with pleasure. "I remember you telling me such stories, Mother. Oh, I do. I missed that so much."

Kanda thought: I wasn't there. The story of someone else's story – who knows if it happened anything like that? But it seems they enjoyed it happening like that.

They sat and talked all together a while longer about nothing and everything and nothing. Then Morna got to her feet. "I'm tired," she said. "Aren't you tired, all of you?" Part of Kanda thought: tired? I could sit forever listening to you, looking at you, Morna my love. Sal was the same: *my sons! My sister!* but she too was yawning. Calian was yawning and yawning. Kanda thought: we have done a great number of things today, Calian especially has done...extraordinary things. She needs to sleep.

Remember what happened when she was overtired before, Kanda thought, thinking of Mannan's and Camryth's swords. Family they might be, but if they go back to telling that tale of their mighty deeds, *we killed and hacked and cut and cut...and the bride...and the bride's women...we do all know where this is headed.*

"You do look tired, Mother," said Mannan. "We should let you sleep."

Sal went to say something, *no, I'm fine, I want to stay sitting beside my sons*, probably, certainly, but Camryth said, "We have all the time in the world now to be together, Mother. We went away to learn the arts of the stone spear and the crane spear and the whistling spear and the three-pointed spear, that even Father could not teach us, and now we're home again." He frowned. "We met Aunt Morna, and we…we…." He almost went to itch his ear with his foot as a dog does; almost his nose seemed to twitch. "…And we…. But now we're home again. We'll stay at home with you now, Mother, don't fear."

"The secrets of the stone spear and the crane spear are well known now to me," said Mannan proudly. "The red spear and the three-pointed spear hold now no mysteries for Camryth."

"We can show you the stone spear and the crane spear and the whistling spear and the three-pointed spear, tomorrow, if you like," said Camryth. He got up, and for a moment he seemed to be going to fall onto all fours to trot out with tail wagging. He frowned. Looked at his hands. Strange. I thought I had…. Well. Anyway. No matter. He looked at Mannan questioningly. Mannan looked back, scratched his ear, shrugged. "Well. Anyway. Come on, Mother, we'll show you up to your bedroom."

All getting up now, yawning, stretching, rubbing eyes, *oh I'm tired, yes*, no one wanting to be left to speak alone to another, Kanda so desperate to be alone with Morna and so reluctant, all wanting to stay together and wanting to flee and wanting to be the first and the last to bed.

Good night, Morna. Good night, Mother. Good night, Morna, good night…cousins. Good night, Calian. Good night…Morna. Good night… Dellet. Good night, everyone.

And the hall had a guesthouse besides with many fine chambers. Beds hung with green silk and beds hung with red velvet, and carpets and tapestries on every wall. Windows with a view of lush gardens, rich with fruit trees. The city was faded, a hall set in fields and orchards, set in meadows and wild woods. A practice ground for Camryth and Mannan to show off their sword skills and their spear skills, a stable for horses… Morna had restrained herself from a kennel for hunting dogs. Servants with the faces of the market traders led Kanda to her bedroom, checked she had water in a jug to drink from and water in a bowl to wash, turned back the furs and blankets and sheets. The jug was carved from a single huge ruby. The bowl was carved from a single huge pearl. Her bed robe was white silk. Dellet's bed robe was green silk. A panoply stood at the foot of the bed waiting for Kanda's armor. She thought a long time before she hung her armor there.

It did look very fine. She stood and looked with pride at it.

Dellet said, "Kanda."

Dellet said, "Kanda, wife."

Kanda said, "Del-my-heart." She took his hand in hers.

Rage words about to burst out.

Tear themselves out.

"Kanda: no," said Dellet. "Don't speak of it."

Kanda whispered, "Morna." Vomited it up.

"You with all your magic. You with all your power. Ah, Kanda, wife." Dellet stroked Kanda's hair. "So many things you've seen and done. Some things even you have to accept." She struck the pillows and struck the bed and gnashed her teeth together and sobbed into her husband's arms. Then she at last grew still.

They held each other tight in the huge bed, small as children. There were no more words either could say, so they said nothing. Lay huddled together in a bed almost as big as the house they had helped build, in a room that glowed with dark and lightless light.

"Kanda, wife." "Del-my-heart." Said it without speaking until he fell asleep and she must have fallen asleep.

CHAPTER FIFTY

When Kanda woke the next morning, Dellet wasn't there. His clothes were gone from the chair he had left them on. She was frightened he had gone away. Been taken away. Her clothes were gone too; a beautiful white gown with gold trim and a pair of soft doeskin boots sat in their place. She left her armor and helmet on the stand, but strapped on her sword.

Her lost sword, Iath, *Kind Strength*, would have looked lovely against the white dress. This dress too had been made for that nameless woman she had dreamed she once had been. She tried to count the days she and Morna had been together, after she had first told Morna about Roven and her life as one of the Six and before Morna had died. Three days? Four? Ten? It was hard to remember even that. In one of the stories I told Morna about Roven, she thought, did I mention that my sword Iath was gold? Did I mention a white dress?

There was no one about in the guesthouse or in the feast hall. Kanda stood in the hall doorway a while. The city rose half-formed beyond the feast hall's walls, towers, domes, trees, half there, half ruined, thin as smoke. It might be clouds piled, as she had often seen great battles and cities falling in the clouds when a storm threatened or when she simply stood with her face to the wind. Sounds, occasionally, drifting upward, sounds and scents, snatches, a crowd talking in muffled voices, a bell's faint peal, a ghost-perfume of fresh bread or fresh shit.

"Hello, Mother. Good morning."

She spun around.

A column of light, a creature of gold, her eyes' feasting.

"Hello, Morna." Keep her voice soft. Good morn-morn my good Morn-Morn my heart's morning's best and best.

Morna said, "Did you sleep well? It's late. The others thought you needed to sleep. You looked so…so tired, last night."

So old, I think you mean, Morna, Kanda thought. Not as you remember me as timeless all those years half a year ago. She said, "Where is everyone?"

Hug her, hold her, never let go.

But she only stood and looked at her daughter.

Morna said lightly, "They're on the practice field. Mannan and Camryth are showing Calian the stone spear and the crane spear and the whistling spear and the three-pointed spear and some other kinds of spear even beside that. I tried to watch them, but I can't see myself how it's different from any other spear I've seen. They throw the spear. It hits the target. They cheer. Unless the art is in the different cheering? But Calian is fascinated."

Kanda said lightly, "Yes."

"Calian is…." A little laugh and lightly lightly speaking, "Calian is so young. I always thought of her as tall and vast and grown. Like a giant."

Lightly lightly laughing laughing. "Yes, well, she is like that," Kanda said.

"I had not realized that Sal had got so old," said Morna.

Lightly lightly. Laughing.

Kanda said, "Having children makes you tired and old."

Silence. Then Morna said in a rush, "But I remember you so clearly, Mother. Dellet – my – my father-that-was – he looks the same." Morna paused. Then she said, to Kanda's astonishment, "That's not true at all. I always thought of him having a beard and redder hair. A bit more like your hair, I suppose, thinking about it, like…they'd got muddled in my memories. You and him."

"He's never had a beard," Kanda said.

"I know. I know that, I've always known that, but in my memories, when I try to picture him—"

Silence.

Silence.

"You can't blame him. Dellet. You can't blame him," Kanda said. "Of all of us, he is the least to be blamed. It was my sword that struck you down." She said, "We all thought you were dead. All four of us."

"You and Sal and Calian all struck me down," said Morna.

Silence.

Silence.

Silence.

Silence.

May we never have to speak another word again.

"It's done," Morna said. "You did it. My father rescued me from it and brought me up." She said, "What more is there to say? What do you want me to say?"

Everything, Morna.

Nothing.

Empty things.

"Shall we go and find them?" Morna said. She took a few steps with the yellow flowers swirling around her. Then she stopped, looked at Kanda, said, "That story you told last night…it was very foolish. It was a fine story. Made everyone laugh. But I heard a story about Lord Morren and Lord Gallyn and an enchanter, too, once. More exciting, maybe, but not quite as good. An enchanter who came against Roven with an army following behind him, fell beasts and demons and dragons with bronze claws. He fought Gallyn, almost defeated him. Knocked Gallyn unconscious from his horse. He fought Morren, almost defeated him. Struck Morren so that he dropped his sword."

She said, and Kanda was genuinely unsure if she was being cruel and mocking or not, "Do you know that story?" she said.

Kanda said, "I might know it." And she looked at Morna, and she looked at Morna, and she looked and looked and looked. She looked at the silver roof and the golden walls that Morna had made, and the beautiful gardens, and the beautiful white dress. She looked at the yellow flowers opening at Morna's feet.

"But the enchanter didn't destroy Gallyn or Morren, Morna. He nearly did, but he wasn't strong enough. Gallyn got back on his horse.

Morren picked up his sword. They killed the army following, the fell beasts and the demons and the dragons with bronze claws. I killed the enchanter myself."

A frown on that lovely shining forehead. "You did? Father always said it was Kestre who killed the enchanter."

"No…."

A shrug. "Are you sure? He described it so well, Kestre's yellow hair all flying…. But it's a better story, then, if it was you."

Are you sure! "It was definitely me. I think I can remember such things." But now I see Kestre's yellow hair flying…. Kestre with a beard and redder hair, perhaps. Are you sure?

A horror, sudden, overwhelming, creeping up suddenly but it had been there in her heart a long time crouched there coiled waiting. An old woman in her last years, her mind beginning to fail, to forget the present. Like Amraen, she was returning in her mind to the dreams she had had in her youth. Creeping up suddenly, and it had been there in her heart a long time crouched there coiled waiting, and she received it now without surprise like an old long-resented friend. The past, the stories – so much more vivid, more real now, than the world she now lived in. I remember killing warriors, dragons, I lose myself in those memories, forget I no longer have that strength. I remember – I dream it. I tell tales, mere words, and think them the truth. Children, farmers, kind people with hard-worked hands – they seem to me to be warriors, I kill them, I think I do some great deed. For a little while I know the truth, if I am told it. Then again I forget. I curse my daughters for strangers, because they are grown women. I tell them they are evil, because I do not recognize them. The things they do…they are not child things, and so I say I do not recognize them. I see Calian fighting monsters but I cannot recognize her, I think she is a child fighting a child's kind things. My grandsons are grown men old enough to have adult sons themselves. Boast of their deeds of blood and horror. Start up in concern at their old grandma's doddering. Stories of the past that I fold myself into. Stories that others tell and I pretend I was there or they were there and it was real and true. Great cities, humble villages, dragons, farmers, great enchanters: they all blur into memories of joy and blood. I killed my enemies, and Kestre killed our enemies, and it gets mixed up into one. *Do you remember a village, a city, a kingdom, we massacred, Amraen? Do you remember one monster rather than another, Kestre my lost friend?*

She said, "Now you say it, perhaps it was Kestre. People got the two of us muddled, sometimes, someone told the story about her perhaps, or about me, or she told the story and I remembered it over the years as a story about me. Who knows? One of the Six killed him, anyway; perhaps Kestre and I did it together; anyway, it all ended well." One of us killed someone.

Morna grown up; Sal grown old; Sal's sons as old as Kanda is or once was. Here's Morna, fairest, brightest, finest, see her sneer. Her father is not grown old.

They went to find the others. In the practice field, the two great men leaping to throw spears, Calian learning to throw spears as well if not better than the two men. Dellet watching with a look of wary fear and wary admiration, as a man might watch a wolf bring down its prey. Sal shining watching her sons.

"Look at this," Calian cried when she saw her mother. "Look at this." She leapt, twisted like a salmon, a spear as tall as she was in her right hand. The spear flew, it made a spiral, it caught the light – sun light? some light – it made the light within itself, perhaps, or the light was made and drawn in Calian's leap and Calian's throw. The spear was as water, wood and bronze could not move so, flow and pour and flicker so. The spear was as smoke. The spear was as mist. Not a spear to draw blood from the wind, this spear; rather, this spear was itself the wind. It struck its target, a man made of straw and wood. Went through it cleanly, buried itself in the earth beyond.

"Well done, Calian!" Camryth shouted.

"Well done, Calian," said Mannan. He had the sulky voice of one who has not quite mastered the thing another has just effortlessly managed. Morren had made that voice sometimes at Kanda and Palle. Child-Sal had made that voice when Calian as an infant had managed something for the first time that previously only Sal could do.

"Well done, Calian," Kanda said. The stone spear or the crane spear or the whistling spear or the three-pointed spear or some other kinds of spear. Who knew?

Calian: she rushed over: "The bright spear, Mother! Camryth taught me!"

"It is…astonishing, Calian." The arts of killing had not been named and practiced so in Roven. The purpose of a spear (the point of a spear, Gallyn would say, every time, as if it was the funniest thing), the purpose of a spear was to defend the wielder at a safer distance than the sword, to kill an enemy that must at the last be killed. Many things had names in the Hall Roven, but only if they were worth naming. "Wonderful, Calian."

"Isn't it?" Calian was smiling at her new cousins. Sal's sons, therefore in her mind they were no different to Sal and therefore in her mind they were no different to Calian herself. Warriors, like Kanda and Calian. They had appeared before her fully formed rushing to embrace their mother: she could not therefore fully understand what they were.

"Nobody knows these skills but Camryth and me and you," Mannan said, exultant, "because we used these skills to kill our teacher after she'd taught us." Which was a warrior's bravado, the kind of thing a warrior boasts of. And so comically phrased, and said knowing it was comic – that it must have been a game, not the truth.

Kanda watched them teach Calian the crane spear and the stone spear and the three-pointed spear and some other kind of spear the name of which she didn't catch, all of which were indeed only the same thing. More kinds of spear than Kanda had thought possible.

At last Morna said, as many young women would have said and after much longer than many young women would have waited to say it, "This is even more boring than before," Morna said. "Shall we go riding, Mother?" She looked at Sal, transfixed watching her sons at their sporting, at Dellet. "You and me, Mother, just the two of us?"

Kanda said awkwardly, "I don't think—" I mean – something, I mean, I don't think—

"I'd like to," Morna said. "And this is very dull, you know it is."

Calian glared. Kanda said hurriedly, "I wouldn't say dull."

"We could ride and ride and it would be good," Morna said.

The air shimmered around Kanda. Gleamed. Beyond the practice field, damp greenness rolled itself before her to the horizon. No city, no forest and wide river, only green stuff for horses to run together on and on. Sunlight caught the folds of the land. Low stopes, low hills. Low hedges, little streams that flashed from the earth like the wings of insects, set for a horse to leap. If the earth is the bones and flesh of a human body, this green spreading land to ride with Morna was the bones and flesh of a rolling child, safe and soft. Only a blurring in the far distance where the earth and the sky met together. Both unreal. To the east, to the west, to the north, to the south.

Dellet said, "Go on, Kanda. I'll stay here to praise Calian and make sure she doesn't do anything too dangerous."

A very wise man, Dellet. Like Kanda, he saw the words that pushed at Morna's lips, that Morna herself did not know she wanted to speak.

Unlike Kanda, he wanted Morna to speak them. Kanda thought for a bitter moment: it always falls to me. "But I did the hard part, Kanda, keeping Calian away," he says. A hollow laugh at that. But he doesn't know.

"I'll make sure Calian doesn't hurt herself," Dellet said. "Try to. You go with…with Morna."

So Kanda could only say, "Yes."

Mother and daughter went to the horse field. Morna in the horse field whistled. Two horses came galloping. A white mare, mane plaited with red ribbons. A white stallion, crowned in gold, mere skin and bones, long dead.

"The best of horses," said Morna. "These two."

"I thought…that horse was…." A joke? A game? Mockery?

"I like him," said Morna. "He and I, we rode here in less time than it took you to kill me."

Kanda took a long deep breath. Said, in a voice that was harsh because it was breaking, "Morna: why are you doing this?" Said, in a voice that was only a whisper, "Can you not see that we are punished?"

The lovely face crumpled. Not lightly laughing: filled with grief. "I wanted...to see you," Morna said.

"Why?" One word. Must. Be spoken. Then still dead silence.

Morna whispered, "Why?" Whispered like the dead.

Still and silent and more dead silence.

"You created this place, Morna. This hall this city this kingdom, all of this you made, for us. We all hear the cruelty in your voice. Then the happiness in your voice. Like you can't decide. So why? What do you want with us?"

"Why?" Morna only whispered again.

"Do you want to cut out my heart and give it to you? Because I will, I would. I cut out my heart on the day I killed you, Morna. Do you need me to show it to you, give it so you can lock it away in a box? Cut off my hair, rend my clothes, tear my face with my nails? Raise the grief song, 'Mare, mare, henket; mare that is only *despair, mighty ceaseless quenchless all-consuming sorrow*; henket that is only *death. How young she was, how splendid, how beautiful and strong. Night has covered my eyes. There is no joy in my face.*' I will bare my breasts, beat my breasts with my fists, scream to the skies; if you had had a grave to be buried in I would lie there with my mouth gnawing the earth of your grave mound. Crawl on all fours, hunched forever over your grave. Raise the funeral pyre, throw myself into the fires, your dead bones and my living bones together burning, my heart burns, my womb that held you burns. Live and die and die and live with grief for you for you for you for you. Stab myself in my heart and my womb for you again again again again again.

"Is that – what you want from me?"

The lovely face looked at Kanda. A pause, and then Morna said very quietly, "Yes."

She said slowly, "That is what I want."

She turned away, looked down at her hands.

She said, "But, as you say, I have no grave."

She said, "So it doesn't matter, does it?"

Mother and daughter stood together and the horses stood side by side near them, the living horse and the dead horse.

I'm sorry I'm sorry I'm sorry. But there aren't enough words and enough breath to say it as many times as it must be said if it is to be said. And still at the end there would be angry words pushing at Morna's lips.

It's a word. Only that. *Sorry.* Like *father* and *mother* and *love* and *changed* and *done.*

Whisper. Shout. Don't listen.

"Come," Kanda said. "The best of horses. Let's ride. Ride fast as the wind. This kingdom you've made – it is beautiful, Morna. A fair fine place. Let's ride through it. See it. You show it to me, the trees, the fields, the rivers, the houses. Come. I'd like that." Talk on, prattle, like the rain washing away dogshit. A trick a parent learns. Which she always hopes will one day work. Reached out, touched Morna's arm – just. Morna in the horse fields with the wind blowing her fair hair, how fair, how fine, Morna her *golden* daughter is. And all I said is true, Morna, believe that. Was true from the day I killed you. And I loved your father once, and I see in you now how much he loves you.

"You want to see it? Really?" Morna said. Worse almost than the 'why', as her eager voice was worse almost than the dead voice and the bitter voice.

Kanda patted the white horse's neck. It should be a black horse, Morna, a black mare, that also you or I have got wrong in our memories. "Of course I do. You made it," she said. "I want to see it all." She said, trying to laugh, trying at least to smile, "Think of Sal. And you said yourself this would be more interesting than having to admire Calian's spear work…."

This wild magic, hardest of all hard things, exhausting. So we go on, like the end of a battle when you stand on a pile of corpses, and you can't say…there are no words you can say for what you feel and how you are changed. You killed and bathed in bloodshed, killing was your bread, your hearth fire warm in the evening, your plate was *break-skulls*, your cup was *cut-them*, your bed was *wound-deep*. Slaughter was your heart's joy. Murder was your heart's delight. You stand with your feet planted in a field of corpses, blood you have sown, men's bodies, more bodies than a farmer can sow grains of wheat. The fighting ends, you stand triumphant; your sword is raised in red and shining hand. The fighting ends, you must turn away step down from heaped-up corpses. Wash the blood from hands and face. Eat, drink, yawn, scratch, search out a cloth to blow your nose. Crack a joke. Hug my daughter close. Pretend we can move on. Morna in the horse field eager, strong and fast leaping onto her horse. Kanda in the horse field full of old misgivings. Slowly carefully mounting up.

Morna's dead horse could run like the wind in winter. Once, Kanda had a horse that could run that fast. She kicked her heels – that's both Kanda and Morna – as one the dead horse and the living horse leapt to rush. The living horse should be a black mare. Perhaps. Their horses trampled the green stuff and the scent their hooves raised was fragrant; the sound of their hooves churning the damp earth was sweet. Ah, a fair land, a fine land, this kingdom of Morna's making! The fields were full of wheat and oats and rye and barley, the ears of wheat were as large as Kanda's fist. The streams were deep and clear. The trees were great and tall and spreading. The horses dead and living leapt and ran through them. The trees were hung with dark full leaf-bloom of thick late rotting summer, and with golden fiery leaves of autumn, and with fresh golden early summer green. Great lush clots of flowers, on trees and banks and sweetly scattered through the fields and on the streamsides, flowers gold and silver, white and red. Kanda's hair streamed as a banner; a war banner too was Morna's hair. The horses ran together as one horse racing, a living horse and its dead shadow cast there where its hooves broke the earth; faster than the wind, those horses; they ran as fast as thoughts. In that rushing riding together there was something between Kanda and Morna like and not like speaking, and almost or at least edging toward becoming like something. They rode with the fast rush and the running the thunder of hooves and the scent of earth thrown up thick hard clods and clots on and on with all the world spread beneath riders and horses trampling, rode with the wind licking up their hair and the horses' plaited manes. The sunlight burst through branches flashing slanted as eyes that blinked and winked and closed. The taste of the sky on Kanda's lips. They rode until they came to the river where it spread wide as outstretched arms, silvered, gentle, softened, with a fatness to it, calm and heavy, richer, older, ready, dying – for there, at last, the river ran to meet the sparkling sea.

So there, at the end, at the edge, where this world ended, they must stop riding.

Morna touched her mother's hand.

"You have your sword, Mother?" Morna said.

"I do." Since they rode through the gates of the white marble city, trampling horses' blood and human blood beneath horses' hooves and human feet, in Morna's halls and Morna's gardens, sporting, resting, feasting with her family, Kanda had not gone without her black sword that could kill monsters.

Morna reined her horse, turned it, pointed to the hearth smoke and the bread-baking smoke and the city's rising shining lovely towers. "The two of us, Mother. Just the two of us, we could ride there, break upon village or town or city, heedless. Such destruction! Greater. The greatest. Farmers, traders, makers, merchants: we could kill them all. You and I, alone, together.

"You've fought beside Calian, beside Sal, even beside...beside my-father-that-was. So now it can be you and I, together, side by side. Fighting. Killing.

"What do you think?"

Ah, the hope was there in Kanda! We could! We could!

Kanda put her right hand to her sword hilt. Not Kanda's hand *went* to her sword hilt. Kanda moved her hand, placed it there. Knew what she did. Closed her fingers tight. Cold metal quickly warming. The leather grip that smelled of her skin and sweat, shaped so long to her hand. A pleasure, hidden and dirty: to grasp her sword tight, squeeze her hand around the hilt, then smell the metal and the leather on her hand.

I have fought beside Sal and Calian. Now I could fight beside my youngest fairest child. Three daughters I can catalogue: Sal, I am proud of her, she has shown bravery, resourcefulness, compassion, she has given me two strong grandsons; Calian, I am proud of her, she has shown her mettle, she is a greater warrior than I was at my best; but Morna is the third and the last and greatest, she has given me this world to live in, she cares for that one I loved so deeply, she is the greatest warrior that now lives.

Morna pointed to the south where the sunlight flashed on a springhead, lit up golden a cluster of houses. A baby was crying; a woman sang a comfort song. Morna said, "There. Just the two of us. Shoulder to shoulder. Look at it. Waiting. My father taught me such skills that I could show you."

So much work to build that longhouse. So quickly, Kanda could burn it. Such beauty in the fires. The walls and roof all burning. Sheets of flame. The scent of burning pinewood.

The sunlight shifted. Fell in longer, fainter rays. Not longhouses but a hall with storerooms and houses huddled round, a high wooden wall. Better things to loot there. More people for killing. She was practiced in killing them.

"Or there?" Morna said. "I missed it before. Those men – those dogs, I mean – those dogs went too slowly, I heard the noise you were making, but no, the dogs had to sniff and cock a leg and dally about. From what I saw after, it looked like fun. I wish I'd been there with you and Calian."

Kanda thought: it was, Morna. Oh it was. I wish you had been there so I could have seen all three of you in your glory.

"But the best," said Morna. "Or so Father always tells me – the best…."

The city. The towers, the streets, the palaces, the gardens. The people, gold and silver, stately as ancient kings. Kanda in her mind saw herself riding through the streets with blood rising to her horse's forelocks. As in the villages, people fled from her in terror. Unlike the villages, there were so many people there to kill. She and Morna could spend days in the city wallowing in bloodshed. She and her first husband had spent days. She could raise a fire to melt the very stones until they shone like sun-on-water. Liquid stone and liquid flesh. All she and Amraen had seen in their memories and dreams.

"We could," Morna whispered. "We could. Oh Mother. Please." The fires blazed in Morna's eyes.

Golden.

Those days were the best days of Kanda's life, and always would be. Freedom. Joy such as she had never known. A long time since Ikandera Thygethyn had brought a city to ruin. The city waiting, spread before her, hungry for her sword. Once with her husband. Now with her husband's beloved child.

"No, Morna," Kanda said.

With a great effort, Kanda took her hand from her sword hilt. Took up her horse's reins, turned it away. "That time is past, Morna. That time can never come back. At least—" she looked at her daughter. Saw the crushing disappointment on her daughter's face – "it would be very easy to bring it back. Far easier than the quest I am on. I know that."

She said, "But I don't want it back, Morna."

"But I thought— But— I hoped—" Bloody tears, sliding down Morna's face. "I wanted to have something with you," Morna said. "That Calian and Sal had."

Kanda said gently, "I know you did, Morna." She said after a moment, "Thank you, Morna. It was kind of you." She held out her hand to her daughter. "It was very kind of you, Morna, my love. If I—

"It would have been – good. If—

"Once, yes, it would have been a wondrous thing."

They rode back to Morna's hall, with its white-painted wattle-and-daub walls and its yellow reed-thatch roof.

Thus ended an adventure that had almost happened. Always, in her heart, Kanda would wish that it—

It—

Hush now.

Don't speak of this.

CHAPTER FIFTY-ONE

Amazingly – or not, given everything Kanda knew of Calian from birth onward, and everything Kanda had briefly seen of Camryth and Mannan – the arts of the crane spear and the stone spear and the whatever they were, the apple spear and the piglet spear and the blahblahblah spear and yet more spears still were still going on. They had barely noticed Morna and Kanda had gone. "Oh well done, Calian," Dellet was saying as Kanda sat down beside him. "Even better than the last time."

At least, Calian and Mannan and Camryth hadn't. Sal was certainly looking bored now even at her sons' great prowess, she had the face a parent never loses that's half hoping her child will fall down and graze its knee so they can go home; Dellet looked like he'd agree to the child breaking its leg in three places, if it meant they could go home soon.

"Look at that!" Mannan shouted. "Well done, cousin! If that had been a real man, you'd have taken his guts out. Wrapped them round the spear shaft like a streamer flying, and gone on another spear's length."

"Mannan!" Sal said. "Camryth!"

"It's a wickerwork doll, Mother," Camryth said. He picked it up. Took out the spear. Danced it. "Look, Mother, it's quite unharmed apart from the hole Calian made in it."

"Which means we've not been hitting it hard enough," said Mannan. "Put it down so I can hit it."

"No," Sal said, "no, no, no, don't hit it while your brother's holding it. Mannan!"

"No," said Dellet. "No, Calian, don't, let him put it down."

Calian shouted, gleeful, "Oh, look at that! What a blow! What a strike!"

But even the art of the apple spear and the piglet spear and the blahblahblah spear and many other kinds of spear besides must finally be exhausted, and even Calian and Camryth and Mannan must finally be exhausted also. Just about. Kanda was herself beginning to fear it would take a serious injury to make them stop their sporting, and beginning to hope the injury would happen soon. But finally Mannan took the head off the straw man with one throw of the something spear, and Camryth applauded, and they decided they'd probably finished.

"Let's go back to the hall and find something to eat," said Mannan. "We can show you some more tricks tomorrow, cousin."

A loud "Yes!" from Calian. So pleased with themselves and with Calian that two gray tails seemed to wag.

"There's the sword arts; the stone sword, the wild sword, the winged sword, the bright sword. . . ."

"I thought you were great warriors before," said Sal. "But these skills you've learned are wondrous."

"They are, aren't they?" Mannan said. Not one for modesty, that one, it seemed. (Which, when Kanda looked at him, was probably fair enough.)

"I can't wait to show Father these new skills we've learned," Camryth said happily. "He'll be amazed too, I think. Even him."

Sal made a noise. Camryth saw Sal's face. Said, confused, "What is it, Mother?"

Kanda thought: be still. Be silent. Don't speak, don't think. She looked, and tried not to look, and looked. At Sal. At Morna. At Sal. At Sal's sons.

"Your father's dead, Mannan, Camryth," Morna said.

Morna said, "Your mother killed him."

CHAPTER FIFTY-TWO

Sal let out a cry.

"Don't you know?" Morna said. "I thought she must have told you."

"That—" Camryth looked from his mother to Morna and back again. "Mother? What does she mean? You and Father kissed us goodbye together when we set out. 'We'll see you soon,' you said."

"Our father is the greatest warrior and the noblest man now living," said Mannan. "Nothing can kill him."

"Our father is the greatest monster and the wickedest man who ever walked this earth," said Camryth. "Not even the Six Swords of Roven together could kill him."

Sal let out a gasp. She fell to her knees and her tears ran down her cheeks. Her tears were red as blood and black as black ash.

"You're lying, Morna," Mannan said. "See how much you're hurting her. Stop lying like this. Father is at home waiting for all three of us."

"Tell her, Mother," said Camryth. "Tell her. You stood side by side, kissed us both goodbye, said you'd see us soon. You cried because we were going away again. Father comforted you." These great strong warrior men: how small, like children, how frightened they looked, how confused, like children, staring at their mother. "Tell her, Mother!" Camryth said. "Tell her!"

And Camryth was the wiser one, the clever one, Kanda had seen that quick enough, Mannan was the greater warrior but he looked for cunning and wise words to Camryth. But Camryth stared blank and lost in utter confusion. "Tell her, Mother. Tell her. Stop her saying this. You stood side by side, you and Father, you cried because we were going away and Father comforted you. Stop her saying this, why is she saying this?" And Mannan was the slower thinker, simpler, not stupid exactly but certainly not rich in cunning words and plotting, but he looked at his mother and he looked at Morna, and at last he said as certainly as stone and bronze and death are certain, "Our father is dead and our mother has killed him."

Camryth buried his face in his hands with a howl.

Blood ran from the knife that hung on a leather cord around Sal's neck, that she had used to strike down her husband Geiamnyn.

A pause, a silence, watching mother and son and son.

"The moment she struck your father down, you both changed into dogs," said Morna. "You ran wild as dogs until I found you and changed you back into men."

She put her left hand on Camryth's shoulder. She held out her right hand to Mannan, gently touched his arm. "When you were still dogs, you met your mother, she did not recognize you any more than my mother recognized me. The scars you bear came from that meeting." She said sadly, "I'm sorry. I didn't want to tell you this."

"That's a lie, Morna!" Calian shouted.

"It's the truth. I didn't want to tell you," Morna said again. "I'm sorry, that I had to tell you."

And Kanda knew somehow – that it was the truth.

Camryth raised his head from his hands. His face was like a beast's. He howled in his dog voice. Bared long sharp teeth. Then he said slowly and very calmly, "Turn me back into a dog, Morna, cousin, if you have any kindness in you. My mother does not deserve to be killed with spear or sword. As a dog, I can tear my mother's heart from her chest and eat it. She does not deserve to die by a human hand."

Morna took a breath. To work some magic? To do – something?

Mannan leapt. Stood in front of his mother. Drew his sword.

"If you touch my mother, Camryth my brother," he shouted, "I will kill you. If you are a man, I will cut your throat. If you are a dog, I will cut off your head."

Camryth shouted back, "She is our father's murderer! If you try to defend her, I will kill both her and you."

Ah, those words again. *Mother. Father. Child. Love.*

"I'll kill you first. I'm a better swordsman than you, Camryth," Mannan shouted.

"So I've been told since the first day I held a sword," Camryth shouted back. "But you, brother, I'll kill with a sword, like a man."

Camryth's sword was in his hand also. Dog's teeth and a man's sword. Mannan's sword moved, flew, to meet it. The two blades rang together. Both men cried out. Sal cried out. They stood with swords locked and eyes locked. Huge as trees, these fine men. A darkness, like smoke, rising between them.

Turn them back into dogs. Collar them and hold them. Rabid, raging, slobber dripping from their mouths. And both were half a dog and half a man, and both were soaked and red. Heat boiled, blood pounding, hearts pounding loud like drums. The ground upon which they stood made hot from their sudden building hate. But, rabid and raging as they were, foaming fierce, set on killing, their hearts were locked together like their swords and eyes. Each waited, still as stones, for the other to strike first.

Their shadows fell long upon the green of the practice field one shadow. A single man, unformed, rough sketch of head and arms and legs and body, as a child might look half-formed within the cradle of a womb. As each must once thus have looked.

A lifetime, Sal had spent in the dark with Geiamnyn, a life long enough to raise twice over this half-formed child to manhood. A lifetime, Morna had spent in the dark with that *empty* one her father, a life long enough to grow so beautiful and cruel. Far longer, Mannan and Camryth stood with swords locked. On the very edge of fighting. One breath more and they would be fighting. Neither dared to move.

Kanda had drawn her own sword. Saw that Morna too had drawn her sword, and Calian. Poor Dellet sat with his hands pressed over his eyes. Sal herself only crouched behind Mannan, as frozen as her sons. Her eyes were open but she seemed to stare far off into nothing, or into herself or into her sons' childhoods.

Morna's absurd yellow flowers spread across the practice field. Thicker and thicker, changing the green to shining gold. So many flowers they lit the family's skin gold. Curled around Mannan's and Camryth's strong legs.

In Kanda's mind the flowers rooted the two men there. Bound them to the green rich earth. Covered in flowers, overgrown, two statues in an abandoned garden. Forever, they could stay like this. But even as she thought this, the two men began to fight.

No telling which moved first. Neither. Both. So well they knew each other. So well-matched. At the same moment both drew back, leapt, met, struck, leapt. Without need to speak or challenge, without needs thinking. As they would have run and moved together as children, broken together to run one left one right and leave their parent staring – left to stop Mannan falling into the nettles, or right to stop Camryth falling into the bramble patch? Left to catch Camryth and make him put his shoes on, or right to catch Mannan and make him wash his face? Their swords crashed together, over, over, loud and pealing as a ring of bells. Mannan pushed forward; Camryth retreated; three, four, five steps. Camryth pushed forward; Mannan retreated; three, four, five steps. Pressed so close neither could strike the other, bared teeth so close each breathed in the other's breath. Both hissed. Swallowed in his brother's hissing. Blinked at last – weary-eyed from watching – their eyelashes almost brushing each other's eyes. A shout from both, the same shout the same moment; both leapt back to land with sword raised exactly a spear shaft – a stone spear shaft, a crane spear shaft, a whistling shaft spear, a three-pointed spear shaft – apart. Each balanced exactly, set in exactly the same pose. Three great breaths each from two chests heaving. Both turned their head to the right and spat. One great breath, one roar from two voices. Four strong legs leapt to meet. Two swords crashed. So hard the blow that both blades shook together. Seemed to join together, the bronze forced together as one blade. The two men pushed, they too seemed joined, the flesh of their bodies melting into one. Mannan's sweat dripped to cool Camryth's forehead. Camryth's sweat dripped down Mannan's arms.

Such silence around the two men, Kanda could hear two sets of teeth grinding.

Drip of sweat. Grind of metal against metal. Grind and creak of bone against bone against bone against bone. Pushing each other. Forcing each other. Camryth slipping backward, pushing forward, Mannan slipping, pushing. Drip of sweat.

Kanda's sweat and tears.

Calian's sweat and tears.

Dellet's sweat and tears.

Sal's tears and tears and sweat and sweat.

A crunch. Teeth or bone or metal. A shout, both triumph and pain, two voices in one voice. The two men leapt back apart. Their swords flashed as they leapt. Closed together, jostled, and their swords struck and rang. Leapt apart.

But this time Camryth was one breath slower than Mannan. His leap one hair's breadth shorter. His sword jerked a little as he held it ready, where Mannan's sword flowed.

A single drop of blood ran down Camryth's right arm.

Mannan stared at the wound he had made. His eyes were empty and white. He closed his eyes. Shook his head. Mannan leapt and Camryth leapt. The two men closed in a thunder of bronze. Like a hammer working, both struck and struck and struck.

Sal cried something. Wordless. Soundless cry. Kanda found herself clenching her body with every sword stroke. Her hand burned, her feet itched to trace out the pattern the two men's feet traced as they fought. She felt Calian beside her tense, struggling – as if the two of them also could, should, fight like this.

Fight with Mannan to destroy Camryth, she thought, for Mannan was fighting for Sal's life as well as his own. She had known these two men a few days, she had not liked either of them. It should be the easiest decision in the world.

Yet: her eyes met Calian's, just briefly, a flash between them: we could cut Camryth down in one heartbeat, and we too would not need to speak to do it. As one sword, one arm, we would strike. Yet…Sal's keening, wordless, soundless, on and on so loud it hurt. Blood on Sal's right arm to match Camryth's wound. Now the two men closed and their swords crashed and they both hissed, when they drew apart again both were gasping, blood ran now from Mannan's left shoulder, and blood showed on Sal's left shoulder through her dress.

Now Mannan was a little slower, a little heavier on his feet, his sword a little weaker in his hand. Now Camryth roared in triumph in the same voice as Mannan roared in pain and fury. Now they closed again, their feet trampling blood and flowers, and blood was running from Camryth's face and Mannan's right hand and their mother's hand and face.

Now Camryth's right thigh was wounded. Now Mannan's right thigh. Now both were panting and slick with sweat. Their eyes blinded. Their mouths dumb. Fixed together in their rage. Pressed, grunted at each other. Creak of metal like the grind of two stones. Creak of their flesh. Camryth shifted, slight faint movement, sword and muscle yielding, Mannan pushing his brother one step back. A crack as the pressure of their bodies loosened. A chink of light between them. Their swords flew up both together, both shouted. Braced to strike.

Mannan was taller than his brother, stronger and heavier in the muscles of his arms and his legs. But Mannan's foot slipped in their pooling blood and the weight of his body carried him falling. He stumbled, went down on his knees. His sword dropped from his hand at the shock. And Camryth cried in triumph and wonder. Raised his sword.

CHAPTER FIFTY-THREE

Camryth's hand trembled, and he raised his sword to kill Mannan. Mannan cried out and threw up his arms as a shield. Camryth brought his sword down to kill.

Kanda and Calian were there with their swords drawn, and they would kill him or he in his rage and grief would kill them.

Camryth's sword came down, down, bright and killing, gold and fine his blade shone. As gold and fair as Mannan's golden hair. As fair to look at as the setting sun or the rising sun. Camryth's sword met and cut Mannan's handsome face. A wound opened like the sun's wounding. A twist of Camryth's wrist now would take off Mannan's handsome head.

Camryth stopped. Still and frozen. The wound just opened in a long fine trickle of blood. Camryth's sword was a hand, touching, holding his brother's face.

One two three breaths.

"Get up, brother," Camryth said.

"Fooled you!" Mannan would roar, and he would leap up and laugh at Camryth as boys do. *"Tricked you!"*

"Get up, brother," Camryth said.

Mannan said slowly, "I would rather you killed me. Brother."

"Get up," Camryth shouted.

"If you want to kill our mother, I would rather you killed me first," Mannan said. "I don't want to live now."

"Get up." Camryth's clever voice was stupefied. His clever face was struck dumb. "I wouldn't have – I wouldn't have hurt either of you," Camryth said. "Not really." Such confusion. "You can't think—

"My brother," Camryth said, "get up. Please."

Mannan raised his head then. How like his father he looked, so full of rage. But so much grief in his face. Then – a kind of peace, a gentleness, in his face. He reached out his left hand. Clasped Camryth's left hand as his brother held it out to him. The two stood together. Clothed in each other's blood. Fell into each other's arms embracing. Again, their blood and their sweat mixed. My brother my brother. My friend. Arms and thighs and faces cut and bruised and pained. They looked at each other's wounds in a kind of horror, then a kind of wonder, then with pride.

"Told you I was the better swordsman," said Mannan, "always was, always will be."

"You!" said Camryth. "I was winning."

"Yes, that's true, I'll grant you – but look at the wound I made on your thigh. Even losing. You can command a company better than I can, Camryth, but I'm the better swordsman one on one. Admit it. There's more of your blood on me than my blood on you," Mannan said.

Together they turned to Sal. They clutched at her like infants, fists clenched into her skin. Their blood and their sweat covered her and their blood and their sweat and the clasp of their hands gave her some stranger healing. For the blood and the wounds vanished, and it seemed to Kanda that Sal's face was younger than she had been before her sons fought. But she stood uncertain between them, dared not meet their eyes.

"I didn't mean it…." Camryth said. "Didn't mean…I mean, I did mean, but I didn't mean…I mean…."

"Hush, Camryth; hush, Mannan," Sal said. "Hush, you two, my wild sons."

Mannan said, "You really killed him?"

Sal said, "I did."

Camryth said, "Are you sorry for it?"

Sal said, "I am."

She said, "Not for myself. Not for him. But for you two, I am."

A pause, and a looking, and a thinking, these two huge great warrior men like desperate eager boys. Sal stood between them thin and worn. Said nothing. Said nothing. They clasped their right hands together all red and bloodied, and kissed their mother's cheeks.

"I mean…there's worse endings," said Mannan. "I think."

"There's probably worse endings," said Camryth. "If we think long enough."

"You killing me and Mother, for one," said Mannan. "Then where would you have been?"

"True," said Camryth. "Worse off than I am with only my father being dead, that's where I'd have been."

"Also, our father was a murderous old bastard," said Mannan. "Don't think many people would disagree enough to mourn him."

"Our father was the greatest warlord who ever lived in all the world," said Camryth. "But we always knew he'd end up dead in a ditch."

"If Mother hadn't killed him, one of us two would have ended up killing him," said Mannan. "You know how it goes."

"Or he'd have killed us," said Camryth. "That's sometimes how it can go."

"Speak for yourself," said Mannan. "I'd have killed him if he'd tried it."

"True," said Camryth. "You would at that."

"I'm mean…it's awkward," said Mannan. "I'm not saying it isn't."

"But that's the way of it," said Camryth. "When you live like we do and he does. Did. We'll just have to ignore it."

"Pretend it didn't happen," Mannan said. "Just that someone killed him."

They clasped their mother's hands tightly, four big men's killing fists over Sal's thin worn clenched killer's hands. "Mother?" they both said together, "we can do that, can't we? Say yes?" They kissed each other's hands and their mother's hands.

Until Mannan looked at Morna standing in all her golden beauty, and Camryth looked at her. Both raised their hackles like the dogs they had been. Both growled like dogs. Bared their dogs' teeth.

"Why?" Camryth said. For all his cleverness, his cunning and wise words. "Why? Why? Why? Why?" Like a crow cawing or a cow lowing or a dog's bark. Until Kanda wanted to shout to make him be silent. Like two stones being hit together, and as meaningless. "Why? Why? Why? Why? Why? Why? Why? Why? Why? Why? Why? Why? Why?"

And Morna…shrugged.

CHAPTER FIFTY-FOUR

Mannan took up his sword.

Camryth took up his sword.

Morna took up her sword.

Mannan's sword was beautiful and brilliant. Camryth's sword was beautiful and bright. Morna's sword was more beautiful than all the stars and the moon and sun and the rain and the mist and the harvest morning and the harvest evening and the sweet summer dew and the cool summer wind. More beautiful than an apple on the tree or a flower in the meadow. More beautiful than a blackbird can sing.

Morna met Camryth's and Mannan's swords both together, parried both swords, forced both men back. She moved as the light moves when the breeze shakes the willow tree. As the corn moves as the traveler passes, the stems bend to show paler silver that flows and ripples across the fields, it seems as if an army is passing there, a thousand men each stretching their hand to bend the corn stems, but there is only the gentle rustle of the wind in the cornfield, the play of color and the drift of cloud and the curved lines of the earth and the light.

So delicate, dancing, her feet seemed barely to touch the ground. Her lovely hair flying out around her, her silk skirts, the flash of her jewels; she smiled, she laughed as she fought. Her sword was at Camryth's neck and at Mannan's shoulder, at Camryth's chest, at the muscles of Mannan's thigh. They could not wound her. Couldn't touch her. She twisted and flickered between them, she was unreal to their crude blows. As well try to cut a single thread from her gown or a single hair from her head.

Mannan shouted in fury. *Strong* as a bull, and he could not land one stroke. He thrust, jabbed, stamped, lumbered. His sword snapped out, he roared. Morna fluttered away from him. His right arm was bleeding, his left arm hung useless. Camryth was wilier, *Fierce*, not merely hacking without thought. Morna knew how to twist and taunt him, tempt him with clever moves and dancing steps.

She was like a flame reflected on a sword blade. Like a drop of blood on a knife point.

The yellow flowers grew so thick and spread so far, a carpet of gold beneath her dancing feet.

Kanda threw up her sword, let out her cry. Dropped her sword. Raised up her sword. Lowered her sword.

She had no idea what to do.

Fight to save Morna! Who did not need saving! Fight to save Camryth and Mannan! These monstrous men! Fight to…to fight these three, the two men indeed great warriors, Morna greater than any even Kanda at her best…thus fight…for the joy of fighting!

Sal shouted, "Help them! Mother! Calian! Help my sons!" But Sal's voice was terrible. Sal who had helped care for Morna almost as a second mother since the day Morna was born.

"Help Morna!" Calian shouted. "We should help my sister! Kill them, the monsters!" But her sword too wavered in her hand, for she knew that any injury to Mannan and Camryth would break Sal's heart.

Camryth let out a groan, stumbled back. Clutched at his belly. His left hand clenched there. Black blood and red blood poured out. The flowers that grew at his feet rose up to hold him, trip him. His blood stained their petals. Their roots drank up his blood. Sal screamed and screamed and screamed and tore her face.

Yellow flowers, and a young man fallen in battle, and a mother's keening.

Mai, that is *despair. Mighty ceaseless quenchless all-consuming sorrow. Grief.*

Thus Kanda had made many women scream.

Thus Kanda or Sal soon must scream.

Thus, Kanda thought watching Morna with pride, with wonder, almost with envy, thus Sal soon must scream.

"This is so stupid!"

Calian raised her bronze sword. Leapt. With that sword, she could kill…anything. Monsters, children. Thus Kanda and Sal cried out together, knowing she would kill one of their children.

All of their children, Kanda thought. A village of them. A city of them. Armies.

Calian spun, her sword whirling. The stone sword, the wild sword, the winged sword, the bright sword. One of these swords struck Mannan in the chest, sent him crashing backward. Calian twisted; she was an eagle surely, she seemed to sweep and turn and fly. She sent poor injured Camryth sprawling; rammed him over so he rolled wallowing in the flowers like a bull calf. She saw Mannan, furious, staggering to his feet again, his face grim as thunder, no other word for it, his teeth set, his sword…the only word was throbbing. The stone sword, the wild sword, the winged sword, the bright sword. All these arts and more Mannan turned on Calian. All these arts and more and better Calian met stroke for stroke, turned back on Mannan. Some other kind of swords, the blahblahblah sword, the I forget its name sword, the please this is so dull sword. She lashed at him, parried him, he struck hard with all his mighty hero's *strength* but she was not where the sword was, she had moved like…the only word for it was lightning, she was out of Mannan's sword's reach then like lightning she struck back at him. Camryth rose – half rose – staggered – reeled – crawled – to ward his brother. Calian darted left and right and left and right. Mannan's sword cut the air so close to her heart, to her arm, to her stomach. Her sword cut his hand. His wrist. Knocked him falling back. Forced Camryth back.

And Morna! Her face – exultant! Her sword – rejoicing! She tossed back her hair to fight beside her sister. This giant that she had so envied and aspired to be like. So long, so often, she must have dreamed of this.

Her joy was shattered when Calian struck her.

Morna was the better of the two. Stronger. Faster. But Calian knocked Morna hard so that Morna fell backward. Morna's right arm was wounded.

Mannan tried to get to his feet again. Tried to deal Calian a blow.

Calian knocked his sword from his hand.

Morna steadied herself. Tried to deal Calian a blow.

Calian knocked her sword flying.

Camryth went down on his belly. Didn't bother trying.

He dropped his own sword at Calian's feet.

A new and mighty lesson it seemed Calian had learned from her terrible cousins and her terrible mother and her terrible sister and her terrible killing. That it is possible, if you really try, if you work hard enough, to fight…without killing.

"You will not break my mother's heart or my sister's heart or my father's heart again, any of you," Calian said.

CHAPTER FIFTY-FIVE

Here we are again, then. A family standing in a field of flowers, yellow flowers, staring at each other, while the blood drips. Only this time no one was dead. Only three of them might be described as…embarrassed? Confused? Humiliated?

Humiliated.

That would be it.

"Oh, come on," said Mannan. "I only taught you that trick this morning." Of the three Calian had defeated, he alone seemed willing to speak. "What was I thinking?" Mannan said.

Morna went to move. Pick up her sword, or untangle her hair, or something. Calian whipped her sword to point at Morna's throat. "Stay still." Calian turned to look at Mannan and Camryth. Her sword was still at Morna's throat and it moved a little as Calian turned her head, and Kanda winced and clenched her fists and bit her lip.

"Oh stop it, Mother, obviously I won't hurt her. Like these two stupid men saying they wouldn't hurt each other. But Mannan, Camryth: if you start fighting my sister again, you can turn back into dogs for good. And Morna my sister: if you don't stop being so horrible to everyone, you can be a dog too. See how your father-that-is likes that."

The yellow flowers were beginning to wither. Calian wiped her sword carefully on the grass.

"We are on a quest to find the Hall Roven," Calian said. "Find it and rebuild it. We need to leave now. We're stayed here too long. If we could only stay in that lovely village and that – I won't say kingdom – that feasting village a few days, we've stayed here far, far too long. We have to find Mum's sword, and Mum's old name, and a great high hall with a roof of gold and walls of silver that shine brilliant in the sun. Wonderful, rarey things my heart desires. We won't find them here."

Calian sheathed her sword carefully. Adjusted her boots. "Come on, then," said Calian. "Let's go now. Lela's village was boring, and Amraen's village was sad, but this place is worse. Come on."

She began to walk. Away from her own sister Morna. Away from Sal's great fine warrior sons. And Dellet began to walk with her. And Dellet took Calian's hand in his as they walked.

"We'll come," said Mannan. "Unless we find something better to do on the way."

"A wedding feast, or a dragon to kill, or something like that," said Camryth.

"A sport and a great destruction," said Mannan. "It's been a long time since we had one of those."

"Even a small and weak and pathetic destruction, a few houses, a barn maybe," said Camryth.

"We've never tried making something," said Mannan. "Building something not tearing it apart."

"Could be interesting," said Camryth.

"We've never done anything of use," said Mannan after a moment. Then he said, "Grandmother. No, no, that doesn't work. My lady Ikandera Thygethyn, greatest of our late father's friends, greatest by far of all our late father's many, many sworn enemies – he always thought, you know, it would be you who killed him – anyway, what was I saying, ah, yes – my lady Ikandera Thygethyn, honored grandmother – no, no, I can't say that any more than I can call that wild warrior 'Aunty Calian' – my lady Ikandera Thygethyn, Kanda – yes, that's it – Kanda, honored and best of all. May we come with you, escort our, um, ah, our poor widowed mother, at your side, protect her from dangers, to find this place that you are seeking, that does indeed sound a fine and lordly place?"

"We'll try not to destroy it," said Camryth. "Honestly. We'll try. We're great and mighty warriors the pair of us, I'm sure we can be of use. Of some good."

"And we'll try not to fight with Morna or with Calian," said Mannan.

"We'll go and get your horse saddled, Mother," said Camryth. For the first time, he looked uncertain. "...*Old White Nose*, I think you call him?"

"Perfectly good hero's horse's name, that," said Mannan. "I think?"

The two men took their mother's hands. Mannan on her left, Camryth on her right. Beware them, Kanda thought, for all they seem but Sal's children and thus but young and foolish, harmless things. In particular, she thought, beware Camryth; he has a dog's fangs still, that one, and a clever tongue. The three began to walk, Kanda's daughter and Kanda's grandsons. Sal looked small and thin and happy, beside her terrible beloved children.

"Well, Mother?" Morna said. "What are you going to say to me?"

Kanda closed her eyes. In her mind, she saw the Hall Roven just as Calian had described it. In her mind, she heard a blare of trumpets. A crystal bell. A horn ringing. The beast from which that horn came, she had hunted.

Almost, almost, so close, she could hear the murmur of sound that was her old name when she was the greatest of the Six.

"You will come home," she heard the Lord of Roven say to her in her mind.

"Morna," Kanda said. She held out her hand to her daughter. "Morna: you have a thousand years to wait before you can see your father again." She said, more terrible words, defeat and pain and hope in them, "I am sorry for that, Morna, that you must wait that long."

She paused, then she said, "Will you come with us, Morna my love?"

She paused, then she said, "Please?"

The wind blew Morna's lovely hair. Yellow flowers grew thick around her dainty feet. The ground shook.

A shining city of white marble, and a hall of gold and silver and dung and thatch – falling to rubble. Fallen to dust.

Forgotten. Like so many things that are long gone and done.

CHAPTER FIFTY-SIX

They walked through a forest, following the River Wenet the River Wend. Apples hung from the trees' branches. Golden apples, silver apples, apples made of pearls and diamonds and silk thread. Birds in the trees: gold birds, silver birds, birds with ruby wings. A fox ran across the path ahead of them. It was made of gold. A crow burst up from a tree branch. It was made of jet. It didn't caw, it sang and sang and sweetly oh so sweetly it sang.

Kanda and Morna walked together, a little behind the rest. After a little while, Morna said, "I'd like to tell you – about my life with him," just as Kanda said, "Morna – I'd like you to tell me—"

They both laughed, and neither spoke more of the things both wanted to say.

The gold and the silver shifted into greenness growing. They walked through the forest along the bank of the river that was lush with green things. Mannan ahead of them stirred up the scent of nettles by striking the plants with a stick. Calian ahead of them yelled because a bird had shat on her backpack. The trees grew vast and spreading, oak trees tall as the towers of a great city, tall as the columns of a king's hall and as richly hung with ferns and lichen and moss. Wet-stink, mud-stink, damp-in-the-air-water-scent. They came to a place where the riverbank curved like an arm embracing; a willow tree bent with the wind setting its leaves to shiver the water; yellow flowers; a muddy river beach. Six white swans bobbed on the water in the green-gold shallows. On the far bank six white trees in blossom, may trees, dark twining trunks and flowers like stars that smelled of old rotted meat.

Morna stopped. Turned to her mother.

"Wait, Mother," Morna said. They watched until the others were almost out of sight.

Morna took out the hunting horn. Sounded it.

A horse neighed. Such music of its hooves as it came running out from the trees.

A white horse. Red saddlecloth, head trappings of bronze and red enamel. Gold bridle. Gold bit. Sharp spikes on the bit.

It stopped before Morna and Kanda. Snorted, stamped. Eager to ride to war and blood and ruin with one of these two great warriors on its back.

"I'm sorry, horse," Morna said. "You would have carried me across the world, I know you would. You the horse and I the rider, and how fine it could have been. My mother and I as the greatest of warriors, and you to bear me." She said with all her bright malice, "Blame my mother, not me."

The horse neighed, and stamped, and bent its head. It turned its eyes to Kanda, and it seemed to be pleading.

"Ah, my mother would have ridden you to better killing than I could dare dream of, horse," Morna said. "I know and you know well, and she knows. But, alas, that will never again be."

The horse crumbled down away to bones and horsehide. Old and long dead.

The horsehide wrapped itself around the bones. The bones crawled across the horsehide.

A man stood up. A dead man, wild eyes, wild hair. Such pain in him. He looked at Kanda with the same confusion Mannan and Camryth had shown when they had ceased to be dogs and returned to being men.

Kanda knew him.

A murderer, indeed, a bad man, a wicked man, a killer. A warrior once in her army, one who had wallowed in red slaughter, one who had delighted in destruction and bloodshed.

One who had *wanted* to be something more than only killing. *Wanted* and *wanted* and *wanted.*

"Amraen," Kanda cried in grief. "What is this? I left you with Jeha, returning to your home. Such hopes you had. What is this now? How can this be?" She cried out to Morna, "But he was with me, alive, only a few days ago. He was the one who was so afraid of the ghost. This is some further cruelty that you are working, Morna. Some horrible game and trick. Stop it.

"Stop it!

"But you were happy, Amraen," she cried. "At peace in your…your kingdom. You danced with Jeha, she smiled at you and her blue dress swirled like a kingfisher's wings. When the dance stopped you ruffled Ylil's hair. All right, yes, Ylil hated you doing that, but it's hardly a monstrous thing. You asked if I would dance with you myself. There were crumbs stuck on your chin. You were a kind man, in your way. No worse than many.

"Not this."

The man only stared at her.

"I am afraid to see it," he had said to Kanda of the ghost. "In case…."

Ah, Amraen, Kanda thought. I led my army once to destroy a great city with walls of white marble, and you followed me, fought for me. Wonders, marvels, rarey things and even useful things a man could find there, all the heart desires, a grave cloth for a child, even, a man could find there, before I destroyed it. But you died that day in the fighting.

Not even in the fiercest of the fighting. At the back of the back rank. A poor weakling among my warriors, that man Amraen. *Feeble as a sapling tree. Brittle as the miscast bronze. Dauntless, unstinting, he gave his share, no man will say of him. Never in the front ranks he shone.*

She thought: a horse would have been of more use.

"You could have lived a long life in your village, Amraen. Married Jeha – or asked her, at least. Watched Wyn and Ylil playing in a puddle. Sat with that fat old dog at your feet." She said, despairing, "Why are you not in your village, Amraen?"

The man opened his mouth, but no words came from him. Only a sound like the grinding of stones. So much, so hugely, he had *wanted.* Dreamed, grasped, tried and tried and tried and tried to make real his *wanting.* But such horrors he had seen when he was alive and a warrior in Ikandera Thygethyn's service. All the flames of all the world were in his eyes reflected. All the blood of every battle ran from him as water runs. A little while, Ikandera Thygethyn had lived peacefully, a little while, the length of a childhood; but even so very greatly *wanting*, Amraen could not live in quiet peace. Tried and failed all his life and tried and failed every day in his death and the horror was with him, so much he *wanted* to live.

Morna drew her sword. Held it raised, pointing toward Amraen's throat. "Run, you," she said.

He began to run. Faster. Faster. He fled away into the trees.

In the distance, a hunting horn sounded.

The man for whom that horn rang, Kanda would never stop hunting.

Morna looked at her mother. Took her mother's hand, squeezed her mother's hand tight as they walked to catch up with the rest who were slowing and waiting on the path ahead.

"Come on, Mum!" Calian shouted. "What are you two doing back there? We've still got to find your sword, and your old name, and a great high hall with a roof of gold and walls of silver that shine brilliant in the sun! Hurry! We haven't got all day!"

She shouted, "Also you need to clean this bird shit off my bag, it's really disgusting, Mum."

"We're coming," Kanda said.

And they walked all together, old ones, young ones, grandparents, grandchildren, monsters, heroes, killers, dead, living, walked on, went on. The river grew wide and slow, the air smelled of sea salt; the river changed and opened and was no longer a river but the lazy waters of an estuary with the woods tumbling to cliffs and coast where the world ends. The path ran before them north along the edge of the world following the shore. The sun sank in the west into the sea that was gold and bronze and fire and bleeding wounds, and they went on.

CHAPTER FIFTY-SEVEN

It was a spring day in the Hall Roven. The mud lay thick and the puddles spread to ruin the fair maidens' fair silk kirtles, but the crocuses were in bloom white and purple and yellow as egg yolks, and the birds were trying to find reason to sing. The trees were black and green with wet and moss and the shedding of winter, the world was waking to mud and new things. Wheat in the fields just growing – like stubble on the earth's face. Gray sky, gray clouds, gray water where the floods had lapped. The Six rode out through the gates of the Hall Roven with no especial joy themselves but no pain either, for it was, oh, days, since they last went on an adventure, and it was not actually strictly speaking raining that morning. Just a little damp in the air, as Palle often said.

They must go, besides, for a summons had come. A village but a few hours' ride from Roven, filled now with fear. Death and bloodshed and terrible unspeakable things. The summons had come with the dawn, the sun had barely risen above the trees when the Six were riding. A few hours, no more, for them to reach the village: almost a pleasure ride, easy, not a long weary questing. A track that led there (well, almost led there), at the end a village on a low hillside; pinewoods dark as old honey; the land swept down beyond to a great spread of marsh. All peaceful, gentle, quiet (gentler, quieter, more peaceful, than the argument between the Six when they had briefly lost the track). The clouds broke as they rode toward the village; pale sunlight fell upon the marshes and turned them to the beating silver of a dragonfly's wings. The village stood peaceful, not even a wall around it, the sunlight caught its buildings so that they too shone.

"Beautiful," said Kestre.

"Perhaps…it was only a false alarm…." said Erenan. "Look at the beauty here, the peace…."

"I can see the sea!" said Gallyn. Positively crowed Gallyn.

"I saw it first!" said Morren.

"I saw it first," said Palle. "Actually."

But at the edge of the village the horses stopped and would go no farther, they stamped at the ground and made to flee. The village looked prosperous, the houses sturdy longhouses, an orchard, a well-made bake oven, a barn. There was no sign of any trouble here. Only a great silence and an emptiness. Then a man shouted loud and sudden, a door banged closed or banged open, from somewhere nearby came the plashing of a spring.

Kanda said, "Search the village."

A clatter as of stones falling. A crash as of swords beaten against swords. Gallyn's horse reared and shrieked as if a blow had struck it – and there, on its flank, a wound opening as if a blow had struck it hard and deep.

"I felt it!" Gallyn cried, wheeling his horse round, searching. "Something passed so close to me I felt the warmth of it, and the breeze of it as it struck. There was a man there beside me, attacking me."

Gallyn stroked his horse's neck, soothed it, let the blood dry. "Brave-hearted one, brave strong one, heal now."

But a cry from Morren, for his horse too bucked and the blood came flowing from its breast. It kicked and ran, Morren shouting; when Morren had it under control again his companions saw that wounds had opened on Morren's arms. "A blow, a blow!" Moren shouted. "A cutting blade! But I was, I felt – nothing! Just a shadow, a flickering as if I blinked, before my eyes."

And hands gripping Kanda's legs, trying to pull her from the saddle, and hands gripping and shoving at Erenan's legs.

Erenan cried out in horror, "What is this evil?"

The Six wheeled their horses, drew their swords, but the horses were maddened now, they snorted with nostrils red and wide, they showed all the wide whites of their eyes. They kicked and skittered as cuts opened on their flanks, their legs, as invisible hands slapped and tripped those horses, as invisible claws jabbed at them.

Kanda leapt from her horse Henef, as she leapt she cried to the horse, "Run, swift one! Flee this place!" Henef, Queen of Mares, swiftest of all horses, neighed in answer, fled and was gone. Kanda swung her sword Iath, gritted her teeth against invisible swords, against invisible punches and clawings and kicks. She swung: she struck something, she felt her sword bite, she saw blood on her sword blade. The Six lashed their swords wild, thrust, stabbed, hacked. They cut the air like cutting cloth. They cut, and sometimes they felt their swords meet flesh, and sometimes they would see the blood mark their sword blades and mark their own hands and bodies, and often they would feel cuts and blows. Curious, it seemed, how easy it was to kill without sight of what they were killing. There must be a thousand of these foes packed close around them.

But the bodies fell at their feet, and they were the bodies not of great monstrous creatures but of men. Their hands bloodied. Their teeth bared and bloody, to rend and eat human flesh. Not swords in their hands but farmers' tools.

"What are they?" Kanda cried. A blade cut her, she threw up her sword to ward it off. A child fell at her feet. Dead. "Oh! No! No!" Kanda cried.

Kestre said in anguish: "These are the people of the village under some spell that we are killing!"

"Don't hurt them. Merely ward them off," Kanda said. Hands ripped at her arm; she felt teeth close sharp as any wolf's or dragon's teeth. She kicked and punched, shouted, cursed, but the teeth would not let go, long clawed hands ripped into her, a blade stabbed her chest. More hands, more mouths, more blades, and kicks and punches could do nothing, and – would you believe it? – curses could do less than nothing.

And so Erenan cried out: "They will not stop fighting me. I cannot stop from killing them," and Kanda cried out at the same moment, "I cannot but kill them! They will not stop, they will not let off from attacking me," and Palle the wisest of the Six cried out, "We have no choice. Still, knowing what they are, we must kill them!"

Kanda could see them now as she cut them down, men, women, children, again and again she cut them down. She cut harder, fought harder, all her heart and her mind bent now only on killing men, women, children. Her sword shone gold, her power flowed through her, they came at her, she killed them. Men, women, children: weak things.

"Make them stop!" Kestre screamed. As if she, also, was a poor weak thing with no power in her for good.

"Make them stop, please," Palle begged. Such a wise strong man, a great warrior he, no fear in him. And the tears ran down his face and his hand shook until he barely held his sword.

Kanda looked around the village. Looked with her eyes. Closed her eyes and looked with her mind.

The villages ran to fight her, hacked into nothing, broken bones, they were being killed and killed and those they loved were cut down before their eyes but they would not stop fighting and trying to kill. And there, in the center of the village, a longhouse stood strong and well-made – and a track ran from the gates of the village to the door of the longhouse, and the track was wet and black.

Kanda left off the horror of the fighting, went toward the longhouse. Gratefully, she fled the fighting, though she knew that what waited for her in the longhouse would be worse. The entrance to the house stood open, inside there seemed only darkness. From inside came the smell of something dead and unburied, rotten, but in the dark she could hear a living man's dry breath.

"Show yourself," Kanda said. She meant to shout her anger and defiance. "Show yourself": she croaked it, whispered it, her words were like dust.

A light flared in the longhouse. Light enough to see by. No shadows cast.

Six strong wooden posts held up the longhouse. A rope hung from the largest of them. A dark thing she could not look at hung from the rope.

"There! This is the source of the evil!" The worse of all curses. Death had soaked into the tree that post was made from. Men's heels had drummed dying against that tree.

"Destroy it!" Kanda shouted. "Help me!" Her companions came running to join her. They stopped in the doorway, horror caught them, they saw the gallows tree with the man hanging from it. They cried out, could not enter the house. The villagers pulled and tore and dragged at the Six until it seemed the Six were drowning in human flesh.

"Destroy it!" Kestre shouted. "Yes! It is the source of this curse!"

Kanda struck the house post a great blow with her sword to cut it down.

The blow rang up the bones of her arm, rattled in her teeth. Did not harm the wooden post.

Again, harder, she struck the post. Her sword struck with such force the ground trembled, the force of her blow made her teeth gnash together so that she bit the inside of her mouth and her tongue.

The wooden post was unharmed.

She struck the post so hard she felt her right arm was almost broken, a pain shot through her skull as if she had been struck on the head, she dropped her sword.

One tiny chip in the wood of the post.

Her fourth blow, Kanda knew, would have smashed the post to pieces. But her fourth blow would have broken every bone in her sword arm, and her sword besides, and cracked her helmet and her skull from her chin to her crown.

She roared her war cry, ran at the post, tore at it with her bare hands.

Tore at it and fought with it and broke her fingernails against it. Wrestled with it.

Almost bit at it.

The post rocked. The wood creaking, crying. Kanda's feet slipped. She heaved and struggled, the wood tore back at her, ripped her skin. She cursed.

She braced herself. Howled her war cry. Tore and pushed.

Pushed.

The house pole trembled.

The pole fell with a crash.

Kanda gasped, panted, ached ached ached. Pulled splinters out of every finger. Spat out wood dust.

The people of the village sighed. Fell to the ground.

They fell slowly. Heavily. Their faces were twisted in the horror of what they had done and what had been done to them. They were so raw with pain that they had lost their human shapes. They lay soft and dead.

But Kanda had thought…thought….

"They have peace now," Kestre said. "These wretched ones, these cursed ones." She said sadly, "We should bury them."

"A hard thing it is," Palle said, "that they must suffer, rather than the one who cursed them."

"They built a house from the tree on which they hanged him!" said Kanda. She did not know why she felt suddenly so angry at the people of the village. "They brought a curse upon themselves by doing this thing."

"No, no, Kanda," said Kestre. "That is not true. You know it. You cannot blame them. They did not know that tree had been used as it was."

"No one would do such a thing, Kanda," Morren said. "The people of this village merely found a strong good tree to build a house from. A strong tree is needed to build a house – and a strong tree is needed, too, to hang a man who has committed great evil."

"There was a curse upon this village," Kestre said. "We broke it. Freed them."

"It would have been worse for them if we had not killed them," Palle said. "You know that."

Gallyn said, "They would have been forever monsters. They would have killed many others until they were destroyed. That is why we were called, remember? To save others…from them."

Morren said, "We had no choice but to kill them."

Erenan said, "That is how it must be, sometimes, in the doing of high deeds."

Kanda was silent a long time.

"Is it?" Kanda said.

They found their horses waiting for them on the edge of the marsh.

Rode back to the Hall Roven.

ACKNOWLEDGMENTS

As always, there are so many people, ten times a thousand people and yet more, whom I need to thank for helping me write this book. Everyone who has previously been thanked by me, consider yourselves thanked again.

A special mention to Nick Wells, Don D'Auria, Olivia Jackson and the rest of the team at Flame Tree Press. I am honored to be published by people who care so deeply about beautiful books.

Adrian Collins at *Grimdark Magazine*, and Beth Tabler, John Mauro and his daughter at *Grimdark Magazine* and Before We Go Blog, for the amazing support they've given me.

Shauna Lawless, Adrian Tchaikovsky, Christian/Miles Cameron, Peter McLean and Gareth Hanrahan for the most amazing reviews and for writing amazing books themselves.

The Fantasy Hive, Spells & Spaceships, Run Along the Shelves, SFF Addicts and many other blogs, vlogs, podcasts and websites, for more amazing reviews and for the support you give to the whole SFF community.

Gourav Mohanty and Oliver Cheetham, for giving me fresh hope.

Everyone who took part in the British Fantasy Society Charity Auction for Save the Children. There is much good in this world, and you all proved it.

The ever-growing FantasyCon and BristolCon usual suspects.

My family for just about accepting the need for me to write books.

And deep personal thanks to Jenny Hannaford, Allen Stroud, Karen Fishwick, Kate Byers and Judith Katz.

ABOUT THE AUTHOR

Anna Smith Spark is the author of two critically acclaimed fantasy series, the grimdark epic fantasy *Empires of Dust* trilogy and the folk horror high fantasy *The Making of This World Ruined* series, as well as the standalones *A Woman of the Sword* and *In the Shadow of Their Dying*. She writes lyrical prose-poetry about war, love, landscapes, and war. Her writing has been described as 'a masterwork' by *Nightmarish Conjurings*, 'an experience like no other series in fantasy' by *Grimdark Magazine*, 'literary *Game of Thrones*' by the *Sunday Times*, and 'howls like early Moorcock, converses like the best of Le Guin' by the *Daily Mail*. Her favorite authors are Mary Renault, R. Scott Bakker and M. John Harrison.

Anna has a BA in Ancient World Studies, an MA in Cultural and Social History and a PhD in English Literature. Her particular areas of historical interest are ancient Greece, early Medieval Britain, and ancient and medieval Central Asia, with a particular focus on women's lives in ancient and medieval societies. Her writing is very influenced by her studies, with many references to the literature and culture of these periods.

The previous book in this series is *A Sword of Bronze and Ashes*, described by *Publishers Weekly* as 'an enthralling tale of female power'.

FLAME TREE FICTION

A wide range of new and classic fiction, from myth to modern stories, with tales from the distant past to the far future, including short story anthologies **Beyond & Within**, **Collector's Editions**, **Collectible Classics**, **Gothic Fantasy Collections** and **Epic Tales** of mythology and folklore.